Note on the Author

Mairead O'Driscoll was born in Co Offaly and now lives near Midleton, Co Cork with her husband, Leonard, and her son, Tim. *A Moment in Time* is her fourth novel. *Pebble Cove* (2006), *Absolute Beginners* (2007) and *Where the Heart Is* (2008) are also published by Poolbeg.

www.maireadodriscoll.com

Acknowledgements

A Moment in Time belongs to so many great people so it is with enormous gratitude that I acknowledge the contribution made by all of you. The past year has been one of enormous joy – and joy is magnified a thousandfold when it's shared.

As ever, it is Len who has kept the show on the road from beginning to end, with a constant supply of love, encouragement and understanding – not to mention a gentle nudge when my eyelids were drooping.

My darling little Tim – a bundle of energy and the most wonderful little fellow in the whole world – I can't remember what life was like before you.

To Mam, Dad and all the gang at home, as always, thank you for all the support in the past few years – your love and attention is appreciated every single day.

To my mother-in-law, Nonie – as well as being a great friend, you are a fantastic granny as well!

To my friends, who know already what they mean to me – you are irreplaceable as well as being great fun. I will never forget your support and the joy that you've shared with Len and me since Tim's arrival.

To my agent, Ger Nichol, for her support and understanding.

To all at Poolbeg, especially Paula Campbell and Gaye Shortland for your patience, hard work and for making my dream come true yet again. Paula, the elements *did* come together at last.

To my fantastic colleagues (present and past) at Midleton

Health Centre for your unstinting loyalty and great company – I will always remember your kindness and the power of your good wishes.

To Jess, Ronan and all at Midleton Books for the fantastic launches and for being part of this exciting journey – your support has been invaluable and much appreciated.

To the most important people ever – the readers who have plucked *Pebble Cove*, *Absolute Beginners* and *Where the Heart Is* off the shelves and made the characters become real in the best way possible. Thank you to all the readers who've taken the time to write and email – it means the world to me to know you have enjoyed my work.

Finally, my wonderful Len and my fabulous little Tim, thank you for sharing all of my dreams.

To Len and Tim,
Love is . . . knowing you are both there when I wake up
every morning.

1

Laura Gordon's tummy was already like a map of the moon with all the bruises reaching varying shades of age. She found a patch that hadn't already been the victim of a HCG injection and winced as the tiny needle punctured the skin. It was getting harder and harder to tell herself that it would all be worth it in the end but she did tell herself this as she withdrew the needle, just in case the effects of negative thinking or the lack of positive thinking would have a detrimental effect on the treatment. Barry, while generally admiring his wife's dogged optimism, occasionally allowed a rare flash of cynicism to reach the surface and wondered out loud now where all the positive thinking had got them thus far.

"I mean, when it *does* work we'll be saying it was all the positive thinking, but what about all the times the treatment failed?" Logical as ever.

"Well, there's no point in doing it if we don't believe it's going to work," Laura answered stoically. "I mean, statistically, it has to happen eventually."

She grinned at him, knowing full well that her argument

1

about statistics was well off the mark. Barry, an engineer, kept telling her that their one-in-four chance of conceiving with IVF had already been passed by at this stage. Now on their fifth go, they'd come to look at the possibility of success as little more than chance.

"If you had a mathematical brain you'd be dangerous," he smirked, holding out the yellow Sin Bin to her. Laura popped the needle in and watched as he carefully closed the lid without snapping the permanent lock. "What about dinner? Will we go out for a change?"

Laura looked up at him from under her mop of dark, unruly curls. "No, we'll stay in and eat beans on toast. The bill came earlier."

Her husband sighed and reached into the little hardwood letter-holder on the worktop.

"Great to be rich," he sighed, his eyes flickering over the embossed notepaper that announced that they would need to pay €4000 to the Assisted Reproduction Clinic in advance of their treatment cycle on or before their next visit. "At least we can afford it – sort of. Imagine being in this position and *not* being able to afford the treatment?"

"Well, we're not exactly the Bundesbank –"

"You know what I mean." Barry's idea of being well off was having enough money to live as they liked, but not necessarily to be actually well off. All the motivational books that his wife read indicated that this laissez faire attitude was precisely why they would never be rich – you got exactly what you settled for, whether that was Michael Flatley territory, Simon Community territory or, as in their case, something in between.

"I know – and if we'd had kids ten years ago, imagine what we would have spent on them by now." Laura was smiling as she said this. It had become a joke now and was one of their longest-standing justifications for the extortionate cost of the fertility treatment – the fact that people who did have children were spending all their money on childminding and nappies anyway. In their case, the only difference was that they just didn't have the benefit of the actual children yet. It was a game they played, Laura knew, to keep them from getting utterly depressed and giving up on it altogether.

Barry was poking around in the fridge now in search of something that could be classed as dinner material. His strawberry-blond hair was sticking up at angles from his head, something that happened when he was working but that he generally didn't notice unless Laura drew his attention to it if he happened to be leaving the house.

"Chorizo, natural yogurt . . ."

Laura, meantime, had her head stuck in what they called the "provisions" press.

"Pasta, tinned tomatoes . . . grand so, we'll do the pasta dish."

She pulled out the necessary items and watched as Barry headed for the vegetable rack. Onions and garlic. It occurred to her that they were like two clockwork toys the way they moved around the kitchen in unison, each doing a bit to complement what the other was doing.

Laura, a great believer in self-help books, wondered suddenly if there was "space" for a baby in their relationship. One of the books that she'd read had mentioned a girl who was looking for the perfect partner but who had failed to make space for him in her life. It was only when she'd started to sleep on one side of the bed, leaving space for her potential partner on the other, that she'd finally met the man of her dreams. What if she and Barry were so self-sufficient that they didn't "need" a baby enough?

"Give it here," Barry said now, taking the bag of pasta from her hand. "You go in and watch the news – you're tired-looking." He pushed a lock of fine, curly hair back from the side of her face and kissed her gently on the cheek. "Go on."

Laura realised that she had been standing frozen in the middle of the kitchen considering whether she and her husband of ten years might be working against the laws of nature by inadvertently excluding a child from their world by being too close as a couple.

"Okay so." Laura wandered off in the direction of the sitting room, not to rest from the effects of all the drugs that she was pumping into her body, but to consider this latest possible explanation as to why a perfectly healthy couple like them couldn't conceive as simply as other people did.

The television created a soundtrack to her thoughts and the delicious aroma of the onions and garlic went unnoticed as she slouched on the soft leather sofa mulling over the way that she and Barry led their lives. They discussed things, they made decisions and mostly they stuck to the plans that they made. What if their lives were too neat and ordered? What if they should be having disruptions and passionate arguments and wonderful making-up sessions? What if it was *that* kind of thing that provoked sperm and eggs to unite, rather than the type of calm, almost sedate, existence that they seemed to see as normal?

"Dinner's up!" Barry shouted from the kitchen, startling Laura from her reverie. At the same time, the pre-set alarm on his phone rang out and she realised that she'd spent over half an hour pondering the cause of their infertility with no real conclusion.

"Steroids," Barry prompted, just in case she hadn't heard the annoying jangle of the alarm.

Laura never forgot her injections but often only thought of her additional tablet medication as soon as her head hit the pillow – hence the seven o'clock phone reminder.

"Coming!" she called out, the pungent scent of the chorizo and tomato sauce hitting her at last. She knew she'd enjoy the simple pasta dish that was a favourite for both of them. And at least the nausea that was bound to visit her in the next week

4

hadn't hit home yet. She hated the full, bloated feeling that she experienced every time, yet it would be a small price to pay for success.

It *would* happen eventually and it *would* be worth every bit of it.

2

Orla Carmody-Merriman looked with satisfaction at the white and ivory flocked wallpaper that peeked subtly from between the tiers of newly painted cream shelving in the main reception room of her home in Barretsbridge.

She'd waved goodbye to the decorator a few minutes earlier, having paid him handsomely for his two hours' work as well as treating him to a giant slice of her pear and almond tart with a huge dollop of cream on the side. Barretsbridge was a village of only a few hundred residents and the risk of being let down by a tradesman at the last minute would always be reduced if word got about that certain houses paid up smartly *and* made sure that a worker was properly looked after. The Bretts were well known for gossiping about the people they did work for and Denis would be no exception to the family rule – and if he was going to blather all over the village then Orla was determined to be the last person who'd be found wanting.

As it was, Denis had spent half an hour shooting questions at her about the extended Carmody family, in between gulping large, noisy mouthfuls of tea and digging into the pear tart.

"What about that sister of yours? The one living in the city? Has she any family yet?"

"Laura?" He'd made it sound like she had a selection of sisters. "No, none, yet. How are all your own gang, Denis?"

"Ah sure, grand." Denis Brett was never too inclined to give away much about his own circumstances – he was more a collector and distributor of other people's business. "And Donal? What about him? Any sign of him settling down?"

There was as much chance of Donal settling down as there was of Peter Stringfellow giving up his social life but Orla wasn't going to go into too much depth on that subject. She hardly knew what her brother was at half the time anyway, although she had great hopes for his relationship with Amanda Harris, a secondary-school teacher who seemed to have the kind of firmly ordered life that Donal needed to straighten him out.

"Not a sign, Denis. Did your Shirley have the twins yet?"

That'd shift him once and for all, nosy old bugger. As far as Orla had heard on the local grapevine, the brassy Shirley had been spotted on more than a few occasions in the dubious company of Pat Joe Cleary, a married father of six, after which news of the twin pregnancy reached the main street of Barretsbridge

"No sign of them," Denis answered shortly. "Well, I'd better get off. I have to take out a bathroom suite for Brig Moloney. She's getting a Whirlpool bath for herself, no less."

Tell the whole village, why don't you, Orla felt like saying. But she held her tongue, knowing full well that she'd need the handyman's services on another occasion.

Now that Denis had brought up the subject, Orla resolved to phone Laura and organise a little lunch to see how she had fared with the latest round of treatment. Maybe she was pregnant right this minute, something that hadn't occurred to Orla until right now. She was so used to Laura and Barry having the more unfortunate type of news that she'd get an almighty shock if her sister ever did get pregnant.

In fact, she hadn't even realised how far into the treatment Laura was until Gavin had started to fill her in on it the previous evening, discussing it all as if he were a fertility expert himself. He'd come out with it after dinner when she'd asked him something about whether he'd be meeting Barry for a drink on Friday evening, as they often did after work.

"Not sure," he mumbled, reaching for the remote control as he scanned the sports supplement to see what was on Sky. "They're in the middle of treatment so he mightn't be around on Friday."

"You never said!" Orla's attitude was accusatory considering it was her sister they were talking about.

"He mentioned it the other night in the pub, that's all." Gavin had half an eye on the television.

Orla couldn't believe that he hadn't talked to her about this already. "What did he say? How long ago did they start it?"

As far as Orla could gather, it had been a few months since the previous round of treatment and she knew the whole cycle took about eight weeks from beginning to end. Laura was usually secretive about the end date, the part where she did the pregnancy test, and Orla hated being left out of the loop.

"I'm not sure when they started – they're at the injection bit still, I think. Barry said they wanted to do a cycle before Christmas or otherwise they'd have to wait until well into January. The clinic closes for a good bit over Christmas so they wouldn't be able to get their scans or whatever." He'd closed the newspaper now and was looking quite animated as he explained the details that Barry had given him over their pints in The East Village.

Orla, immediately, was jealous of this intimacy that had sprung up between her husband and Barry. Gavin's use of the word "cycle" and his familiarity with the routine of the fertility clinic suggested to her that the two men discussed the subject in more detail than she'd imagined they would.

"So when will they know? If it's worked, I mean."

Even though the birthday dinner she was planning for their mother was a bit away yet, Orla liked things to be under control. She knew that Laura and Barry tended to "bow out" a bit from everyone for a while when one of their treatments didn't work.

Laura, in the days when she used to talk to Orla a bit more about it all, had explained that they needed time out to recover and get their heads together again. Just as well, thought Orla. In light of her brother Donal's generally juvenile behaviour at family gatherings, the last thing they needed at the anniversary meal was Laura and Barry to be subdued as well.

"I'm not sure. I didn't ask, to be honest. I suppose another few weeks. They'll only be having the egg collection this week."

Gavin was saying all this so casually that Orla was utterly gob-smacked. Half the time he wasn't listening to what she was telling him about Lily and Rose yet he was clearly listening intently to the vagaries of fertility treatment from Barry.

"What does that mean?"

She hated the fact that Laura had never explained anything like this level of detail to *her*, yet she still couldn't bear not knowing. She'd glanced in the direction of the television then to make sure her twin girls weren't listening, knowing full well that the conversation could be repeated, most likely skew-ways, to twenty Junior Infants before long.

"The injections are to make the ovaries produce loads of eggs. They know by the scans when they're ready to take out. They do that under a light anaesthetic and then they put them with the sperm in the lab for a few days. If they grow on all right, they put the embryos back in and hope they take." Gavin had it all off pat.

"How do they know whether they take or not?" Orla was fascinated now and was beginning to feel sorry that she hadn't ever asked Laura properly about the details.

"They do a pregnancy test about two weeks after they go in," said Gavin, "and it's either positive or negative."

"And did Barry just tell you all this?"

"Not all the last night. He talks about it now and again, if they're in the middle of it." This was the first Orla had heard of it and she'd resolved there and then to Google the IVF process as soon as Gavin was gone to work the following morning.

She hadn't though and now she was standing in her main reception room mulling it over instead of getting on with her own things. What with the painting of the shelves and all her other priorities, she hadn't time to be Googling IVF. For now, she would have to put Laura and Barry out of her mind, with more pressing matters immediately at hand. All she had to do to complete her mission was get someone in to replace the old wrought-iron light fitting with the new cream enamelled chandelier whose crystal droplets would sparkle elegantly in the newly refurbished room. Thanking God for nine-foot ceilings, Orla reached for her little pink book of phone numbers. Luke Tidey's red van would be outside the door within forty-eight hours of her ringing him if the last time was anything to go by. He'd spent two days installing the electronic gates and had expended more time inside eating dark-chocolate brownies than he had at the end of the driveway where he should have been. He'd done a good job though and Orla had no hesitation in getting him back to sort the light fitting.

After seven years in the house, she still wondered if there was a better title for this spacious room than "the main reception room". At the beginning, she'd been determined not to refer to it as "the sitting room", a name that conjured up images of small council houses with sofas that were called settees and miserable brick fireplaces. "Parlour" reminded her of big, stuffy *Upstairs Downstairs* houses and "front room" was like saying that it was the Good Room, implying that the other rooms were somehow less good. Which in her case, they definitely weren't. "Living room", one of Gavin's suggestions, wasn't quite formal enough for a space that contained a piano and two antique Queen Anne chairs among the furniture.

Now that the girls were getting older, they'd started saying things like "It's in where the piano is" or, as Lily had announced recently when Orla was chasing a missing schoolbag, "It's in under the chair with the funny legs." If she didn't think of a suitable name soon, her five-year-old twins couldn't be blamed for starting to call it a sitting room, as their new friends in Junior Infants most likely called theirs.

Taking a final glance at her blow-dried hair in the ornate gilt mirror that graced the space above the Spanish marble fireplace, Orla admired its glossy contours. She used to wear it at chin length until someone had remarked that her delicate skin tone and almond-shaped eyes were almost Oriental. Somehow pleased, she'd since opted for a sleek, slightly shorter bob that enhanced the jet-black, glossy strands. She thought of Lily and Rose now with their identical shiny caps of hair as she closed the heavy mahogany door that led to the spacious tiled foyer.

The obsolete light fitting was driving her crazy now that everything else had fallen into place the way she'd envisioned it. What Orla would really like would be for Luke Tidey to come that very evening and replace it with the new one before Gavin got home from work – that way she could present the room to him in all its glory without the ugly, outdated black fitting marring his impression of the elegant room she'd created. He'd have to love it, after all the research and planning she'd put into it.

On autopilot now, Orla dredged up the sweetest, most cajoling voice in her repertoire and dialled the electrician's number.

3

Donal Carmody let out his breath slowly lest Amanda would hear it on the other side of the car park that now separated them. She was getting into her own car at last, a new, sporty Corolla that seemed to mock him and define the great divide between them. Donal himself drove an ancient Volvo that had once been his father's but that had come his way ten years ago when his parents had decided to invest in a brand-new model. His getting the old cast-off Volvo was supposed to have been a temporary measure at the time but somehow Donal couldn't see the benefit in upgrading it. Especially when he was driving a taxi most of the time anyway.

According to Amanda, this apathy was his greatest fault. Not his indifference about the car specifically, but a general lack of motivation that had only a little to do with his mode of transport and a lot to do with engagement rings and plans for the future.

He watched now as she reversed carefully out of her parking slot and exited the car park without so much as a backward glance. She was irritated with him more than anything, he suspected, accusing him of "time-wasting". It sounded a bit Victorian the way she said it, as if she could be promised to some other eligible squire if *he* hadn't insisted on marking her card. He'd voiced this by way of lightening things a bit but the comment had only served to elicit a look of exasperation and a resigned headshake.

"You really need to grow up, Donal."

The evening sun had been shining in through the car window, lighting up her features and glinting on the strands of her well-groomed, chestnut hair. He'd become used to the results of the GHD but realised that he preferred her hair in its natural, wavy form. "I really am finished with you but, for your own sake, you need to start acting like you're in your thirties rather than your teens."

This had been her parting shot and Donal was now sitting alone in his car like the chastened schoolboy she clearly thought he was. The empty crisp packets and sweet wrappers in the side pocket of the driver's door had bulged out and overflowed onto the mat beneath his feet, something that Amanda had seemed to find endearing six months ago when they'd first met. Now she'd apparently decided that the generally chaotic tenor of his life was a sign that he was never really going to behave like an adult and commit to a future with her.

"Arrested development," was the phrase she'd used, spat at him in disgust when he'd explained again that he really wasn't in a position to make a decision, that in fact he hadn't really even thought about it too much. Donal had figured that he was being honest and had felt that he should at least be given credit for that much. He'd said so, provoking another round of "I can't believe I'm actually hearing this!" from his now ex-girlfriend.

If he'd felt relief a few moments ago when she finally closed the door of the car behind her and strode purposefully towards the Corolla, he now experienced a surge of defiance.

"Fuck you!" he called out loud in the direction of the red-and-white barrier at the exit of the car park. It reminded him a

13

bit of the way he used to give the headmaster a two-finger signal as soon as his back was turned in English class, causing the rest of the lads to break into muffled snorts of laughter. It disappointed him now, though, that there were no responding sniggers to make him feel even a little bit better.

4

Laura rested her elbows on her knees and emitted the kind of deep sigh that she now knew was specifically associated with the discovery of yet another failed IVF treatment. The feeling had been there from the moment she woke – that dull, flat ache in the pit of her stomach that signalled the start of a period – yet she'd remained on in bed in the hope that if she didn't actually *see* the evidence, then it wouldn't be happening.

Now she was delaying again, sitting quietly on the closed toilet seat with her heart thudding. Putting off the moment when she had to say it out loud and shatter both their dreams yet again. Barry, simply because of the stealth with which she'd exited the bed and secreted herself in the en suite bathroom, was still blissfully unaware that that there would be no pregnancy this time.

Laura had talked to other women who'd been through IVF and at least she now knew that she wasn't alone in hating that moment of having to break the bad news again. Of all the burdens of fertility treatment, Laura had thought she was unique in thinking that this task of telling someone you love the truth was the most difficult of all. Not the daily injections or the steroid highs, not the hot flushes and menopausal lows of the down-regulation of her hormones but that simple moment of looking at Barry in that way that could only mean one thing. Again.

She thought it was interesting that she didn't even have to use words any more. Just as well, she surmised, looking at herself in the mirror. No words could describe the bleakness she felt, even though no trace of it could be found if she studied her face dispassionately. She actually looked quite *normal*. Something this bad was so deep that it didn't just appear on the surface like an allergic reaction – it gouged a great big hole in your soul instead.

She opened the bathroom door, knowing that Barry would have felt her absence from the bed by now. He had. Their eyes met just as she'd expected, the question in his there against his will. Laura just sighed, letting the tightness in her mouth and the glittering of her eyes do the rest. Proper tears had become a superfluous contribution at this stage.

Like Laura, Barry too had learnt how to deal in body language. Resignation had become a trademark for him by now.

"I know," his wife responded stoically, curling into the warm, secure circle that he made for her, "our day will come."

5

"Well?" Orla slid into the booth opposite her sister, her neatly shaped eyebrows raised in anticipation of the news that would follow. She wasn't one to waste time, especially when it had taken her a full week to organise a proper lunch date. She'd had so much going on and Laura hardly ever answered her mobile.

Laura sighed now, raising her own eyebrows – not so well plucked – in conjunction with a resigned twist of her mouth.

"Oh, Laura, I'm sorry. I don't know what to say." This was rare for Orla and she followed it up immediately with a series of statements that might just get across to her sister how truly sorry she was that yet another IVF treatment had failed. "I can't believe it, *really* I can't. I mean, they did say that it was a one in four chance but I thought that was all just statistics. I thought it would *have* to work *eventually*."

Orla's speech became highly emphatic when she wanted to get something across and Laura did appreciate the fact that she wished her well, even though her sister had no real idea of what it was like to not be able to have her own child. As ever, Orla was getting highly if belatedly involved and would soon start a line of quizzing and questioning that Laura really wasn't able for. It wasn't that she wanted to exclude Orla – it was more that she and Barry had been over this ground endlessly in the past few days and she really wasn't fit to go over it all again.

"So did we. But it's just one of those things that can't be explained, I suppose," she said mildly, hoping that Orla would take the hint and drop the subject.

She cast her eyes around to see if any of the waiting staff were within eye-catching distance, already sick of talking about the matter. She knew that Orla thought she and Barry were very blasé about the unrelenting failure of the IVF cycles but what her younger sister didn't realise was the amount of time that they spent going over and over things until they were weary of wondering why it should be them who had this miserable bad luck.

"Don't *say* that, Laura." As Laura had expected, Orla looked horrified that her sister was able to dismiss such a momentous incident as "one of those things" – surely it was worth at least a few sobs and a bout of tears? "It's a big thing, this. *Even* if it is the fifth time, it's still important."

As if she didn't know *that* already. Laura's thirty-seventh birthday was approaching, bringing her ever closer to the forty milestone that would necessitate a reconsideration of their fertility treatment if it hadn't worked in the meantime. When she heard people talking frivolously about their biological clocks ticking away, Laura knew that they hadn't ever engaged in the process of fertility treatment, a world in which the hands of time seemed to move considerably faster than they did in the real world.

"I know, I know. Will we try and order?" Laura finally caught the attention of a matronly waitress who definitely enjoyed the best of Finnegan's delicious fare, from the look of the precariously stretched buttons on her navy-and-white-striped uniform.

"Oh. Okay so."

Orla looked disappointed that their conversation was to be interrupted for something as trivial as ordering food, despite the fact that it was she who had persuaded Laura to meet for lunch at the prestigious South Mall restaurant. Laura, deflated from a week of exhaustive soul-searching with Barry, would have preferred somewhere quieter than the busy "be seen" Finnegan's, although she did console herself that at least they had a booth.

"Now, ladies, have you had a chance to look at the menu?"

The matron was standing over them, her bust protruding like the prow of a ship and her pencil poised in anticipation. She had yet to find out about Orla's penchant for always wanting something that wasn't on the menu.

Laura, as ever, knew exactly what she wanted. "I'll have the liver terrine to start and the monkfish with potatoes and veg, please."

"And you, Ma'am?"

Laura sat back as the waitress jotted down her order and stood over Orla waiting for a choice.

A deep frown creased her sister's perfect forehead as she gazed studiously at the menu.

"What does the Goat's Cheese come on? It's just that I have a gluten allergy."

"It's a lightly toasted baguette, I'm afraid," the matron replied sympathetically.

"What about the spring roll – is that deep-fried?"

Orla had a Gall Bladder Scare, as she called it, after having her twin daughters and was obsessed about high-fat foods ever since. Barry kept pointing out that Orla had always been phobic about fats and anyway nothing had been diagnosed for definite.

"It is, dear. The smoked salmon roulade is nice, I must say."

Laura bit the inside of her cheek to suppress a grin. The waitress, helpful as she might be, was going nowhere trying to persuade the fastidious Orla to eat something that was effectively raw.

"Oh, God, no. I couldn't have that at all." A shudder was

emitted before a final settlement was reached on a small green salad with a light vinaigrette dressing. Next it was the turn of the main course.

"Is it cod for definite or that other thing? Hoki? I'm wary of that."

The matron sighed, no doubt wishing that she hadn't been so efficient in approaching their table in the first place.

"It's definitely cod. Chef can serve the sauce separately, if you like." Clearly an intelligent judge of people, she'd anticipated that Orla was unlikely to want something as rich as a white-wine and blue-cheese sauce draped all over her fish dish.

"That's fine then – I'll have the cod with sauce on the side. Oh, and what kind of vegetables are on today?"

Orla, needless to say, had a certain degree of Irritable Bowel Syndrome, again self-diagnosed. Laura, who'd had nothing since breakfast, was beginning to despair of ever getting a bite to eat. She started to pray that Finnegan's was the type of restaurant where a bread-basket would appear before the first course.

"Runner beans, puréed carrots with poppy seeds and roasted butternut squash."

"Just the carrot then, thanks. And a jug of water, please."

Satisfied at last, Orla resumed their chat about Laura's predicament as soon as their still-smiling waitress had disappeared from sight.

"So what's next? Will you do it again?"

Orla's mind, even in childhood, had always been fixed on the next thing rather that what was going on in the present. Laura always realised just how much of the trauma of her situation went over her sister's head when Orla imagined Laura jumping ahead to further treatment even before they'd had a chance to recover from the one just gone.

"I'm not sure," Laura answered noncommittally. If she said yes then Orla would want to know when exactly that would be. "Probably," she added when she saw the wheels of Orla's imagination stir into motion, wondering if perhaps Laura and Barry had finally had enough and were on the verge of giving up.

"Well, that's good. I mean, you have *loads* of time left yet."

"That's true. We'll have to give it a bit of a break for a while though, money-wise as well as everything else. Anyway," Laura said brightly, leaning over a little to allow a young man to place a scrumptious bread-basket on the table, "enough about all that. What are the girls up to these days?"

Orla smiled, her genuine pleasure in her five-year-old twins evident. "Saucy as anything now they're in Big School."

Laura giggled. "I suppose playschool is 'only for babies'?"

Lily and Rose, for as long as they could talk, had deemed any toy, game or TV programme as only fit for babies as soon as they themselves had outgrown it. It had been their favourite phrase for at least two years now and was one that Orla and Laura often used when discussing their brother Donal and his frequently immature ways.

"You'd think they were in college. They even had an exam last Friday. I know it was only colouring inside the lines – but still! They're loving it, especially Rose. I think she'll come out of herself even more when they start to make their own friends." Lily had always been the more dominant of the twins but Rose, as far as Laura could see, was catching up fast.

"What about Claudia? Is she in the same class?"

Claudia Arnold, also five, had been specially picked by Orla as a "friend" for the girls almost as soon as she was born, more for the fact that her mother was an orthopaedic consultant at St Angela's University Hospital and her father a veterinary surgeon than because they were Orla and Gavin's nearest neighbours in Barretsbridge.

The edges of Orla's mouth turned down immediately. "The classes are divided in alphabetical order so Claudia's in the first group, which goes up as far as F." Obviously the Merriman girls, or Carmody-Merrimans, as their mother insisted on, had missed out on the elite section of the class.

"Pity," Laura commiserated, all the while thinking it was no harm to have Lily and Rose mixing with everyone in their class rather than just the well-heeled Claudia.

"I'll tell you who they *are* sitting next to," said Orla.

Laura, halfway through her second slice of sourdough, paused for the momentous revelation. Orla hadn't laid a finger on the bread, she noted. "Who?" She couldn't wait to hear what bad influence was next to her nieces.

"Carlene Tidey, no less! You know, one of the Tideys from The Terrace." The Terrace was one of Barretsbridge's less illustrious addresses.

"Is she Rachel's little one?" Laura remembered that Rachel Tidey had had a failed holiday romance with a Turkish fellow a few years previously and had wound up with a wonderfully tanned baby who'd been the talk of the village at the time. It occurred to Laura now that a star-crossed holiday tryst might sound a bit outrageous to the hypersensitive citizens of Barretsbridge while to her and Barry, a baby was simply wonderful no matter how its existence came about.

Orla lifted her elbows to make space for her minute green salad as the waiter approached and waited for Laura's terrine to be placed in front of her before continuing.

"She's gorgeous-looking naturally. But as bold as brass. Imagine Lily said the F word the very first day she was put next to her? They called her Carlene after Johnny Cash's step-daughter, apparently." Orla grimaced at what she considered to be a serious lack of class – her own children had been named to match her sweet-scented, floral home.

Laura thought it was a lovely name but had to giggle at Orla's outrage. "Better than Shania or Britney, I suppose." She took a bite of her terrine which had come with a red-onion marmalade and a small selection of greens much the same size as Orla's entire first course. "This is gorgeous. What's the salad like?"

"Wait till I try it." Only then did Orla have her first nibble of rocket after gingerly shaking off most of the dressing. "Delicious."

No wonder she's so petite, Laura thought as she reflected on her own scrumptious platter. But after the last gruelling round of medication the last thing she was going to do was deny herself the pleasure of a proper meal. Orla had always had much more self-control than her older sister when it came to looking after her body, enduring punishing routines in the gym almost as soon as the twins had been delivered.

"What did Gavin make of the F-word incident?"

She was grinning as she asked this, knowing full well that Orla's husband wouldn't take this aberration in manners half as seriously as his wife would. Gavin was as mild as Orla was hyper, mostly sitting back and doing as he was told. As well as earning enough money to fund his wife's ambitious lifestyle, of course.

"The usual – thought it was hilarious until I reminded him of the seriousness of it. The next thing you know they'll be looking for jam sandwiches. I got him to have words with the two of them over it – you know, well, it's only a matter of time before Rose moves on to whatever Lily has started. That was the end of the DVDs for that weekend."

Laura was laughing now, mostly at the idea of a complacent Gavin being forced to hand out a serious telling-off. "Did either of them say it since?"

"They did not!" Orla pushed her salad aside unfinished and leaned in to Laura again. "What about adoption for you and Barry? You're great with the girls, both of you. Wouldn't it be more of a guarantee than going through with the treatment again? At least you'd *know* you'd be getting a baby at the end of it."

Laura and Barry always said that if they had a doughnut for every time they heard this they'd be able to do a documentary as the Ten Ton Couple. What was it that made the general public think that the idea of adoption was so simple? That it was as easy as deciding on getting a house extension or building on a sunroom? They seemed to conveniently forget that there was a child, a real, live person involved, who'd have to be transplanted from somewhere just to satisfy the need of a couple like Laura and Barry. And no one seemed to understand that Laura and Barry weren't yet able to give up on the need to have their own child, something that most couples had an automatic right to. It wasn't that either of them had anything at all against adoption, it was just that it wasn't what they'd envisaged for themselves the day they'd made a commitment to be together for life.

"It's just not for us right now, I suppose," she said mildly in answer to her sister's sudden onslaught.

The remains of their first course had been removed and Orla was searching her face intently across the table. Laura had known this conversation was bound to surface at some stage but today her sense of loss was too acute to deal with it.

"How do you mean?" There was a touch of sharpness to Orla's voice, a slightly raised edge that meant the question had been considered for a while. "I can't see why you wouldn't at least consider it."

Laura knew they were on dangerous territory and glanced towards the kitchen in the hope of seeing their next course materialising miraculously. No such luck, however. She faced her sister wearily, aware that somehow her and Barry's feelings on the adoption process were transpiring to be a problem for Orla's already delicate sense of self. Laura had read enough self-help books to know the inevitability of what was coming.

"It's not that we have anything against adoption, Orla," she reassured her. This was true and Laura told herself firmly that she and Barry shouldn't have to defend their decision to anyone. Nonetheless, she didn't want to make Orla feel undervalued in any way. "I suppose we're still holding out hope of having our own baby. If it was a case that there was a physical reason why we can't conceive, then maybe we'd have given up before now. Who knows?"

"But what if nothing happens with the treatment and you've left it too late to adopt? Have you thought of that?"

Orla's eyes were bright now and Laura really felt like telling her to mind her own business. She and Barry had never interfered with her and Gavin's family planning, after all.

Thankfully, the same young waiter arrived with a large tray bearing their fish dishes as well as their side orders and a fresh jug of water, giving Laura time to gather her thoughts.

"We *have* thought about it." It occurred to Laura that she was getting like Orla now, with all her stressing of words to get her point across. "It's a risk, I admit, but we're willing to take it rather than just clog up the waiting lists for the sake of it. It's not fair on couples who definitely do want to adopt."

This last bit wasn't strictly true. The fact was that she and Barry had already made their decision, mostly because of a strongly felt belief that they would one day have their own biological child. This, although Orla probably wouldn't believe it, didn't mean they had no respect or understanding for the couples who chose to adopt, often in preference to the grindstone of fertility treatment. In fact, it was a topic constantly up for discussion at the support group they attended at the assisted reproduction clinic.

"So basically you'd rather have no child at all than set up with an adopted child?"

Orla dug her fork into the unfortunate piece of cod, her face obstinate and sullen. Laura wondered how they'd moved from Pleasant Lunch to Minefield in such a short space of time. Orla could be like a pressure cooker, though, and clearly this issue had been building for some time.

In the aftermath of yet another dismal failure, Laura too felt like a ticking time-bomb of frustration, something that Orla probably hadn't discerned so intent was she on pursuing her own line of inquiry.

"That's *not* it, Orla." Her teeth were a little more than

metaphorically gritted. "There will never be a situation where Barry and I are happy with 'no child', as you put it. But we've chosen not to adopt – it's a big decision and we didn't make it lightly. Although you seem to be offended in some way about it!" If she was good at anything, Laura was good at staying calm under pressure – she'd had to be over the years – but Orla was really testing her with her wounded look.

"This is *not* about me," Orla hissed, "so don't try to make out that I have an issue with it. It's you and Barry who have an issue, if you ask me." She was visibly upset now but this wasn't Laura's fault. It was Orla, after all, who'd brought up the subject.

"I didn't ask you, actually." Laura tackled her monkfish, focusing on the delicious creamed potatoes and crispy vegetables for a few moments. She was getting sick of stepping around Orla and her sensibilities – it wasn't Orla, after all, who was sitting here with no child to call her own.

Orla blinked, clearly taken aback at her sister's sharp riposte. As always, her response to a challenge was to deflect it back on the other person. "You're going to sulk now?"

"No, Orla, I'm not sulking. I'm enjoying my lunch and wondering why you're so bothered about what we do about treatment or adoption or whatever."

Orla, unlike her sister, completely ignored the cod that she'd made such a fuss about and rolled her eyes dramatically. "I can't understand you, that's all. You go on about wanting a baby so badly but yet you mustn't want one all *that* badly if you're able to dismiss adoption so easily."

Her voice was challenging now, something that Laura normally wouldn't rise to but today wasn't exactly the best of days. If Barry were here, he'd have told Orla to give it a rest long before this. So too would Gavin, for that matter.

"Orla! Firstly I'm not asking anyone to understand me. Secondly, we don't 'dismiss' adoption. Some of our good friends have adopted children. Not to mention that some of our family members are adopted," she added pointedly, really pissed off now at Orla's assumptions. "And lastly, do you really think any of the decisions that myself and Barry have to make are done 'so easily', as you put it?" Laura knew it was useless to try and get through to Orla just how devastated she and Barry were every single month but, for once, she didn't seem to be able to exercise the control that was needed to prevent a major altercation with her sister.

Orla looked as shocked as Laura had ever seen her, probably because Laura never lost her cool with anyone but mostly because she'd been the cosseted baby all her life and nobody had ever before taken her to task so forcibly.

Laura however, was on a roll. "Now we can finish up this conversation and get on with our meal or we can pay the bill and go home. What'll it be?" Laura felt like the sinister barman in the anti-drink-driving advert as she said this and briefly imagined recounting it later to Barry.

"Well, there's no need to get into a huff," Orla blundered. "Can't we just have our lunch and stop going on about it?"

Laura smiled grimly. Orla would certainly never come out the wrong side of any situation, with her ability to twist things around to making it the other person's fault.

"Grand so," she gave in peaceably. The least she could get out of it was to enjoy her lunch, even if she did have to eat it through gritted teeth.

"Anyway," Orla continued briskly, as if their heated little exchange had never happened, "we have to talk about the Seventieth next week. It's all planned but it's just getting the logistics right for the night."

Laura wondered whether there was some impostor God up in heaven that really had it in for her. The thought of sitting down in some overpriced, pretentious restaurant to celebrate a birthday that her mother really didn't want celebrated at all made her feel like a worn-out, see-through old blanket. Orla, for whatever reason, insisted on having some kind of "do" for any occasion that she could think of, regardless of whether anyone else felt it was necessary or desirable.

Iris, the recipient on this occasion, had mentioned more than once that she didn't want any fuss about her upcoming milestone. Orla, characteristically, had dismissed these hints claiming that *everyone* wanted a Big Birthday marked, whether they admitted it or not. Hence, the immediate Carmody family were to be herded into Chez Louis to be force-fed joviality at Orla's insistence.

"What logistics?" Only Orla could think there was some kind of action plan to be put in place for eight adults sitting down to dinner.

"You know, what time to arrive, etc." She waved her hand in a general fashion as if to cover a myriad of different problems that could arise before they ever got a bite to eat.

Only lately, Laura had heard Lily advising Rose to "switch your ears off" when their mother was giving out about some misdemeanour or other. She now knew the value of this as she switched her own off and waited for salvation in the form of the dessert menu.

6

"Well, how was Bree?" Barry greeted her with a smile and reached over to hit the On button on the kettle, knowing full well that his wife would be stressed after an intense lunch with her younger sister. If it wasn't for her sharp, jet-black bob, Orla Carmody-Merriman would be the identical twin of the highly efficient perfectionist Bree Van de Kamp in *Desperate Housewives*.

"If you think tea is going to do the job after the lunch I had you're sadly mistaken!" Laura pushed her curls, now standing out in unruly disarray, back into place and plonked herself down at the kitchen table that Orla insisted on calling deal instead of pine.

"We'll open a bottle of wine for dinner so. Were you in Finnegan's until now?" Barry rinsed the teapot and added tea leaves, observant of the need for a very strong brew. It was half four now so he knew it must have been a marathon session, probably with Orla obsessing over some chandelier or wallpaper sample.

"I was not! An hour and a half was bad enough. I called in to Dr Ellis and got a sick cert for next week – I think I need a bit of a break and I've only two weeks annual leave left."

"Jesus, Orla must have been at her best if you needed a sick cert after her." Barry placed two mugs and a packet of HobNobs on the table before settling himself opposite his wife. "What was she on about?"

"Honestly, Bar, she's the best in the world but, really and truly, she'd try your patience at times. She's been on to me about adoption before but she went at it hell for leather today."

Barry smiled wryly, knowing full well how forceful his sister-in-law could be once she settled her mind on something. He often wondered how Gavin put up with all the schemes and plans his wife came up with, although it seemed he didn't actually have to participate in much as long as he agreed and admired and paid.

"Go on."

Laura sighed, hating to be starting another bitching session about her younger sister, with whom she normally had a fairly good relationship. "I suppose I have to understand that she has a thing about adoption but I don't see why our decision should make her feel personally insulted. I think she feels that if we're looking down our noses at adoption, then we must be looking down our noses at her in some way."

"But it's a totally different situation," Barry protested. They'd been through all this before, numerous times. "Your parents already had children, Laura. They adopted because they wanted more after what happened. We have a whole other thing going on."

"*We* know that but Orla seems to see it as some sort of blanket solution to everything."

Laura knew that Orla had always prided herself on the fact that she was somehow special because of the fact that she'd been adopted by the Carmodys at six weeks old. In those days, she was the only adopted child in Barretsbridge and because she was younger than Donal by five years, she'd been petted and made a fuss of like the Great White Hope. Now, it seemed, Laura and Barry were taking the shine off it all for her, undermining her in some way because, in her eyes, they were effectively saying that adoption was something to be dismissed rather than celebrated.

"Well, if that's the case, why aren't her and Gavin out adopting children themselves? Woody Allen's at it. And Brad Pitt, for God's sake! If it's good enough for him and Angelina, you'd think that Orla would be on the next plane."

Laura could understand why he was so annoyed. "It's just her way. Nothing's any good to Orla unless it's endorsed by everyone else."

"Well, that's *her* problem, surely? Or does she want us to adopt a baby to make her feel good about herself? Is that it?" Barry, normally fairly mild-mannered, was usually able to laugh off Orla's notions and was always the one to help Laura put things into perspective but this really seemed to rile him.

Laura smiled at last, despite the fact that her husband was almost blowing his top. "I suppose that's it, to be honest. Of course, when I suggested it was Orla who had the issues rather than us, I got blamed for putting it all back on her!"

Barry snorted at this. "Good old Orla, never in the wrong. It's a great way to be, I can imagine. What was the wind-up of it?"

"I have to admit I lost it a bit with her," Laura confessed. "I told her we could either change the subject or just go home. That shut her up – you know how she likes to be seen in Finnegan's."

Barry shook his head at the idea of his wife getting irate. "Can't blame you, to be honest. And at least something shut her up!"

"Well, it didn't actually. She started on about the birthday dinner then. Organising logistics, whatever that was about."

"I'd almost forgotten about that," Barry admitted. "Here, we should just forget about her and tune out until we're lined up like kids in Chez Louis. Will we abandon cooking and just get a Chinese?"

"Good idea. *And* we'll open that bottle of wine you mentioned – only check whether we have a strong one in stock!"

7

If there was one thing that Donal really couldn't stick, it was the Organised Family Gathering. He'd even given these events capital letters in his head, they were so significant for him because of his dread of them.

Needless to say, it was never Donal himself who was the organiser. All the birthday celebrations for either of his parents, all the achievement do's, like when his mother had got a distinction in the Archaeology Diploma, all the anniversaries, were masterminded by Orla.

Donal's younger sister actually thought that she was doing everyone a service by booking meals and inviting friends and neighbours to buffet meals and Masses but, from Donal's perspective, she was just busily filling her time because she had nothing better to do.

This time it was his parents' Ruby Anniversary, being organised well in advance, despite the fact that there was still the seventieth birthday for his mother to get through. Orla had even explained to him that Ruby meant the fortieth anniversary of their wedding when she'd phoned him on his mobile at work.

"It'll only be a meal out – we'll do Chez Louis again," she'd said. "Family anniversaries are a bit more private, I think?" This was phrased as a question.

"I wouldn't know, to be honest . . ." Donal himself had never had any call to wonder whether things like birthdays or graduation ceremonies were filed under "public", in contrast to other events that might be classed as "private". Orla categorised everything.

"Well, look," she continued, a notebook in her hand, he imagined, and probably a few pencils stuck in her hair for effect. Surprisingly, Orla actually had exactly the same jet-black hair colour as he and Laura did, something his mother had explained was due to the Adoption Agency's policy of matching children as best they could to the family that they were to arrive in.

Hair colour, in the case of the Carmody children, was where the similarities ended. Laura's was all curly and ringletty, Orla's neat and precise in its customary sharply cut bob, while Donal's was more about being unruly, unkempt and always seeming to need a good cut according to his younger sister. Their height too defined the biological tie between Donal and Laura. Orla was like a petite China doll beside her siblings.

"Eight is just right really. Chez Louis doesn't take large groups anyway so we'll be a nice, civilised table. And we can have a drink there after the meal. They serve –"

Donal's inattention meant that he only grasped the "eight" word a few beats after Orla mentioned it. Fuck. He'd been meaning to tell them about Amanda and now Friday night was looming, never mind this distant anniversary meal Orla was plotting.

"Now look, Orla, do we really have to –" Maybe putting off the anniversary would save him another round of lectures about settling down. He'd actually only had one lecture from Amanda herself and even *she* hadn't actually mentioned settling down specifically but Donal, with a heightened sense of anticipation, felt that he'd already experienced his sister's exasperation and didn't need to physically hear it out loud, blaring into his ear across the mobile airwaves. This must have a name, he thought absently, this syndrome of imagining a lecture so often that it was as if you'd physically felt the effects already.

"Ah, don't start, Donal!"

He could visualise this very clearly – Orla rolling her eyes as if he was a child refusing to eat his Coco Pops. Not that Orla's household had any truck with Coco Pops. It was all low-GI cereals and organic bread in that house. Donal actually hid his cereal boxes on the rare occasions that his sister arrived around to his flat.

"This goes on every time," Orla went on. "It's the least we can do to acknowledge that Mum and Dad are married forty years. Now we can go somewhere else if you want but it's not easy to decide on something that they'll like . . ." She trailed off, her technique for giving him a moment to consider the error of his ways.

"I know that," he acknowledged, his feet resting precariously close to an overflowing ashtray. The taxi base was a dive but at least he wasn't having to listen to the fares rabbiting on as well as listening to Orla.

"So what are *you* planning?" Orla continued, ignoring his comment. "Organising something any minute, are you? What? A hot-air balloon ride, I suppose!"

Orla always got sarcastic when she was wrong-footed and Donal loved riling her. As usual, she'd bypassed him and gone ahead with booking something, then rang him to "discuss" it as if she were asking for his opinion on what would be a good plan.

"You always just assume that I won't organise anything, don't you?" He was getting a bit indignant now at the presumptuousness of his sister, more secure now that they were away from the subject of Tables for Eight.

"So what'll we do then?" The challenge was in Orla's voice

now and Donal went from secure to cornered straight away. Now *he* had to come up with something.

"I'm not saying it's not a good idea," he began hesitantly, hating himself for backing down rather that saying confidently that, yes, he'd be booking a hot-air balloon ride later in the day. Except, as usual, Orla was right. Iris and Paddy Carmody only liked certain things, among them buffet lunches, special Masses and meals in certain restaurants. They definitely wouldn't want something left of centre and anyway, the kind of exciting, different celebratory presents took an awful lot of organising.

"So I'll keep the booking at Chez Louis then?" Orla punctuated this with a sigh as if to say "We still had to do this the hard way, didn't we?" No wonder she was so expert with Lily and Rose.

"Grand so, but Amanda won't be there." He'd put it off there for a while but it was out now, sort of, anyway.

"What? You won't be bringing Amanda?"

The silence that he let develop served him well. Orla cottoned on immediately so at least he didn't have to admit it.

"Is it off? What happened? Ah, for feck's sake, Donal, when are you going to cop on?"

He noted that she hadn't waited for answers to the first two of her questions. She just jumped in and relied on "form", as she called it, to assume that it was Donal who'd put the kibosh on the romance, as usual.

"What? I should just marry someone for the sake of it? Is that what everyone wants? It'd be handy, I suppose, for making up the tables at restaurants!"

"It's not about tables of eight, Donal! Anyway, I can change the booking to seven." As ever, Orla backed down a little when she was challenged.

"Look, leave the booking, okay?" This was getting more awkward by the second and he was pissed off at himself that he hadn't tackled the problem a bit sooner. "I'll . . . ah . . . bring someone."

"Someone?"

"A girl."

At least Cleo Morgan, who he'd been seeing for the past two weeks, would be a bit of a laugh, even though he wasn't exactly sure that she'd be willing to be paraded at a small family meal after only a few dates. On the other hand, he'd need some bit of light relief to soften out the stiffness that usually pervaded such evenings.

"What?" Orla was clearly astounded at this radical change of plan. "We'll have to tell the others – you can't just arrive with someone that nobody knows from the back of a bus, Donal. Who is she, anyway?"

It was like being questioned by the school principal, Donal recalled from his youth. "Cleo's her name. Look, you'll meet her on Friday, okay?"

"But Donal –"

"And, yeah, I will put on a shirt and tie," he added, before she got started on *that*.

"Ah, Donal, don't be like that. I'm only –"

"Look, I have to go – this yoke's crackling here." He hoped that she could hear the electrical buzzing from the desk that meant another call to the dispatch. "I'll see you soon, okay?"

"Okay so. And I'll definitely keep the booking for eight people?" She sounded a bit less sure now.

He'd dented her confidence in the plan, he knew, and felt guilty suddenly.

"Definitely," he sighed before hanging up.

Orla would be on the blower to their mother and probably Laura straight away with the Amanda news and for that, if nothing else, he was grateful. The deed was done now, and at no great inconvenience to himself. All he had to do now was phone Cleo.

8

"Honest to God, Gavin, you'd think he was five instead of thirty-five. He has to be dragged to everything and still he puts up this protest as if he was being pushed off the Number One spot for organising things. And now I find he's broken up with Amanda and is dragging someone called Cleo along instead!"

Orla was perched on the edge of one of the Queen Anne chairs that stood opposite the sofa her husband was sprawled across, her forehead creased with annoyance.

Gavin Merriman looked up from *The Examiner* and gave a knowing, slightly wearied, grin. "Donal, I presume?"

"Who else but Donal would sound surprised that his parents' fortieth wedding anniversary would actually have to be celebrated? Oh, and then slip in the fact that Amanda has gone by the wayside to be replaced conveniently without a by your leave to anyone. How many is that, do you think?"

"How many what, Mom?"

Lily was all ears suddenly. Her Uncle Donal was being discussed, that was clear. And if numbers were being discussed simultaneously, it probably meant that two of something was being bought for herself and Rose. "Are we getting something off him?"

Rose twisted around from where she was lying on the floor watching a *Lazytown* DVD. She too was gazing at her mother with interest.

"How can two girls who had a birthday very lately be looking for more presents?" Orla thought the girls got plenty as it was and was often a bit annoyed at Donal for arriving out of the blue like a big child, usually late in the evening, with Barbie dolls and noisy games that drove Lily and Rose crazy and upset the sleep schedule that she'd so painstakingly cultivated since they were born. Christmas and birthdays were fine but Donal had no concept of order and could well produce some spectacular new toy a week after their birthday.

"We're just asking," Rose piped up, notwithstanding that it was Lily who'd been eavesdropping in the first place.

"Well, no more asking and no more listening or it'll be bedtime," their mother announced firmly. It was still ages from their usual bedtime and they hadn't even had their bath yet. It was enough to make Rose order Lily to "zip up" under her breath in a tone that suggested a new phrase just learned in the schoolyard.

"And he's definitely bringing this new girl? If he comes at all, that is." Gavin continued the conversation about Donal as if the aside with the girls hadn't happened at all. Orla was used to dealing with them and he had no intention of interfering with a perfectly good working arrangement.

"Of course he'll come. Doesn't he always? After messing around and causing some big kerfuffle, of course. It'd be no good without that."

Orla was wound up and at the same time annoyed with her brother for being able to rise her the way he did. She often wondered if he did it on purpose but Gavin assured her that it was just the way he was and that he didn't like the idea of being herded around like a black sheep.

Orla's retort to that was to point out that there would be no need to herd Donal anywhere at all if only he decided now and again to take the lead himself. And if there was one thing that was anathema to her brother, it was being proactive in any shape or form. Donal had spent his youth being dragged out of bed every morning by their mother and cajoled into going to school. No wonder he couldn't be bothered to make an effort in life now that he actually had a choice.

"Where are we going for the anniversary, anyway?" Gavin asked mildly, used to one occasion running into another in the planning diary. He was always saying that the only way to get Orla off one of her Donal rants was to distract her with details. She agreed with him mostly, especially when he'd point out that her plans were highly likely to come to fruition whereas trying to figure her brother out was a hopeless waste of time.

"Chez Louis again. You know Mum and Dad – it's either there or the Westpark. And that'll be mobbed with people who know them and would probably be odd about not being invited. And there will be a bit of a time lapse between the birthday dinner and the anniversary." Normally, Orla wouldn't organise to use the same venue twice in a row.

"What about Laura and Barry?"

While Gavin was frequently as exasperated as Orla was regarding her older brother, he had great time for Laura and Barry. He even went for a drink with his brother-in-law after work now and again, something that pleased Orla's sense of family cohesion greatly.

"They'll be no problem, although I think Laura's a bit down after the last IVF. Did Barry say anything?"

Orla had resolved to keep away from the subject of fertility treatment with her older sister since they'd coasted onto the subject of adoption during their disastrous lunch in Finnegan's. It still shocked her that Laura and Barry seemed to have completely ruled out the idea of adopting a child if the treatment failed to produce their own biological child, although she wasn't too inclined to admit this to Gavin who would probably tell her that "they" should mind "their" own business. Gavin was like that – totally non-confrontational and more inclined to say "we" when he really meant "you" when warning Orla off something she was getting involved in.

Orla, understandably in her own view, was immediately insulted. Laura hadn't been able to explain exactly what it was that made the concept of adoption so distasteful to herself and Barry, leaving Orla feeling indignant at somehow being relegated to the role of a second-class citizen. Their conversation had concluded with a tight-lipped Laura saying it was just the way they happened to feel about it and the subject hadn't been revisited since, nor did it seem likely to be.

"Well, hopefully they'll be all right for Friday night."

"Hopefully, they'll be all right, full stop," Gavin sent back mildly before returning his attention to the sports supplement.

Orla gazed at the top of his head, the greying strands disguised by the shortness of his haircut and felt slightly guilty about Laura and Barry's predicament. Having children had come easily to her and Gavin and, as far as she knew, there was nothing physically wrong with either her sister or her husband. What would it have been like if she and Gavin had had to face IVF?

Orla sat for a moment and imagined herself taking the daily injections and organising bottles of tablets according to the time she'd have to take them. Going up and down to Cork for the scans wouldn't be too much of a problem, she figured, especially if one didn't actually have children to ferry around and sort out. All in all, it probably wasn't a hugely difficult process to manage, but then she'd always found herself to be good at coping when it came to facing into complicated things. Organising was what she was good at after all.

On that note, she shifted her thoughts away from her sister's problems, aware that she too had things of concern going on. The landing, for a start, needed attention and as soon as she settled for definite on a colour scheme, she was planning to get Denis Brett onto it.

The handyman annoyed her no end with all his snide little comments and questions but it was an unfortunate fact that the old busybody was tasty in the extreme when it came to decorating. She studied his most recent handiwork now as Gavin perused the sports pages. The wallpaper he'd applied behind her new shelf units was done to perfection and she had to admit he was the only man for this next job. It would be a small price to pay to have to listen to him gabbling on, as long as her new flocked wallpaper would be spot on.

9

Cleo, in a situation like this, would definitely be more entertaining and interesting than Amanda.

This was Donal Carmody's reasoning as he waited for his new girlfriend to join him in the car. He'd have gone up to the door and rung the doorbell, only it was already half seven when he'd left his own flat. Instead, he'd phoned her as soon as he was approaching Patrick Street so that she'd be ready and waiting. She wasn't, as it happened, so he pulled into the loading bay on the street and sat back and relaxed. It was no longer *his* fault that they'd probably be late arriving.

He imagined her getting ready inside, choosing from the reams of coloured beads that hung off the wooden knobs on the headboard of her bed. She wouldn't be fussing the way Amanda surely would and this, Donal had to concede, was a big part of why he'd ended things with Amanda in the first place.

The seventhieth birthday dinner had been mentioned casually to her around the time that Orla had organised it and Donal himself had forgotten about it until Amanda had posed in a fitted black dress with a lace back one evening and asked if it'd be suitable for his mother's birthday night out.

Donal had nearly collapsed. Firstly that she'd evidently filed away the date in her head for all those months and secondly that she'd been thinking about what she'd wear and if something would be "suitable". It was all beginning to sound a bit like Orla for him, very organised and pressurised. He'd told her it was a lovely dress, of course, but the damage had been done.

Everything she said or did after that made him feel squeezed. Suddenly he noticed that she asked things like whether they'd go out the following evening or stay in and get a take-away. As far as Donal was concerned, there was no need to think about take-aways until you got hungry. Wondering about it a day earlier was plain weird.

By the end of the Week of the Dress, he was feeling as if a tight band was being drawn around his throat. The last straw came on the Friday when Amanda had told him over the phone that she'd got a wedding invitation in the post that morning. It was six weeks away, yet she was telling him about it as if he should put it in his diary or something. Later that evening, he arranged to meet her after work in the car park and had told her that their relationship was over. The relief he'd felt was almost overwhelming.

When he'd met Cleo Morgan in Scott's the following evening, she was like a breath of fresh air. She certainly wasn't the sort to be bothered about weddings and what to wear for someone else's birthday party. Cleo sold ethnic and fun beads from her small shop on Patrick Street. She wasn't fussed about clothes and, as far as Donal could make out, wore whatever came to hand.

Cleo appeared now at the shiny black door that stood next to the equally shiny door of Beady Eye. She lived in the large flat over the shop because it was handy and available and she didn't have far to go when she closed up her business at half five in the evenings. Donal admired this and wished fervently that there was a vacant flat over the dingy Go Cars office where he worked.

"Hi there!" Cleo slipped into the smooth leather seat of the Volvo and leaned over to kiss him on the lips. She looked a little different this evening, probably because they were going to Chez Louis.

"You look nice," he complimented. She did, in a long, black gypsy-style skirt and a fitted black jacket with gold buttons. Her same style was evident but without the usual array of reds, yellows and blues that he loved. She still had black boots on, he noted, although not the clunky Docs that she wore in the shop every day.

"Thanks." She smiled as he pulled off from the kerb.

"You smell nice too," he commented. The scent was new to Cleo but did remind him a little of his sister Laura, which wasn't ideal.

"You're all compliments this evening," she teased. "It's my favourite – I only wear it for special occasions. You look nice too, by the way."

He glanced over at her and grinned. "Orla insists on a shirt and tie for these things." He'd worn the black trousers that he sometimes wore to work when his boss, Joe Crowley, got a figary about the drivers smartening themselves up. Orla, he knew, would notice that his tie was navy and not matching anything but it was the only one in the drawer that wasn't creased.

"Remind me again who exactly will be here, Donal. I hope your mother doesn't mind me just arriving out of the blue." For the first time since he'd known her, Cleo looked slightly anxious.

"I keep forgetting you haven't met them all. Orla, as I said, and her husband Gavin. She usually leaves the girls at home for these things in case they make a show of her. My other sister, Laura, will be there as well with Barry – he's an engineer. And Mam and Dad, of course."

"Thank God you're not from a family of twelve!"

"You can say that again."

Although Laura or his parents rarely interfered with him, he couldn't imagine being saddled with another few sisters like Orla checking up on him. He was about to say as much now but decided against it on the grounds that he might frighten Cleo off and make her want to be brought home again. And whatever else he needed tonight, Donal needed Cleo in Chez Louis.

If he was on his own, Orla would be quizzing him about Amanda and getting back-up from their mother saying things like "Isn't that right, Mum?" every second. She would be really bothered about what was going to become of him if a nice girl like Amanda wasn't going to make him settle down. With Cleo there, they definitely couldn't be harping on about Amanda and he knew from past experience that they'd soon forget about her.

"Chez Louis might be a bit stiff," he said apologetically now. He didn't want the free-spirited Cleo to think that it was the kind of place he was into or she'd think he was a real stuffed shirt.

"Good food though," she said thoughtfully. "And I love the way you're practically hidden behind the plants."

Donal was surprised that she'd been to Chez Louis at all, considering just how Bohemian she was in contrast to the formal, stilted restaurant. If it wasn't for Orla, he was sure that none of his family would ever have been there. And it wasn't just the expense that prohibited many people from going there – it was the intimidating sense of restraint that settled about the place like a gauzy scarf thrown over a lampshade. Subdued was a word that suited Chez Louis.

"You're right about the plants. I hate those places where you're out on the middle of the floor like you're on show." Donal shuddered at the memory of some of the pretentious places that Orla had booked in the past. He glanced at the clock on the dashboard and was heartened to see that they still had five minutes to get to the restaurant. Traffic was light so they were sure to make it on time.

45

"Are we okay for time? I thought I'd be ready sooner but it was late opening this evening and there were a few stragglers that I couldn't shift."

She looked sorry that she'd held him up a bit and Donal was surprised. She wasn't a fussy sort of person at all and if *he* wasn't bothered about being a few minutes late then it was hardly worth her while fretting.

"We'll be grand. They'll be looking at the menu for a while anyway."

If there was one thing he liked about the restaurant, it was the comfortable seating area with the old-fashioned brocade sofas where diners were offered an aperitif while they perused the menu. On more than one occasion, he'd been able to text Laura to order for him while he then slipped in just as they were being seated.

"What does Laura do? For a living, I mean."

"She works with the Council now in the housing department. She used to be a social worker but she gave it up a few years ago."

Donal had thought she was mad at the time to want to be tied down behind a desk instead of being out driving around calling on people as she used to do as a social worker.

Cleo was interested in this. "I read that about people getting out of social work because it's so stressful. There was a good article about it in the *Irish Times* the other day. There's a huge shortage now, apparently."

"I thought she had a right cushy number, to be honest. She wasn't office-bound the way some social workers are. She did a lot of home visits and that sort of thing." Donal was still perplexed at the need for a change at all.

"But imagine what she was dealing with. I know it's mainly in Dublin but some of them have even been attacked at work. And it's not exactly the most popular of jobs to be in. A bit like traffic wardens, I suppose."

Donal hadn't thought of it like that before. "But there are pitfalls to every job," he reasoned as they pulled into the leafy avenue that led to the front door of the restaurant. It was just eight o'clock. "Look at what I have to put up with! People think taxi drivers are solely responsible for every road work that gets in their way and then when they ask you to take a short-cut they accuse you of ripping them off with the fare."

Cleo laughed at this image of Donal as some sort of con artist who put up diversions and road-blocks on purpose as they alighted from the car near the front door of Chez Louis.

"See," Donal informed her, still grinning at the fact that he'd amused her, "if you leave it late enough you'll always get a spot right next to the door. Which is one of the *benefits* of being a taxi driver."

Cleo took his arm, still laughing. "You must be seriously burdened with the weight of that kind of knowledge."

Feeling debonair and in control with the beautiful, smiling Cleo on his arm, Donal pushed open the glossy green door, nonchalant now about facing what he sometimes thought of as the firing squad.

10

Orla took it all in at a glance. The Volvo was the first thing that struck her and the fact that it hadn't even been washed to make it a bit more presentable. Its ancient off-white paintwork was bad enough on a good day. Covered in mud and grime, it looked like something that would be left in the side of the ditch after a rally race. And Donal, of course, *would* have to park it almost in the porch.

"Oh my God – it's the Wicked Witch of the West he has now!" Orla whispered urgently to Laura.

They were sitting next to each other on one of the squashy, upholstered sofas by the window and Orla had had her neck craned for the past five minutes for Donal's arrival. Now she'd spotted this tall, thin creature with the shocking streaky hair and black ensemble getting out of his car.

Laura swung around to check out her brother's latest girlfriend, not too bothered what she looked like on account of the fact that they never lasted more than a few months anyway. "She doesn't look too bad."

"Ah, Laura, would you look at the boots! And the hair could

48

do with a run of a brush." Orla couldn't fathom how her sister could fail to take in such obvious details when they were staring her in the face but Laura had been distracted since they'd arrived anyway. And it wasn't so much the Bohemian get-up of this Cleo that Donal was landing in on top of them that irked Orla. It was the way she was laughing her head off with her boyfriend as if she wasn't a bit bothered that she was imposing on a close family gathering at short notice. And she hadn't even bothered to dress for the occasion. Clearly, she'd never set foot in Chez Louis before now.

Laura looked again between the draped chintz curtains and grinned. "We've seen worse with Donal."

"True," Orla agreed, "but she looks a bit giddy. We'll have to listen to talk about the planets all evening, I suppose." Cleo looked like she should be selling hand-painted scarves on Patrick's Bridge.

The next thing she knew, Donal had breezed through the glass-plated door that led from the elegant hallway into the comfortable waiting area, Cleo clinging to his arm with a broad smile on her face. Orla thought she looked like someone just out of bed after a good seeing-to, as Donal would probably describe it. She shuddered at the thought but was convinced it was the reason the smug and glowing couple were late.

"Hi, folks," he greeted, the grin still in place. "This is Cleo, everyone."

Cleo, to give her credit after this less-than-proper introduction, smiled politely and reached out to shake hands with Iris first.

"Hello, Mrs Carmody, happy birthday."

At least she has manners, Orla conceded as her father stood up to introduce himself and the others. How typical of Donal to abdicate even that little responsibility.

Laura moved over a little on the sofa as soon as the introductions were complete and made room for Cleo between herself and Orla.

"Thanks," Cleo smiled, obviously grateful to Laura for this friendly overture. "It's lovely here, isn't it?"

Laura agreed and gave Orla a pointed look as if to spell out that Orla's initial assessment was well off the mark.

Orla, although the remark hadn't been addressed to her, replied that it was indeed lovely and offered Cleo the menu to look at just as the maître d, arrived to offer the latecomers an aperitif and take their order.

"White wine, please," Cleo said, smiling politely at him.

"Are you ready to order yet, Madam, or would you like a moment?"

To Orla's shock, Donal's inappropriately dressed girlfriend didn't miss a beat. "The quail, please, to start. And I think I'll have the seafood medley with potatoes."

"Marvellous," the maître d, nodded. "It's salmon, monkfish and hake this evening. And the soup is Spanish Tomato and Chorizo."

"I'll just have the consommé, please."

Orla was fascinated and continued to observe her target as Donal's order was taken. Cleo hadn't so much as looked at the menu.

Laura was suddenly chatting away to her new companion about where she lived and Orla glanced over at her parents to see how they were coping with this latest addition to the family circle. Iris, as ever, was looking around vaguely while Paddy was sitting there smiling as if it was all just wonderful.

Gavin and Barry, she noted, were listening intently to a still-grinning Donal. It was obvious that he was telling them all about the mysterious Cleo, seeing as not one of them had set eyes on her up to now, or even heard of her for that matter. It annoyed Orla that she seemed so relaxed in the situation, despite the obvious differences between her and the rest of them.

She herself was wearing a black Amanda Wakeley knit dress with a deep scoop neck and the pearls that she kept for special occasions. Laura, who normally didn't like formal dressing, was at least wearing a floral Monsoon dress and turquoise wool shrug that looked well on her.

Orla glanced again at Cleo's boots. The fact that she seemed to know the menu by heart indicated that she'd been here before yet the fact that she wore laced boots that went halfway up her calves under a hickey gypsy skirt spelled out that she hadn't a clue about the appropriate dress code for a Michelin-starred restaurant.

Perhaps she was the type who didn't pay her own way in exclusive restaurants, Orla concluded, knowing that there was a certain type of girl who knew exactly how to pay for an expensive night out. Although in that case she wasn't going to get much value out of Donal with his cold beers and take-aways.

Determined to get sitting next to Cleo at the table, Orla stood up smartly as soon as their table was called. She'd find out the lie of the land in no time.

Laura was quite happy to be placed next to her brother's new girlfriend when they were seated in the dining room. Cleo, so far, was easygoing company, something that was badly needed as far as Laura was concerned. Orla was already wound up over Donal cutting it so fine and seemed to have taken a bit of a set against poor Cleo, as if it was her fault that Donal could never be early. And she'd been shooting dagger looks at Gavin and poor Barry for egging Donal on earlier as he told them all about meeting Cleo in Scott's.

Laura, comfortingly, had Barry on her other side. Donal, she noted, had plonked himself on the end, probably in an attempt to remove himself from Orla and Iris who were seated towards the opposite end.

"Donal tells me you work with the Council," Cleo began now as they waited for their first course to arrive.

Her eyes, Laura noticed, were a deep green. Her matching green eyeshadow served to accentuate their unusual colour as did the dramatic eyeliner that ringed her upper and lower lashes. Laura, whose own make-up regime was much more tame, decided there and then that she was going to experiment more.

"Yes, in the housing department. It's always been considered to be the most boring of places but it seems to have revved up in the last few months with so many people losing jobs and getting into arrears."

The two women chatted away about Laura's work and the current economic crisis that had washed over the country so suddenly. Barry joined in when their food arrived and Laura was glad to be able to focus on normal subjects instead of having Orla quizzing her about the adoption thing again.

Cleo told them all about her business on Patrick Street and was entertaining company as she spoke about some of her more eccentric customers. She sold beads and jewellery-making accessories as well as designing some pieces herself. She sourced many of the beads from African countries that she'd actually travelled to in the past and spoke a lot about Fair Trade products that Laura and Barry certainly knew very little about.

"I do children's parties as well, which is great fun. People book me to go to their houses and do jewellery-making as entertainment. For girls obviously!"

"That's fantastic," Barry enthused, "although I wouldn't fancy being in a room with twenty or thirty screeching children."

Cleo laughed. "I figured that out the hard way! I only do a maximum of twelve children now, so I can give a proper portion of time to each of them. And they have to be six or over. Imagine how tempting it is to put a coloured bead up your nose?"

"Has it ever happened?" Laura could just about visualise the chaos and the distraught trip to the A&E.

"Another hard lesson," Cleo laughed. "People think I have an easy job but it's not without its stresses!"

"Try being a social worker," Laura grinned, thanking the waiter quietly as he removed her now empty plate. She'd ordered the quail as well and it had been delicious. "I was in court more than I was in my office!"

"No wonder you got into something more regular," Cleo commiserated.

Laura rarely spoke about her days as a community social worker but found Cleo to be an interested listener and talked more about it now than she had in years. Their sorbet arrived and the tangy lemon and lime drew murmurs of appreciation the length of the table.

It was great too to be able to have a few glasses of wine, something that was denied to her for the duration of the IVF cycle. She'd mentioned this to Orla once and had been told smartly that if she were pregnant, she wouldn't be able to have a drink for the whole nine months. Laura hadn't had the energy to remind her that a baby was worth giving up the occasional glass of wine for. Fertility treatment, on the other hand, bred a resentful sort of self-denial. All the effort, time and again, but never the reward at the end.

Despite the fact that these gatherings as organised by Orla were more often than not fraught with tension for one reason or another, Laura found that she was actually enjoying herself. She and Barry had had a heavy week of discussion about what their next step would be as regards the treatment. Laura, after her trip to the GP's surgery earlier in the week, had tentatively formed a plan that she felt would make a difference but Barry was still undecided as to the wisdom of it. It was no harm to have a night off from their considerations.

Laura glanced down the length of the table towards her mother as Barry and Cleo started chatting about the state of Patrick Street with litter on Saturday and Sunday mornings. Iris was half-listening to Orla who was leaning in closely, no doubt trying to make a few hissed comments under her breath about Cleo. All the while, Iris's gaze was somewhere in the middle distance, a small frown creasing her forehead as if she were concentrating hard.

Laura knew that Iris wasn't concentrating at all and wondered if Orla ever realised how little their mother seemed to enjoy all the birthdays and anniversaries. Laura, needless to say, could read the emptiness in her mother, even though she herself didn't actually have a specific child to miss. But she did know what it felt like to go to christenings and First Communions and feel the sharp loss of knowing that there was something missing that she and Barry badly wanted. God only knew how Iris felt to be celebrating with her family gathered around her.

"The lamb, Madam?"

Laura jumped a little as the waiter appeared at her elbow. Barry noticed and gave her the smallest of winks. She looked around to find that everyone had been served during her little daydream. The lamb looked delicious and she pushed away the maudlin thoughts that had encroached on her evening so suddenly. Even Iris was tucking in.

Donal was amazed at how well it was all going. Apart from Orla's disapproving glance at her watch as he and Cleo arrived, it hadn't been too bad. Barry and Gavin had been all ears to hear where he'd come across a stunner like Cleo and she and Laura were chatting away as if they'd known each other forever. He'd purposely sat as far away from his mother and Orla as possible, lest they start questioning him about his intentions towards Cleo. That kind of thing was always tedious in the extreme at this stage.

His father, to be fair, never commented at all unless something upset Iris in some way. He watched them now as Paddy exchanged his oval dish of vegetables with the one next to Iris's plate, speaking quietly to her in between admiring the food and décor and complimenting Orla for organising it all. There was probably something the matter with Iris's vegetables and Paddy would eat them himself rather than make a fuss that would fluster his wife. It was that way all the time, with Paddy smoothing out any little problems that arose for her, while keeping the show going at the same time.

His mother looked a little jittery, Donal thought, recognising the familiar signs in her slightly flushed cheeks and the subtle darting of her eyes. Paddy, generally jovial by nature, tended to become even more buoyant whenever something was bothering Iris. Over-compensating, Orla called it. Donal wondered what exactly was bothering his mother this evening. For many women, reaching seventy would probably be some sort of milestone but Iris, he sensed, wasn't too bothered about what age she was. He looked away from his father's earnest face and bald head, this attentiveness towards his mother making him feel guilty somehow. He had a vague memory of a time when she was less frail and distracted-looking.

He decided to focus instead on his well-done steak. It was enough that all of them were grateful in a cautious way for the normality of being out in a restaurant eating dinner together, even though he knew that it was only Orla who felt the need to put it all to the test. There was already the Ruby Anniversary in the pipeline. He tipped the contents of his vegetable dish directly onto the plate, imagining that Orla would think this was uncouth or something. He didn't care, nor was he bothered about the next Chez Louis night out. Now that she was settled in, at least he'd have Cleo to get him through it.

Iris didn't know why it was that Colman Broderick made her feel so unsettled. As far as she knew, *he* hadn't spotted *them* yet, the Carmody family out enjoying themselves. She'd seen him immediately, tucked away in a corner with his wife.

Paddy thought she was wrong but Iris was sure that the solicitor would be judging them, particularly herself and Paddy. It was a bit much, this expensive restaurant, she felt. But it was what Orla wanted and the least she could do was to come along and try to enjoy herself, although she wished that Colman Broderick knew that she wasn't actually sitting here having a whale of a time.

Paddy was forever saying that people didn't think like this, that there was no reason for her to be ashamed of getting her hair done or going on a day trip with the Community Council every year. It didn't stop her dreading these things – in fact Paddy's insistence that she *deserved* a treat or a day out only served to make her feel worse.

Her husband leaned back a little to allow the waitress to remove his plate and she immediately started to feel panic rising in her chest as she became exposed from Colman Broderick's position. Paddy, thankfully, resumed his position as soon as he realised. If their solicitor had turned in their direction at that moment, Iris would have had to meet his eyes and nod or smile. The thought of it made her feel nauseous.

Paddy had told her, under his breath so that the children wouldn't hear, that he'd do the talking if Colman noticed them and approached the table. This was reassuring, definitely, but the idea of him asking if they were celebrating was there in the back of her mind. If it was Orla's birthday, for instance, she wouldn't feel so bad. But the thought that someone from Barretsbridge would know she was out in Chez Louis, of all places, celebrating her *own* birthday made her feel embarrassed.

She dragged her thoughts away from Colman Broderick and what he might think of her and tried to focus instead on Orla's chatter. She was great, organising all this, even though she had the girls and Gavin to look after. The least Iris could do was concentrate.

Laura watched her mother surreptitiously and knew exactly why she was so fidgety. She'd noticed Colman and Audrey Broderick sitting at a quiet table by the window as soon as they'd been called to their own table and now realised that poor Iris was finding it difficult to settle while there was someone from Barretsbridge in the restaurant. Paddy, of course, was in hovering mode, minding his wife as if he was expecting a giant wave to wash her away at any moment.

Even though this was nothing new, it wearied Laura all of a sudden. Her mother's life had been a waste to some extent, to say nothing of the effect that this near-paranoia had had on all of them.

The school sports day, for one thing, had been an annual nightmare, with the run-up every year being almost worse than the event itself. Orla had always insisted that their mother be there like everyone else's. Laura, preferring the quiet life, always thought it would be better if Iris just stayed at home, if that was what she wanted. Donal, of course, never had an opinion either way. Paddy, in his most reasonable voice, would reassure Iris that there was no need for both of them to go, adding that there was no such thing as Sports Day when *they* were at school and they'd done all right for themselves.

In the end, Iris usually managed to attend, but the stress of the preceding week had always taken the good out of it for Laura. Watching Paddy guiding her mother carefully around the sports pitch, avoiding this one and that one, had been so distracting that she used to wonder why she didn't just do as Donal did and not get involved in any of the races at all. Orla, oblivious to the stress her mother was under, would enter every event and get a medal in most.

Watching her mother now, Laura realised just how exhausting her life must be. Her every move was tied up with what someone might think. Iris rarely shopped in Barretsbridge, tending to do even her grocery shopping in the city rather than have too many people "knowing her business". Anything that she was involved in was only done with Paddy's encouragement, especially if it was something local, like the Community Council. Even her own birthday, in the company of her family, couldn't be enjoyed properly because there was someone they knew in the restaurant.

Sighing, Laura turned her attention back to her chocolate roulade. Her mother wasn't going to change now, that was for sure. It was way too late in the day for that.

Orla watched the scenes playing out around the table and felt something tighten inside her. On the face of it, everything was going to plan yet she had that familiar feeling that she was just on the edge of the action.

Iris, characteristically, was fussing quietly although Orla couldn't imagine what the matter was. She was used to Chez Louis, which was why Orla had chosen it in the first place.

Laura, far from being devastated after the failure of the IVF, was chatting animatedly with Cleo. Somehow, this created a current of annoyance in Orla – how well her sister could make the effort to get to know yet another of Donal's fly-by-night girlfriends and yet not want to confide in her own sister about the things that were going on in her life. Laura's curtness during their lunch in Finnegan's still hurt, especially when Orla had first-hand experience of things like adoption that *should* be relevant to Laura.

Donal, of course, was the centre of attention with his brother-in-laws this evening, as was the case whenever he produced yet another interesting girlfriend that he could show off for a few weeks. Orla felt like kicking Gavin under the table for giving her brother so much notice.

The food, it had to be said, was excellent but Orla was slightly disappointed that the rest of them weren't more bowled over by it. They all complimented it of course, yet Orla sensed that none of them really appreciated the effort she'd made to get the evening just right. She'd already noticed Iris having some little quibble over her vegetables.

Pulling herself together, Orla realised that she still hadn't got the measure of Cleo Morgan, mainly because the seating arrangements, despite her best efforts, had conspired against her. Not one to be easily thwarted, she leaned forward now in her plush upholstered chair.

"Laura? Cleo? Ladies' room?"

11

It was the day after Iris's birthday night out and Laura and Barry were still recovering from the extended evening with Donal and Cleo in the East Village in Douglas. Orla and Gavin had left directly after the meal so that they could take the baby-sitter home and Paddy and Iris had gladly gone with them. Donal, as usual, wanted to carry on for drinks.

Laura, stretched out on the sofa after a late lunch, was talking her husband through the scheme she'd discovered the day she'd called into her GP for a sick cert after her lunch with Orla in Finnegan's. Her husband, new to the concept, was still a little dubious.

"Honestly, Laura, I still can't make my mind up on it. It *is* a good idea and we definitely need a holiday but what if anything went wrong? You know, even getting a clot from the flying or something?"

"Everything would be sorted out before we go. I'd be started on all the meds and everything. It's mostly just the egg collection and the embryo transfers they actually do there. We'd be back home for the pregnancy test."

Barry was sceptical about this latest notion, Laura could see. It was just a matter of convincing him.

"Is it safe?" he said. "That's all I'd want to know."

Laura hadn't said anything to Barry about the idea of doing what was termed Overseas Fertility Treatment until she'd researched it properly. The more she'd found out, however, the more convinced she was that it was the right thing to do. She'd been browsing through a magazine in Dr Ellis's surgery when she'd come across the article on combining a cycle of IVF with a holiday on a Caribbean island. The clinics were first class and everything was organised for the client, from flights to hotels to complementary treatments that would induce relaxation during the treatment cycle.

"I asked Dr Ellis about the safety aspect that day and she seemed to think it was all above board. She even knew a few couples who'd actually done it. Some of the clinics are affiliated with the NHS."

"It'd be great to do it all without the pressure of anyone keeping track of us, that's for sure." Barry was beginning to hate the well-meaning "Any news?" that some people felt obliged to ask childless couples, finding it harder and harder to answer in the negative.

"Tell me about it! We could just say we were going on holiday and let that be that. I can't be doing with Orla attacking me again."

She could see that Barry was coming around to the idea and was thrilled that he'd at least consider it. Orla's attitude to their decision not to adopt a child had been the last straw for Laura. Going abroad for a holiday combined with IVF seemed like an ideal way to take a break in a relaxed environment and something that might just be the key to having the treatment work for a change.

"I wouldn't be keen on India or places like that," Barry stated firmly.

"Dr Ellis was saying that Barbados is the most popular place for overseas treatment. I'd never even heard of this before and I know it sounds a bit outrageous, Bar, but it's definitely worth looking into."

Barry stood up and stretched, his hair, as usual, all over the place. It was a miserable day outside and they'd spent the best part of the day lounging around with the papers until Laura had broached the subject of the "holiday".

"I'll get the laptop and we'll do a bit more research," he announced decisively. "We can always ask some of the clinics to send us brochures or whatever they're called in this game. If we can find out what drugs they use and whether the procedure is pretty much the same as here, we'll have an idea of how safe it all is."

"Okay, so. I've looked at a good few of them already and a lot of the websites are very good. I'll make more tea while you log on."

"We'll have to look at the cost as well – some of them are probably crazy prices, Laura."

Barry, as ever, was level-headed about what they could realistically afford in terms of treatment cycles. At the end of the day, they still had a mortgage to pay.

An hour later and with a second round of tea and Kit Kats inside them, they'd narrowed the possibilities down to three fertility clinics, two of them in Barbados and one in Cyprus. They'd emailed each of their choices for further information, requesting telephone consultations with the treatment co-ordinators to discuss the finer details.

"That's all we can do for now, I suppose." Laura closed the laptop and slid it under the sofa, glad that they'd made a start on a new plan at least.

"Just in time for *The Clinic*," Barry reminded her, glancing at the clock.

The gritty medical drama was Laura's favourite television viewing and the only thing to be doing on a wet October evening.

Barry threw another log on the fire and settled himself next to his wife. "We could do with a bit of sun."

"We'll have to pick the Days of Sun Fertility Clinic then," Laura giggled, amused by how little gravitas the title gave such a serious enterprise. The correct meaning had probably got lost in translation, making it sound a bit evangelical.

"We'll see," Barry said, shushing her as the opening credits began to roll. "We might just be in Barbados for Christmas."

12

"Are you sure now, Donal?" Orla wanted to make *dead* sure that her brother would definitely baby-sit before she gave up her search of the teenagers of Barretsbridge. Her usual girl, Sophie Conway, had announced that she had her own eighteenth birthday party on the same night as the Architectural Society Annual Ball and Orla was in crisis mode. She'd spent a fortune on a dress and a small mortgage on a pair of purple Christian Louboutin shoes that she had every intention of displaying in Broomfield Hall on Friday night.

"I said I would, didn't I? And Cleo texted to say she'll come to keep me company and do a Bead Party with the girls."

Orla had enough on her plate without Donal organising some sort of party. "A Bead Party?"

"Yeah, she does them on Saturdays for birthdays and things. She said she'll bring a rake of big, colourdy ones to keep Rose and Lily entertained."

Donal was delighted with this by the sound of him, probably because the responsibility of getting his nieces off to bed after he'd stuffed them with sweets and made them hyper with jumping on beds would now be halved with Cleo.

"I thought she had a *shop*?"

This was what Orla had gathered from the others after the night in Chez Louis but she hadn't actually been able to get Cleo to herself long enough to find things out properly, despite trying to corner her in the Ladies' while Laura touched up her make-up. Gavin said they talked about the economy and the recessionary state of the country a lot when he and Barry had been talking to her towards the end of the meal. Orla had found this hard to believe.

"She does have a shop. But she gives the parties as well – makes a fortune at them, actually."

Donal was as proud as punch of the fact that his girlfriend strung beads at children's parties. Orla thought of Mr Lolly, the clown to whom she'd paid €150 to entertain the troops at the girls' last birthday party. All very fine, but she couldn't see herself dating him.

"Right," she conceded, moving on. "So what time will you be over? We'll need to be leaving here at half seven." It was difficult to pin Donal down to hard facts sometimes.

"Grand so," he said equably. "The shop closes at six and I'll be finished at six as well. We'll come straight over."

Orla scribbled a quick note on the pad by the phone to remind herself to text Donal around lunchtime on Friday, knowing he was apt to forget all about his promise if something more interesting came up. "And I'll have them fed, Donal, so there's no need to bring too much in the line of sweets, okay?"

"Grand so," he said again and Orla actually felt a little wave of affection for him. He was good in his own way, kind and obliging to the last. But unfortunately without the sense of responsibility that would define anyone else as an adult. If Iris and Paddy had been available, she would have asked them to baby-sit. But seeing as they were going to some Community Council thing the same night she'd had to resort to Donal.

"Okay then, see you around seven on Friday."

Purposely treating her brother like a child, Orla specifically repeated the arrangements the way it advised in all the parenting manuals so that the details would sink into his head. "I'll leave dinner in the oven for you. And thanks, Donal, you've really got me out of a hole."

Orla rang off and sighed with the relief of it. Sophie had really given her a shock with her sudden withdrawal of services, so close to the night of the Architectural Ball of all nights. The ball was an important occasion in Orla's calendar every year and one of the events that she put most effort into. It was all right for some of the attendees, young graduate architects who went for the craic and the fancy meal. It was more serious for Orla, with Gavin being a partner in an actual practice and not just an employee. As his wife, Orla had a certain standard to maintain. This year, the choice of Broomfield Hall was a magnificent one and she was really looking forward to sweeping up the steps on her husband's arm with the sheer organza coat that she'd be wearing over her dress gliding behind her. The fabulous shoes would give her a necessary few inches in height.

She needed to collect the girls from school now and wondered if she should tell them about the Bead Party that they were in for on Friday evening. On second thoughts, it mightn't be wise to give them too much advance notice in case Cleo failed to turn up. She seemed a bit flighty with all that wild hair, pale make-up and overdone eyes.

She was still mulling over the mystery that was Cleo as she touched up her make-up for the trip to the primary school. Although she rarely, to borrow a phrase that she'd heard on one of her TV shows, met anyone more important than herself at the school gates, she never left herself in a position where she was anything less than perfectly groomed. Having more belief in Nurture than in Nature, it was important to her to be there on time, well turned out, as an example that her girls could aspire to in later years.

The sudden peal of the doorbell annoyed her, not least because it signalled an interruption of her thoughts on Donal's latest squeeze. Hoping it was a Jehovah's Witness that she could shift off the doorstep fairly smartly, she was annoyed to find PJ Madden, a neighbour of her parents', in front of her when she opened the door.

"PJ! How are you keeping?" The last she'd heard, the elderly man had taken a break from the Community Council to have a prostate operation. Judging by the familiar black clipboard under his arm, he was back in action again.

"Great, thank God. I'm glad to catch you, Orla. Have you a few minutes to spare?"

Without even having to glance at her watch, Orla knew that she didn't have much more than five minutes before she'd have to leave to collect the girls but she wasn't going to say that to PJ, whose position on the Community Council had benefited her on more than one occasion.

"Of course, PJ. Come on in."

She held open the door and ushered him into the hall, taking care to prevent him progressing to the main reception room for fear he'd get too settled. He was probably looking for a donation, something he knew full well he'd get.

Orla had no difficulty when it came to helping the fundraising efforts for any community project that would improve the facilities in her immediate surroundings, especially if it was something that would be of any advantage to Lily and Rose into the future. The Council's last project had been the creation of a footpath that ran the whole way from the village to just beyond Orla's house on the outskirts of Barretsbridge.

"Thanks, Orla. I just wanted to have a quick word with you ahead of the Council meeting on Friday evening. It's a bit delicate so I just wanted to test the waters, so to speak." PJ, normally a straightforward man who didn't tend to beat about the bush, looked a bit uncomfortable.

Orla, figuring that this latest project must require a bigger donation than the usual €50, decided to put him out of his misery to speed things up a bit.

"Have you a project on hand, PJ?"

PJ, starting to look a little relieved, shifted the clipboard from under his left arm and shuffled it between his hands. "We have, Orla. And I know your father and mother will be coming down to the meeting on Friday so I thought it might be better to discuss it with you first."

Orla, who was on every committee in Barretsbridge *except* the Community Council, was baffled. PJ, on a roll now, continued.

"It's about Kiely's Corner, you see." He hesitated and Orla knew exactly why he was here. "We're trying to make the village a bit safer – speed ramps and pedestrian crossings – that sort of thing. Especially with all the trucks tearing along the main street from the quarry. Some of those drivers don't know the meaning of the word safety!"

"You're right on that," she agreed emphatically. A pedestrian crossing would certainly be an improvement at the precarious junction where Main Street met River Street but she could see how PJ and his colleagues on the committee would be reluctant to bring it up at the meeting in front of her parents. Whatever about her father, the thought of her mother sitting there in the Community Centre listening to a discussion on the safety of Kiely's Corner didn't bear thinking about. And clearly PJ and his cohorts were also aware of Iris Carmody's delicate feelings on the subject.

PJ nodded, his next sentence confirming Orla's impression that it wasn't just her own family who stepped around Iris's feelings on the matter of Kiely's Corner. It was almost a conspiracy theory at this stage, she thought fleetingly.

"I wondered whether it might be a bit upsetting for them to have it talked out at the meeting?" he continued, eyebrows raised.

He was clearly looking for Orla's direction on the matter and she wondered what he would think if she were to tell him that she, despite being their *daughter*, would be just as reluctant as anyone to broach the subject. That her mother, after three decades of effectively pretending that nothing had happened, wasn't likely to engage in a sit-down discussion at this stage. And that her father, skirting around the issue for as many years by way of not upsetting his wife, would definitely be averse to opening up the old wounds.

PJ, meanwhile, was looking to her for guidance.

"That corner certainly needs something done with it," she said eventually. "Would you get a chance to talk to Dad about it before the meeting, do you think?"

If PJ took the course of action she was suggesting it would mean that she wouldn't have to deal with this herself, nor would she have to admit to him that her relationship with her parents was such that a simple issue such as this couldn't be discussed in a civilised manner.

"Would that be the thing to do, do you think?" PJ looked a little more sure of himself now.

"It would, I think," Orla told him convincingly. "You might catch him later if you're going to the funeral." Jimmy Prendergast from The Terrace was being buried later in the day and Paddy would definitely be attending. It would be a good opportunity for PJ to talk to him alone as Iris never went to funerals.

"That's that then," PJ said, nodding briskly as if to confirm the plan to himself. "There needs to be some sort of traffic calming put in – it should have been done before now but there was never enough money in the pot. And the County Council aren't too bothered about a little junction in Barretsbridge."

He sounded regretful to Orla's ears and she smiled warmly to let him know that, even at this stage, the work the Community Council was doing would be appreciated. "Better late than never. And if it prevents another accident . . ."

"True, true. I'll be off now, Orla and let you get on." His job done, PJ was now anxious to be on his way.

"Thanks again," Orla reiterated as she closed the door. Alone now, she sank down on one of the antique upholstered hall chairs and for the first time in a long time allowed the questions to filter through her mind. What was the big deal? What was such a secret that the whole bloody village had to tread on eggshells? And what was so wrong with *her* that, even after all this time, she was still on the outside looking in?

13

By seven o'clock on Friday, Orla had gone from high excitement to calm serenity and back to high excitement again.

First there had been the crisis when she realised that the pattern of her lace-topped hold-up stockings could be seen through the sheer material of her dress. That had all been sorted after she phoned Zita in Bridal Dream and sourced a pair of stockings without the lace decoration at the top. Gavin had been sent into town to collect them as soon as he'd arrived in from work. When he'd landed back with the new stockings, the outfit came together as she'd imagined it and Orla was floating on air.

Her hair was glossy and precision-straightened. Her make-up was porcelain. And the fact that she had no lumps or bumps to hide in her clingy dress was testament to the three bowls of All-Bran that she'd eaten every day for the past four days. She hadn't faltered all week and was looking forward to the meal later, even if she couldn't afford to splurge on the dessert.

Now, everything was plunged into chaos again with no sign of Donal and his mobile not being answered and texts not being replied to. She'd sent him a message earlier in the day and hadn't been particularly surprised when she didn't get one back. That was Donal. Now it was almost ten past seven.

Everything was ready, granted, but it'd be nice to have a few minutes for a proper "hand over". Dinner for her two baby-sitters was in the oven as promised and Rose and Lily had had their tea. They were also in their pyjamas and Gavin had read them a story so that there would be no nonsense about waiting up for them to come home. And they'd both been seriously warned about behaving. Orla wanted to give this warning to Donal as well.

"He's here, he's here!" Rose shot out of the kitchen with Lily after her as soon as the flash of headlights was evident through the glass panels at either side of the front door. They weren't able to reach the latch yet to open the door so they wedged themselves up against the glass to peer out and make faces at their uncle. They also needed to suss out this new girlfriend who'd be helping him to mind them.

Orla sighed inwardly as their sticky fingers clung to the polished glass. Monica wouldn't be around again until Thursday and she'd given the glass panes a thorough clean only yesterday.

"Gavin," she half-whispered, "open the door and show Cleo into the main reception room. I want to fill Donal in properly."

What she really wanted was to be a bit stern and serious with her brother lest he give the girls permission to do something radical – like phoning their school-friends as soon as the beads appeared. She couldn't say this in front of Cleo.

Five minutes later she was still spelling out to Donal things that she wouldn't even have to warn her eighteen-year-old baby-sitter about, while Gavin entertained Cleo and the girls stared at her wide-eyed.

"Orla," Donal said finally, an exasperated grin on his face, "will you just go, for God's sake or the Ball will be over by the time you get there! We'll be fine. It's not rocket science."

If there was one thing Orla hated it was being told that parenting and housekeeping wasn't rocket science. Who exactly were all these rocket scientists and had anyone ever put them in charge of a 4,000-square-foot house and twins at the same time? Now, however, wasn't the time to get into this with Donal.

"Fine," she said shortly instead and gathered her small, glittery purse from the kitchen table. Her organza coat was draped carefully over the sofa in the reception room and she sincerely hoped that Gavin wasn't sitting on it at this very moment. She had no intention of putting it on over her deep-purple, silk dress until she was alighting from the car outside Broomfield Hall. "I'll just say hello to Cleo for a moment."

Donal followed her towards the front of the house where Cleo was perched on the edge of the sofa, just inches from Orla's expensive coat. If she leaned back just a little, she'd crush it to pieces. Orla doubted that she'd even noticed it.

"Hi, Orla," she greeted her immediately. "It's lovely to see you again." It was almost a month since their first meeting in Chez Louis.

"It's very nice of you to come over, Cleo," Orla replied graciously. The girl certainly had more breeding than her appearance suggested and Orla was at a loss as to what to make of her.

"You look great," Cleo complimented her now, "and what a fabulous coat – I'm terrified sitting here in case I crush it to bits."

"Oh, it'll be fine," Orla said blithely as if it didn't matter a bit. "I suppose we'd better get going, Gavin." Orla was anxious to get at a good table with appropriate people but her husband was stretched out in a fireside chair as if he hadn't a notion of going anywhere.

He grinned at Cleo now and stood up obligingly. "I almost forgot I was going anywhere for a minute there. Only I'm starving!"

"Have a lovely time." Cleo smiled from Orla to Gavin as Donal wrestled with trying to balance Rose on one foot and Lily on the other.

72

"Enjoy," he panted and looked relieved when the girls hopped off to kiss their parents goodbye.

Orla gave them both a quick hug before removing her coat carefully from the sofa and heading for the door.

"Be good," was her final warning to her offspring.

"So, now so," Donal announced as soon as the door had closed behind Orla and Gavin, "what are we up to tonight?"

This was what Rose and Lily loved about their Uncle Donal. He never ordered them to do things – in fact *he* actually asked *them* what the plan was. As usual, they had it all thought out.

"Well," Lily began importantly, "we have a few things lined up."

Donal caught Cleo's eye and suppressed a smile.

"Yeah," Rose continued. "We were thinking of making Krispie Buns first, then after that we could have a midnight feast with Krispie Buns and some sweets maybe."

She trailed off hopefully at the end. Donal hadn't produced the sweets just yet, maybe because Cleo had distracted him, but she imagined they'd appear at any moment.

Donal considered this proposal for a moment and knew full well that Orla would have a fit if he started making buns at this hour of the evening. He didn't know how to make them anyway, although he figured that Cleo might. Now was the time to divert them with the *pièce de resistance*.

"Would you believe, I don't even know how to make buns . . ." he began.

"It's okay, we know!" Lily started to shout. "We'll show you, Uncle Donal!"

Rose was hopping up and down yelling, "We know, we know!"

"But," Donal continued over the din, "Cleo brought something special for you." He grinned over at his girlfriend and back at the twins, both of whom were looking at him cynically. There couldn't be anything better than making buns.

Cleo, at this point, reached for the bag she'd brought with her, a bag that the girls had noticed earlier and had imagined was some sort of weird handbag. There were beads all over it and it had two wooden handles. She held it up and shook it a little so that they could hear a rattly noise from inside. They stared at her solemnly, wondering what was going to appear.

"I only do this on special occasions, you know," she told them mysteriously, putting it down again. A small smile played over her face.

Donal joined in, "And everything has to be organised first – so you'll have to be very good and wait until Cleo has her dinner. Okay?"

"Okay," they chorused obediently, now interested seeing as Donal thought it was a big deal.

"Have you ever been to a Bead Party?" Cleo had already asked Donal to check this with Orla in case they'd already seen her at some of their friends' houses.

"No," they echoed. Neither of them knew what a Bead Party was and even Lily, normally afraid of nothing, was too overawed to ask.

"Good," Cleo told them briskly. "We'll have great fun." She explained to them about stringing the different coloured beads onto the cords in whatever pattern they chose and the fact that they could make necklaces for their mother as a surprise and maybe even one for a friend at school. "How about that?"

"Brill!" Rose screeched, clapping her hands. Lily shouted "Class!" a word she'd heard from one of the cooler of her classmates.

"But me and Cleo have to have our dinner first, remember?" Donal was determined to be strict as Orla had ordered and not let them away with murder. "Now, do ye want to watch a DVD for a while or come out to the kitchen for a snack?" He'd save the sweets for later.

"DVD!" They were like a pair of parrots.

Donal grinned and told them to pick a film. "And no fighting," he warned.

"I'll be getting set up in the kitchen while you're watching that," Cleo smiled as the *High School Musical* crew sprang into action on the television screen. The girls lay on their tummies in front of it, gazing up at Gabriella, their heroine.

"We'll be good," Rose promised for both of them.

Donal was already halfway out the door and Cleo followed close on his heels.

"I've never seen them so obedient! They'll be like mice until they see the beads. Let's see what's for dinner." Donal opened the oven and a waft of spices hit him.

"Indian," Cleo murmured appreciatively. "What can I do to help?" The table was already set for two.

"The plates are even warming for us," Donal grinned as he lifted the cast-iron pot out and placed it on the worktop, followed by the Denby plates. He'd told Cleo already about how organised and perfectionist his sister was and here was the perfect example.

Cleo noticed the two serving spoons that Orla had left out and started to ladle the aromatic chicken dish onto the warmed plates. There were naan breads as well and another smaller pot which she imagined contained rice. Donal took these over to the table and was about to plonk them down on the polished surface when Cleo squealed at him to stop. Swiftly she selected a trivet from a neat stack beside the cooker.

"We don't want to ruin the table with a heat ring," she warned and Donal rolled his eyes.

"What'll you have to drink? There's always plenty of wine and beer here." Donal opened the double-fronted fridge and selected a Miller for himself, his eyebrows raised at Cleo.

"I'm fine," said Cleo, sitting down. "I might have a glass of wine later but I'll have water for now."

Donal pulled out a bottle of Ballygowan and reached into one of the presses for a crystal tumbler, noting just how immaculate everything was in the kitchen. There was a formal dining room as well for special occasions but Donal found it scary in the extreme with its book-lined walls and plush upholstered chairs.

"This is gorgeous – I presume Orla made it herself?" Cleo was already testing the creamy Korma.

Donal roared laughing. "Orla makes everything from scratch – even the cereal – she has big boxes of it in the pantry." Orla made her own granola, mixing and baking it for hours in the oven before storing it in a large airtight container.

"There's a pantry?"

"Oh yes, for 'dry goods'!"

Donal had imagined that pantries had gone out of fashion the day fridges were invented and had been fascinated when Orla had shown him her house plans in the early days. Needless to say, there was a utility room as well.

Cleo, whose own kitchen was a narrow, galley affair that just about hosted the necessities, just smiled in amazement and carried on eating. After a moment, she looked up incredulously. "And the naan bread? Tell me it isn't home-made!"

"You can check all the presses – and the fridge. I bet you won't find a bought pack of naans." Donal was deadly serious. Orla made all her own bread, even complicated things like focaccia.

Cleo looked at him in disbelief. "I thought only Indian chefs made their own naan."

Donal was about to reply when an unholy shriek emanated from above them. Like a shot he was out in the hall calling Rose and Lily, knowing that the sound hadn't come from the sitting room.

"*Heeeelp!*"

"*Heeeelp!*"

He mounted the stairs two at a time in response to the fact that *both* of his nieces were calling for help. Cleo followed him, her dinner forgotten on the table. Donal followed the sound to the master bedroom where he found Rose ashen-faced on the bed and Lily standing over her draped in bracelets and necklaces of all description.

"We were only playing dress-up," Lily began defensively while her sister continued to howl from her perch on the now-crumpled coverlet.

"What happened? Rose, are you hurt, is that it?" Donal was in a panic but couldn't see blood or anything else obvious.

"My nose! It's stuck in my nose." The howling wound down to a sob as Donal tried to look up her nose and get the full story at the same time.

"What is, Rose? Lily, what's up her nose?" He could see something all right but it looked like a little spike.

Rose, seeing her uncle's alarm, took up the full level of screeching again.

Lily, aware that she might be about to be blamed, looked brazenly from Donal to Cleo. "It's only an earring. A pearl earring," she clarified.

Poor Rose was poking at her nose, her face a mask of panic.

"It's okay, Rose, leave it or it'll get even more stuck," Cleo soothed, taking control of the situation. "We'll be able to get that out no bother, won't we, Donal?"

Donal was shocked enough without Cleo thinking he was going to extract a foreign object from Rose's nose but thought it best to wait until calm had been restored before announcing that. Already, Rose was settling and Lily had joined Cleo in the comforting of her sister. She was now kneeling beside her twin on the bed rubbing her head solicitously, all business now that she wasn't going to be blamed for the incident.

"Don't worry, we'll get this old thing out of your nose and we'll have a treat and our Bead Party, okay? You do have a treat, Uncle Donal?" Cleo prompted.

"Definitely," Donal managed. Action on the nose thing wasn't expected straight away at least. "Two Kinder eggs, two

Creme Eggs and some jellies – enough for a midnight feast actually." He was delighted when Cleo winked her approval.

"Well, that's brilliant," Cleo enthused.

The girls looked at her to see if they were right in thinking that an earring up a nose wasn't as big a matter as they'd thought it was.

"Will the earring be all right?" Rose sounded a bit nasal but not too bad considering.

"I think it's a Good One," Lily explained, holding up a little velvet box.

Donal looked at his girlfriend for confirmation, although he suspected that there wasn't much in Orla's jewellery box that wasn't "good".

"It looks like an expensive one," Cleo mused, checking out the remaining earring, "and that means it'll be much easier to get out. Now, will we all go downstairs and we'll decide what to do?"

Rose slid off the bed gingerly. "Okay so."

Lily hopped down too, looking a bit cocky now that no-one had specifically blamed her.

Downstairs the girls were luckily distracted by *High School Musical* again so Cleo and Donal were able to hold a muttered conference.

Donal was already shattered from the drama and the thought of having to phone Orla to tell her they were on their way to the A&E to have her best earring removed from Rose's nose.

"I'll be killed. I can't believe they got up the stairs without us hearing them."

He was pale at the thought of having to inform his sister that this had happened almost as soon as she'd left the house.

"It'll be grand."

Cleo looked completely confident and Donal began to wonder if she was thinking of removing the earring herself. He knew Orla would go crazy if she did, especially if Rose needed plastic surgery or something afterwards. A professional job was the only option.

"Cleo, you don't know Orla . . ."

"Look, Donal, it's only a matter of being able to grasp the stem of it. My cousin lives here in Barretsbridge – she's a doctor. We'll ring her and see what she says. It can't be too difficult."

"I don't know –"

Cleo looked at him sceptically. "Do you really want to get Orla and Gavin home from a big night out?"

In truth, it was the phone call and hysterical response that he was dreading most. He knew that Rose was in no real danger but Orla wouldn't believe that until she'd come home to investigate herself. "I don't know about –"

"Look, I'll phone Jessica and see what she says. You keep an eye on them." Cleo headed to the phone.

Donal wasn't reassured. Even if this doctor cousin of Cleo's called over to remove the earring, he was sure that Orla would still go mad over it. Gavin, as usual, would be perfectly reasonable and would probably say that children did this sort of thing all the time.

Lily and Rose were as quiet as mice in the front room. It astounded him that they could go from hysterical to normal in such a short space of time but then he remembered that their mother could do the same thing in reverse in seconds too.

"How is it now?" He tried to sound casual and not-too-bothered, a tone that had seemed to work when Cleo used it in the bedroom.

"Okay," Rose answered. She sounded fine, as if she had a mild head cold.

"It's the earring we're worried about," Lily added dolefully.

"The earring will be fine – and so will your nose, Rose," Donal reassured them.

Orla would probably have to send the earring to some expensive jeweller for fumigation or something before she wore it again. "I think we'll have the Bead Party as soon as your nose is sorted and then we'll have the midnight feast."

The girls didn't know the clock yet so they didn't actually know what midnight was. As far as they were concerned, a midnight feast was any illicit eating of sweets after their bedtime.

"Wow!" they squealed in unison.

Donal winced, afraid the screeching would drive the earring further up Rose's nose.

"Right so, girlies," Cleo announced, joining them at last. Donal hoped he wasn't about to hear anything too dramatic. "You never told me that you were Best Friends with my cousin Claudia."

Lily and Rose looked at her open-mouthed.

Lily, characteristically, spoke up first. "Are you really Claudia's cousin? Are you not too old?"

Cleo smirked at Donal. "Well, her *mammy* is my cousin. So Claudia's actually my second cousin. And her mammy says she'll be over in a minute to take the earring out," she finished triumphantly.

"Who's Claudia?" Donal asked. He wasn't used to having to keep track of his nieces' friends.

"Claudia Arnold," Lily piped up. "She's *nearly* five and her mammy is a doctor."

"She fixes broken legs," Rose added. "I'm not sure she knows about noses."

"Doctors know everything," said Cleo.

Donal looked at her doubtfully.

"Jessica lives in the brick two-storey at the end of the road," she told him. "She's in Orthopaedics but she has a small forceps in her bag that she thinks will do the job. She's on her way over."

"And she knows Orla?" Donal needed to know that Orla wouldn't go bonkers if this Jessica was some mad quack that happened to live in the same area. He knew how fussy she was about who the girls consorted with.

"Of *course* she knows her, Uncle Donal. When Claudia comes

for a play-date, Mrs Arnold gets coffee with two spoons of sugar." This was from Rose.

"Yeah. And sometimes her bleeper goes off and she says 'Have to run.'" Lily said this in an imitation posh voice and Rose giggled like mad.

Donal figured that if this Jessica was a doctor and had a posh accent, then Orla would definitely approve of her being called to deal with the emergency. He imagined it would raise Cleo's status with her as well, by association. He had a sense that his sister disapproved of his girlfriend, probably because she was just slightly Bohemian and didn't quite fit in with what Orla's idea of "normal" might be. A doctor in the family might just alter her perception of Cleo, if Orla's usual standards were anything to go by.

"Great." He grinned gratefully at his girlfriend just as the doorbell chimed. "I'll get it," he insisted as both of his nieces jumped up at once.

"You two stay put here," Cleo instructed before following Donal into the hall and closing the door firmly behind her. She kissed Jessica on the cheek before apologising for interrupting her evening. Donal had already introduced himself.

Jessica, as tall as Cleo and extremely elegant in a fitted red dress, just grinned. "Claudia found a bag of calf-nuts over at Peter's brother's farm once. Needless to say, one went up each nostril. At least Rose stuck to one side!"

Donal was impressed at her calm demeanour. "I have to admit I would have panicked completely if Cleo wasn't here. I'd have probably phoned 999!"

"Well, if in doubt . . ." Jessica reassured. "Will I take a look at her?" She had a small black Gladstone bag with her, something that would surely impress the twins.

"Be my guest," Donal invited, opening the door of the front room. "Do you need me to get you anything?"

"Nothing at all. Hi there, girls. I hear there's been a wild party going on?" Jessica smiled at both Lily and Rose and they visibly relaxed at her jovial tone of voice.

"Well, the party hadn't exactly started. We were just bored waiting so we decided to get dressed up a bit." Lily was pointing at her sister's nose as if this explained the obstruction.

"Well, let's get you lying down, Rose, and we can get this thing out pronto. Cleo tells me you're having a Bead Party?"

Rose stretched out obediently on the sofa while Jessica opened her bag discreetly and slipped on a pair of fine rubber gloves. Donal could see a little instrument, not unlike a pair of scissors, emerging and hoped that Lily wouldn't be traumatised looking at the procedure being carried out on her sister.

Jessica knelt beside Rose and asked her to close her eyes while she examined her. "And I wonder would you be able to get your sister a glass of water, Lily, while I'm having a look?"

Lily scuttled off importantly.

"Now, Rose, I'll just have a peep, okay?" With that, Jessica grasped the stem of the earring and withdrew it slowly with the forceps.

"Is it very far in?" Rose muttered, eyes still closed.

"Well, would you believe, it just slipped out while I was examining you!"

Rose's eyes shot open just as Lily re-entered the room with a tumbler of water full to the brim. Jessica held the earring aloft with the forceps.

"It's out?" The patient sat up, looking half-disappointed.

"Just like that? But I wanted to see!" Lily sounded bitterly hard done by.

Jessica was very apologetic that it was all over so quickly. "I can't believe it myself, to be honest," she told them. "I've never seen anything so quick in my whole career."

"Really?" Donal questioned earnestly, impressed at her management skills. "We were just lucky then?"

"Very lucky," Jessica confirmed.

"And the earring?" Cleo looked at it with concern.

"That'll be fine too. I'll just have to sterilise it before it goes back in your mother's jewellery box." She proceeded to clean the earring carefully with a tiny alcohol swab before handing it to Donal.

"Thank you very much, Mrs Arnold," Lily said primly.

She looked more relieved about the earring than she did about her twin's nose, Donal noticed.

"Would you like a cup of coffee?" Rose was now deciding to play hostess to her rescuer.

Jessica disposed of her gloves and rubbed her hands with alcohol gel that she squeezed out of a small clear bottle. "No thanks, pet. Just look after yourself for the evening and I'd recommend no shouting or running around. Have a small treat maybe and get to bed early."

Jessica winked subtly at Donal and Cleo – she knew full well that only medical instructions regarding the need for calm would prevent the twins from being hyped up over the incident for the rest of the evening.

"Thanks, Jess," Cleo smiled as she and Donal showed her to the door. "You're sure you won't have a coffee?"

"I'd better get off or Claudia will have Peter running around like a lunatic. It's nearly her bedtime."

Donal thanked Jessica profusely for coming to their rescue and for her cunning advice that there be no rough and tumble for the rest of the evening.

"It'll save me having to call order later! It was great of you to come, Jessica – I'd have hated to have to call Orla and Gavin home."

"I'm glad I was able to help," Jessica smiled. "And it was nice to meet you, Donal – Cleo would have kept you under wraps for another while if this hadn't happened!"

They said their goodbyes and Donal and Cleo waited at the door until Jessica was safely into her car.

"Thanks, Cleo, you're a star," Donal said, hugging her as soon as the door was closed.

"No bother," she grinned. "That's the thing about twins – there's always a companion to get into bother with!"

Donal froze a little at the uncanny truth in her comment, a sudden flashback stopping him in his tracks for a moment before his mind closed the frame as quickly as it had opened it.

"Kitchen, girls," he ordered briskly, back in the front room. There was no way he was letting them out of his sight again.

"Proper order," Cleo commented, clearly amused at this new, strict Donal. "Now can we finish the dinner and get this party on the road?"

"It's the least you deserve – only this time I'll be more vigilant!"

Happily, he herded the twins ahead of him and followed Cleo towards the kitchen, mesmerised at his luck in avoiding the dreaded phone call to his sister. For that he was truly grateful.

14

As it happened, it wouldn't have been too much trouble at all to have phoned Orla and Gavin to deal with the crisis. Considering that they ended up leaving Broomfield Hall at half-nine anyway.

If the pain in her temples hadn't been quite so bad, Orla might have been able to overlook it and carry on with the evening, especially when they happened to be placed beside Tony and Renate Barton at one of the better tables. And although they were placed a few seats down from the Elverys, it was still gratifying to be sitting *practically* next to the president of the Architectural Society and her husband, a Circuit Court judge.

Everything had been going fine until she'd felt the familiar dull ache starting just above her ears. It had been happening for the past few days and Orla imagined it was the price she was paying for the effects of eating nothing but All-Bran to look sleek in her clingy dress. And in that case, the meal would kick into her system soon and resolve the problem. In the meantime, she excused herself as soon as the first course had been removed and made for the luxurious Ladies' room. She'd spotted complimentary miniatures of Ballygowan water on display there earlier and she'd provisionally packed a few Nurofen into her tiny handbag.

Now she was back at the table, trying hard to put the nagging pain out of her mind as she listened in fascination to Renate Barton talking about the upcoming airing of a television show that she and Tony would feature on.

"It's just good timing," Renate was saying of the opportunity to showcase their architectural practice to the nation. "People are genuinely interested in eco-housing now."

Her husband and business partner grinned boyishly. "When we started out it was only rich hippies who were interested in solar panels and straw-bale insulation. Now people can see that it's about saving money as well as considering the environment. And thank feck, I say!"

"Tony," his wife admonished as Gavin and the others at the table laughed.

"It's true," Gavin insisted. "There are plenty of people out there who think that global warming is one big conspiracy theory. But tell them they can save a few bob on their electricity bill and they're down to B&Q like a shot looking for a solar panel. I can only imagine the response to a passive house that needs no heating at all!"

"Well, thank God it's caught on at last or we'd have had to move to Finland to make a living!"

Renate was typically understated about their venture but Orla knew from Gavin that she was far from complacent in her business acumen. Normally, Orla would have enjoyed being part of such lively and intelligent banter but this evening she was finding it difficult to concentrate, never mind contribute.

Now the main course, salmon for Orla, was arriving and she couldn't bear the thought of it being placed in front of her. Eating it would take all of her willpower but she needed to have something substantial if she was to shift her gnawing headache. It had crept up to the crown of her head now and she wished they were at the latter end of the night with the possibility of slipping home early.

"... must be enjoying it?" She jumped when she realised that Renate was asking her something but she hadn't heard enough of the sentence to figure it out.

"Sorry, Renate, I didn't catch that." Orla prided herself on being a good conversationalist and hated being caught dreaming.

"Having a bit of free time to yourself now the girls are at school," Renate repeated with a smile.

"It is great, I must admit – although it's only now that I have the free time I realise how neglected the house has become over the Toddler Years. So there's plenty to catch up on." Orla hated people thinking that housewives were women of leisure and took pains to cultivate her image as a busy co-ordinator of family life.

"Tell me about it," Renate laughed. "That Derek Stewart from the TV programme wanted to 'meet the architects in their own beautiful home'," she paused and rolled her eyes dramatically, "and Tony had to tell him we were renovating to put him off. You wouldn't believe the state of the place with two teenagers."

Tony chipped in at this point. "At least we were able to control them when they were toddlers, Orla. It's a psychology degree I need now."

Orla grinned weakly, unable to muster a response beyond, "It's all ahead of me."

She could sense Gavin looking at her curiously and knew he was surprised that she wasn't her usual vivacious self. The salmon darne in its white wine and tarragon sauce looked huge and unappetising, although Renate and Tony were now tucking into theirs.

"Gorgeous, as ever," Renate enthused.

Orla picked a little of hers and swallowed it without even chewing. The vegetables she definitely wouldn't be able to touch. "Very nice."

The lights, normally subdued and discreet in the Broomfield Hall dining room, seemed to be particularly bright this evening. She wished she'd had the sense to bring two Solpadeine with her as well as the Nurofen, which didn't seem to be kicking in at all this evening. Glancing discreetly at her diamond-studded Raymond Weil she noted that it was twenty-five minutes since she'd taken them. The thought of a darkened room came to her suddenly and she knew that if it didn't abate soon, the headache would drive her home before the glittering auction even started. The dancing afterwards would be out of the question. Even the darkness of the interior of the car would be welcome right now.

As the meal moved along, she fielded questions and made the occasional comment, frighteningly conscious that this headache was a problem she'd created herself. She'd probably washed all the minerals out of her body or something with the ten pint-glasses of water that she consumed on each of the last four days. Following on from that thought, she remembered an episode of *ER* where this woman had drank so much water that her brain became swollen somehow and she ended up brain-damaged from it.

By the time the Black Cherry and Kir Royale Roulade was placed in front of her, Orla was imagining herself being looked after by anonymous carers in a nursing home while Lily and Rose were looked after by an *au pair* and the house went to rack and ruin because Gavin couldn't cope. It was a frightening thought and the worst of it all was that she'd caused the whole thing herself with her stringent detox programme.

She couldn't tell Gavin, that was for sure, or he'd lose the head about her starving herself. But neither could she allow herself to collapse here in Broomfield Hall in front of everyone. She'd have to get some minerals into her system and that was the Holy All of it.

Cursing the fact that her vegetables were now gone and that the condiments had been removed, Orla decided that at the very least she'd have to eat the pudding, despite its lack of appeal right now. She felt nauseous from the pain that now felt like a pulsating vein that might burst at any minute. She imagined her brain swelling slowly as she dug her dessert spoon into the cream-filled roulade.

"Orla?" It was Renate, touching her lightly on the thigh and whispering. "Are you all right?" She sounded concerned and Orla was surprised that she'd noticed anything amiss.

"I'm fine," she mustered, despite the fact that she couldn't manage her usual gracious smile. "Why?"

Renate looked at her as if she were a child in kindergarten and continued to speak quietly and clearly, her voice so low that Orla could barely hear her. "You're as pale as a ghost and you've hardly touched your food. Will I pour you a glass of water?"

"No!" The last thing she needed was more water. Then she realised how harsh she'd sounded and amended it with, "Thanks, I'm fine, really. Just a headache – and the other!" She rolled her eyes for effect to indicate that her period, although in reality not due for another week, was particularly inconvenient this evening.

Renate's face assumed a sympathetic stance. "No wonder you haven't touched your wine. It always makes things worse."

Orla agreed vehemently, glad of an excuse to cover her discomfort as well as being grateful for the distraction. "It does, doesn't it? I've taken some Nurofen so I should perk up a bit soon."

"You'll have to get earplugs for the auction if it's Johnny Loughran again this year!" The charity auction was generally hosted by a local celebrity and last year the Cork-born tenor had boomed his way through thirty lots, oblivious to the fact it wasn't the Opera House he was dealing with and that most of the audience went away with burst eardrums. The thought of enduring the same performance with a splitting headache made Orla's head hurt even more.

"Well, if it *is* him, I'll have to persuade Gavin to make it an early night. Johnny nearly blew the head off me last time – and that was without a headache."

Renate smiled sympathetically at her and Orla realised then just how nice a person she was. They'd met at plenty of functions before but, because she was a professional architect and businesswoman as well as a mother-of-two, Orla had always felt slightly intimidated by her. Not only did she, probably very efficiently, do the same job as Orla did but she also ran a busy practice with an equally busy husband. Tonight, Orla recognised just how empathetic she was.

"Well, you have to look after yourself, especially with two little fairies tearing around the house at 7 a.m. – if they're anything like mine were at that age. And the Architectural Society will still be here next year, plus or minus Johnny Loughran."

Orla knew that Renate was right. It was only another night out, even if her new shoes had barely got an outing. If her head didn't improve soon, she would have no choice but to leave early and, strangely, the night meant more to her than it did to Gavin anyway. She glanced over at him now but he was chatting animatedly with Pearse Elvery who'd stopped to lean over Gavin's chair for a word, presumably on his way to the bar. It was a well-known fact that Morag Elvery's esteemed husband had a fondness for expensive brandy and vintage port.

"Well, when you put it like that . . .!"

She was grateful to Renate for giving her an out, especially if there was any chance that she'd faint or have some sort of seizure from brain-swelling. The more her head throbbed, the more she thought of the wisdom of getting out of Broomfield Hall before she made a show of herself and Gavin altogether. She didn't know whether she felt better or worse having forced herself to eat the rich roulade. The nausea was still there but she felt marginally more secure at the thought of the nutrients that would be absorbed into her bloodstream and hopefully reach her brain soon.

"Tea or coffee?"

The young waitress was looking expectantly at her now and Orla tried to work out which beverage would be best under the circumstances. Coffee, as a stimulant, might just expedite a seizure if one was imminent. Tea, on the other hand, contained all sorts of tannins as well as caffeine, although it probably wasn't as potent.

"Tea, please," she decided, hoping it was the right decision. At least Renate was fully aware of the fact that she was suffering from a headache, in the event that an ambulance would have to be called for her. Otherwise, the paramedics would think she'd collapsed from something else and might neglect to do a brain scan. Panic began to well up in her and she ordered herself to stop thinking like this.

She'd had the Nurofen and something to eat. And as soon as she could get a moment to speak to Gavin, she'd be on her way home to the peace and quiet of her bedroom and two Solpadeine.

"Have you a baby-sitter in," Renate asked now, "or did you farm them out for the evening?"

"My brother and his girlfriend are looking after them so hopefully they're not dancing on the ceiling as we speak. He's a bit over-enthusiastic at times."

Conscious of the fact that she'd barely contributed to the conversation all evening or asked Renate anything about *her* family, Orla tried to pull herself together a bit. "Your boys are old enough to take care of themselves, I imagine?"

"They are not! If I didn't ask my sister and her husband to 'drop in' they'd have everyone on the road in for a party. They're highly insulted, of course, that they have to have a caller to check on them but it's just not worth the risk. Keeping a well-stocked drinks cabinet is expensive these days!"

Orla smiled half-heartedly and hoped the girls would be in bed by the time they landed in Barretsbridge. She hated the fuss of leaving early but her head felt like it would burst if she didn't get away soon. Making discreet contact with Gavin would be her next manoeuvre and she didn't know how she was going to manage to fill him in without making too much of a fuss.

"I might just tell the others that one of the girls has a bit of a temperature rather that make a scene about feeling unwell." She hoped Renate would understand.

"I'll pop to the Ladies' as soon as dinner is over and give you a chance to speak to Gavin if you like. He can sit in here for a few minutes."

Orla couldn't believe that Renate could be so accomplished and so nice at the same time. "Thanks, Renate. I hope we'll be able to have a more fun evening next year. And sorry for being such a drag."

"No need to apologise. Now, here's Johnny – unfortunately for your head!"

With that, Johnny Loughran took to the stage.

"Ladies and Gentlemen, it's wonderful to see you all again this year. Before we begin our auction in aid of Cork Children's Fund, I'll give you a few moments to stretch your legs and shake out your wallets! Last year we raised a substantial sum for this worthy cause and we're hoping to top that here tonight." His cheesy grin and foghorn voice seemed to light up Orla's head like a lighthouse beacon and she closed her eyes briefly before Johnny completed his spiel. "See you in ten, folks!"

"Ten years, I hope," Renate hissed irreverently into Orla's ear. "I'll head off now. And go straight home to bed, okay? You really do look a bit shook. And next year's a date?"

"Definitely," Orla said warmly, touching Renate's arm. "Thanks for the support all evening – and sorry I'm leaving you to Johnny's charms."

With that, Renate winked at her and resurrected a little shiny handbag from under the table before leaving the table. As soon as she'd vacated her seat, Orla raised her eyebrows at Gavin.

"You look a bit pale, love. Hang on and I'll come around

beside you." Excusing himself from the greying matron next to him, he came around the table and slid into Renate's empty chair.

"Headache," Orla explained quickly. "And it's blinding. I'm really sorry, Gav, but we might have to go home. I took two Nurofen but they might as well have been Smarties."

Orla leaving a party early was a first and she could see the concern on her husband's face at this departure from character.

"I'll just say goodbye to Tony and Morag and we'll head off," he said. "Pearse is still at the bar."

"Just say one of the girls had a bit of a temperature before we left and we're anxious to get home. I don't want to make a fuss, Gavin." Orla didn't like to lose face in front of people that she'd normally be trying to impress and was glad when Gavin just nodded and squeezed her hand under the table.

"No bother. Give me a minute and we'll get you home to bed. Are you okay to walk or will I hold your arm?"

"It's not that bad," she said immediately, although it nearly was and she would be grateful for his arm as soon as she got out of the hotel. "I'll get my things together."

It took all of five minutes to extricate themselves and suddenly she was away from the noise and into the coolness of the foyer. The lights were brighter though and she closed her eyes momentarily as pain shot down the back of her neck. The thought that the brain-swelling she'd induced with her detox was already advancing almost made her weak but she clung to Gavin's arm and kept walking, aiming for the sanctuary of the car. As soon as she got home, she could eat a packet of crisps and anything else salty that she could find in the house. Sodium, she remembered now, was the important mineral that she'd washed out of her body with all the water. And her high-fibre, All-Bran diet hadn't helped.

The night air and blessed semi-darkness soothed her almost immediately, as did Gavin's reliable presence beside her.

"I'll be fine now, Gavin," she announced stoically, catching sight of his worried face as he opened the car door for her. "Just get me home."

Orla closed her eyes gratefully and lay back on the smooth leather seat, hoping that if she *did* die tonight of an unexplained illness people would remember her arriving at Broomfield Hall in her floor-length organza coat and her purple Louboutins.

15

Even now, over a month later, Donal still couldn't believe his luck at how well the potential baby-sitting disaster at Orla's house had worked out. Every time he looked at Cleo's beaded bag it reminded him of it.

He shoved the bag off the end of the black leather sofa now, stretched out his legs and switched over to *Top Gear* while he waited for her to get ready. Things were going well with Cleo so far. She was relaxed and easy-going which was what he liked about her. No fussing around about things like what to wear and what time they were going at. Tonight, they were meeting the lads in The Lobby for a few drinks. More than likely there would be some band on but he hadn't got around to looking in the paper to see who it was. But as Mick liked to point out, they'd know when they got there.

Jeremy Clarkson was getting involved with speed testing the new Jaguar and Donal's mind wandered off. It was a repeat anyway that he'd seen a few times in the taxi base during the night between call-outs so he wasn't bothered.

It still amazed him how cool and collected Cleo had been over the earring getting stuck in Lily's nose. If Orla had been there, it would have been a hysterical nightmare with Orla and the twins screeching and Donal being blamed for the whole thing. As it stood, Orla had arrived home to find the girls sound asleep, the earring restored to its proper resting place and the house tidy on account of Cleo picking up discarded toys and all the paraphernalia that went with stories at bedtime and last-minute things that just had to be shown to Donal.

In fact, it had stunned him to see just how little the whole episode had bothered his sister overall. The least he would have expected was that she'd have quizzed Cleo about her exact relationship with Jessica Arnold but instead she'd gone straight to bed citing a headache. Donal wondered if she and Gavin had had a row or something, considering it was a first to see her leaving a function early.

Now, he and Cleo had been invited to baby-sit again tomorrow night, probably so that Orla could pick up the threads of all the information she had missed out on the last night. Donal was only too aware that it must be Cleo's influence that was the cause of him being asked to baby-sit again so soon – normally he was only asked in dire emergencies when there was nobody else to fill in. And Orla hadn't been there at all the afternoon they'd taken Lily and Rose to the park so she'd really missed out on her Guantanamo Bay routine to date.

Whatever had been up with Orla the last night had been out of character, although Gavin had been his usual affable self – Orla had insisted on him staying up to chat to Donal and Cleo while she retired to bed early.

"Ready!" Cleo announced now, emerging from the bedroom and startling him into hopping up from the sofa. It was probably having Orla in his mind that made him feel guilty about having his feet up on the leather – with shoes on.

He looked at his watch and saw that it was already half-nine and hoped that the lads would have been able to keep seats for them. Although Cleo wasn't the type to complain about having to stand all night, Donal himself hated it because his six-foot-two frame meant his back would be aching from having to keep bending to talk to people.

"Grand so, we'll take off."

He collected his keys from the sideboard near the door and noticed two sets of earrings laid out on pink tissue paper. "Are they for the girls?"

Cleo nodded and started to laugh. "Don't look so alarmed! I know you're a bit traumatised by anything to do with earrings but I think they've learned their lesson. I promised them I'd make earrings and bracelets to match their necklaces. I'll do the bracelets for next time."

"They have it good! Gavin says they're like two dolly-birds going off to school in the necklaces as it is. Imagine what they'll be like now."

"I thought Gavin wouldn't even notice whether they had necklaces on or not," Cleo said, looking at him curiously.

"That's only the impression Orla likes to give to make herself feel important. She likes to think that if it was left to Gavin the kids would starve or something. He'd be well on the ball if only he was let get stuck in now and again."

Cleo was putting on lipstick in the gilt-framed mirror over the mantelpiece. "I suppose. Maybe he's just too quiet for her?"

"He likes a quiet life, which is a different thing entirely. Sometimes it's better to agree with Orla rather than have her go on and on about something. But Gavin's far from a push-over."

"Yeah?" Cleo had replaced the lipstick in her handbag and was now ringing her already made-up eyes with eyeliner.

Donal wondered what it was she'd been doing all this time if she still hadn't finished her make-up. "Well, he runs his own company for a start. And I know he's a bit of a soft touch where Orla's concerned but he must be successful enough for her spending not to make too much of a dent in his wallet."

"I suppose," Cleo said again. "Come on or it'll be time to go home again!"

Donal snaked his arms around her waist suggestively. "Well, we could always just stay in . . ."

"Enough of that!" She took his hand and dragged him out of the flat. "Plenty of time for that *after* you've bought me a drink."

Donal grinned and followed her, delighted with his life.

16

Orla pedalled harder, knowing that she'd probably end up having to eat dessert later at the Barton's house. She'd been so grateful to Renate the evening of the disastrous dinner at Broomfield Hall but had been embarrassed afterwards that she'd made such a fool of herself. It surprised her then that Tony had phoned Gavin at work to invite them to dinner tonight. And although she was still a little mortified about the last time they'd met, Orla was looking forward to redeeming herself with Renate sooner than she'd expected.

Needless to say, the stupid headache that she'd created that night had abated as soon as she'd reclined in the darkness of the bedroom and pumped herself with some salty crisps from the Treats Box that she kept under wraps from the girls. It had been a lesson for her to start her preparations for a big night out well in advance in future and not leave it to the last minute. The Broomfield Hall episode, terrifying as it had been, would put an end to any notion she'd have again about cutting corners with bowls of bran and glasses of water. God only knew how the celebrities managed for the Oscars.

She still got her normal headaches – one was even starting

now as she pumped away at the pedals of the exercise bike – but nothing like the one she'd had that night at the Architectural Society dinner. And today she had a perfectly good excuse for a headache.

It galled her to have had to ask Donal and the precious Cleo to baby-sit but as Gavin kept going on about "the facts being the facts" she'd had very little choice in the matter. She'd even had to invite them to stay over tonight in case their evening with the Bartons would turn into a late one as Gavin hoped.

The past few weeks had been a bit of a nightmare, with Gavin going on and on about the recession as if it was something that was going to stop the whole world in its tracks. Orla didn't see how cutting down on baby-sitting expenses and "slowing down a bit" on getting people in to do what she considered to be essential jobs around the house was going to somehow prevent the country from collapsing but Gavin was insisting and she at least had to be seen to be co-operating to get him to shut up about it. Although, she'd *had* to insist on at least completing the project she'd started – namely the stairs and landing. The last thing she needed was to cancel that old Granny Grunt Denis Brett and having him hinting to the citizens of Barretsbridge that the recession was hitting the Carmody-Merrimans.

It was a war mentality, that's all, as far as Orla was concerned. It wasn't as if Gavin was going to get rid of his precious car or anything. But he had to look a bit serious and give talks about business tightening up and money not growing on trees to make himself feel better about the apparently dire state of the economy and people forming dole queues all over the place.

She'd have loved to have gone out and bought something new to wear to the Barton's house this evening but imagined that Gavin would put on his disapproving face again. She'd be getting her hair done later – enough in the line of preparation as far as her husband was concerned – and he was already being odd about the tickets for the Russian Ballet that she'd ordered online for one of their Christmas nights out.

Orla examined her arms as she gripped the handles of the exercise bike and wondered if they were getting a bit flabby. She wasn't quite thirty yet but all the same it was never too early to worry about bingo wings. If she smartened up, she'd be able to get in fifteen minutes on the rowing machine before she had to leave to get to the hairdresser.

As soon as she stepped off the bike, dizziness hit her. Terrified of fainting and causing a scene, she bent down carefully and re-tied the laces of her Nikes to allow the blood to return to her head. It did, almost immediately, and she stood up gingerly and took a deep swig from her water bottle.

As well as the dizziness, she still had the mild headache at her temples but decided that was more from annoyance at Gavin than any undue strenuous activity. And now that the light-headedness was resolved, there was no reason she couldn't do even five minutes on the rower. From the look of both Renate and Tony, they both enjoyed their food and Gavin had mentioned that Renate was reportedly an excellent hostess. That usually meant creamy sauces and rich desserts, things that Orla was determined to work off *before* she consumed them, rather than having to spend the whole of next week with regrets.

As luck would have it, there was a rowing machine free almost straight away and she set to, intent on preventing any future flabbiness that might beset her upper arms. She'd have to think of something to bring as a gift to Renate tonight as well, although with Gavin's new budgetary flair she'd probably have to rifle through her stock at home and see what she could come up with.

At least she was the type of person who was well prepared for any eventuality – even a recession. She often bought things that she might need to use as impromptu gifts and stored them away in the wardrobe of the spare room, just in case. There might be a crystal candlestick there, she mused, or even a bottle of good wine that they could bring with them.

The more she thought about the sudden necessity of having to raid her collection of standard gifts rather than buy something special for the Bartons, the more annoyed she became and the more her temples ached at the irritation of it all. Gavin was being petty and mean over a few little essentials and as soon as tonight was over she had every intention of talking to him about it. Well, maybe she'd leave it another few weeks, considering the Stairs and Landing Project, she amended. But she certainly wasn't putting up with it long-term.

Sweat broke out on her chest and back and she imagined the grams of fat evaporating away as she rowed vigorously. Another thing she was irked about was this new frugality about going out so much and having to cut down on getting a baby-sitter so often. It was fine for Gavin who was out all day but what about *her* being stuck in the house from morning until night? And if she didn't keep using her and paying her well, then Sophie, her regular baby-sitter, would just take off to someone who would. It was all very fine of Gavin to talk about getting Donal or their parents now and again but how reliable was her brother when it came down to it?

Despite the fact that it had all seemed to work out, Orla hadn't forgotten the fact that Donal and Cleo had been responsible for an earring getting stuck in Rose's nose the last time they were in charge.

Orla hadn't yet had a chance to get to the bottom of how exactly Jessica Arnold had become involved in the whole saga, even though she'd made a concerted effort to target Claudia's mother at the school gates for the past month. On every occasion that they'd overlapped, however, there happened to be some other mother present and Orla hadn't wanted to bring it up and give the impression that her home was so chaotic and disorganised. Or that her brother was stupid enough to leave two five-year-olds unsupervised.

Tonight, she'd be able to get the full story out of Cleo herself, despite the fact that she still couldn't seem to like the girl. There was something overtly sexy about her that put Orla off, something about her wild, abandoned-looking hair that suggested she might just be as wild and abandoned in bed.

And the way the girls were so taken with her was another bug-bear of Orla's. As far as Lily and Rose were concerned, Cleo was the belle of the ball with her beady necklaces and promises of matching accessories. She was like the Pied Piper with her hippie bag full of God only knew what and Donal and the girls were like lapdogs around her. Even Gavin was all about her which was a miracle considering that he barely took any notice of his own children half the time.

Fuelled by her increasing irritation at Gavin, Orla was rowing so hard at this stage that she'd become dizzy again and had to stop for a drink. The coolness of the water helped her to regain her composure a little and when she glanced at the large clock on the wall opposite her, she realised she only just had time to shower and get herself into town for her weekly blow-dry. Normally, she didn't go to the gym on Saturdays for this very reason.

Standing up suddenly brought the wave of light-headedness back again and she stumbled a little as she crossed the non-slip floor. Mortified, she pulled herself together and stopped to take another swig of water. Tilting her head back to sip caused her to tighten her muscles and a quick spurt of pain shot through her neck. Cursing herself for pushing herself too hard, she continued her progress to the changing area and sat for a moment on one of the slatted wooden benches to steady herself.

Looking back, she probably should have eaten a little more for breakfast this morning but she hadn't wanted to pig out too much in anticipation of the meal later. Now, she was regretting it a little.

Eventually, her head settled a little and she hopped into the shower, conscious that she might miss her hair appointment if she dawdled any longer. As soon as tonight's dinner was over, she was going to devise a proper diet and exercise plan. This dizziness thing was becoming a bit inconvenient.

17

Barry planned to try and slip into bed without waking Laura but as soon as the bedroom door opened she popped her head up from under the duvet.

"Well – good night?"

Barry had been out for one of his occasional drinks with Donal and Gavin and although it wasn't too late, Laura had work in the morning.

"Grand," he whispered as she turned on the bedside light. He proceeded into the walk-in closet but left the door open so he could tell her about the events of the evening, surprising as they were.

Laura sat up, wide awake now but not too bothered. Tomorrow was Friday so she didn't mind being a little tired at the end of the week. She hated going to bed without Barry and, on the rare occasions that she did, she loved waking up to welcome him home properly.

"Anything new with the lads?" she asked.

"If I said the words 'Donal' and 'girlfriend' in the same

sentence, what would you think?" He stuck his head out and rolled his eyes heavenward.

"Ah, this is ridiculous! There won't be any women left on the face of the earth to try out if he continues at this pace." Without Barry actually having to spell it out, she knew that another of her brother's girlfriends had departed the scene.

"And the comedy is that they're always actually nice – however he manages it."

Laura shook her head in wonderment and made room for Barry in the bed. In his absence, she'd deviated over to his side and now there was a cold bit when she moved back.

"Fecker," she complained, "I've warmed your side!"

Barry grinned smugly and settled himself in. "Come back for a cuddle then."

"So what happened this time?" Laura quizzed, snuggling in next to him. "Cleo didn't seem like the type to be pushing for commitment. That's usually the problem."

"This one was a new departure entirely. Apparently *she* broke it off with him. How about that for a turn-up?"

Laura sat up, as incredulous as her husband was. "Don't tell me Donal was looking for commitment? He'd have to be on a stretching rack before that'd happen!"

"He was all upset about it." Spotting the disbelief on his wife's face, he amended this. "Well, as upset as Donal gets. 'Put out a bit' is probably a better way of describing it. She told him it was all getting a bit 'cosy' for her. Donal's blaming Orla now for asking them to baby-sit a few times. Poor Gavin was all embarrassed at being the cause of the break-up."

"He didn't say that in front of Gavin?"

Having asked the question, Laura answered it herself. "Of course he did. He's such a child, blaming Orla and Gavin. If he didn't want to baby-sit, he didn't have to – or at least he didn't have to insist on bringing Cleo. It probably *was* a bit much, especially with Orla quizzing the poor girl."

Barry didn't look convinced. "I wouldn't have thought she was the type to be too bothered about that kind of thing. I thought she'd be delighted with a 'free spirit' like Donal."

Laura was still amazed that someone had had the opportunity to finish a relationship with Donal before he'd done it himself. "Unprecedented" was probably the best description for it.

"Strange all right," she had to admit. "So there will be high drama now over the anniversary dinner and how many places are booked. Unless he gets someone new by the time it comes around."

Barry laughed. "I don't envy Gavin having to tell Orla it's all off. She'll freak if he brings another new one for us to have to get to know!"

"Well, it is getting a bit tedious. As you say, most of them are actually nice so you tend to make an effort to get to know them but it's starting to seem a bit pointless when they last a few months and then disappear."

"Gavin says that Rose and Lily will be disgusted. Apparently Cleo used to bring them fancy necklaces and things. They'll melt Orla's head now about her whereabouts."

Laura grinned, imagining the faces on the twins at being told that the supply of necklaces had run dry.

"So what did you do all evening?" Barry asked now.

"Nothing spectacular. Simone rang about the therapies so I made an executive decision on acupuncture and counselling."

Simone was the treatment co-ordinator at the fertility clinic in Barbados that they were planning to visit in a few weeks' time. Part of the package included a range of complementary therapies that would enhance the IVF treatment and hopefully improve the chances of success for them. They'd talked long and hard before reaching a decision on going ahead with the overseas treatment but now that it was actually organised, both of them were almost looking forward to it.

"Will we be able to fit it in around everything else?"

"It should be no problem – they do scans, egg collections and embryo transfers in the morning and everything else after lunch. I thought the counselling sessions might be a change of scene?"

Up to now, they'd both declined the offer of counselling at the Assisted Reproduction Clinic but maybe this time a fresh approach was warranted. Normally Laura just partook of the other complementary treatments like acupuncture and reflexology on an ongoing basis with Barry getting a run of sessions before each treatment cycle in order to optimise their chances.

"I'll try anything once," Barry agreed, yawning.

Laura turned off the light and snuggled down beside him.

"I suppose we should keep practising?" he murmured, running his hand along the inside of her thigh.

Laura laughed softly in the dark and snaked her arms around his back. "I suppose we'd better . . ."

18

"Hardwick Street, is it?" Donal called over his shoulder as the tall, slender blonde ripped open the door of the car and launched herself into the back. He'd picked her up at the same time the past two mornings but this was the first time he'd had to beep the horn outside the house.

She smiled, her face flushed from rushing and her hair considerably more dishevelled than he'd seen it previously. "As fast as you can. I slept through the clock for the first time in my life!"

The phenomenon of sleeping it out wasn't at all strange to Donal, who did it regularly. He grinned at her in the mirror and told her as much.

"Then you clearly don't have the same working environment as I do!"

She already had her mobile phone in hand and was dialling as she spoke. "Hazel, Susan here. Sorry but I'll be a few minutes late. You go ahead if you like and I'll deal with the supplier. Emilia can give him a cuppa if he arrives before I do."

She scrunched up her face and grimaced apologetically at Donal.

"Sorry about that," she said as soon as she'd hung up. "I hate people yelling into mobiles all the time but my car's in the garage and I seem to be all over the place this week."

Donal could hear her scrabbling about in a massive handbag as he negotiated College Road and its never-ending road works.

"What time do you have to be in?" he enquired, not liking the look of the tailback he'd just joined.

"Nine?" This came out as a not-too-hopeful question. "Don't tell me it's like this the whole way in!"

She was brushing her hair as she spoke, its long white-blonde strands flying out around her head with static from the heat in the car.

"Unless we're very lucky with the lights, I can't see you getting there on time. And there's no point in trying any other route – there are road works everywhere."

"I might as well sit back and relax then. No point in getting stressed."

Donal liked her attitude, not being one for much in the line of stress himself. They chatted away as she methodically put on her make-up with the help of a small compact mirror and the car inched slowly along the jammed streets of Cork City.

"At last," Donal announced as he finally pulled up outside Talking Heads, the city-centre hairdressing salon that he presumed was her workplace.

"Thanks a million. I might be seeing you again if they don't hurry up in the garage." She handed him the fare and hopped out of the car. It was ten past nine and he could see that there were customers already lined up inside the window. Donal pulled out of the loading bay he'd temporarily parked in and hoped that Susan didn't get an earful from her boss.

As soon as he was back in the barely moving traffic, he called in to say that he was free again and hoped that his next fare would be as pleasant as the last. He was heartily sick of people giving out about the extortionate price of taxis, as if it was *his* fault. The traffic, of course, was also the fault of taxi drivers according to most of the general public.

Normally he just let it go over his head but today he wasn't exactly in the mood. Orla, on the ball as ever, had been on the phone at half eight wondering what his thoughts were on an anniversary present for their parents. At that hour of the morning, Donal's only thoughts were on his next cup of coffee but he didn't dare say that to his sister who would have been up and dressed to the nines since seven.

"What do *you* think," he'd countered when she'd quizzed him as to whether he'd thought about it at all. He hadn't, knowing that Orla would have thought of the perfect present about a year ago and would be only dying to reveal her idea.

"Well."

When he heard this for a start, he knew he was right about her having it all planned. He could hear the deep breath she always took just before launching into something elaborate.

"Rome. What do you think? It'd be five days, four nights. I looked up hotels in the centre, near everything really. I think half board would be best – that way they wouldn't have to be rushing back for lunch. There are a few tours they'd like so we could book those in advance –"

"Are you sure they'd go?" Iris was always a bit fussy and delicate about trying out new things and unless this had been mooted already, he could see her baulking at the idea.

Orla, of course, had it covered. "Mum was talking about it last year – seeing the new Pope and everything. They missed seeing the last Pope in Galway that time, remember?"

Donal did indeed remember the Youth Mass in Galway and the arrival of Pope John Paul – it was on TV at the time. Bishop Casey, later found to have fathered a child with his American mistress, led the singing, accompanied by Father Michael Cleary, who was similarly shamed after his death for having produced two children with his housekeeper. Subsequently, Donal's memory of the event was now somewhat tarnished.

"That's grand so." He knew better than to disagree, aware from past experience that he'd only be annihilated for not making any effort himself. "Is it okay with Laura and Barry? Money-wise, I mean? With the treatment and everything."

"Of course it'll be okay," Orla snapped indignantly. From this, Donal took it that they hadn't yet been consulted. "They'll only be paying a few hundred. Well, less than a thousand anyway," she amended.

"It's a good bit, Orla. I'm not saying *I* mind, but it might be a lot for them. I was watching *Ireland AM* the other morning and there were a few people on talking about the price of fertility treatment. It's mental, Orla, that's all I'm saying."

Orla, clearly stung by his comments, answered him back sharply about being such an expert and muttered something about watching too much daytime TV.

Defeated, Donal gave in. "Well, see what they have to say. I have no problem – just tell me when you need the money."

"And the other thing, Donal . . ."

He knew what was coming and was surprised that she hadn't actually rung him before now to tackle the subject. It was a few weeks since he'd split up with Cleo and there hadn't been a word out of Orla about it since. The last time he'd seen her was the evening that they'd baby-sat the girls and for once Orla had been chatty and interested instead of dismissing his girlfriend out of hand. Now Donal knew that she'd be put out about her departure. Not to mention the subject of the upcoming anniversary meal.

"What?" he put on a weary, resigned voice so that she'd know he didn't want to be quizzed about it.

He could hear her deep, indrawn breath down the phone. "The anniversary dinner in Chez Louis?" She sighed now for effect. "What will I do about the booking? I mean, with Cleo gone and everything . . ."

If Orla was pissed off about Cleo not being there at the table with them, Donal certainly was. Things were always more tense when they didn't have someone new to be polite and jovial in front of.

"Do whatever. I don't mind."

"Well, that's no answer, Donal." Her voice had taken on a shrill tone that often made him wonder how Gavin put up with her at all. "If you're bringing someone, I need to know in advance."

"Well, I can hardly tell you if I don't know myself! Just leave it for the moment, okay? We can always cancel one place at the last minute, can't we?" Orla made everything so complicated. What was the big deal about having to know now, so far in advance?

"Well, we can't be inflicting new people on Mum left, right and centre, can we?"

Donal was exasperated at this stage and let her know by sighing deeply into the phone. "*You* won't be inflicting anyone on her – it'll be me, *if* I decide to bring anyone. And I'll tell you in plenty of time if I am, okay?"

"Fine."

Sounding slightly mollified at this apparent concession, Orla had hung up fairly smartly on the pretext that she'd ring Laura straight away.

Donal thought about it all now and still imagined that a thousand euro would be a lot for Laura and Barry under their present circumstances. Although he had never actually spoken to them in detail about the treatment that they appeared to undergo on a fairly regular basis, he heard bits and pieces of it from Gavin and Orla from time to time. And despite his younger sister's disparaging attitude, he'd been genuinely shocked at the prices mentioned by the participants on the *Ireland AM* feature.

It was typical of Orla to just assume that everyone had the same access to money as she did. Gavin worked night and day, as far as Donal could see. He was an architect and probably earned a fortune, which was just as well considering the lifestyle they led. If it was up to Orla, the house would be renovated every month instead of practically every year as seemed to be the case at the moment. Donal was always amazed at the amount of projects she had on the go, all copied out of glossy magazines that were up to the minute with style.

He knew it would put a right fly in the ointment if Laura and Barry thought the holiday to Rome was beyond their budget. It was at the limit of his own and he had no great commitments. When he'd been with Cleo he'd been spending more, going out at night for dinner and to pubs. Since their break-up, he'd been more inclined to have a take-away and a few cans in the flat.

Even meeting the lads at the weekend had dwindled a bit, what with all his friends being tied up more and more. Billy had been available until his wife Rhona became pregnant but she seemed to be sick all the time so he was inclined to stay at home on Friday and Saturday nights. And Mick was becoming more and more preoccupied with that Jennie girl that he'd met the weekend they all went to Killarney. No wonder he could afford to dole out a thousand euro for his parents' anniversary present.

His radio had begun to crackle after that and he'd pushed all thoughts of Orla and her grand scheme out of his mind. He'd soon find out from her whether it was a flyer or not and no doubt she'd have a back-up plan in place if the Rome idea failed. If so, he'd just hand over the money and let her get on with it.

19

Laura heard the suddenly flattened tone of her sister's voice and knew that she was the cause of an elaborate plan biting the dust.

"It's just a bit much for us right now, that's all. I'll talk to Barry, definitely, but I imagine he'll think the same."

Orla, characteristically, was persistent. "It *is* their fortieth. I thought we should do something a bit extra for that."

The pause at the end of her sentence was palpable, even over the phone.

"It's not that it's not a good idea, Orla. I think it'd be great and I'd love if we could afford it but we've just booked a holiday for ourselves and we wouldn't be able to manage the two." Laura knew instinctively what Orla's next move would be.

"Oh." Pause again, as if she were completely perplexed at it all. "I thought you were broke after the IVF. Where are you going?"

Under normal circumstances, Laura could have simply explained that they were going abroad for treatment this time but she and Barry had agreed to keep it to themselves. They'd had enough of Orla's opinions to date and they certainly didn't want to hear her thoughts on a foreign fertility clinic.

"Barbados. We'll be going in December. We really –"

"What!" The shriek that Orla gave nearly split Laura's eardrums in two. "You can't be. What about the anniversary dinner? You *have* to be here for that. What date are you going?"

Orla in demanding mode was a frightening entity and Laura started to wonder almost immediately if she'd be able for the secrecy of their fertility holiday at all.

She and Barry had had a telephone consult with the treatment co-ordinator and had booked their flights on the basis of Laura's menstrual cycle dates, allowing for a few days either side. But she couldn't see Orla buying into the rigidity of this plan.

"Calm down," she instructed now, her voice becoming tinged with exasperation against her will. Orla meant well but she was in the habit of organising things to suit her own schedule and then getting snotty if herself or Donal couldn't fit in with them.

"*No*, Laura, don't tell me to calm down! This has been booked for ages and now you and Barry decide to swan off on holidays!"

Laura nearly started to laugh. She and Barry hadn't been on holiday for nearly five years while Orla, on account of a dedicated mother-in-law and a husband who earned a mint, was able to get away twice a year, not counting her "weekend breaks" as she classed the little trips to places like Paris and Amsterdam. Laura didn't necessarily covet her sister's freedom – fertility treatment was a choice that she and Barry had made – but it stung to be accused of "swanning off".

"Will you listen, Orla? We'll be there for the dinner. We're flying back before it. Okay?"

"Oh, right." Orla sounded almost deflated that there was no fly in the ointment to fuss over after all. "And you're going to Barbados?"

She clearly had an opinion on this, probably the fact that a holiday on a Caribbean island was more expensive than a package deal to Lanzarote. The implication was, of course, that if she and

Barry could afford a luxury holiday, then surely they could afford a measly €1000 towards an anniversary present for their parents. And from the proposed itinerary that Orla had outlined at the start of their conversation, it was patently obvious that the holiday was going to cost much more than the original estimate.

The injustice of it nearly choked Laura. And though she was sorely tempted to tell Orla the truth, she knew she'd regret it when the saga of the present was over. The best thing for it now was to create a diversion.

"Is there anything else that they'd like, I wonder?"

Mostly, Orla needed to be in charge and tended to get cross if Laura was seen to shoot down her idea and come up with one of her own. Today definitely wasn't the day for Laura to come up with an alternative.

Slightly pacified, Orla took a long, deep breath, audible to Laura on the other end of the phone, and made a song and dance about considering this. Laura decided that she wasn't going to apologise for not being as wealthy as her sister and sat back at her desk in the Housing Department to wait for the second best proposal. It was just as well she was the senior housing officer, considering the number of long-winded phone calls that Orla made to her at work about things that really could be discussed in the evenings when Laura didn't have a mountain of housing applications to get through.

"There *are* a few things they mentioned," she announced importantly. "I'll have a think and get back to you. I really thought you wouldn't mind doing the Rome trip for them."

Guilt was another one of Orla's not-so-secret weapons, used often in the face of being thwarted by one of her siblings. Donal tended to be the victim of the guilt trip more regularly on account of him chopping and changing girlfriends, thereby causing anxiety and confusion to their parents.

Orla was of the opinion that Iris wasn't able for the regular introduction of new partners and that Donal should just settle down. Even a long-term partner, while not ideal, would be better than all the uncertainty in the lead-up to family gatherings.

Laura had had three phone calls already on the subject of Cleo but, as far as she knew, Orla hadn't tackled Donal on it yet as Gavin had apparently warned her not to interfere. It was possible that she'd quizzed their brother by now but Laura definitely wasn't going to ask for fear of another earful.

"And I *don't* mind," she stressed now on the subject of the Rome trip. "But we just don't have the money for it right now."

She couldn't believe how slow Orla was to let this one go and wondered suddenly if she'd gone so far as to hint to Iris and Paddy that a trip to Rome would be forthcoming. And if that was the case, she knew that Orla wouldn't be the one to shoulder the blame for withdrawing something already promised.

"I'm sure Barbados isn't cheap." A pertinent silence was allowed to develop again before she continued. "Anyway, I'll think of something. Look, I'll go back to the drawing-board and let you know what I come up with."

Laura had had enough of the martyrdom. "And I'll have a chat with Barry and see what *we* come up with. We can go out for a drink some evening and have a chat about it and decide, okay? And if Donal's around we'll get him in on it too."

Orla snorted disparagingly at this. "Donal has difficulty deciding to get up in the morning, never mind having an opinion on something like this."

"All the same," Laura insisted firmly, "It'll be no harm to chat about it anyway. I'd better go, Orla, and get some work done. I'll talk to you over the weekend."

"Grand so, talk later."

Relieved, Laura hung up. As she often did after such a phone call, she wondered for a moment how Gavin dealt with his wife's constant demands. Orla was the best in the world and ran a fantastically organised house in which Gavin rarely had to lift a finger, yet it was go, go, go all the time.

And Laura wondered now what he thought of forking out a heap of money for the proposed Rome holiday. Granted, Cole & Merriman were bound to be doing well but with the current economic downturn, many established businesses were feeling the pinch. The Civil Engineering group with whom Barry worked had already let all of their contract workers go and no doubt Cole & Merriman Architects were in a similar position as the construction sector dwindled alarmingly. Not that Orla would recognise a recession if it came up and bit her on the ass.

Laura grinned now at the thought of anything having the audacity to bite her sister on the ass and turned her attention back to the mound in her New Applications basket, aware that the recession was certainly biting someone, if the list of new people looking for council housing was anything to go by.

20

"Well, I have to say I see her point. From what Barry tells me . . ."

Orla, viciously chopping vegetables for her signature *Coq au Vin*, slammed the knife repeatedly against the granite worktop, causing bits of onion to go flying off in all directions. "Oh, for feck's sake, if I hear another word about fertility treatment I'll crack up! Donal was on about it this morning, then Laura. Now you're starting."

Gavin, rarely one to disagree with his wife, made a mild protest, all the while anxiously watching her progress with the knife. "To be fair, they don't go on about it too much. And it is expensive. I'm not sure that *we* should be laying out that much money all at once either."

"I can't believe you just said that! It's their anniversary and it's very poor if we can't do something proper to celebrate it. End Of!" She stared at him viciously to let him know that this really was the last she was to hear of scrimping and saving over her parents' anniversary. "And as far as I can see," she continued, "half the country is getting fertility treatment. I mean, it was on

Joe Duffy the other day that one in six couples have trouble conceiving so it's not as if they're unique or anything."

Orla was heartily sick of hearing about Laura and Barry's "predicament", which was what Iris tended to call it rather than get into any lurid descriptions of what might or might not be wrong.

Gavin sighed, annoying Orla further. "In the end of the day, if they can't afford to contribute to Rome then that's it. We'll have to leave it be and think of something else."

"You mean, *I'll* have to think of something else." She swept her ingredients into a shiny Stellar pot. Regardless of how cross she was at her sister, it wasn't going to interfere with the perfection of her delicious chicken dish. "It's not stopping them from going to Barbados," she announced sourly.

"They could do with a holiday," Gavin said, as if he couldn't see how ludicrous it was that Laura and Barry could on one hand afford a two-week winter holiday yet were saying that they couldn't come up with a few measly euros for a decent anniversary present. "When are they going?"

Orla knew by now that he always changed the subject when he was getting sick of a particular topic but this was important and she was having none of his diversions.

"Not sure when they're going exactly. They'll be coming back the morning of the anniversary dinner, that's all I know. They'll probably end up with a delayed flight and the whole evening will be a disaster. You'd think they'd at least have gone the previous week or waited until afterwards."

"Well, at least they'll be there. Any further news of Donal?"

Orla pushed her hair back behind her ears and gave the snort that she usually reserved for conversations about Donal.

"I asked him on the phone this morning whether he'll be bringing anyone to the dinner but of course I didn't get an answer. It's hard enough to get him to decide about something as simple as a present, never mind something as complex as a dinner reservation. Anyway, once he breaks it off with them, there's no going back so unless he gets a replacement . . ."

Orla had studied her brother's "form" over a number of years and had never once seen a repeat performance once he'd moved on from a girlfriend.

Gavin picked at a bowl of nuts and raisins that Orla had left out for the girls to nibble after school and for what seemed like the first time this evening, agreed with his wife.

"What they see in him is beyond me," he commented. Donal wasn't exactly Mr Suave, yet he seemed to have no shortage of good-looking women for his gloriously short-lived relationships.

Orla sprayed her anti-bacterial cleaner over the worktop in short, sharp bursts and raised her eyebrows in disbelief. "You know how charming he can be when he wants to. He's all Mr Nice Guy so long as they're not expecting an engagement ring!"

Orla herself had been engaged at twenty-three and couldn't understand how these girls were so taken in by Donal. Her own first thought on meeting the likes of him would be to wonder why he wasn't settled already at this age of his life. Donal was thirty-five now and hadn't a notion of engaging anybody. Any girl who wasted her time hanging around waiting for a commitment from her brother didn't merit a modicum of sympathy as far as Orla was concerned.

"I suppose," Gavin conceded. "What time will that be ready, do you think? It's just I told Bob I'd check on a job he's involved in this evening. I could nip out now and get it done if that's going to be a while."

"Does it have to be done this evening?" Gavin had arrived home earlier than usual when a meeting with the Church Renovation committee in Barretsbridge had been cancelled so Orla had had high hopes of getting in an hour on her treadmill before dinner.

She hated him going back into the office in the evening and

actively discouraged it whenever she could. He needed to spend more time with Lily and Rose, for a start. The girls were having "free play" in the playroom for an hour while Orla cooked dinner for herself and Gavin but she expected him to have some interaction with his daughters now that they were no longer babies.

Lily had already quizzed her as to why some of the children in the class only had mammies and she was determined that her girls would at least know the difference between a single-parent family and their own well-rounded two-parent one. Although if it was left to Gavin, God only knew what they'd think after a while.

"There's a deadline for tomorrow and Bob will be in the Bons all evening. Deirdre has to go in this evening to have her veins done in the morning."

The Bon Secours was Cork's only private hospital and therefore the only port of call for someone like Deirdre Cole having a minor procedure carried out.

"Dinner'll be ready around six so be sure to be home before then. I'll get the homework over in the meantime and leave the stories to you." Orla was firm on the need for educational, politically correct stories before bedtime.

"Grand so. I have the files in the car so I shouldn't be too long. I can do up the report after dinner."

"I'll see you later so. And no later than six, okay?" She stuck out her cheek for a peck and turned her attention back to the cooker as Gavin detoured to the playroom to promise the girls their stories for later.

As soon as she heard the door slamming after her husband, Orla's thoughts returned to the subject of her parents and the anniversary present. She honestly couldn't see the difficulty for Laura and Barry, both of whom worked full-time. She had no idea what either of them earned but George Lee, the national broadcaster's economic correspondent, was forever going on about the burden of Public Service pay on the increasingly overwrought economy. Laura, therefore, was most certainly on a decent salary and Barry was a senior engineer at this stage. All this poor-mouthing was getting a bit tedious.

21

"What planet is she on, in the name of God?"

Barry was only hearing about Orla's Rome holiday idea from Laura while they waited for Kevin and Noelle in the comfy reception area of their favourite Thai restaurant. They often met here after work on Friday evenings, especially if the fridge was empty and either of them had had a busy week at work. Barry's colleague, Kevin Daly, had detoured to the Unified Bank to collect his wife from work while Laura and Barry waited on their table.

"Planet Orla, of course," Laura answered in mock surprise, wriggling a little in the squishy leather armchair to straighten the narrow, fitted skirt that she'd worn to work. Normally she wore trousers but she hadn't been able to resist the black silk suit with its nipped-in jacket that actually accentuated her waist and made the most of her slightly apple-shaped figure. "You know, the planet where everyone is rich and are generous with their favours," she continued. "Not to be mixed up with Planet Laura where the natives are miserable and spend all their money on luxury holidays to the Caribbean while their elderly parents die for want of a high-end trip to Rome."

Barry raised his eyebrows. "Is that how it is? I presume you filled her in on the details of the 'luxury holiday' to clear your good name?"

"I did not! It's bad enough that she has opinions on almost every aspect of the fertility treatment to date, but to actively invite her judgement on this latest madness would have been fatal."

Laura was rarely sarcastic but she was realistic enough to know that Orla would always be critical of something that she simply had no understanding of. Right now, she was focused on the anniversary and her tunnel vision would have kicked in.

Barry sipped his Singha beer, his face disbelieving at Orla's latest expectation of them. "I know we agreed to keep it quiet to take the pressure off us but I wouldn't have minded you telling her, Laura. Does she really think we're meanies?"

"So it seems. I know she'll calm down and be all sorry for implying that but it's what she thinks. It amazes me that she has no concept of money, for one that worked in the Credit Union in her day."

"It's all very fine dealing with other people's money and the Credit Union in Barretsbridge is hardly Wall Street," said Barry. "I wonder how Gavin feels about all this?"

Barry was of the opinion that Gavin wasn't half the soft touch that Orla had him down for. The two men got on well and Barry thought that, while Orla had a fairly long leash as regards spending, her husband had a good handle on the finances nonetheless.

"Well, he must be in agreement," said Laura. "I know you say he's no fool but –"

"Sir? Madam? Your table is ready. This way, please."

Starting to feel a very definite hunger pang at the delicious spicy smell of the restaurant, Laura hopped up and followed the dainty Thai waitress in her traditional clothing. She was forever wondering if every woman in Thailand was this petite and dainty or whether it was just the ones that worked in the Siam Thai in Cork. They were shown to their favourite table, by the window overlooking the River Lee, just as Kevin and Noelle appeared, their faces rosy from the stiff breeze outside.

"Just in time – I'm starving." Barry was divesting himself of his suit jacket as their friends reached the table.

Kevin laughed knowingly, removing his own jacket and settling in next to Barry as his wife kissed Laura in greeting. "When are you *not* starving? Honestly, Laura, you must spend the whole time grocery shopping."

"I know, but look at the figure on me." Barry patted his tummy, almost concave, and grinned. "Like Beckham, boy, not a spare ounce of flesh."

It was true. Barry had the sort of metabolism that gave him a physique often described as a "greyhound build". No matter how much he ate, he never put on a pound.

Noelle, perusing the large ornate menu, paused to giggle. "All the research now is saying that it's good to be pear-shaped. We live longer and have healthier lives." She wriggled in her seat, indicating subtly the ample bottom that she and Laura spent considerable amounts of time discussing.

Kevin looked at her in amazement. "So that's it? No more 'Does my bum look big in this?' conversations?"

"Don't even go there," Barry warned.

"I didn't say it wouldn't be mentioned again! I'm just pointing out that it might be an asset when I'm seventy or eighty, that's all."

"What about apple-shaped?" Laura was intrigued at this latest research, much of which Noelle got from her sister-in-law who was a nurse in St Angela's. Kevin and Barry were engrossed in the menu, trying to avoid getting into a big health discussion that might make them feel guilty about the Thai Red Curry in its cauldron of spicy, fat-laden coconut milk.

Noelle's chestnut pony-tail swung authoritatively. "Apple-shaped is *not* good. More heart disease, more diabetes, more everything really."

"Jesus, that's a bad start." Laura, with slim hips and legs that Noelle envied, couldn't seem to tone up her slightly wobbly waistline no matter how many Pilates classes she attended. It was only when they'd read that some people are Pears while others are Apples that she'd decided to accept what nature had given her and get on with it.

"Having said all that," Noelle continued, "which would you rather happen – die young or spend the best years of your life with a fat arse?"

The two of them burst out laughing, leaving their husbands mesmerised. Kevin mumbled something about this being the first time that fat arses were a laughing matter. Barry nodded in agreement as the waiter approached.

This was more like it, Laura thought as she sipped her wine and waited for her order to be taken. A good laugh and a chat with their friends was what she and Barry were really about and the feeling of relaxation she felt just now put Orla and her plotting into perspective. A few drinks and a bit of craic with no demands and criticisms was surely what everyone needed at the end of the day.

After a general consensus, they ordered a large platter of assorted starters, with Laura immediately bagging the little sweetcorn cakes in their sweet chilli sauce. Kevin and Noelle, as usual bickered over the satay skewers while Barry demolished everything else.

"Friday night at its best," was Kevin's verdict as the last of the peanut sauce was mopped up. "Were you telling Laura about Arthur, Bar?"

"What about him?" Laura turned to her husband expectantly, knowing that whatever antics the office joker had been up to this week would surely be good entertainment.

For once, where Arthur Lewis was concerned, Barry looked grave. "Yeah, I didn't get a chance to tell you earlier. He was let go today – a month's notice – it's 'last in, first out' territory."

Laura was shocked. It was common knowledge that Dardis

CE had dispensed with most of the contract workers that they'd employed during the unprecedented property boom and it was certainly no secret that any companies involved in the construction sector were contracting their operations in line with the general downturn in the economy, but to start making permanent employees redundant put a new face on it.

"That's desperate. I didn't know things were that bad. What about everyone else?"

"That's what I asked," Noelle interjected, refilling her own and Laura's wineglasses. "Only last year you were both snowed under with work and now suddenly there are less and less people needed."

Kevin nodded in agreement, his hand roving over the dark stubble that covered his jawline. "I suppose we're lucky in that all our work is focused on the environmental side of things but the lads on the big construction jobs are starting to feel it. Most of the work coming in is in the environmental area."

He was backed up by Barry on this, both of them being involved in water quality, sewerage and waste-water engineering as well as landfill sites and incineration.

Laura shuddered. "To think we used to joke about neither of you being involved in nice, glamorous things like housing and fancy public buildings. It's becoming less and less of a joke."

The conversation had taken a more serious turn and they discussed the alarming economic downturn as they waited for their main course to be served. Laura, of course, saw the reality of more and more people facing housing difficulties, with the banking sector in crisis and the possibility of getting a mortgage becoming more remote. Suddenly, couples who might in the past have taken it for granted that they would buy their own home were now applying to the council for low-rent accommodation.

"We're seeing it every day too," Noelle confirmed. "Up to recently, almost anyone who had a job could walk in and get a mortgage but with companies laying off people all over the place, there are fewer of the applications being approved. Of course, I'm the Big Bad Wolf who has to break the bad news."

Noelle was a mortgage broker with Unified Bank but only a few weeks previously she'd told Laura and Barry that she no longer even had the authority to approve the most basic of applications. Everything went to Head Office now, she'd said, with the bad news arriving back for Noelle to break to her customers.

A silence developed as their steaming main courses were placed in front of them by a flurry of the petite women that Laura and Noelle so envied. Conversation ceased momentarily as each of them dug into the bowls of sticky rice. Both women attacked their platters of creamy Beef Paenang while Barry and Kevin made haste to demolish their green and red Thai curries.

"What about your brother-in-law?" Kevin asked eventually, directing the question to both Laura and Barry. "Do they still have work coming in?"

Laura allowed Barry to answer this one, seeing as he and Gavin tended to discuss work quite a bit whenever they met for a drink. Although she often wondered how they allocated enough time to talk about anything other than the latest Arsenal goal.

"It's tight enough with them. They've let the contract workers off like everyone else but they have a few big jobs on that'll keep them going for a bit. Not much new business though, Gavin was saying."

Noelle was interested, considering that she too had an interest in the fate of property development. "Is it mostly housing design they do?"

"Half and half. Gavin takes care of the private housing side of things and Bob Cole does mainly public buildings and the bigger projects. They'd tendered for a few things lately – libraries, for instance – but they've had word now from some of the government departments that a lot of the public buildings are on hold for the moment."

"That's unfortunate," Kevin observed, "especially if you've put a heap of time into getting drawings together. It's money down the drain if you're not even in with a chance."

As the others talked on, Laura wondered for a moment if Orla was concerned at all about the way in which business in all construction-related areas was tightening up. She and Barry had certainly discussed it and, although there was very little fear of him losing his job, they were glad nonetheless that at least one of their salaries was coming from the Public Service.

Noelle took up the thread of conversation, remarking that, as well as large government projects being cancelled, there was less and less money floating around for the kind of exclusive homes that Gavin had been flat out designing for the past ten years.

"You should hear Gavin on that topic," Barry agreed. "He's been turning away business for the last five years that he knew he couldn't commit to properly. You know, people who'd done well in property development and had the money to spend on the Dream Home. They're still getting the calls but a lot of people want just extensions and renovations now."

"Smaller job, smaller profit," Kevin completed, tipping the last of his curry sauce over the remains of the rice.

"Feckin' hell, it's all doom and gloom these days," said Noelle. "There's nobody happy only George Lee!"

They all laughed at the truth in Noelle's statement. The normally poker-faced economic correspondent on the main evening news was relishing the bad news stories that he seemed to be doling out day after day.

"That's only because nobody wanted to listen to him for years and now he's the main man," Laura laughed. She and Noelle exchanged grins, having agreed ages ago that George was sexy in a student/lecturer sort of scenario.

"Well, if things go on the way they are we'll be able to fantasise over Sexy George for a long time to come," Noelle giggled. "More wine?"

Kevin snorted in disbelief. "You've had enough as it is if you're starting to fancy George Lee! Strong coffee would be more like it."

"Better than bloody Beckham," Barry reminded him, only too delighted to get on to the recurring topic of why women fancied David Beckham, now well past his prime according to their expert opinions.

"We've told you – it's the smile," Laura reiterated as their waiter approached to take their dessert order. "Who cares whether he has two left feet?"

This prompted a football discussion from which the girls happily disengaged as soon as their coffees arrived.

"Kevin was telling me about Barbados," Noelle said quietly now. They had spoken briefly about it before but this was the first time they'd had a proper chat since a definite decision had been made. Laura and Barry had agreed that Noelle and Kevin would be their only confidants in this latest mission, knowing that they would respect whatever choices they made.

Laura paused from nibbling her after-dinner mint. She knew her friend would give an honest answer. "What do you think?"

"I think it's great. You need to get away, for a start. Plus, you won't have all the pressure of people asking you how the IVF went. What they don't know won't hurt them."

Laura knew that what Noelle really meant was that at least she wouldn't have Orla in her ear.

"That's it mainly," Laura said, relieved. "I'm actually looking forward to it, would you believe? The last time, we went into the IVF feeling a bit sceptical, which is why we needed a change this time."

Noelle sipped from her minute espresso cup. "So what's the line-out? Is the procedure the same as it is here?"

Noelle had a pretty good idea of what the process entailed, considering that she and Kevin had themselves had to look into the option of IVF in the past. And although they'd decided against going for fertility treatment, they were both accepting of the road that their friends had chosen.

"It's basically the same – we even asked Dr Carroll in the ARC to have a look at the programme for us, just in case. He thought it was pretty standard so we were happy with that. I'll start the preliminary meds here and we'll actually be in Barbados then for the first scan."

"The Down-Regulation scan?"

Laura nodded. "We'll have the egg collection there and –"

Here Noelle interrupted with a giggle. "You always make that sound like you're a little farm girl out on the prairie collecting eggs in a basket! Sorry . . . go on."

Laura was laughing at this vision of herself. "Revise that. Don't forget I'll be in a tankini this time!"

"Sorry about that, Missus! I presume you'll be flying back after the embryo transfer? And the test will be here?"

"Yeah, we'll have a few days there after the embryos are put back so we'll be able to chill out a bit. And it breaks up that long two weeks where we're waiting to do the pregnancy test."

It was so nice to be able to talk about this in a civilised manner to Noelle, instead of having to tread on eggshells and defend herself to Orla all the time. Laura sometimes felt a bit disloyal that she was closer to Noelle than she was to her own sister but Barry kept reminding her that opening up about the most important thing in their world shouldn't have to be the minefield that it was with Orla. Laura knew he was right about this.

"That's for sure. And being away from work and all the mundane things like housework has to be a good thing. I have a good feeling for you this time." Noelle, as always, was encouraging and warm in her support.

"Thanks. What about you? Any developments?" Laura accepted another espresso from their waitress and sniffed it appreciatively.

"Not a bubble," Noelle sighed, adding milk to her coffee.

"And I can't keep plaguing the social worker or Kevin says we'll get a penalty point!" She rolled her eyes in her husband's direction at this. "He's right, of course. If I'm put down as a madwoman we'll never get a child."

Noelle and Kevin had actually met at an outing set up by their local Cystic Fibrosis support group and had, unfortunately as Noelle often stated, fallen in love instantly. Considering that Kevin's niece was a sufferer, as was Noelle's niece, it had seemed prudent for them to embark on genetic testing before they started their family. As they'd feared, both of them carried the gene for Cystic Fibrosis.

Like Laura and Barry, they both wanted children but were reluctant to take the chance of going ahead with a pregnancy. And as Noelle was always quick to explain, it wasn't that either of them had a problem with caring for a child with the illness. Their fears were more related to a child having to suffer and the risk of losing that child in early adulthood. Despite the fact that CF was more common in Ireland than anywhere else in the world, healthcare services for sufferers were among the poorest.

Genetic counselling had thrown up the option of using the IVF technique to produce a number of embryos that could be tested for the presence of the gene but both Kevin and Noelle had been shocked at the idea of having to choose a healthy embryo and the trauma of discarding the rest. All of the embryos would be a part of both of them, effectively a child, so destroying them would never be an option for them. Eventually, they'd decided to forego having biological children and were proceeding with adoption instead.

Laura was sympathetic to her friend's plight, knowing exactly what it felt like to want a child so badly. "I still can't believe how long the time-scale is for assessment. Couples are growing older on the waiting list!!"

"If we'd known how much shorter the waiting lists are in other places I'd have used Mam and Dad's address. It would have sped things up by about a year."

Noelle's parents lived in Waterford where, it was reported amongst their circle of potential-adoptee friends, the whole process took a mere three years as opposed to the four it took in Cork.

"It's horrendous. The health minister is always on about equality. Where's the equality in that?"

Noelle laughed. "Hold on now! That's my line. Kevin is sick of hearing it. At least we're in the process now, that's the main thing."

"It's still hard to wait, though," Laura acknowledged.

"Same old, same old," Noelle said philosophically.

Kevin and Barry, having drained their teacups and gone as far as they could with their football analysis, had paid the bill and were preparing to leave.

"Will we just come back for ye in the morning?" Barry wanted to know.

"I'll ask if they serve breakfast," Kevin added, by way of hurrying them up in anticipation of a crowded cab office.

"I know, I know, we've 'done enough chatting for one night'," Noelle parodied before her husband got a chance to say it.

"Don't worry – I can ring you tomorrow for a proper chat!" said Laura.

On this note, they made their way out onto the street, laughing together as they did most Friday nights. Laura and Noelle were always saying that they'd better do as much socialising as they could *while* they could. One day soon, they always said, they'd be far too busy with their babies to get out on a Friday night.

22

"I've decided that there's just no point in going ahead with the holiday to Rome if Laura won't agree to it."

They'd just made love and now Orla was propped up on one elbow filling Gavin in on her new plan. He'd been a bit of a pain about the cost of the trip all week, even from their own perspective, so she had no choice but to drop it. Yet, she hadn't wanted to give in too easily or he'd be curtailing budgets in all directions given a chance.

The girls were downstairs watching their Saturday morning DVD but she was always mindful of one of them arriving up to have a dispute settled at an inopportune moment.

Gavin didn't look too surprised, she noticed, at her quick withdrawal of the original gift idea.

"I'll be going to Dublin anyway next Friday," she continued before he had a chance to comment, "so I'll think of something in the meantime. It'll be nice to get them a gift that they wouldn't get in Cork."

Orla went to shop in Dublin regularly, although her husband always pointed out that there was almost nothing available there that couldn't be sourced in Cork city or online at this stage. "Tea in The Merrion," was always Orla's answer to that.

"Well, you'd better keep the gift more reasonably priced than the holiday. I don't think Iris and Paddy expect anything too OTT anyway."

Orla's features sharpened at the perceived criticism. "It wasn't OTT! It was pretty reasonable if anything, for a five-day stay in Rome. Just because Laura and Barry have other priorities I'm made to feel unreasonable."

Gavin sighed, his facial expression indicating that he was sorry he'd commented at all. "All the same, it was a good bit of money by anyone's standards."

Orla threw her legs out of the bed crossly and pulled her silk robe off the chaise longue at the foot. "Don't you start. I never heard such a song and dance about anything in my life." She tightened the belt viciously and stared down at her husband, annoyed at him for not supporting her.

Gavin slid up into a sitting position and settled the pillows behind him. "I'm only saying. It's a month's mortgage repayment for us – probably more for Laura and Barry considering we had a free site from your dad."

"Well, they could have had a free site too, if they'd wanted. It's not my problem that they ended up buying a site in Blackrock instead of building on a perfectly good one here." With that, she strode purposefully into the large en suite bathroom leaving Gavin shaking his head.

Orla was fuming as the sharp needles of water hit her on the shoulders. She often wondered why she bothered doing all the communal stuff in her family that Laura and Donal chose to ignore. It wasn't as if they were remotely grateful for all the trouble she went to. It occurred to her that if she fell down dead in the morning, the whole family network would probably disintegrate. Her mother would just float along as she always did with her husband dancing attendance on her as if she was an invalid. Laura would just continue her insular little life with Barry. And Donal . . . well, Donal would merely saunter through life as he always did, only reacting to situations that got in his way. His dead-end job, a few cans of beer, a night out with the ever-dwindling posse of lads and the occasional superficial relationship that he made sure to end if it looked like it was beginning to amount to anything – that was Donal down to a T.

Orla cursed when she realised that there were only the dregs of her favourite Ghost shower gel left in the bottle. Gavin, she knew, was apt to use the first thing to hand if his own shower gel had as much as fallen to the floor of the shower stall. She squeezed out the last of it and made a mental note to replace it from the stock she kept in the little Louis 16th bureau next to the double basins. Meanwhile, she continued her fantasy about her family falling apart if she were to disappear from the equation.

Laura would probably visit Iris and Paddy once a week and maybe meet her mother for coffee or lunch midweek. She certainly wouldn't help with the grocery shopping like Orla did every Friday morning as Laura was under the impression that it wasn't a good thing to take Iris's independence away.

Orla couldn't argue with the fact that her mother was physically mobile with her own car but knew that she liked her Friday mornings with Orla picking her up, helping her to choose her groceries and especially putting them all away neatly for her. If it was left to Iris, *she'd* leave it to Paddy and things would be shoved haphazardly into presses with dried goods going next to tins and no order at all on items like eggs that really ought to be refrigerated but would probably be placed in a bowl on the worktop for handiness.

Donal too would be useless, she imagined. Apart from the very occasional bit of DIY, he did nothing to contribute at the moment. And even at that, Orla usually ended up getting Denis Brett, the local handyman, to come and re-do it after him. So he'd be precious little use in the event of Orla's untimely demise. He would probably arrive home for Christmas dinner all right, so long as someone else prepared it, but that was about it.

Orla scrubbed and exfoliated as her mind trailed through the possible devastation of the Carmody family as a whole should she not be there to organise its smooth running. The only satisfaction in the whole thing was that none of them realised the extent of her efforts right now so looking down from heaven at the inevitable chaos would be a treat.

As soon as she turned the shower off, she could hear the squealing noises coming from the bedroom. Lily and Rose had evidently had enough of their DVD and were up looking for entertainment.

Making a mental note to change the sheets as she did every Saturday morning, she dried herself briskly and rubbed in the rich Crabtree & Evelyn body crème that made her skin so silky. Letting up on exfoliation and moisturising was one slippery slope that she planned never to go down. The very idea of papery arms and gritty elbows made her shudder.

"Clothes on," she instructed as soon as she'd wrapped the robe around herself again and opened the bathroom door. "Everything's left out on your beds."

Whatever outfits Lily and Rose were to wear the following day were always left out the night before by way of making them independent. It also saved a racket about wearing this and not wearing that at the weekend and after school.

Both of the girls giggled madly and continued hopping up and down on the bed while Gavin walloped them with one of the expensive down pillows that had cost an absolute fortune in BT's.

"Gavin!" she admonished in frustration. It was his morning to spend time with the twins and Orla thought the least he could do was organise something constructive for them. Pillow fights were all very fine but educationally their value was surely limited.

"What? This is important – they've scored twice. I'm not stopping now!"

Orla had no idea of what the scoring system consisted of but if one of those pillows burst, it would be her bursting Gavin's head as well.

"What about that exhibition in the Blackrock Observatory? Did you look into it?" Orla had seen an advert for some kind of space-age thing in the facility in Blackrock Castle and though it would be an ideal experience for the girls. The park was all right now and again but they might actually learn something about the planets at such an exhibition.

"I didn't," Gavin admitted, hauling his legs out of the bed, "but I can have a look at their website and see what time it's on."

"Are we not going to the park? I told Melinda we'd be there," Rose wailed. Melinda, no doubt named after the Page 3 model Melinda Messenger, was Rose's new best friend. If that was the case, then missing a trip to the park mightn't be such a bad thing, Orla mused.

"Dad might be bringing you on a special trip instead," Orla cajoled. This would make Gavin pull his socks up a bit.

"But I *said* we were going to the park. Melinda will be waiting for us," Rose wailed.

"Well, if you don't arrive, she'll know you're not coming," Orla told her daughter logically.

Lily looked a bit relieved at the idea of Melinda being knocked off her sister's radar, even temporarily.

Gavin made his way to the bathroom, turning to raise his eyebrows and to mouth "Melinda?" to Orla behind the twins' backs. Orla had to smile. Some of the names of the children in Junior Infants were indeed amusing, mostly suggesting their parents' interests and aspirations. There was even a Bianca, clearly a reference to *EastEnders*, a soap that Orla watched only rarely.

"Go on now, hop down." She shooed the girls off the bed so

that she could strip it down and let it air while she dried her hair and got her make-up on. She was actually going to have her hair blow-dried later that morning in Talking Heads in town but there was no way she was going to go out like a scarecrow in the meantime. It would be the one time she'd bump into someone on her way down Hardwick Street to the salon.

Gavin's mobile rang out from the bedside locker as she started to comb mousse through the glossy strands of her hair. She sincerely hoped it wasn't a work call at this hour on a Saturday morning. She'd always had a strict policy of no work at the weekends for her husband but lately it was starting to infringe on their lives more than usual. She doubted if Deirdre Cole let Bob away with it.

She wondered what had possessed her husband to tune it to a Benny Hill ringtone and turned on the hairdryer lest he hear it and get diverted from his duties with the girls. If it was work, then there was the possibility of her blow-dry being cancelled.

By the time Gavin emerged from the shower, the message tone had already come and gone and Orla sincerely hoped he wouldn't notice it until he'd looked up the schedule for the exhibition and promised the girls the trip. What could be so important at work that it couldn't wait until Monday morning?

To her disgust, the first thing he did was check the phone.

"Ah, blast." He was listening to the message and talking at the same time. "Deirdre's been kept in the Bons for another few days for tests on her gall bladder. And there's a report that needs doing for a meeting on Monday morning –"

Orla interrupted before he got any further. "That doesn't mean *you* have to do it. He can't keep taking advantage like this. You already did that job for him earlier in the week."

"To be fair, Bob was great when the girls were born. He took a load of work off me that time –"

Orla snorted. "That was five years ago, Gavin. Surely he isn't pulling that one?"

"I didn't say that," Gavin retorted. "But we have a company to run and clients to keep on side. And in this day and age, we need all the clients we can get. It's only while Deirdre's knocked out – it'd be a bad job if he wouldn't cover for me if you or one of the girls were sick!"

"Okay, keep your hair on. I'm only saying he needn't think you're a push-over, that's all."

Gavin wasn't usually so defensive about his business partner. In fact he was often the first to give out if Bob was being precious about one of his own big, elaborate projects while Gavin slogged away at the smaller, yet lucrative, housing projects.

"Look, I'll give him a call back and tell him I'll go in for an hour or two this evening. I'll get it done quicker in the office. What time will you be back at?"

"Around half two, I suppose," she answered grudgingly. She had hoped to swing by Brown Thomas after she'd had her hair done. "Don't forget about the girls."

"I'll look that up first and then ring Bob, okay? And I won't stay too long in the office," he promised as he made his way into the well-ordered closet to get dressed. Orla resumed drying her hair, envious of her husband who didn't have to contend with make-up and hair styling after his shower.

Gavin had the laptop out over breakfast, something that was normally prohibited, and looked up the exhibition while the girls looked on wide-eyed and munched the granola and fruity yogurt mix that Orla liked them to eat on weekend mornings.

"Half eleven is the first session," he announced eventually. "We'll even be able to send an email to whatever planet we want. So the sooner we're finished breakfast, the sooner we'll get there. We can look at the magnetic field things if we have time to spare, okay?"

Orla was slightly appeased by this show of enthusiasm but wondered if her husband would just let the girls tear around the park every Saturday morning while he read the *Irish Times* on a bench if she didn't prod him into doing something more productive.

"What about next Friday?" he asked now. "Are you driving?"

Sometimes Orla took the train for her Dublin trips but this time she'd decided to drive on account of Denis Brett coming on Friday morning to start the wallpaper on the landing. There was absolutely no way she was taking the chance of having to leave the handyman in the house while she rushed off to catch the train. Denis was definitely the type to nose in drawers and cupboards so that he could report to all and sundry that Orla Carmody was on the Pill or any other bit of information he might come across.

Plus, whatever gift she decided on for her parents might be too bulky to carry around all day so driving was definitely the better option on this occasion.

The Christmas trip was earlier than usual this year on account of the anniversary dinner taking place and all the organising that went with it, not to mention having to be available to Paddy and Iris for the next few weeks while Laura and Barry were away.

Crucially, Orla planned to get some of the Christmas toys before the *Late Late Toy Show* made everything a "must have" so that they were snapped up. At least she could return to the car to stow things throughout the day.

Gavin nodded when she told him this, using well-coded language in relation to the Christmas toy shopping.

"I'll put it into the diary when I go in this afternoon so Kelly won't schedule any meetings for Friday afternoon."

"You won't have to rush too much anyway. I'll drop them over to Mum's after school for a sleep-over. You can pick them up Saturday afternoon sometime." She rolled her eyes then in amusement. "*Donal's* going to bring them for a treat in the morning, if they're good, so two or three o'clock will be fine."

She thought Gavin looked a bit stunned to have no role in this grand scheme but Orla knew well that by Thursday evening there would be a song and dance about a meeting that might run late on

Friday or some job to be completed on Saturday morning. It was easier to plan for her overnight stay in Dublin without factoring her husband into the equation at all. And anyway, the last thing she wanted was him arriving home early on Friday and getting involved in a chat with Denis Brett who was highly likely to comment on the price of the top-of-the-range wallpaper that she'd picked out.

"I'll try and get home early anyway," said Gavin. "Just in case there's any drama."

"Just in case we want to come home from Granny's, you mean," Rose piped up. She'd obviously had her ears cocked the whole time.

"Well, we won't," Lily confirmed. "She's letting us make Rice Krispie Buns and a chocolate-biscuit cake. And we'll be staying up late and getting hot chocolate."

"So there," Orla said to Gavin. "No need to come home early at all!"

Gavin grinned. "That's me not needed then. I'll get a man-flick instead so."

This would be his chance to watch a DVD that Orla wouldn't look at in a month of Sundays.

"What's a man-flick?" The twins asked this in unison, as they so often did.

"Nothing. Is the breakfast finished? Get your coats on ASAP and we'll take off."

The girls ran off to the utility room, squealing excitedly, to get their warm coats while Gavin and Orla finished their coffee.

"You'll be home Saturday evening?" This was typical of Gavin and Orla had a good mind to say she'd be staying Saturday night as well. The thought of having to do the bed and bath routine on Saturday evening was enough for him – he'd never manage to get them up and dressed for Sunday Mass as well.

"It'll probably be late, after nine I imagine." She intended to get in a full day's shopping before facing the four-hour drive back to Cork.

143

"We might go to evening Mass then and get a DVD for after. It'd save you getting up on Sunday morning."

Orla was stunned at the idea of Gavin organising Mass and wondered what clothes he'd dress the girls in. Probably the same clothes they'd had on all day and muddied in the park with Donal.

"I'll make sure and leave out their good clothes then," she stated firmly, getting up from the table.

Not for the first time, Orla realised how handy it was to have Monica coming to do the housework every Thursday. Getting the big things like the floors and the bathrooms sorted out left Orla free to carry out the kind of quality mothering duties that she felt were more important than slaving over housework. Not that housework wasn't important – it was, or rather it would be if it wasn't done.

And not that Monica had to slave over anything. Oh no, Orla made sure that the Polish girl was paid properly and had a break every four hours like a proper employee, despite the fact that she insisted on being paid in cash on account of not having a PPS number or whatever it was that was required to be a tax-paying member of the workforce.

Orla considered herself to be a fair and reasonable employer but had been determined from the outset not to be seen as a pushover either. It was a delicate balance, she thought as she began to stack the breakfast dishes in the dishwasher. Particularly when Monica did a certain amount of hours in a few other houses in Barretsbridge. It wouldn't do at all to have it said that Orla Carmody-Merriman was anything less than a pleasure to work for.

23

Susan Hegarty was nothing if not efficient but the whole car thing earlier in the week had really put her off the radar. Subsequently, she'd spent most of the morning trying to decide between putting her feet up in the kitchenette or tearing out on her lunch break to buy a birthday present for Hazel's little fellow, Kenny.

She'd meant to go into Smyth's toys and get something interesting the previous evening but the garage had finally phoned to say her car was ready, so that naturally took priority.

But glad and all as she was that she was mobile again, it didn't solve the problem of the present, especially as Hazel was calling in to the salon in Hardwick Street later in the afternoon. If she didn't get something at lunchtime the birthday would have come and gone by the time she saw her boss again so she'd decided that she could sacrifice her leisurely lunch for one day.

Now she was standing in the children's section of Next, bamboozled by a vast array of outfits for one-year-old boys. It occurred to her that the clothing range would make any toddler far more stylish than any of the men she knew, although at the rate she was going any man, stylish or not, would be welcome.

Glancing at her watch, she figured she'd better make her mind up or she'd be at the receiving end of one of Orla Carmody-Merriman's imperious looks. It was already ten to one and Orla would be landing in Talking Heads at half past for her weekly wash and blow-dry. Susan knew from experience that Orla was never late and certainly wouldn't be soft-soaped by one of the juniors with cups of coffee if her stylist hadn't arrived on time.

Plus there was the small matter of a take-away sandwich to pick up in O'Brien's sandwich bar on the way back.

She was just on the point of settling on a tiny cords, shirt and waistcoat ensemble when she heard a familiar voice behind her.

"He'll look like Guy Ritchie in that one."

Susan swung around to see who she knew that actually had an opinion on miniature male clothing and came face to face with the taxi driver who'd been ferrying her to work all week.

"Do you think?" She looked doubtfully from the little checked shirt and tweed waistcoat to the cheeky grin of her critic.

"Only messing," he told her, still grinning. "It'll look fantastic when he's out shooting on his estate."

"It's not *that* pompous," Susan protested, still holding the hanger aloft. "Anyway, who made you an expert on children's clothes?"

She took in the large Next bag he was carrying and was disappointed that he appeared to have children. She noticed again how attractive he was – albeit in a scruffy sort of way.

"I'm not, I'm afraid," he smiled. "What age is your little fellow?"

"Oh, he's not mine at all – that's the problem. I'm buying for my boss's little boy, he's a year tomorrow. What ages are yours?"

He rolled his eyes, a deep blue she noticed, and held up his bag apologetically. "I've none either. All the purchases are for me on this occasion."

Susan smiled, a little relieved to know that he didn't have

children, although she knew this wasn't necessarily a sign that he was actually single. "You'll be pleased to know that I got my car back last evening. It never got as much appreciation as it did this morning!"

"I'll bet. It's one of these things we take for granted."

He shifted out of the way of a harassed-looking lady with a twin buggy, giving Susan time to look at him properly. She liked tall, lanky men and Donal was just such. Today he had on jeans and a series of tops and T-shirts layered over each other, a look that Susan also liked. She knew his name was Donal from hearing the dispatcher checking his whereabouts over the radio in the car for the past few mornings.

He looked at her quizzically now, his head tilted down towards her. "I was just going to go for something to eat. I don't suppose you'd like to join me?"

Disgusted, Susan cursed inwardly. Of all the days to get a lunch invitation, the day of her slot with Orla Carmody-Merriman was not the most feasible. If it was any other customer, she would have asked one of the other stylists to take over but Orla was not a client to be discommoded on a whim.

"Believe me, I'd love to," she told him, "But I'm due back at work. I only shot out to get this. And now I hear it's too 'Guy Ritchie'."

"No worries. I thought you might be in one of those jobs with a nice leisurely lunch break."

She hoped she wasn't imagining it but she thought he too looked a bit disappointed. On impulse, she tried on what she hoped was a cheeky smile. "I wish! However, I'd definitely be in the market for a stiff drink at half five, if you're still in town."

She knew this kind of thing worked in films but in the children's department of Next it would probably go down like a lead balloon so she braced herself a little, just in case.

"That sounds great," he said immediately. "What about Scott's?"

Susan smiled, a genuine non-cheeky smile this time. "Scott's it is then. Now what should I do about this?" The little country-squire outfit was still dangling expectantly from its hanger.

"I *was* only messing – I'd wear that myself."

Susan, seriously under pressure for time now, decided that Lord of the Manor wasn't the worst look that little Kenny Deegan could be seen in and turned in the direction of the pay-desk.

"I'll see you at half five then," she said. "And I'm Susan, by the way."

He smiled. "Donal Carmody. See you in Scott's, Susan."

Susan, grinning like Julia Roberts at this stage, gave a little wave. "Later."

As Susan was tearing along the street with the carrier bag bashing against her leg and her heart beating furiously from her romantic encounter, Orla was striding up Patrick Street after a quick sconce in the Laura Ashley shop in Merchants' Quay. She bought nearly all the girls' clothes there and kept a constant watching brief for new stock whenever she was in town.

She'd seen nothing of interest today for Rose or Lily but what she had seen was a woven rug in a deep cream with a faint red and navy pattern running through it. It was just the kind of thing she needed for the second guest room but she'd changed her handbag to a smaller one this morning and didn't have her measurements book in the Vuitton one she carried now.

A repeat trip might be on the cards later in the week to view the rug again when she had more time *and* the correct measurements for the floor of the bedroom. For now, she had her hair appointment with Susan.

It had taken her a while to get used to a new stylist but after two years Orla was satisfied with her. She'd been going to Hazel Deegan for years, back in the days when she had only one salon. Now Hazel had six, spread across the city as well as in some of the towns on the outskirts of Cork, and spent her time moving between them. She'd recommended Susan, the new manager of Talking Heads, Hardwick Street, as a replacement stylist for Orla.

Orla lowered her head a little and walked smartly past the Beady Eye shop as she rounded the corner onto the Grand Parade. A covert glance inside as she passed the door, wide open even at this time of year, revealed Cleo perched dreamily on a tall stool gazing into space as a surprising number of customers browsed.

Orla couldn't figure out how anyone could actually make a living selling coloured beads and was more baffled as to who exactly would wear them. Apart from children, of course.

When Cleo had been dating Donal, Gavin used to tease Orla about her obvious dislike of the girl. Everyone else liked her, despite the fact that she never made an effort to converse properly, instead just drifting in and out of conversations with comments that everyone thought were interesting.

"Good point, Cleo," Barry would nod, frowning as if she'd just given away the Third Secret of Fatima.

Gavin was fascinated with her thoughts on the development of Patrick Street, the city's main thoroughfare. Admittedly, every shop front *did* boast a gaudy sign and a display of mobile phones or contained yet another British chainstore clothing outlet but Orla was of the opinion that just because Beady Eye was an "indigenous industry" didn't mean it was of any benefit in restoring the former class of the majestic street.

Cleo's sense of self-importance had always made Orla want to smirk but she knew that her other loyal fans would disapprove. She could never take her as seriously as the rest of her family seemed to. Calling herself a businesswoman while she was dressed in an ankle-length, tie-dyed skirt with more layers than a wedding cake, with which she wore gaudy hand-knitted jumpers and Doc Marten boots! Orla doubted that the girl even showered, judging by the condition of her hair. Yet, according to Donal at the time, her business was highly lucrative, although that apparently wasn't enough to keep him interested in a long-term relationship.

She mentally shook Cleo out of her head and marched on briskly towards Hardwick Street, her heels clicking a little on the uneven footpath. As ever, she'd made sure to park in Merchants' Quay and walk the rest of the way for exercise.

She'd even dressed for it, knowing there was no point in high heels that would mean she couldn't burn off the calories she would probably gain later in the evening. Fitted grey tweed trousers were teamed with a fine cashmere sweater that wouldn't present any bulk under her short, baby-pink trench coat.

"Hi Orla, good timing!" Susan, her stylist, was approaching the black and gold front door of Talking Heads, laden with Next bags and what looked like one of the take-away sandwiches from O'Brien's Sandwich Bar.

"Susan, hello. Doing a bit of shopping?" Orla made it her business to be nice to people in the service industry, feeling that to do otherwise only showed that one wasn't used to accepting a service.

"A few last-minute bits on my lunch-break," Susan confirmed, holding the door for her.

Orla thought it was a bit unprofessional of her not to be in place to receive her client at the appointed time and glanced at her watch. It was one twenty-eight, two minutes before her appointment.

"Take a seat, Orla, and I'll be with you in a moment. Would you like a coffee?"

Emilia, a skinny Eastern European girl, appeared and looked expectantly at her as Susan disappeared to divest herself of coat and shopping bags.

"Coffee, please," she said, turning her attention to Emilia. "Black, no sugar."

Orla prided herself on discipline, which was probably why Susan's late appearance had irritated her just now. Shopping on her lunch-break was a little juvenile, something that maybe the less-experienced juniors would be at whereas she would have expected someone like Susan to be in control of her environment at all times. She was the manager, after all, and if she couldn't manage to get her shopping done outside of working hours then it was unlikely that she was adept at managing a busy salon. Orla hoped that Hazel Deegan had her under surveillance.

"Now, Orla." Susan had reappeared, this time with a touch of lip-gloss in place. "Just a wash and blow-dry, isn't it?"

Orla *had* just booked a wash and blow-dry but while grooming her hair this morning she'd come to the conclusion that it actually needed a trim as well.

"A light trim around the edges, Susan, I think. I noticed this morning that it's getting a bit scraggy. And a deep condition as well, for the ends. I think they might be getting a little brittle."

"That's no problem, Orla. I'll ask Emilia to take you over to the sink and we'll get you washed. Going anywhere nice tonight?"

"Only to the Opera House for a show. We'll get something to eat beforehand."

"That's lovely. Now, I'll leave you in Emilia's capable hands. See you in a few minutes."

"Thanks, Susan."

Orla sat back, determined as always to enjoy her weekly sojourn in Talking Heads. The deep condition would give her time to sit back and relax for twenty minutes with the heat of the lamps warming her scalp. She felt only slightly guilty for deciding on the cut and conditioning, aware that Gavin was waiting for her to get home so that he could get off to work. She could even have refused the coffee to speed things up a bit but that was yet another slippery slope she had warned herself never to go down. She worked hard all week in the home and the least she could have was a break at the weekend.

Susan gritted her teeth and maintained her professional smile until she'd moved away from Orla Carmody-Merriman's chair. A cut *and* a conditioning treatment when she'd only booked for a blow-dry was a bit outrageous by anyone's standards. On a Saturday afternoon. It had been all Susan could do to keep from saying that they were heavily booked and that she really couldn't fit it all in today. Which was what Orla would have heard in any other salon on a busy Saturday. She was a regular client, however, and one who tipped the juniors well.

Orla was so imperious, with her glancing at her watch earlier as if to make some point about time-keeping. Susan wondered who the poor unfortunate Mr Merriman was, imagining it would be no easy ride to be married to her.

24

"Make sure and do everything right now," Barry laughed as he departed the house the following Friday morning.

Laura was still tucked up in her dressing gown and planned to watch *Ireland AM* on TV3 with a second cup of tea before getting ready for her trip to Barretsbridge. Barry was right about having to get everything spot on though. It was Orla's shopping trip to Dublin this afternoon and Laura had offered to do the grocery shopping with her mother, knowing full well that Orla would be thinking that Paddy and Iris would be left to starve if it wasn't for her.

It amazed Laura that Orla never wondered how their parents could manage other things, even minding Orla and Gavin's children, yet their shopping and numerous other jobs had to be organised for them. Paddy went out for a drink on Friday evenings to the local and Iris went to her flower arranging on Thursdays without anyone having to supervise, although if it was left to Orla they wouldn't be left out at all.

The previous winter she'd been insisting that they both wear personal alarms in case they fell inside the house, despite the fact that they were both fully mobile. They'd resisted, rightly so to Laura's mind, but it was inevitable that the subject would come up again this year.

It was only half seven in the morning, yet Laura was already feeling guilty for lazing around. Half nine was plenty of time to be over in Barretsbridge to collect Iris, but no later or Orla would be ringing the house to make sure Laura had definitely arrived. And no doubt she'd be checking the presses as soon as she got back from Dublin to make sure everything was in the correct place. Barry was right. She *was* like Bree from *Desperate Housewives*.

It was shaping up to be a busy day. Laura had taken an annual leave day and planned to get some housework done in the afternoon. There was a festival on in the city and, if Barry wasn't too wrecked, they might meet Noelle and Kevin later for a few drinks in town.

Two hours later, after another cup of tea and a bit of a rush getting ready, she was pulling up outside her parents' house.

Iris was all ready when Laura went in.

"We'll have to hurry now," she said anxiously, tucking a warm, chenille scarf that Laura had given her into the collar of her tweed coat. "Orla will be dropping the girls off at three."

They were only driving the ten miles into Cork but Iris was already anxious about getting home. Although Orla liked to think it was in her nature to be a worried, fretful type, Laura remembered a time when their mother wasn't anxious at all. In fact she'd been just the opposite, letting them tear around as much as they wanted and never panicking about their whereabouts. Of course, it had all come to a rapid halt but Laura was convinced that she just needed to regain her confidence, not be cloistered as she'd been for years by Paddy and now by Orla.

"We'll be fine. It'll only be twenty minutes in and out," Laura reassured her.

Iris, her face pale and thin from years of unnecessary worry, wasn't convinced. "We'll have to get parking somewhere though."

Laura knew that there would be no problem getting a parking space in any of the multi-storeys in town and reminded her mother of this.

"You're right, I suppose," she gave in grudgingly. "Have you got the bags? I only have three. Will that be enough?"

"Of course it will," Laura told her gently, knowing full well there would be many more things to worry about before they ever got to use one of the eco shopping bags. "We can always buy an extra one there if we're stuck."

Eventually, after a series of concerns about whether Paddy would have soup or tea for his morning snack, and a litany of assurances from Paddy that he'd be fine for a few hours, they were on the road.

"Mind, Laura, there could be ice on the road this morning," Iris warned as soon as they joined the dual carriageway.

There hadn't been a warning of ice or even a good frost on the weather forecast so far this year but Iris always predicted the worst. December wasn't even in yet and although it was certainly cold, it was a bright morning with a brash winter sunshine slanting low under Laura's windscreen visor.

"It's not too bad this morning," she answered mildly. "Have you anything else to get in Cork besides the groceries?"

"If we're near Marks & Spencer, we could get your dad some of those socks with the loose tops on them. He could do with a new cardigan as well, come to think of it."

"We'll go to Merchant's Quay so," Laura decided. They could park in the vast multi-storey and do all their shopping under the one roof. Laura needed things for her upcoming trip to Barbados and although she was on a tight enough budget, she'd be able to pick up some M&S underwear and a new swimsuit.

"That'd be grand," Iris agreed, starting to look a bit enthusiastic at last.

Twenty minutes later they were getting to grips with the groceries in the large, bright SuperValu, with Laura taking the opportunity to do her own weekly shop as well. She knew well Orla would disapprove of this, expecting her to be pushing the trolley for her mother rather than each of them managing their own.

"Would they have any of those home-made sausages, do you think, Laura?" Iris was looking at her anxiously.

"We'll go up to the meat counter on the way to the till and you can ask. They usually do on a Friday."

Laura noticed this any time she went shopping with her mother – the fact that she held back and wanted everything to be done for her. Yet she drove to the hairdresser's every Saturday morning to have her fine grey hair set on rollers.

"Grand so," she said, satisfied that she'd been advised on what to do. "And we'll go to Marks and Spencer after that?"

"We might even manage an early lunch or at least a coffee if we smarten up," Laura said, dropping a bag of porridge oats into her trolley.

Iris started piling in single packs of Handi-Oats, little pots of porridge made up in individual portions that were, to Laura's mind, outrageously expensive.

Noticing Laura's incredulous expression, Iris continued to add portion after portion to the trolley. "Orla said I should get these instead of the big bag to save cooking. It's dear enough, though, getting fourteen of them every week," she mused.

Laura though that Orla needed a kick up the ass if she was starting to discourage Iris from cooking a proper breakfast, especially something as simple as porridge that she'd been making her whole life. She decided to say nothing, knowing that Orla would reinstigate it next week even if Iris was persuaded to buy a proper pack of porridge oats today.

The funny thing about Orla was that she wouldn't let a convenience food inside the door of her own house and she was always citing her home cooking as the reason Rose and Lily were never sick.

They moved along the shelves, with Laura becoming

progressively more aware of the reason why her mother was so bamboozled by the idea of the grocery shopping these days *and* why she was worried she mightn't be back by three o'clock.

She spent a full five minutes searching out a particular type of egg that had "extra omegas" in them, something that Orla, apparently, had said was essential. Ordinary eggs were no good now, according to Iris. Laura wondered exactly how someone put these omegas into the eggs and thought it was all a bit suspect. Surely an ordinary free-range egg was as nutritious as it could ever be? Next up was butter and poor Iris had Laura searching out one that lowered cholesterol and definitely had no *trans-fats* in it. Laura didn't know exactly what a trans-fat was but did know that both Iris and Paddy had their cholesterol levels checked every year and both were well below the "magic number" of 5. It wasn't that she didn't think healthy eating was important but it was bad enough that Orla was obsessed with calories and grams of fat without Iris, already anxious about all sorts of things, being a nervous wreck on that account too.

Eventually, after a discussion on whether the orange juice was from concentrate or not and whether there was aspartame in Lucozade, they made their way towards the checkouts.

"I forgot the sausages. I'll just nip over to the meat counter."

Before Laura knew it, Iris had shot off in search of her sausages, leaving Laura in no doubt as to her mother's abilities if only she was allowed to fend for herself a little.

As soon as the groceries were loaded into the car, they made their way into M&S. Laura, in search of new underwear, pointed Iris in the direction of the men's clothing, right next to the lingerie section, and set about picking out something nice for herself for what she'd begun to see as her second honeymoon.

It was actually a nice change to have a morning off work, she realised – even if the pleasure was marred ever so slightly by the fact that Orla would probably be checking up on what was and wasn't done properly. Because she was a fairly straightforward size 12, in no time she'd picked out a knickers and bra set in a delicate, floral pattern as well as another set in fine black lace. She hadn't seen a swimsuit that took her fancy but she had plenty of time to look again before Barbados.

"I'm all sorted. I got him two pairs of grey and two of blue," Iris announced triumphantly, reappearing next to Laura half an hour later. She was talking about the loose-top socks that Paddy liked and Laura could see that she'd also picked out a charcoal-coloured fine wool cardigan.

"I'll just pay for these," Laura told her, heading for the pay point. "The café doesn't look too busy," she added looking along the wide central aisle towards it.

"Have we definitely time?" Iris was following her, looking at her watch at the same time.

"We'll be well back before three," Laura assured her, feeling sorry for the fact that Iris was clearly anxious about every aspect of her day.

"I suppose you're right," Iris agreed perkily. "Sure it's only gone twelve. I might get a bit of that bacon quiche if they have any – it's nice heated."

Now that she was satisfied they had enough time, Laura knew her mother would enjoy herself. She just needed to be assured that things would be fine, that was all.

If Orla could have seen Laura and Iris sitting back in the M&S café with their tea and pear tart, she'd have been even more annoyed than she was at this very moment.

That was the thing about Denis Brett. While she had to agree that he was good at his job once he got going, it was getting him going in the first place that was the challenge.

Laying out clearly her exact requirements was essential, of course – it was just that there was no such thing as giving him his instructions and letting him get on with the job. Oh no. As soon as Orla presented him with the wallpaper and started to explain exactly which areas she wanted papered and which bits he would need to paint in a complementing colour, Denis started interjecting with his usual catalogue of questions and comments.

The unfortunate element of today's job was the fact that Denis was planted on the landing, which meant that Orla had to pass over and back in his path as she went about her preparations for her night away in Dublin.

She'd sensed that he had something brewing almost as soon as he'd stepped through the front door, armed with his ladders, brushes and buckets.

"I'll take these up while you're making the tea, Orla," he called out, making it sound as he was doing her a favour. If she hadn't been so sure that he'd tell the whole village that she wouldn't so much as spare a cup of tea she'd have a good mind to tell him the kettle was on the blink and leave him to his own devices. Only too aware of the way he gossiped between one house and the next, she'd gritted her teeth and buttered two thick slices of Tea Brack.

Minutes later, he was laying into the fruity cake while frowning up at the vaulted ceiling to let her know just what a complicated job this was. So complicated, Orla thought cynically, that it would definitely be more expensive than the average ceiling paint job.

"Your mother okay?" he mumbled, chomping away on the brack.

Orla resisted the urge to start picking the crumbs off the carpet and wondered why he was so interested in Iris's welfare. Denis never made a comment that wasn't leading somewhere.

"Grand, thank God. I saw Shirley the other day with the babies. They're beautiful."

"Great little fellows," he agreed. "Noisy little feckers, though."

Orla knew exactly how noisy newborn twins were and had some sympathy for Denis's wife Rita who was probably rearing the two small boys for her daughter. Orla had noticed it was she rather than Shirley who seemed to be pushing the double buggy around Barretsbridge most of the time.

"I know all about it," she nodded. "Now, Denis, around the windows . . ." She paused to indicate the two narrow, stained-glass windows and the central picture window of plain glass that flooded the large space with light.

"I'd say it threw her a bit?" he said. "Your mother, I mean," he added when he saw Orla's quizzical look.

"What did?" It was sometimes nigh on impossible to follow a conversation with Denis and today was one of those days.

"Father Hardiman."

Orla could see Denis watching her carefully, sussing her out to see if she already knew about whatever it was that *he* knew.

Sometimes Orla mumbled non-committedly to give Denis the impression that she was in tune with his bit of gossip, just to take the wind out of his sails. The subject that he'd just introduced, however, was one that she probably wouldn't be able to bluff on.

"What about him?" She looked him straight in the eye, ashamed almost of her eagerness to hear something new about the priest who'd left Barretsbridge so many years ago. Her heart started to beat a little faster in anticipation of whatever small piece of information she might hear.

"Died," Denis announced triumphantly, aware now that he was the first to bring the news of the cleric's demise. "A heart attack, I heard. He was in a nursing home, you know."

Denis loved being the first with any kind of story but, Orla knew, this wasn't just as simple as a former parish priest of Barretsbridge passing on. Denis's demeanour said it all as he waited for her reaction.

Orla's pride, always her greatest support in times of stress, didn't desert her now.

"Pity," she answered vaguely. It wouldn't do at all to let Denis Brett know that she was actually upset in some way at this news.

"A pity my arse," Denis snorted. "A pity he wasn't gone years ago, more like!"

Orla was shocked at this outspoken spiel from Denis. Not that he wasn't always fairly vociferous – it was more that he was usually more cautious, tending to elicit comments from the other person before giving his own opinion.

"Well, I suppose he was elderly . . ." Orla let the sentence trail off, wanting to hear more but not wanting to give him the satisfaction of asking. If Father Hardiman was dead now, then part of the puzzle that had formed a backdrop to her life was gone.

"Eighty-two, it said in the paper. There was a big, long-winded death notice in *The Examiner*." His voice was openly disparaging now.

Orla's heart did another little jump. She often bought the paper on the way back from her school trip if she had to stop for milk but this morning she'd been rushing back to get the house in order before she left for Dublin that afternoon. Her parents, though, got *The Examiner* most days. She wondered now what effect this news would have on them and whether her mother's trip to town with Laura had gone ahead at all.

"I didn't have time to get the paper at all today, Denis." Orla's urge to get to the bottom of the Father Hardiman story was getting stronger by the second. "I imagine most people will have forgotten him – it's years since he left the parish," she added as casually as she could.

"He's one fellow that'll never be forgotten – although there's some people that it suits. I bet your mother and father remember him well!"

Orla wished that she could just come out and ask but after years of hearing vague mutters and cut-off sentences in relation to the former parish priest, she was embarrassed to admit that she'd never been told about the part he appeared to have had in her brother's death. Darren, her adoptive brother, was never spoken about within her family, never mind anyone else pertaining to him. It seemed ridiculous but that was just the way things were. She felt a surge of anger now that she was, at thirty years of age, beating about the bush with Denis Brett to find out something that she should be privy to as a right.

"It's different for us, I suppose." Orla had always been good at improvising.

Denis gazed up at the ceiling again and Orla was half-afraid that he was going to drop the subject of Father Hardiman altogether.

"Well, it was a bad job, I'll say that. It wouldn't happen nowadays, which is no harm. In those days everything was covered up. No-one was going to blame a priest for anything or have him up in court. They were like gods in people's eyes. And there was no-one going to stand up as a witness anyway against a priest."

"I suppose not," Orla admitted, still not fully aware of what exactly she was talking about.

She remembered the first time she'd heard the name and gleaned that there was some mystery about this Father Hardiman whom she'd never even met. She'd been in Miss Rogers' class so she must have been six or seven. It was the day the school photographer had come to take photos and Orla's class had been brought down to the assembly hall by their teacher to join up with any older brothers and sisters for the group shots.

Mrs Collins, Laura's teacher, had been on hand with a hairbrush to tame the more unruly heads of hair before the photos were taken. Donal, of course, needed a good brush out to make him presentable. It was just when the three of them were finally posed that Mrs Collins had stood back next to Miss Rogers and commented on how well the three Carmody children looked.

Miss Rogers, the softer of the two teachers, observed that Donal was a picture with his big mop of curls.

"A beautiful child," her colleague agreed in a voice so low that Orla could barely hear the words. "Father Hardiman has a lot to answer for, when you think that there should be a pair of them."

Orla, a big smile on her face for the photographer, wondered what she meant. One Donal was enough – a pair of them would be a nightmare.

"He has indeed," Miss Rogers conceded, "and the less said about him the better." The tone of her voice sounded somewhere between annoyed and sad, something that Orla thought strange coming from the teacher.

It was only later that evening that she'd remembered the conversation and proceeded to repeat it at the dinner table.

"Imagine two Donals!" she'd giggled, then stopped short when she saw the way her mother's face went all funny.

Finally, after what she remembered as a long silence, her father had explained that there had indeed been another little fellow like Donal, only he was gone to heaven.

"Now, eat up or you won't be any bigger for the school photo next year," he'd ordered firmly.

Orla hadn't got as far as mentioning what the teachers had said about the priest.

Over the years, she'd heard many veiled references to Father Hardiman, nearly always when the speaker wasn't aware that one of the Carmody children was listening. Her parents never mentioned him, nor did they mention the little boy. She'd asked Laura and had only been told that his name was Darren and that he got knocked down by a car.

It had been like this all the time, little bits of information so scant that she always had the feeling that there was something big and scary that she didn't know about. In later years, she'd asked both Laura and Donal but neither of them had much to offer by way of information even though they'd been there when the accident had happened. Both of them, Orla had noticed, referred to the death of their brother as "The Accident", as if the phrase had capital letters.

As for her parents, after the day that she'd asked what the teachers had been talking about, she'd known from their demeanour that it wasn't something any of them were allowed to mention.

Denis Brett, in fact, was the only person who'd ever spoken openly to her face about it and that was only because he was looking for news himself. Orla decided that now was the time to probe a little. It was ridiculous but maybe if she had a little more information she could demand that Laura tell her the whole story.

"Your mother and father couldn't do much about it at the time," Denis commented, giving Orla an opening.

"Things were different in those days," she observed. "If it was now . . ."

"Too right! He wouldn't be able to get away with it, no matter who he had behind him. I suppose Farrell will have a front seat at the funeral."

Denis slugged the last of his tea and landed the Denby mug down on his wooden trestle table with a bang. Orla shuddered, imagining a hairline crack, at the very least.

This wasn't the first time that Nicky Farrell, the local Garda Sergeant, had come up in relation to the events of thirty years ago. Orla remembered overhearing a whispered argument of sorts between her parents over a birthday party that Teresa Farrell had invited her to during her primary school years. Iris, her back against the door of the fridge and her arms crossed in front of her chest sounded as determined as Orla had ever heard her, telling Paddy that there was no way that one of the children would ever step over the threshold of Nicky Farrell's house. Her husband, as reasonable as ever, pointed out that whatever they thought of the Garda Sergeant they couldn't take it out on Orla or little Teresa.

"Sure they're only children," he'd reminded her. "They know nothing about what happened."

Typically, Iris had had her way. Nothing was said to Orla but she'd missed the party anyway on account of Paddy taking them all to the beach in Inchidoney for the day. After that, she was careful not to mention Teresa at home, knowing that her father had had something to do with The Accident. She knew this because her mother had had that face on again when she'd hissed his name at Paddy.

Now Denis Brett was mentioning Nicky Farrell as if Orla knew all about his part in the fatal crash. She looked at him over the rim of her own mug and ventured a question.

"Were they in touch over the years, do you think? Farrell and Father Hardiman?" There must have been some sort of cover-up – that much was obvious. Perhaps the priest and the Garda Sergeant had been friends or maybe even related.

"I'd say not. Sure Hardiman was sent on a 'Sabbatical' to Rome in a matter of days and I reckon the bishop would have had him under surveillance any time he came home. He was shifted to Leitrim in the end."

Orla almost smiled at how typical the story was of the Catholic Church's *modus operandi*. Whether it was a child sexual abuse case, a financial scandal or an incident involving a woman, the answer was to remove the priest from the school or parish and transfer him to some remote little village until the furore had died down. The case of Father Hardiman and the death of a five-year-old child in Barretsbridge was clearly no exception.

"Typical, isn't it?" she said. "But the Guards were probably powerless back then as well." Whatever the cover-up was, surely Denis would know something about it.

"Powerless indeed! Farrell got his promotion to Sergeant out of it."

Denis, it was evident, had strong opinions on the subject of Nicky Farrell. Orla remembered now that the Sergeant had been fairly heavy-handed the time that Noel, Denis's youngest, had been involved in spraying graffiti on the wall of the Community Centre.

"He wasn't a sergeant before that?" This was news to Orla.

"God, no. He was a right cocky little fecker when he was stationed here first. I suppose the Superintendent had a nod and a wink from the bishop when everything died down. The next thing Farrell had the Sergeant's badge on him."

Orla wished with all her heart that she could just come out and ask what exactly it was that had been covered up but she couldn't bear to be so beholden to Denis Brett. She'd already let this conversation go on too long. Besides, time was moving on and they still hadn't got to grips with what needed doing on the landing. And she had a mountain of work to do before she picked the girls up from school.

"It's all in the past now," she said, by way of concluding the discussion.

"That's as may be," Denis agreed, "but that death notice will bring it up again for a lot of people."

Orla presumed he meant for her parents and for herself, Laura and Donal.

"Well, there's nothing can be done about it now." She gathered the two mugs and the plate up. "That whole wall there will be for papering, Denis, and you can do around the windows with the Antique White. It'll need a few coats to cover the Sienna."

It was past lunchtime now and she needed to nip out to get *The Examiner.* Only she'd have to drive as far as Rathmollin or Elsie Flynn in the Spar would start to question her in front of everyone. Denis Brett she could deal with in the privacy of her own home. A public enquiry from Elsie was a different thing entirely.

As it transpired, Laura and Iris were home and even had the groceries packed away before Orla and the girls appeared. Rose and Lily burst into the kitchen as if blown in by a tornado.

"Did you get all the things, Gran?" Rose was hopping up and down like a flea, her shiny black hair identical to Lily's. And Orla's, Laura noticed now.

"Rice Krispies, chocolate and Golden Syrup," Lily added for good measure.

"Oh Lord, I forgot the Rice Krispies," Iris announced in mock horror. Both faces dropped. "But Laura remembered to put them in," she chuckled, causing the twins to squeal with delight.

"If there's going to be that kind of noise made, there might be no buns at all," Orla warned. She took the cup of tea that Laura handed her and sat down at the kitchen table, the twins now quietened. "Thanks. So how did ye get on in town?"

She sounded sharp today, Laura thought, probably because Laura had been treading on her turf with Iris and the shopping. She was probably dying to see into the presses to make sure that everything had been done properly.

"Lovely," Iris piped up, warming her hands around her mug. "I got socks for your dad and one of those lamb's wool cardigans. And we had a bit of lunch in the Marks & Spencer café."

"You must have left at the crack of dawn!" Orla clearly couldn't believe that everything could have been achieved in such a short time without Iris being completely frazzled.

"We were in Merchant's Quay for ten o' clock and it was quiet enough to begin with," said Laura. "It was great to have a morning off."

"So everything's all right then?"

Laura clenched her teeth and smiled at her younger sister who clearly couldn't imagine that they'd managed to get everything they needed in town and get home without any major catastrophe.

"Of course it is, Orla – we had a great morning." It annoyed Laura that Orla insisted on this shopping routine with Iris yet she went on about it as if it was a major task that she had to perform for her mother every week. She looked almost disappointed now that Laura wasn't making a big deal of it.

"What time are you heading off, Orla?" asked Iris.

Iris, Laura noted, had picked up on Orla's chippy mood and was starting to look a little uneasy. Moments ago, she'd been all smiles with Rose and Lily.

"I'll go now as soon as these two settle down." Orla indicated Lily and Rose through the kitchen window where they were digging in the garden with Paddy. "Any other news?"

"Nothing strange," Iris told her. "I got the sausages your dad likes in SuperValu. They don't always have them, you know, Laura."

This was Iris's way of making Orla feel important. Laura didn't mind the implication that Orla would know all about the sausages while she was just a newcomer to the job.

Orla looked slightly mollified at this. "Good. They're the only ones that are any way low in saturated fat."

Laura doubted that her father was bothered about the nutrient value so long as they were tasty.

Orla, satisfied now, was suddenly all business. "Now, Mum. About tomorrow. Will you make sure they have their coats on going out with Donal in the morning? You know what he's like – he wouldn't even notice if they were perished."

"Don't worry about them. You get going now as soon as you can and get there before dark. It's already a quarter past three. They'll be fine." Iris was always worrying about how busy traffic was on the main roads.

"And make sure Rose eats two Weetabix in the morning, Mum, or she'll be constipated for the week."

"Honestly, child, the two of them will be grand . . ." Iris, a faint colour rising to her cheeks, was already starting to look frazzled by all the instructions that her daughter was issuing.

Laura watched the interaction between the two and began to understand what the self-help books meant by co-dependency. Iris needed Orla to take control of things, even though her daughter's forceful personality actually stressed her. Orla, on the other hand felt needed by her vulnerable mother even though Iris's inertia frustrated her a lot of the time. It was the way things had been for as long as Laura could remember.

"She'll be looking for toast if you don't put your foot down," Orla continued insistently, "especially if Lily is getting some. So just tell them it's Weetabix or nothing."

"Grand so."

Iris sounded weary and Laura wondered if Orla was always like this when Iris and Paddy were looking after the girls.

"And if there's any talk about Donal taking them to McDonalds, remind him that he took them the last time – I don't want them getting into the habit of it."

Orla was terrified of either of her daughters turning out to be fat, the way that glamour-puss Gaby Solis's daughter had in *Desperate Housewives*.

"He says he's only going to the playground with them," Iris said defensively, as ever incapable of hearing even the slightest criticism of Donal. Her hands were hovering around her neck at this stage, a sure sign that she was getting stressed. If Paddy had been there, it was at this point that he'd head the conversation onto a less demanding plane.

"You know Donal . . ." Orla wasn't letting up until she'd made her instructions clear, even though Laura thought it was unlikely that Iris would censure Donal if he did decide to do something as outrageous as take Lily and Rose to McDonalds.

"I'll tell him," Iris assured her.

It occurred to Laura that her mother was half-afraid of Orla and her myriad directives. Even she herself was getting stressed just listening. Orla, however, was on a roll.

"And tell him as well to move along fairly smartly from the playground if that Carlene Tidey appears. Talk about a bad influence!"

Orla had been washing her cup vigorously as she said this. She now placed it on the draining board before taking the milk jug off the table and replacing it in the fridge. Laura noticed her disapproving look and the fact that she shifted a few items quickly from one shelf to another before closing the door smartly. This was her way of letting Laura know that things hadn't been put away properly. Annoyed at the fact that her own efforts of the morning clearly weren't satisfactory, Laura felt the irritation rising in her that Orla so often seemed to ignite.

"Honestly, Orla," she said, "you'd think you were going to the moon for a year."

Iris's eyes opened wide at this uncharacteristically snappy statement from Laura. "Get yourself organised for the road, pet," she advised, looking at Orla.

Orla though, was quick to bristle at this perceived criticism from her sister and her mother's repeated requests that she get going.

"Well, I *am* going halfway up the country," she snapped back, glaring at Laura. "*And* I have to make sure everything's done properly," she added smartly, her glance directed this time at poor Iris who was looking more harassed than ever at this sudden flare-up.

"Ah now, Orla love –" Iris pacified.

"It's easy to know neither of *you* have to organise a pair of twins seven days a week!" Organising was at the centre of Orla's world and there was no way she'd leave even a moment of her daughters' time to chance when she was away.

Laura couldn't believe how indignant Orla was – or how insensitive. Laura would just love to have a pair of twins to "organise" seven days a week and from the way their mother's face had changed from red to white, Iris too had been stung by her younger daughter's smart retort.

"What?" Orla demanded now, taking in the silence that greeted her.

"Nothing," Laura said pointedly, letting her figure it out herself. Although, knowing Orla, she'd think it was infinitely more challenging to be in charge of two lovely little girls than to be in Laura's position or even Iris's. Orla always thought her own situation was of more importance than anyone else's.

"Good girl," Iris placated. "You'll be all night on the road if you don't start out soon."

"Fine so." Orla appeared slightly miffed that she wasn't going to be challenged. She tapped the kitchen window to alert her daughters to the fact that she was leaving. As good as gold, they abandoned their grandfather temporarily and paraded into the kitchen to say goodbye.

"Be good for Gran and behave yourselves for Uncle Donal tomorrow. Kiss?" Orla's face softened a little now, Laura noted, as she bent down to embrace her daughters.

Obediently Lily and Rose planted sloppy kisses on her lips before disappearing into the garden again.

"So much for being missed," Orla sighed. "I'll ring later before bedtime."

"Drive safe," Iris advised.

Laura echoed the sentiment perfunctorily.

Her sister, she knew, would never change. Within twenty-four hours, Laura surmised, Orla would be in her element, surrounded by glossy shopping bags.

25

If there was one thing Orla loved it was the peace and quiet of a solitary drive, although today the prospect had lost its gloss a little. It irritated her to see her mother and Laura sitting in the kitchen chit-chatting as if the Friday shopping had been a ball. It was easy for Laura to swan around the Marks & Spencer having a leisurely lunch when she had a whole day off. And from Iris's buoyant good humour, it seemed she knew nothing about the death of Father Hardiman.

Or maybe she and Laura did know and *that* was the reason for their good spirits. If they were aware of it they certainly weren't letting on. There had been no sign of *The Examiner* in the kitchen but that didn't mean that her father hadn't bought the paper today. He often went into the front room to have a read first thing in the morning so the paper could be lying in a crumpled mess on the sofa there as was often the case. One way or another, Orla was none the wiser. By the time she'd arrive back on Saturday evening the news of the priest's death would surely have reached them and perhaps she might glean from Iris's mood just how big a deal it was.

She sighed deeply now and tried to push Father Hardiman and her family out of her head. She was going to enjoy her trip to Dublin without any interference. Lily and Rose were happy as Larry to be pampered and petted by their granny, not to mention the thought of being let run riot by Donal in the morning. Gavin, no doubt, would be happy with his "night off". She'd rung him at work to fill him in on the last-minute details of clothes and routines and promised to ring again as soon as she was checked into her hotel room, hopefully around seven.

Now that the previously bottleneck towns of Fermoy and Mitchelstown had been bypassed, the journey to Dublin was no longer as frustrating as it had been in the past – besides, Friday-evening journeys were considerably shorter time-wise.

The interior of her Audi SUV was cosy and she relished being able to listen to her favourite Westlife CD without Gavin snorting about "ponces" or the girls singing along so loudly that they drowned out Shane Filan.

Orla always stopped at Josephine's in Urlingford, the halfway point on the journey, to have coffee and a snack and even though the little village was now bypassed, force of habit enticed her off the main road towards the busy service station. She was already looking forward to a fresh latte and she needed to top up at the pumps, something she'd neglected to do earlier in the day on account of Denis Brett holding her up with incessant chat.

It was just five o'clock as she slowed down to join the minor traffic queue on the outskirts of Urlingford. Orla flicked off her CD and tuned into Today FM for the news. Matt Cooper would be on afterwards and she always enjoyed the Cork-born broadcaster, unless of course there was some sporting event to concentrate on. Friday Night Eighties would be on after that, a programme she loved, although on this occasion she imagined she would have reached the hotel before it commenced.

Finally, after a good five minutes' queuing, she pulled in next to one of the pumps and killed the engine. She sat back and sighed, the sudden quiet in the car soothing. It would be good to stretch her legs and maybe even treat herself to a bar of Green & Blacks organic chocolate with her coffee.

She leaned over to retrieve her handbag from the floor of the passenger seat and was shocked to find her hand coming in touch with an empty space. Immediately her heart started pounding and she swung around to see if she'd left it in the back seat when she was leaving her parents' house in Barretsbridge. It couldn't have been stolen, she reasoned. She hadn't stopped anywhere and the windows had been up all the time.

Undoing her seat belt to lean over properly, she scrabbled under the passenger seat to make sure her bag hadn't skidded out of sight when she'd braked. Her search, however, revealed nothing.

"Shit, shit, shit!" It wasn't like Orla to curse but no handbag meant no money and no cards. In a moment of clarity, she had a vision of the handbag sitting on one of the pine kitchen chairs. She'd obviously left it behind in her rush to get on the road earlier.

She wouldn't be able to fill up on diesel now, she realised, something that started another bout of panic. The late-evening sun had already slipped away and the thought of being stranded was terrifying.

A sharp series of beeps behind her caused her to start. She'd been sitting here panicking and holding up the whole show. Turning the key jerkily in the ignition, she started the car and was relieved to see the fuel hand move up to near the halfway mark. Thanking God that she was in the habit of never letting it run too low, she moved away from the pump area, figuring she'd have more than enough to get her back to Cork.

She'd just have to ring Gavin and tell him she was on her way home. Disappointment sunk her heart to the level of her navel. All this way for nothing, she thought, reaching for the phone. Which, she discovered with a pang, was tucked away in the little pouch at the front of her Italian leather handbag, compounding the disaster. She didn't even have her phone if she got a breakdown.

"Oh, Christ, this is desperate," she groaned out loud. For the first time that she could remember, she was stranded without a plan and suddenly she felt scared and vulnerable. She didn't even have money for a cup of coffee to settle her nerves, a situation that she'd certainly never been in before.

The only thing for it was to turn around and head for home. And although she had no idea of how far exactly she'd get on less than a half tank of fuel, the nearer she got to Barretsbridge the better. At the very least, she might be able to persuade an attendant in a small country petrol station to give her a fill of even €10 to get her home if she really got stuck.

Suddenly, like manna from heaven, she thought of the few coins she kept in the glove box for the shopping-trolley slots. Scrabbling excitedly to get them out, she discovered two €2 coins – enough, she hoped, for a take-away coffee at least.

For the first time in her life, Orla knew what it was like not to have money.

It was a revelation to have to go into a shop and actually check out prices for a change and in Orla's case it was done in a highly surreptitious manner lest someone from Barretsbridge should be there to hear her asking the price of a Kit Kat.

Eventually, she figured that €4 was enough to buy her a medium white coffee and a Turkish Delight. The lattes, she found out, were more expensive than getting a plain black coffee and adding milk.

It was half five before she was on her way again, somewhat calmed after her coffee. She'd made up her mind that when she did get home, she'd phone her mother to tell her the situation but wouldn't bother Lily and Rose with the information that she was back in Barretsbridge. It would only unsettle them when they'd otherwise be having a good night making buns and an exciting morning with Donal being stuffed with bags of sweets and McDonalds. And even if Gavin had picked up a man-flick as promised, he could put it on hold for one night to watch *The Late Late Show* with her.

She sighed deeply as she faced the Cashel bypass for the second time and switched back to her Westlife CD. Matt Cooper was just too depressing at this stage.

It was dark by the time she pulled in at the front of the house but at least Gavin was home from work. It was unlike him to park so haphazardly right up at the front door but he was slightly messy by nature and he wouldn't have been expecting to have to make space for her car as well this evening.

The first thing Orla noticed when she opened the front door was the smell of frying. How typical of Gavin to act like a teenager whose parents were away for the weekend by laying into a big greasy fry that would have spatters of oil smearing the tiles and worktop. She could hear the hum of the overhead fan and was somewhat relieved that he'd at least had the cop to switch it on and save the whole house from smelling like a chipper.

"Gavin!" she called out loudly as she made her way to the glass-panelled mahogany door that divided the hall and the kitchen. She hoped that he wouldn't think she was an intruder and come at her with the frying pan. "I'm back, believe it or not . . ."

If anyone had asked Orla afterwards the exact sequence of events – a policeman taking a statement, for instance – she actually wouldn't have been able to tell them. What she could say she noticed, but not in any particular order, were the following things: that she heard the shower in the *en suite* running at the same time as she opened the kitchen door, that she thought it was strange that Gavin should be taking a shower and frying his tea at the same time and that the barefoot girl in front of the cooker was wearing a pale pink shirt exactly like the one she'd laid out for her husband at half-seven that morning. And to say that she wore it minus accessories was to understate the situation.

What Orla could say for definite was that the same girl clearly did not have a *Le Creuset* frying pan in her own kitchen.

"Do *not* use a stainless-steel implement in that pan!" was what came out of her mouth unbidden. And despite her shock, she was pleased at the icy composure in her own voice. "If you *must* use something, then use the bloody wooden spatula."

It was slow motion after that as far as Orla was concerned. The hair flowing loose down the back of the Pierre Cardin shirt. The pile of eggshells, bacon and sausage wrappers piled up alongside her next to the cooker. The table set for two, albeit haphazardly and without the handmade leather tablemats. The offending stainless-steel spatula hitting the Chinese slates, sending splatters of grease flying onto the bottom of the of the maple kitchen units.

The series of fluid movements whereby this impostor turned around to face her was in slow motion too, a bit like 'The Reveal' as practised at the end of *Extreme Makeover*.

The shock on the girl's face was nothing compared to the shock that registered with Orla when her eyes met the heavily kohled ones of Cleo of Beady Eye fame. It was gratifying, to a certain degree, to see her appalled expression as their eyes locked together for a split second.

It was far from gratifying to start putting together the facts of the matter. Which were that Gavin had evidently brought this girl home to their house and slept with her – or at the very least removed her clothes. Now, after instructing her to cook a fried tea, very typical of Gavin, he was taking a leisurely shower in their *en suite* bathroom.

"You can finish that if you want," Orla told Cleo as nonchalantly as she could manage.

Strangely, she felt a little like Bree Van de Kamp of *Desperate Housewives*, with whom she had often been compared by friends and family, and was a little relieved that she was behaving in a civilised and appropriate manner. Her adversary, on the other hand, appeared to have nothing to say.

"I'll be upstairs if you need anything," she added, the malicious satisfaction she felt at catching the bitch red-handed tempered by the situation she would have to deal with next. She turned on her heel smartly, pleased that she had the kind of heels and the kind of floor that made this move almost flattering.

The shower was still running as she ascended the softly carpeted stairs. If it weren't for the fact of having premature twins five years ago who were apt to wake at the sound of a footfall, Gavin might at least have had the clatter of her heels on bare stairs as a warning.

The bedroom was just as she might have expected it to be, if it was a thing that she'd ever sat down and prepared herself for a situation such as this. She hadn't, imagining herself immune to the pitfalls that other, less thorough, women fell victim to.

A shard of annoyance shot through her that she'd changed the bedlinen this morning, mindful of missing her usual Saturday routine. Now it was all crumpled and no doubt stained in hideous ways she hated to imagine. Worst of all was that Cleo had benefited from the lovely fresh feeling of just-on sheets that Orla herself loved.

Her eyes swept around, taking in the evidence. She loved *CSI* and wished she had plastic evidence bags in which to dispose of the woolly jumper that was strewn in a corner next to Gavin's navy trousers, the gypsy skirt puddled on the carpet and the stripy tights trailing across the bed. There was also a bra that Orla would have thrown out long ago if it were hers, a little grey and forlorn-looking next to the wastepaper bin that stood neatly beside the dressing table. Orla refused to allow her eyes to search for a pair of knickers.

The shower stopped running and her heart started to hammer in response to its silence. She gathered herself together and wondered for a second where she should place herself. Not on the bed, that was definite. The chaise longue, untainted by anything that could be considered evidence, would have to do. She perched on the edge of it, her back twisted so that she was facing the bathroom door, and waited for her husband of almost seven years to appear. Which he did, almost immediately, with a small towel slung casually around his neck.

His face, much as she'd expected, was a mask of horror. His wife – she could see the wheels of understanding turning – was sitting in the bedroom. His lover was frying sausages and rashers in the kitchen.

"Orla!"

Orla took a deep breath and let it out with a sigh.

"Gavin."

26

Good news – or bad, depending on how you look at it," Laura announced as she emerged from the bathroom.

"Period?"

Barry was the sort of man who might never have become so fully versed in the workings of the female body had it not been for the curse of infertility. Now he was happy to discuss progesterone levels over dinner in the evenings and was as tuned in to his wife's menstrual cycle as he was to the Premiership League.

Laura nodded and the white towelling turban wrapped around her hair tumbled off her head. Reinstating it, she settled herself in front of the dressing table to survey her face in anticipation of putting on her make-up.

"It's strange, isn't it?" she admitted. "Normally I'd be dreading it but at least this time it serves a purpose." Laura's period had come exactly on time, making the dates for the next IVF fit in neatly with their travel plans and the scans that were already booked in Barbados.

"That has to be the definition of positive thinking," Barry

teased. "Getting a period so that we can get on with the treatment! Wouldn't it have been twice as good if it hadn't come at all? Then we'd have to cancel Barbados altogether."

Laura glanced up from applying foundation with a damp sponge and laughed. "I *suppose* it would have been better."

Laura had known for the past few days that her period was imminent and was used to schooling herself through the disappointment before it actually arrived. She'd known that the trip to Barbados would be necessary and just wanted to get on with it.

"We'll just have to get ourselves psyched up for it now," Barry said, "and enjoy ourselves in the meantime. Maybe this time next year we'll be too busy to manage a social life."

They were meeting Kevin and Noelle at nine for a Don Baker gig in the city and it was already eight o'clock, something that prompted Barry to urge his wife to hurry up. Barry himself was showered and shaved though not yet dressed.

She giggled at his comment about hopefully being too busy with a baby to be able to go out next year. "That's Orla's favourite thing when she's telling me how lucky I am not to be tied down with children – that at least I can go out whenever I want, to things like the Jazz Festival."

"And when did Orla ever go to the Jazz?" Barry was looking at her sceptically as she plugged in the hairdryer, knowing full well that his sister-in-law wouldn't have a notion of attending a hot and sweaty pub session or standing out in the cold listening to the street acts.

"Even before she met Gavin she used only ever go to the sedate little sessions in hotel foyers where all the 'civilised' people went on Jazz Weekend. She used to go mad if I went to the pubs with the girls to hear proper bands." Laura rolled her eyes and switched on the hairdryer.

Barry laughed at this picture of his wife's precise little sister as he picked out his favourite jeans and a long-sleeved T-shirt in the dressing room off the bedroom. She and Laura were as different as chalk and cheese. Laura was so easygoing and, while she was certainly organised generally, she didn't feel the need to control everyone else as well the way her sister did.

He got dressed for the night out as Laura's hairdryer hummed away, looking forward to meeting up with Kevin and Noelle. Kevin had mentioned briefly over their canteen lunch that he and Noelle had been given a date for the next stage of their adoption process and he was dying to hear the full details. It was difficult to talk properly at work when the lunch area was buzzing with other staff all talking about their upcoming weekend.

"Did I tell you what Gavin was saying about their contracts the other night?" he called out as soon as the dryer ceased its monotonous hum.

This was typical of her husband, Laura thought in amusement. He'd been for a drink with Gavin the previous evening but it would take him the whole week to filter out the information to his wife. She was always teasing him that if she ever happened to be pregnant with quads he'd probably forget to tell people until they'd actually appeared in a buggy.

"No. What about them?"

"They've had a few problems with things that won't be going ahead. Mostly with one-off houses but some big ones as well in Bob's side of the business."

Laura was surprised to hear that the kind of clients that tended to engage Cole & Merriman would be short of the money to get a housing project moving. "Is it people having problems getting mortgages or what?" She was rifling through her side of the shelving units now, searching for a pink top that always looked nice with her best jeans.

"Their clients were mainly people who were selling an existing house for a profit but of course now they're not getting sales as handy as they were. And certainly not at the profits of the past five or six years. People are just staying put and riding out the recession, I suppose. Plus, they're not willing to pay huge prices for design now."

"That'll come as a shock to Orla," Laura commented, stepping into her jeans. "She's been so used to spending whatever she wants that it'll be hard for her to curtail it now. There's been a recession in this house for years so we're used to it!"

Barry and Laura had been doing fertility treatment for so long now that they were used to not having much in the line of spare cash.

Barry grinned at this running joke about their financial status. "I'd say he's worried about that actually. I tell you, I wouldn't like to be the one to have to clip Orla's wings as regards spending!"

"Speaking of spending," Laura said now, changing the subject for a moment, "did you remember to transfer money into the credit-card account?"

While all of their main expenses were covered by the holiday package, they'd still need their credit card for general spending.

"Yeah, I did it online at lunchtime, so we're all set. I nipped out and got the timers for the lamps as well, just in case. Kevin said they used them the time they went to Majorca – it's no harm to give the impression that there's someone at home these days."

It was only a week to their departure date and Kevin and Noelle had promised to keep an eye on the house while they were away. Donal had agreed to drop in as well if he had a cab fare nearby, just so as not to have the post lying on the mat or sticking out of the letterbox.

Needless to say, there was no way that they needed Orla inspecting for dust under the beds and checking for limescale marks on the shower door. Laura giggled now at the idea of all the penalty points she'd accumulate if her sister did get the opportunity for an inspection.

"I'd say Orla will be well put out when she hears we have Donal keeping an eye on the house – you know how she likes to be in on any bit of action that's going!"

"Don't even go there," Barry warned. "She'd have the place fumigated by the time we came back!"

"Well, she must have feck all else to do if that's all she has to worry about. Imagine what it'd be like if she had to go back to work?"

Barry frowned. "Highly likely, I'd say, if things continue the way they do for Cole & Merriman. Especially if she wants to continue the same lifestyle."

Laura was sceptical, knowing her sister only too well. "You know Orla – she'll just put her head in the sand and expect Gavin to sort it out."

"Well, good for her if she can maintain the status quo in the middle of a recession! Now, come on, we're wasting precious drinking time."

27

For once in his life, Donal couldn't believe his luck. Things were looking good with Susan Hegarty and so far they had met each other five times in the past two weeks.

Their first date had extended well into the evening with them walking over to Wagamama for a bite to eat after their drinks in Scott's. Since then, there had been a few nights in Donal's local and another evening in Scott's at a leaving do for one of Susan's colleagues.

He'd even met her boss, Hazel, and found out that Susan was actually the manager of the salon in Hardwick Street while Hazel herself oversaw all six of her salons around the city and county.

For someone so relaxed and casual, Susan certainly had her head screwed on. She owned her detached three-bed house in Glasheen and was thinking of setting up her own salon as soon as she had enough capital to do so. Meantime, she was gaining valuable experience working with Hazel Deegan, a dynamo by all accounts.

For the first time ever, Donal actually felt the lack of a five-year-plan in his life, something that had never bothered him in the least before now.

He wondered if it had been brought on by the whole Cleo episode, something he still didn't understand. They'd been getting on fine, and the sex had been great, and somehow her assertion that things were getting "too cosy" between them didn't ring true. Lately, he'd begun to wonder if she'd finished their relationship because he was "going nowhere" in life.

Cleo herself had certainly been going places, despite what Orla thought of her business. For all that she was a bit of a free spirit, Cleo actually owned the shop and the flat above it and had started a course in some sort of play therapy for children who had problems with manual dexterity in which the fine motor skills of bead-making would be beneficial.

Donal's own career plan was simply to keep his job at Go Cars as he liked the flexibility of the hours and had plenty of time off for socialising. Said out loud, it didn't sound like much but it suited him and to date he hadn't felt the need for anything more. Orla, it had to be said, was always at him about his future and whether he had any intention of buying a house but as he tended to ignore her in most regards it was easy to ignore her advice on his future plans as well.

Cleo *must* have rattled him a bit, now that he thought of it. He'd been almost embarrassed that he was living in a dingy flat when he found out that Susan owned her house. He'd even made an attempt to tidy it and had bought new sheets and a cream duvet cover in preparation for the first night she'd stay over.

He liked Susan for her no-fuss attitude and would like her even better if she was able to come to the anniversary dinner with him. Not that he'd be informing Orla yet. She was gone on her shopping trip this weekend anyway and, although he was taking Rose and Lily to the park in the morning, she probably wouldn't be back from Dublin by the time he dropped them off to Gavin.

Right now, though, he was waiting outside Talking Heads for Susan to finish her shift and close up the salon for the night. The Volvo, clean for a change and for once devoid of crisp bags and sweet papers, was parked in the loading bay outside. He could see her inside through the large picture window, moving back and forth in slim-fitting black trousers and a tight black top with lace sleeves. She opened the door to let the last client of the evening out and winked at him when she spotted the car. Donal grinned back, curiously happy to be here, waiting for her.

28

It was unbelievable, but despite the fact that her husband was standing there naked in front of her and that there was a semi-naked woman frying in her kitchen, all that Orla could think of was the logistics of getting the immediate situation sorted out.

She wasn't thinking about betrayal or whether her marriage could survive this. It was more the practicality of what would happen next. For instance, Cleo's clothes were here in the bedroom. *She'd* have to be gone from the house before any meaningful discussion could take place. And Gavin couldn't have a meaningful conversation in the nip.

Did that mean Orla had to excuse herself for a few minutes? If so, where would she go? Down to the main reception room so that Cleo and Gavin could get dressed? Did this make it too easy, as if she were somehow happy to be complicit in this, as if it was all okay?

"Orla," Gavin said again before she had time to figure it all out.

This time, there was less shock and more regret in his voice. It was quieter, for a start.

"Put some clothes on, at least," she advised with a sigh.

Although the trauma of the aborted trip to Dublin had left her mind momentarily, she was actually exhausted from that as well as this new crisis.

Without a word, Gavin went into the closet, not even attempting to gather his clothes from the floor. He was probably terrified of drawing her attention to the other ones mixed with his, she realised. As if she could fail to notice.

She sat and waited, all the while longing to tear the bed linen off and put it in a 95-degree wash. She wondered what Cleo was thinking downstairs and if she was listening for sounds of a shouting-match.

A few moments later, her husband emerged, this time attired in jeans and a navy T-shirt. He'd put on socks and shoes too, she noticed.

"I'm sorry, Orla." He closed his eyes as if to block it all out and shook his head regretfully. "You knew . . . obviously."

"You think I knew?" Did he think she was mad or what? If she knew already, she'd have confronted him straight away. Or at least she thought she would.

"You came home?" He looked resigned, as if getting caught was inevitable and now the inevitable had just happened.

Suddenly Orla got it. Gavin thought she'd set a trap for him, saying she was going to Dublin and staking him out to catch him in the act.

"I came home because I left my handbag in Mum's. And my phone – otherwise I'd have rung you. I stopped in Urlingford and realised I had no purse so I had to turn around."

She stated all of this simply, wanting him to know that she wasn't devious and manipulative and treacherous, like he clearly was.

He was still standing and normally she'd have felt at a disadvantage as she was sitting on the chaise longue. Somehow, she felt it was the opposite. He was the one standing there with one hand as long as the other. She was poised and contained for whatever would come next.

"I . . . I . . . don't want us to . . . split up, Orla. Nothing like that."

His hair was still wet and he ran his hands through it. He'd clearly forgotten about Cleo downstairs. The hum of the overhead cooker fan below in the kitchen stopped suddenly, making the pauses in conversation more pronounced. "I just –"

"Just what?" Orla interrupted quietly. "Just needed a break of some sort? A change of scene? Something different to me and Rose and Lily?"

She was shocked to see tears coming into his eyes. He moved towards the bed, smoothed the duvet silently and sat down. He buried his head in his hands, elbows resting on his knees and Orla wondered if he was actually crying. His breath was coming in deep gasps and for a moment she wondered if something physical might be wrong with him. She almost asked if he was all right, a stupid question under the circumstances, she realised.

"Everything was just . . . going wrong. Work, the business. Bob was talking about getting out . . ."

Orla thought she'd never heard anything so ridiculous in her life. The business was going wrong so he had to have an affair?

"What has this got to do with anything, Gavin?"

Orla didn't give a hoot now about Cleo waiting patiently in the kitchen for some sort of signal. Let her shiver away in the fine pink shirt with her bare feet freezing on the tiled floor. She really had to hear this.

"God, *everything*, Orla. I didn't know how I was going to keep it all afloat. I still don't know."

He wasn't looking at her as he spoke. He was just staring down at the floor and she couldn't see his face properly.

"I'm not talking about . . . Cleo. I just wanted to get away from everything, that's all . . . I think."

Orla couldn't see any connection between the things he was

saying. He didn't want to split up. Yet he wanted to get away. Something serious was wrong with the business. But none of it had anything to do with bloody Cleo.

"So where *does* Cleo come into all this?"

She could go back to what he was saying about work and Bob "getting out" at a later stage. The Cleo side of things was more important. And more immediate, considering she was still in the kitchen.

At last he looked at her and Orla realised that he actually *had* been crying.

"I don't know – it just happened. I'm glad it's all out now, especially about the business and whatever it is that'll happen."

Orla wasn't getting this. Yes, his affair was "out", as he put it, but nothing about Cole & Merriman had been said properly yet. She waited for him to continue.

"It's only been a few weeks, Orla."

He looked up at her again as if he were asking her to understand that this whole thing wasn't too important or momentous. She said nothing, although she had a fleeting moment of wondering whether she should be screaming at him that it didn't matter how short or long his affair was, it was the fact that it had happened at all that mattered.

"Around the time she finished up with Donal. I mean, it wasn't going on when they were going out or anything."

Orla didn't give a hoot about the possibility of her feckless brother being two-timed. She just wanted to know what it was that had interested her husband in this untidy, disorganised-looking girl downstairs.

She'd done everything right – cooked meals, given birth to the girls, was bright and chatty at parties, was supportive about the business – everything that any woman who wanted to have a long and happy marriage would have done. She hadn't let herself go like some of the mothers at the school gates had, nor had she weighed him down with problems and worries the way her mother did with her father. She was there every evening unlike Jessica Arnold who was on call for the hospital and often left the dinner and bedtime routines to Peter at short notice.

"It just happened," Gavin continued. "I don't know why. I think I just wanted to talk about things mostly but it just sort of . . . developed, I suppose."

For a moment, she'd thought he was about to deny the obvious sexual element to this thing with Cleo and try to convince her that it was all just talking.

"I was here to talk to, Gavin," she said at last, not willing to be dismissed like this. "What was there that I couldn't be told about?"

"I just didn't want to tell you how bad it all was. *Is,*" he amended.

"How bad *what* is, Gavin?"

He was implying that things were somehow bad or going wrong in their life but Orla hadn't been aware of it. As far as she was concerned, they were happy, the girls were happy, they had a good life going out and enjoying themselves. Yes, she was busy with the house and the girls and he was busy with work but surely everyone's life was busy in some way?

"The business – work – money." He looked up at her as if he was trying to explain something to Rose or Lily.

Now Orla, for the first time since she'd come face to face with the reality of her husband's marital deception, became aware that maybe the affair with Cleo wasn't her biggest problem. "Money?"

"I'm sorry, Orla. There's just nothing coming in. Work has dried up and I don't know where myself and Bob will be going from here." He sighed and buried his face in his hands again. "He has his own problems. He told me today they found a tumour on Deirdre's liver so he doesn't even know if he can continue to work at the moment."

Orla was shocked. Deirdre Cole couldn't be more than fifty

and she knew from *All Saints* and the other medical dramas that she watched that liver tumours were not good news. But even if Bob did have to take early retirement, surely Gavin could continue on his own?

"But what about the housing side of things?" she asked. "What about the ones you have on the books already?"

Gavin was facing her now, twisting around on the crumpled duvet as if this, a business conversation, he could cope with.

"Anything that we'd started we finished in order to get some money coming in but we haven't even got paid for most of it. Almost every housing project in the country has stopped, Orla," he explained patiently as she stared at him in disbelief.

"I know *that*," she snapped, annoyed at him for thinking that she was stupid. She had seen all this on the nine o'clock news – it wasn't that she didn't keep herself informed – it was just that she hadn't realised that the collapse of the property market might affect her.

"So you knew this was coming?" He looked almost relieved.

Orla began to wonder if she *had* been stupid. Gavin now thought she'd taken all this in and knew the impact it would have on his business. She hadn't, thinking that the type of clients he dealt with were recession-proof in some way because they were rich. Now she was beginning to see that they were only rich because they were involved in the booming property market and had been engaging Cole & Merriman to design extravagant houses for which there was no longer a market.

"No, Gavin, not like this," she told him stoutly. "I thought we were secure. That we had everything sorted out . . ." She trailed off, hearing how ridiculous it sounded even to her own ears. She hadn't ever asked, that was the bottom line. She'd just presumed.

"The house is safe, Orla, and –"

"*The house?*" She could feel herself going pale, the blood draining out of her face making her feel as dizzy as she had in the gym last week. "Jesus, Gavin, the girls –"

193

"I said the house is fine, Orla. We paid off the mortgage, remember? It's just the money coming in that's a problem. What we'll be living on."

She was beginning to understand now just how serious this was and could see suddenly why Gavin appeared more anxious to explain this than he did about Cleo. She did remember him telling her about the mortgage but it had been around the time they had been deciding whether to send Lily and Rose to the local school in Barretsbridge or whether Orla would drive them to the Gaelscoil in town to give them a better start academically. The mortgage didn't seem important then with all that going on.

"What about the cars?" She couldn't believe she was actually asking Gavin if the SUV would have to be sold. It was like something out of a film, the kind of ones where the scene ended with televisions and sofas being carried out the front door in front of all the neighbours. Although things *couldn't* be that bad.

"Yours is paid for, so it's all right."

Thank God for that, she thought.

"We've had to let all the staff go today, Orla, it's that bad."

"Even Kelly?"

She was utterly shocked when he nodded wearily. Kelly Redmond was the hub of the Cole & Merriman office and had been there right from the beginning with Gavin and Bob. Surely they'd still need a secretary-cum-receptionist no matter how bad things got. Shock was setting in now and Orla badly needed a cup of tea. This was way worse than she could have imagined. She thought of Cleo below in the kitchen and felt like screaming at the fact that she couldn't even go down and put the kettle on.

In the silence that developed, the sudden intrusion of tyres crunching outside startled her. She shot off the chaise longue and darted to the curtains, horrified that a visitor who couldn't be kept on the doorstep would find Cleo downstairs in the shirt and nothing else.

Gavin didn't move as she carefully opened a minute slit in the

now. She'd fallen for it all over again like the big eejit that she was – the married man who hadn't a notion of leaving his wife. Like Jonathan, Gavin would probably say he'd been "mesmerised" by her.

Not mesmerised enough though to sort out the debacle that had happened this evening. Instead, he'd left her standing freezing like a fool in the kitchen while he no doubt explained the situation to his wife. Or maybe that was Gavin's way of resolving things properly. Prioritising his wife and family while his lover stood discarded and half-naked without giving her a second thought.

She was glad of the taxi driver's silence and was even gladder that she'd had the presence of mind to avoid Go Cars. It was messy enough as it was without Donal arriving on the scene. The only godsend was that her handbag had been in the front room – otherwise escape would have been impossible.

It was hard to believe now that only a few hours ago she and Gavin had been tearing off each other's clothes in the opulent boudoir with the chaise longue.

Tears came to her eyes now in the darkness of the car when she thought about what a fool she'd been to think that Gavin Merriman would be any different. But for every minute that she'd stood there in the kitchen, she'd felt more and more like a prostitute who'd been used and then dispensed with. She hadn't even had a shower, a fact that made her feel dirty and degraded – a feeling that she'd become all too familiar with after Jonathan.

And it wasn't as if she'd even wanted this to happen. But as soon as they'd met, there had been an instant attraction that had been impossible to ignore, even with Donal and Orla hovering in the background. Cleo had known that it was out of the question. He was married with two children, a state of affairs that she had sworn she'd never revisit. But that evening in the shop when he'd arrived out of the blue to buy two bracelets for Lily and Rose, she'd been unable to resist the feeling that he needed someone.

That he'd come, not for two Maasai bracelets, but simply for someone to talk to.

Now, of course, he had his wife to talk to, when it mattered most. And no doubt Orla was finally hearing about all the worry he'd wanted so badly to spare her. It occurred to Cleo then that no man had ever cared enough about *her* to be concerned about sparing her from anything. No, she was just a sort of whipping boy that they came to in order to relieve the stress so that they wouldn't have to carry it home to their precious wives.

She thought now of Jonathan Dundon and the sheen of perspiration that would appear on his forehead week after week whenever there was a new development with the impending court case. Phyllis Dundon hadn't known about it until the last minute and by the time it appeared in the national newspapers that the eminent surgeon was responsible for removing a perfectly healthy kidney, the young housewife in question had adjusted to life on dialysis and the ongoing wait for a kidney transplant. It had all been settled for the princely sum of €1.2 million, Phyllis had stood by him for the three-day stint in court and Jonathan had realised just what a wonderfully supportive wife he'd had all along.

The only difference this time was that Cleo had been infinitely more careful, having learned the hard way that family planning was, in the end of the day, a woman's responsibility. This time, there would be no solo journey to Hampstead and no career as a medical student to abandon while she went into a black depression that nobody understood.

Her parents, despite standing by her decision to "take time out" for her travels to the orphanage in Kenya, still didn't understand what it was that had precipitated her nervous breakdown. They were just happy that she finally came back, even if it was to sell her ethnic beads at the Farmers' Markets around Cork. Their decision to buy the building on Patrick Street for her had been a tax incentive. And much cheaper that funding another five years of medical college.

At the time, the worst thing of all had been that nobody knew what she'd been through. She became used to being thought of as a frivolous free spirit who was too flighty and highly-strung to settle down to college life the way her brothers and cousins had. If only she'd been like Jessica and completed her studies and married a nice, reliable veterinary surgeon. And Peter Arnold was just that – reliable, anyway – as she'd found out for herself in the most shameful way possible.

Now for the first time, Cleo was glad that the Jonathan Dundon saga hadn't been public knowledge. To have this happen once was perhaps the act of an innocent young girl being taken advantage of by a powerful and charming society surgeon. To have it happen twice . . .

"Fucking eejit!" She cursed her stupidity out loud unknown to herself.

"What, love?"

She'd forgotten all about the chubby, middle-aged taxi driver.

"Nothing," she mumbled, feeling a frisson of fear at the fact that she'd spoken out loud without being aware of it. The memory of her three weeks in the psychiatric wing of St Angela's felt frighteningly near right now.

"Nearly there now, anyway," he said kindly.

Cleo thought that perhaps he might have noticed her dishevelled state and the fact that she'd bolted into the taxi as soon as it had pulled up outside Gavin and Orla's house. It occurred to her that maybe he even thought she looked like a callgirl and felt sorry for her but she dismissed this thought as being perilously close to paranoia.

All she needed now was to be home and to feel the warmth of a soothing shower washing all the filth and shame of the last hour away. The first thing she would do, though, would be to tear off Gavin Merriman's soft pink shirt and his offensive trench coat and stuff them into her small wood-burning stove.

29

Laura stretched out her legs under the light cotton sheet, waking Barry in the process.

"This is *soooo* the life," she said smugly, watching her husband come alive at last. For some reason, Barry was feeling the jet-lag more than she was but it was time for breakfast and neither of them had thought to place the request label on the door of their apartment the previous evening.

"Any chance of an OJ?"

Barry had had a few glasses of rum in one of the bars and was evidently suffering a little from the generous Caribbean measures. Feeling a bit sorry for him, Laura hopped out of bed and got one of the miniatures of orange juice from the medication fridge that was standard in all the resort's apartments.

"There you go. I can nip over and bring back a breakfast tray if you like. I'm starving and it'll be ages before you surface properly!"

Barry grinned half-heartedly but agreed instantly. "It's your own fault for encouraging me," he reminded his wife.

The past few weeks had been a rush for both of them, with

finishing up at work and organising the holiday so Laura really wanted them to make the most of the opportunity of being relaxed and away from home. Tonight, Barry would be starting his course of antibiotics and would be unable to have a drink after that, so Laura *had* encouraged him to let his hair down a bit.

"Grand so, I'll be back in a few minutes." She pulled on shorts and a floral cotton top and headed for the restaurant to secure a breakfast that they could enjoy on their second-floor balcony.

Crossing the neatly clipped grass to the chrome and glass food hall, she wondered if all the couples she passed were here for fertility treatment. Or if perhaps the clinic offered other services as well. Most of them looked relaxed but she imagined that she and Barry looked the same despite the fact the usual anxiety was still there as regards the number of follicles that she'd produce and whether the eggs would fertilise successfully.

The food hall opened onto an outdoor breakfast area that they'd used on their first morning in Barbados and it was from there that Barry had gleefully spotted people collecting laden trays that they seemed to be carrying back to their rooms. Laura glanced around now and secured a large rattan tray. Now all she had to do was decide what her slightly hungover husband might like for his breakfast.

Five minutes later, she was retracing her steps across the lawn, her tray laden with fruit juice, muesli, pancakes and maple syrup as well as a heavy silver pot of strong coffee.

"Wakey, wakey!" she called out, tipping open the door with her foot. She'd left it ajar on her way out so as not to have to disturb Barry from his bed. Now she headed straight for the balcony to relieve herself of the cumbersome tray.

He sat up immediately and followed her out, anxious for another shot of juice even though he'd polished off the little bottle from the mini-fridge fairly smartly.

Laura grinned. "Juice first, I presume?"

"And coffee," he said, rolling his eyes and downing the large glass of mixed fruit juice in one go. "My tongue feels like one of Ghandi's sandals! Remind me again why I didn't use a mixer with the rum?"

"Because the barman convinced you it was too pure to be messing with or something. And you believed him, of course." She handed him his coffee and poured milk over both their bowls of cereal, the early morning sun already warming her shoulders. There wasn't a cloud in the sky and for a moment she forgot that they were on anything but a well-deserved, ordinary holiday.

"So what's on today?" He looked perkier already and listened as Laura read from the typed itinerary that she'd stuffed in the pocket of her shorts the previous day.

"A scan first at eleven thirty. We could have a swim before it if you like?"

"Mmm. I'll be well recovered by then."

"That remains to be seen."

Barry grinned, then said seriously, "Hopefully some of the other follicles will have matured."

Laura's scan the previous morning had shown twelve developing follicles, eight of which had been mature. The next few days would determine how many "usable" ones would be there for collection.

"Even eight though, if all of them continue to grow, would still be good," Laura mused. "Hopefully they'll be ready for collection by next Monday."

Barry held out his cup for a second round of coffee. "What about the afternoon?"

"I'm going to the counsellor at two and you're booked for acupuncture at the same time. It's very well organised, isn't it?"

Barry nodded, his mouth full of a delicious blueberry pancake. "Very good," he managed eventually. "You always hear people talking about holiday bookings that don't work out the way they were advertised but so far this is spot on."

He was right about it being spot on. The previous morning, an aide had knocked on their door ten minutes before their appointment, offering to walk them over to the scanning room and show them around the facilities that they'd be availing of. As well as high-spec treatment rooms, the complementary therapy block was serene and gently air-conditioned for maximum relaxation. Some of the therapies could even be taken outside in the shade if the client so chose.

"And in terms of the actual treatment, it's practically the same as the ARC. And it's great that we'll be having Janine for the scan again today."

They'd been told that there was a "continuity of care" policy at the clinic so that they wouldn't be seeing different people every day, insofar as it was practical. The sonographer who'd carried out their first scan had been pleasant and efficient and Laura was already looking forward to meeting her again this morning.

"It'll be nice to have the same person," Barry agreed. "I wonder will both of us have the same counsellor?" Barry was booked for a session the following day while Laura had the first in a series of massages.

"I imagine so. God, these are gorgeous." She added a further dose of maple syrup to her pile of pancakes and leaned back in her chair. "You know what? Regardless of the treatment, we really need this break."

Barry reached out then and kissed her. "You're right. It feels like years since we sat back like this in the sun."

"That's because it is years!" Laura laughed. "Will we lie out for an hour before the scan?"

Barry groaned, stuffed now after too many pancakes. "We'll have to. You were a bit heavy-handed with the pancakes!"

It was five to two and Laura was feeling only the tiniest bit of anxiety about her counselling session. She was sitting among the leafy green plants in the reception area having given her name to the local girl manning the desk. A door opened quietly down the corridor and she watched as an elegant lady with chocolate skin and an amazing collection of corn-rows approached.

"Laura? Hello, I'm Grace Cavendish." Her voice was quiet, with precise English and only a slight hint of the Caribbean lilt that had already become familiar.

Laura stood up and found herself, for once, next to someone that was taller than she. "Hello, Grace, it's nice to meet you."

"Please, follow me."

Laura followed her back down the hall and into a large airy room that looked out over the garden with the azure of the sea beyond.

"Do sit down."

Grace indicated a comfortable floral sofa next to a low table on which was placed a glass of iced fruit juice decorated with a colourful cocktail umbrella. Laura smiled at the incongruity of the little cocktail here in a counselling suite.

"It's non-alcoholic," Grace asserted with a smile. "Talking can be thirsty work."

Laura thanked her and settled into the sofa, unsure as to how this would begin.

"You had a scan this morning?" Grace was obviously familiar with the medical routine at the clinic.

"Yes. We have eight mature follicles this morning so we were delighted."

Laura thought that she might need to know whether the treatment was going as planned – or perhaps she even knew already from some other source.

"That's great. I see from your notes that you and Barry have Unexplained Infertility?" It was phrased as a question so Laura nodded and obliged by sharing her own thoughts on that.

"Yes. We'd been trying ourselves for about six months and nothing happened so we decided to get help. This is our sixth attempt at IVF but we had other treatments before that."

Grace nodded. "I see. So you've had a busy few years with this?"

Laura smiled. "That's an understatement! I know there are breaks in between treatment cycles but really it's there all the time."

"Most people tell me that Unexplained Infertility is so difficult because there's always the possibility that you might become pregnant without any treatment at all. So you're actually trying every month."

This, in Laura and Barry's case was completely true. Orla, for one, tended to think that it was all about the IVF and that they could forget about it in between treatments. But they couldn't when there was "nothing wrong" and they might just be lucky if they made the effort every month. Which of course they did.

"That's so true. There's no real 'let up' ever. I'm not sure whether it's harder or easier but, for people with something specific wrong, they might be able to take a mental break in between treatments if they know there won't be a chance of pregnancy."

Grace nodded again and smiled. "The other thing about Unexplained Infertility is that it can be frustrating that there's nothing specific people can do to remedy the situation."

Laura was impressed at the counsellor's understanding of the kind of feelings people in her situation had. Noelle and Kevin were marvellous, having some experience of it themselves but there were a lot of Orla-types who were quick to give glib advice about adoption or IVF as if either option was a piece of cake.

"Tell me about it! Sometimes I wish I had endometriosis or blocked tubes or something that could be fixed with laser or surgery. In our case, we can only keep doing treatment and see if it works."

"That *must* be difficult," Grace acknowledged.

Laura thought for a minute before going on. "It used to be harder. This time around, I feel a bit distracted by the different surroundings, which is no harm. The last few times I was quite anxious, maybe because time is moving on for us as regards my age. I'll be thirty-eight next birthday."

Grace smiled. "It's not *too* old."

"Not for most people," Laura admitted. "But with infertility you have a sense of time slipping away all the time. Generally, I wouldn't be the type to be worried about ageing but I know the treatment will produce fewer follicles as time goes on."

"I can see where you're coming from," the counsellor said.

Grace seemed to be agreeing with everything she said, a far cry from Orla who tended to challenge her all the way.

"As I said, it's frustrating to have no explanation at all. I'm so healthy normally. I'm never sick and neither is Barry for that matter. That's what makes it all so strange. I'm convinced there's nothing physically wrong with either of us, even though the consultant at home says there could be something that just hasn't been discovered yet."

Laura and Barry talked about this a lot between themselves. It was true that they were both on the extreme end of healthy, rarely even suffering from colds or flus.

"And if it's not a physical thing, have you ever thought about what else it is that *might* be wrong, Laura?"

Laura had actually thought about this a lot lately. Initially, she'd kept hoping that, statistically, their one-in-four chance of the IVF working would materialise. It hadn't. So she'd put the fifth failure down to simple bad luck in an attempt to maintain hope and help her to continue optimistically on this occasion. She explained this now as best she could.

"That's something that most couples say – that it's difficult to remain optimistic when they're faced with failure time after time." It was clear that Grace Cavendish had extensive experience.

"There *are* times that I feel like giving up," Laura admitted.

"I can appreciate that. It's a real rollercoaster – up and down all the time."

In this too Grace was accurate. There was the huge build-up

of hope and expectation every month, then the crash at the end when her period arrived yet again. She and Barry often discussed how much longer they could go on taking blow after blow. She told Grace this now.

"And what conclusion do you tend to come to?"

"I suppose we give ourselves time to recover a bit and get the misery out of our systems. But, so far, we've always ended up going ahead with another treatment. In the end of the day, we know there isn't a whole lot of time left in terms of my age."

"It's quite pressurised, this biological clock ticking."

"It is but we try not to let it get to us too much. We look after ourselves quite well. I changed job a few years ago, for instance, to get away from stress so that I could concentrate properly on this."

"So you make as much effort as you can to cope." Grace smiled when Laura nodded at this.

"It's just sensible, I suppose. I mean, if we get stressed about it all, then it's less likely to happen. We just have to take it day by day and see what comes."

Grace smiled sympathetically. "It's hard to resign oneself to having to deal with something like this."

"Well, things happen to everyone," Laura responded, taking a sip from her fruit juice. She was beginning to sound a bit moany and she wondered if the counsellor would think she had a very negative attitude. "I've been very lucky in other ways – meeting Barry, for instance. And we have a lovely home. And I know I give out about it now and again, but my job is fine as well."

"Some of the couples I meet feel a bit short changed that there are other people out there who have lovely homes and good jobs but are lucky enough to have children *as well*."

Laura felt a little bit defensive all of a sudden and didn't quite know why.

"I do feel that sometimes. But I usually end up coming to the conclusion that there are people out there with cancer or whose husbands are killed in car accidents or whatever. Even though this hasn't gone the way we want it to, we're still lucky in other ways."

"True. There are some who might say that worse things could happen than not having children."

Laura sincerely hoped that Grace didn't think this was her attitude. She would hate anyone to think that this was how she felt although she knew that Orla definitely thought she wasn't half cut up enough about it all.

"Well, it's the worst thing that could happen to me and Barry," she said truthfully. "But other people have horrible things going on too, that's all I'm saying."

Grace smiled her enigmatic smile again. "You make it sound like you don't exactly deserve sympathy for this when other people have so much going on!"

Laura felt wrong-footed somehow and tried to explain. "It's not about deserving *sympathy*. This is mine and Barry's problem, that's all. I don't want sympathy from people."

"I can certainly appreciate that, Laura. And it is good to be able to empathise with other people despite everything you are going through."

"I suppose," Laura concurred. "It'd be a bad job not to be able to see outside your own problems, wouldn't it?"

"It would," Grace smiled gently. "But I imagine it'd be equally as bad to minimise our own problems or think they're not as important as other people's."

She was looking at Laura with one eyebrow raised. Laura had to admit that she did tend to diminish the enormity of the infertility, which sometimes annoyed Barry a bit if he was feeling particularly pissed off after a treatment had failed.

"Barry says I'm one of these people who loses a leg and still says what about all the poor people out there who've lost two legs!" She realised now just how well Barry knew her.

"How did you get to be like that, do you think?" Grace looked curious, as if this trait of Laura's was interesting in the extreme.

"I don't know. I'm the eldest at home, so I suppose I did have more responsibility than the others."

"How so?"

Laura thought it was obvious that older children would shoulder more responsibility than their younger siblings. "It's just being the eldest, I suppose. You take it for granted a bit." She couldn't really explain it now that she'd been asked specifically.

"Who else was there at home?"

It was like being in a Woody Allen film all of a sudden. Everything came back to childhood as far as counsellors went and here was the proof of it.

"I've a brother, Donal, who's thirty-five. And a sister, Orla. She's almost thirty and married with two children – twins, actually. Donal's still single." She thought this was a succinct description of her family.

"Your parents aren't living?"

"Oh no," she corrected, feeling foolish. "They're there too. Mam is just gone seventy and Dad's a year older."

"And they're both healthy?"

Laura had no idea where this was going. Surely the state of her parents' health didn't have anything to do with her problem?

Grace just nodded and wrote this down. She'd been making notes here and there and Laura wondered exactly which bits the counsellor thought were relevant.

"There's a biggish age gap between your brother and your sister," Grace noted now. "Do you find you're closer to one or other of them?"

Guiltily, Laura thought of the fact that neither of them even knew why she and Barry had come to Barbados. She was tempted to just gloss over it and say that, yes, they were all as close as peas in a pod. She had a memory then of one of her school teachers preaching about "fooling no-one but yourself" and decided to be as honest as possible now that she was here.

"I suppose I'm a bit closer to Donal, although we don't have

all that much in common. Orla is . . . a bit much sometimes."
She looked up to see if Grace looked like she understood. "She
doesn't really understand the fertility treatment, I suppose. She
has her own ideas on what we should do."

"Is it that she doesn't agree with IVF?" Grace was looking at
her as if this might be quite a normal response.

"No, not that." Laura knew that many people, particularly of
the older generation, had a problem with IVF and the fact that
the Catholic Church considered it to be a mortal sin. "She can't
understand why we don't just adopt a baby."

Grace raised her eyebrows as if asking Laura to go on and
explain further.

"Orla is adopted herself, you see. So I think she feels upset
that we don't seem interested in it. She gets a bit offended
actually."

"I'd noticed in the notes that you haven't started the adoption
process but that doesn't particularly surprise me. Lots of couples
don't see it as an option."

Laura let out her breath, not realising until now that she was
actually holding it in anticipation of Grace starting on about
them not choosing to adopt. It was a relief not to have to defend
their decision for the moment at least.

"It's unusual to adopt a child after having two already,"
Grace commented now. "What does your mother feel about
your decision?"

Laura felt like giggling. Iris didn't care one way or another
what Laura and Barry did or even if they ever had a child or not.
She would nod and try to sound interested if Laura told her
something about the treatment but she never asked about it and
certainly had never asked if she and Barry had considered
adopting a baby. Which was a bit odd now that Grace had
brought it up.

She wondered now what time it was and if there was time left
in the session to go into this. She didn't really feel like getting

into it but was practical enough to know that there was no point in attending a counselling session if she wasn't going to make an effort to be truthful.

"It probably was a bit unusual to adopt another baby when she had us – me and Donal, I mean." She sighed, unknown to herself. "But there was an accident . . ."

30

While Laura was discussing her past with a counsellor in Barbados, Orla was sitting at her kitchen table, pen in hand, planning her future.

If she was to say that she learned anything from the discoveries of last Friday night, it was that any disaster has the capacity to pale into insignificance if placed alongside a greater one. Which was why the realisation that Cole & Merriman were as close to the wall as the new colours that Denis Brett had painted on the stairs and landing had taken precedence over the fact that her husband was having an affair. It was a bit like the difference between a minor earthquake and a full-scale tsunami.

She revised in her head. Her husband *had been* having an affair, seeing as he'd phoned Cleo as promised on Saturday morning and put an end to it. Afterwards, he'd told her that he was glad she'd found out, that he'd known it was all wrong but that, in some mad way, he'd been able to push the thought of the business and all its problems out of his mind while there was something much more stressful to hide.

To Orla, it made a strange kind of sense, although she

imagined that Cleo probably hadn't seen it like that. She felt guilty as a woman and as a supposed feminist that she accepted this explanation from her husband. That his mistress had been a useful diversion which he now no longer needed as his secret was out and he needed his wife to help him get through the next few months if their life as they knew it was to stay afloat.

Their simple dinner of garlic bread and pasta on Friday evening had been accompanied by the most enlightening and frank conversation that she and Gavin had ever had. It was too late now to gloss things over or to talk about things getting better at Cole & Merriman. There were some debts, probably in excess of what they could meet, unless some of the money they were owed started to miraculously appear. This was fairly unlikely, in light of the fact that credit had dried up for many people who'd leaned too heavily on it in the first place. The financial chain had been broken and Cole & Merriman was one of its many casualties.

The staff had been let go, fully paid up at least, that fateful Friday evening, which was why Cleo had been on hand. It galled Orla that *she'd* been chosen as Gavin's confidante when it was Orla's life that was falling apart in the middle of it all. That bit, strangely enough, was nearly worse than the fact that he'd slept with her.

Conversation about his affair had taken second place to their altered financial status on Friday evening but they *had* talked about it, late into the night after Orla had phoned her parents to explain her early arrival home. And to lie to them about needing to do the Christmas shopping in Cork instead the following day. Thankfully, Iris had offered to keep Lily and Rose for a second night, an offer gratefully accepted by her daughter.

Orla, if she'd thought about it for a minute, might have imagined that the discovery of an affair would mean a husband decamping under duress to the spare room. Bizarrely, it was she who suggested that they both sleep in the spare room for the time being. Not the guest room, which would have been a bit unreal, but the en suite room downstairs that had been a brainwave of Orla's for the possibility of an elderly parent having to be looked after in the future.

She couldn't bear to sleep in their own room until it had been decontaminated of any association with Cleo. And there had been so much to talk about, even at three in the morning, that it made sense somehow to make their way to the little wing at the side of the house that had its own basic kitchenette, lounge and even a back door.

Only a few weeks ago, Paddy and Iris had slept here while Gavin and Orla took a weekend break in Faithlegg House. It was incongruous to be turning on the electric blanket to air the bed there in the face of the biggest crisis she'd ever encountered.

They'd lain there side by side in the darkness without touching until there was no more left to say and sleep had finally claimed them both. Of course Gavin had been sorry. Of course he'd said it over and over. And of course Orla had told him there were no guarantees that they could get through this or that their marriage could survive it. But the truth was that Orla knew it would be easier to survive the effects of his disloyalty with Cleo than it would be to lose everything she had built up by throwing the towel in now.

If she did demand that he leave, what would there be to support her and the girls? The business was practically gone and there would be no big divorce settlement to hold out for. There mightn't even be enough to live on if Orla was tied down with the girls and couldn't work. And what would she work at anyway?

The more they'd talked, the more convinced she'd been that a hasty separation wasn't the answer right now. Yes, she needed to sort out her marriage. But more urgently, she needed to sort out her life.

Which was why she was sitting here at the kitchen table on Wednesday morning staring at her list and feeling slightly more optimistic than she had been the last two mornings. Gavin had gone into town to meet with Bob again in order to try and sort out some plan of action. Orla was carrying on with her own plan of action.

The good news, she discovered, was that their everyday spending had been so extensive that she could make enormous savings by just cutting back to basics.

The bad news was that, even with cutting back as far as the bone, there would still be very little money coming in to cover even the essentials.

Sophie, her baby-sitter, was at the top of her list. There would be no social life now anyway. Monica's Thursday cleaning sprees had also been culled, a difficult phone call by any standards, but Orla had explained that she was getting an *au pair* who would be able to do the housework as well. It was a little more than a white lie but reputation was everything and Monica visited half of the houses in Barretsbridge on a weekly basis. Orla didn't want the grapevine to flourish on *her* account.

She'd already called the leisure centre to cancel her membership, citing a back injury that her consultant had insisted on her taking care of. To her wonder, the manager had helpfully suggested that she get a letter from her doctor explaining this. As soon as they received it at The Sanctuary, a refund for the remainder of her subscription could be issued. And seeing as that the remaining six-month period amounted to a valuable thousand euro, Orla had phoned her GP immediately for an appointment. Surely it couldn't be too difficult for a woman who'd carried twins to feign a late-onset back strain?

Of all the calls she'd made this morning, picking up the phone to dial Gerry Cashman's number at the Credit Union had been the most nerve-wracking. She'd been out of the workforce for over six years now and God only knew what had changed in that time but it was the only work she'd ever done and the only start she could make on earning a living once again.

The manager of the Credit Union had been delighted to hear from her. Orla had been a model employee in her day, a fast learner who'd joined straight from her secretarial course and who'd proved herself to be both efficient and discreet in the years she'd worked for him. They moved in the same social circles, so Gerry understood exactly what she meant when she explained that the girls were in school now and she had more time on her hands than she could handle. It wouldn't do at all to say that they were practically broke and that her phone call was a necessity.

"If there was anything part-time going there, it'd be great. I know I'm limited to mornings or evenings when Gavin's at home but I thought I'd let you know that I'm available anyway, Gerry."

"Well, there's nothing right this minute but I'll certainly keep you in mind. The younger girls often don't like the late evenings and Saturday mornings but it might suit you. Would you be able to send in a CV so we have you on file officially, Orla?"

Dismay set in at the idea of disclosing an extended maternity leave that she'd spent decorating the house and a five-year period where her only focus had been Rose and Lily. She knew in her heart the true value of what she'd been occupied with for the last half decade but it wasn't much to write on a CV when you badly needed a job.

"Of course I will, Gerry, although it'll be short and sweet, I'm afraid. My computer skills are good, mind you, but I've been at home with the girls since I left work." There was no point in glossing it over. Better to be up-front now rather than face embarrassment and confusion at an interview later.

She sighed now at the memory of the phone call but dismissed any misgivings she had about Gerry Cashman realising just how badly she needed to go back to work. She'd get her CV, such as it was, together later in the evening. And now that she thought about it, she hadn't exactly been lying idle all those years. She'd done two interior-design courses as well as the first level of a child psychology course. Nothing to do with the world of high finance exactly but at least it showed that she hadn't remained stagnant. It was wait and see after that.

She sighed now and looked dolefully at her to-do list which was still remarkably long.

Starting to do her weekly shop in Lidl or Aldi was the next item and Orla had been shocked to realise that she didn't even know where her nearest outlet was – not that she'd be going to her nearest one, anyway. She'd always shopped wherever she wanted to but it was time for a change of scene to a less expensive option. Her laptop was open beside her on the table and she decided to Google the location of the Aldi and Lidl outlets in Cork county. It would be worth driving a little farther away to avoid meeting the local busybodies.

Minutes later, Orla had made her choice. Youghal was only a thirty-minute drive and it would be unlikely that she'd meet anyone from Barretsbridge there. If she was unlucky enough to bump into someone she knew, she'd have to remember that they too were shopping in a lower-end store and breeze through it with aplomb.

The next item on the list made her heart drop down towards her navel. She was trying to push it to the back of her mind until everything else was looking more sorted but the fact was that she couldn't completely ignore what had happened to her marriage. On some level they had to get back to normal but apart from going upstairs to get dressed and shower, both she and Gavin seemed to be ignoring their own beautiful bedroom. Sleeping downstairs, albeit together, seemed to be a way of putting it all on the back burner until the more immediate financial problems could be unravelled.

It had been easy to convince the girls that she was getting around to painting the bedroom walls, something that she was now fully bent on. Denis Brett, to be fair to him, was always meticulous about storing away any leftover paint and Orla's next task would be to resurrect the leftovers in the garage and attempt to place her own stamp back on the room she'd loved until she'd found it strewn with Cleo's grubby bra and stripy wool tights.

At any other time, Denis would have arrived and dispensed with the paint job in a few hours. Times had changed and there would be no more easily written cheques for tradesmen but Orla herself had plenty of time on her hands and a simple paint job was hardly beyond her.

The thought of herself and Gavin moving back upstairs brought on another sigh and she decided that another coffee was in order. Her lovely silver coffee pot and the lifestyle it represented mocked her now. She knew that she and Gavin would turn things around eventually but right now, with almost no money coming in – and it was as bad as that – the luxuries like freshly ground coffee beans would have to go.

Miserable suddenly, she turned on the radio, needing a bit of light relief for a few minutes from rearranging her life. Although 96FM was her local station, she rarely listened to it but the last few days she'd tuned in out of necessity to pick up on the local job slots that were listed every afternoon. It was twelve o'clock, almost time to pick up Lily and Rose, so she decided to sit back and relish the few moments to herself while the news of the day was reeled out – as if she didn't have enough bad news of her own already.

The gods, though, weren't quite finished with her it seemed. As soon as the newsreader began the lead story of the day, Orla's heart was thumping violently again.

A taxi cab had been crushed by a gravel lorry on Patrick Street, she intoned, with the driver killed instantly. Gardai and ambulances were at the scene and colleagues at the popular Go Cars cab office were said to be "shocked and stunned". The driver's name hadn't been released yet, Orla heard, until family members had been informed.

31

Donal just stood there and watched helplessly as the emergency services started to disband. The ambulance had left and the fact that it hadn't even had its sirens blazing was the most telling feature of the past hour.

Patrick Street had started to free up again, although there were still rubber-neckers holding up the traffic as they slowed down to have a gawk at the mangled white taxi cab and the overturned gravel lorry that was still blocking a certain amount of the street.

The fire truck moved away from the scene now, leaving only two colleagues and the county council workers to cordon off the area until the truck could be examined and moved.

His mobile rang out sharply, the childish ring-tone sounding inappropriate in light of what had just happened. It was Orla's number on the display and he answered straight away, hoping he wouldn't have to deal with some tirade about the upcoming anniversary dinner.

"Donal," she said breathlessly as soon as he answered. "Are you okay?"

"Me?" he responded incredulously. Senan Crowley was dead and Orla was asking him if he was okay.

"I heard it on the news. A taxi cab? Someone was killed, Donal! I thought . . . I thought . . ."

She trailed off and he finally copped on that Orla, and perhaps even his mother if she'd been listening to the radio, had thought that it was he who'd been involved.

"I'm fine, Orla," he reassured her, touched that she'd actually been worried. It hadn't even occurred to him that the crash might have been on the news, much less that anyone would think it was he who'd been injured. "I'm fine," he said again, more to himself than for Orla's benefit.

"You don't *sound* fine. Are you in shock? Were you there? What happened?" It was typical of Orla to ask twenty questions at once and still expect an answer.

"I heard it over the radio in the cab – one of the other lads was driving just behind Senan. A gravel truck went up on a kerb and overturned. Senan's car was just passing at the time."

Donal had dropped his own passenger and diverted to Patrick Street as quickly as he was able, hoping to be able to help when he'd heard Phil's frantic call for an ambulance coming over the radio and Marge, on the desk today, promising to ring the emergency services straight away.

He could hear Orla gasp at the other end of the phone. "Had he a passenger in the car?"

"He'd just dropped her off at the rank. Phil, the other lad, saw him pulling out again just before it happened. Phil tried to get him out but he was right under the lorry. The whole car was crushed."

It sounded horrific but not half as horrific as it had looked.

"He must have died instantly," Orla said quietly. "Who was he, Donal? Was he married?"

Everyone, he realised, would want to know the details.

"Senan Crowley, Joe's son," he explained. Orla didn't know

Senan but she did know that his father, Joe Crowley, was Donal's boss and the owner of the Go Cars taxi fleet.

"God, that's desperate. Was Joe nearby? Was he at the scene when they . . ."

Orla delicately stopped short of asking whether the dead man's father had been there when they cut his only son's body out of the mangled car. He had been, surrounded by his drivers who'd converged on Patrick Street from all over the city to try and help. It was too late of course and all they could do was stand by in solidarity as the truck was eventually hoisted enough for the car to be removed by the fire service. The hollow metal thud of the enormous truck as it was lowered to the ground would stay with Donal forever, echoing another thud from the past that had been threatening to overpower him from the moment he heard Phil Conway's frantic voice calling for help over his crackling cab radio.

"We were all there. But it was too late. Joe went in the ambulance," he finished flatly. There was nothing more to be said and Donal didn't even know why he was still here at the scene. He couldn't leave, feeling somehow that it was disloyal to Senan to abandon him and go. It was too late for that now, when Senan was probably lying in a mortuary at St Angela's, cold already.

"God, Donal, I'm really sorry. I got an awful fright when I heard it was a Go Cars taxi. They said that, you know, on the radio."

Donal thought he heard a little sob in her voice and felt guilty for not thinking of Orla and especially his parents. What would *they* have thought if they'd heard the radio? He thought of Laura then and was glad that she was still away in Barbados.

"I didn't even think to ring, Orla. I was just here all the time –"

"Are you still there? Will I come over and get you? You could come back here and stay the night, maybe . . ."

It was the last thing he wanted but he appreciated her offer all the same. He just needed to go home and adjust or something. Get it all straight in his head. He felt confused and needed to be on his own.

"I'm grand, Orla, I'm just going home now. I might just rest for the evening, but thanks anyway. I'll be home in a few minutes."

For once, Orla let it go. "Okay so," she conceded. "I'll ring Mum and Dad if you like and tell them you weren't involved. And I'll give you a bell in the morning once the girls are out to school."

"Thanks, Orla. Bye."

He hung up before she said any more or thought better about coming over. He just needed to lie down and was glad that Marge had taken an executive decision and told everyone to go home for the evening. Feeling cold and almost shivery, he took one last look at the spot where Senan Crowley had lost his life. Then, for the second time in his life, he had to walk away.

32

Now that she was on a roll, Laura was fascinated to actually be talking about the accident. She'd been almost embarrassed yesterday at the amount of time she'd taken up but Grace had assured her that a double session was no problem if there was something important to discuss. No point in losing momentum, she advised, when there was a free period in her schedule anyway.

And now here she was back in the counselling block again, continuing the story of the Carmody family as if they were some exotic clan in a blockbuster novel. If Iris, or indeed Orla, knew that she was talking like this they'd certainly disapprove but now that she was in the process, Laura didn't really know *why* there was some sort of embargo on the topic.

"And how long afterwards did Orla arrive?" Grace clearly interested and seemed to think that the whole saga was significant in some way to the events in Laura's present life.

"I'm not sure exactly. A few months maybe," she guessed. It seemed ludicrous now when she was asked but Laura genuinely didn't know the exact sequence of events that led up to Orla arriving in Barretsbridge.

"You don't talk about it at home?"

"No! It's never mentioned. I mean, we all know the anniversary but it's not really mentioned." It *was* ludicrous, Laura realised.

"Tell me a little more about the actual day it happened, Laura," Grace probed. "Like, who was where, for instance? And what ages you all were at that stage."

Laura's heart started to beat faster and the waves of guilt ran up her chest and into her face in the form of a deep flush. The fact that she was full of abnormal hormones probably wasn't helping but, regardless of this, the feeling was the same as if it had all happened yesterday instead of thirty years ago.

"It's really just what I told you yesterday," she said, her throat dry.

Grace was waiting for her to expand on this.

"It was a Sunday morning and we were coming home from Mass. I was seven at the time and the twins were just five. I crossed the road to the shop holding Donal and Darren by the hands. Mam and Dad were sitting in the car. But when we came out with the ice creams I was only able to hold Donal's hand because I was holding my cone in the other. I thought Darren was following us."

Defensiveness had crept into her voice. She could hear it and she hated herself for making excuses.

"But he wasn't?"

"No. I told you, he shot across on his own. Myself and Donal were still in front of the shop after . . . afterwards."

She stopped herself from closing her eyes this time and looked at Grace full on to see what her reaction might be. She only ever talked about it to Barry and it was always when they were in bed with the lights off. She hated to think of how he would look at her if they did ever talk about it in daylight.

Grace just nodded, her expression the same as ever.

"And what happened then?"

"There was just commotion. Dad and Mam ran over. Dad

lifted Darren up and was trying to get him to open his eyes. There were so many people there, even before the ambulance came. It was actually the local priest whose car hit him so some people were trying to help him as well. I remember he was shouting and trying to get out of the car and people were telling him to stay where he was. He was probably in shock after what happened."

"And what happened to you and Donal? Did someone come across to get you?"

Laura was shocked at this question. Barry asked things like whether the traffic stopped or who picked Darren up off the road or whether the priest had been distraught. Nobody had ever asked Laura what had happened to her and Donal.

"No. As I said, Mam and Dad got out and ran out onto the road to Darren. Dad picked him up and shook him. Mam was just standing there begging him to do something. When the ambulance came all the traffic stopped and I brought Donal across to the car. I remember feeling guilty about that – eating the ice cream while everyone was around Darren on the road. It was melting, you see," she finished apologetically.

"And what happened then? Did you have to go to a hospital or what?"

Grace, of course, wouldn't know the procedure for sudden deaths in Ireland.

"Mam and Dad did. They went in the ambulance. To the mortuary, I suppose."

She and Donal hadn't ever seen Darren after that so it was just her memory of the Sunday afternoon that had her mother and father arriving at the mortuary of the local hospital with Darren's body.

"And who looked after you while they were gone?"

"No-one, really. The priest was still really upset and everyone was trying to help him, I remember. We were watching it all from the car."

Laura was perplexed now. They'd only been seven and five at the time but her clear memory was of being alone in the back of the car as everything got back to normal on the street after the ambulance and the two guards left. Father Hardiman had been almost hysterical and Laura had a memory of PJ Madden, one of their neighbours, helping him into his own car and driving him away.

She told Grace now about Donal needing to go to the toilet and her wondering what to do, terrified of being gone from the car when their parents got back.

It had been almost dark when she ventured across the road again to the shop to ask the lady behind the counter if Donal could go to the toilet at the back of the small, poky grocery. Laura too was bursting to go but it had seemed a bit forward to be asking for both of them. Donal was only small so it was understandable that he'd need the toilet.

They'd been recognised straight away of course and there had been an almighty fuss by the elderly shop owner. They'd been brought through to the back into a kitchen and then out the back to a small, cold bathroom with green walls. There had been black mould spots at the skirting boards.

Afterwards, the old lady had insisted on them having tea but Laura had refused. They'd need to be waiting in the car in case Iris and Paddy came back. In lieu of the tea, they'd been given bottles of Sport orange, Curly Wurlys and bars of Dairy Milk in case their parents were delayed.

"No-one stayed with you? You were left alone?" Grace looked almost as if she didn't believe this.

Laura felt guilty immediately for implying that she was complaining in some way.

"Well, no – there were two of us. Looking back now, I'd say that everyone thought someone else was looking after us."

"And did you realise that your brother was dead? Or did you think he was just hurt?"

"I don't know," Laura admitted. She thought of the chocolate bars that the shop lady had given to them and felt guilty that she and Donal had been chewing away when Darren had probably been dead. "We were too young to realise that he might be dead. I think we were more nervous about getting into trouble or something. Looking back he probably died there and then."

"You were never told?"

"No, to be honest. It was only later in the evening, when we were going home in the car, that Dad told us that Darren was gone to heaven. That was it. Even now, I'm not one hundred per cent sure whether he was definitely dead or whether the ambulance crew tried to resuscitate him or anything like that."

Grace, she imagined, must think she came from the weirdest family in the world but it was true that the accident had never been talked about in detail. After that initial Sunday evening, there had been the funeral and her memories were of being good in front of everyone and she and Donal keeping their clothes clean. Suddenly, they were back at school, their routine very much the same as it had always been, only without Darren. They'd been a bit of a novelty at first with everyone being nice to them but things had eventually returned to normal.

Except that Donal had started to come out to Laura's bed during the night because he was afraid on his own with his twin gone and the single bed next to his empty. Paddy would carry him back to his own bed before Iris woke in the morning and Laura would keep her eyes closed and pretend she was asleep. That had all stopped when Orla arrived, as Laura remembered.

She told Grace as much of this as she could, especially about the fact that Donal had been moved into Laura's old room and Darren's bed taken away around that time. Laura had been moved into the larger "boys' room" with Orla's big white cot placed next to her single bed.

"Did you mind that? Being moved around?"

Grace, Laura noticed, asked the smallest, simplest of questions and every one of them seemed to get her going on a new thought process.

"No," she admitted. "I mean, my room was the smallest so it was better for Donal once he was on his own. And there was room for a bed and a cot in the bigger one for me and Orla."

"And how was your mother after Orla arrived?"

Laura had explained to Grace the previous day just how frail and nervous Iris had become after the accident. She'd often heard neighbours describing her mother as being "in a world of her own" when they thought that Laura or Donal weren't listening. Laura still thought it was a good description.

"The same, really. Dad did nearly everything with Orla when she arrived. Mam was always worrying that something would happen to her."

"And what did you think of Orla?"

Laura always hated this question from aunts and neighbours. There was an in-built assumption that Laura must have resented the intruder in some way and it was something that she always felt she had to defend, even though the opposite was actually true.

"People always think I must have resented her arriving," she told the counsellor, knowing it was best to tell her the truth, "but I thought it would help Mam so I was delighted. I thought she was different because of what had happened to Darren and that she'd come back to normal once she had a new baby."

Laura felt foolish admitting this now. Of course a new baby wouldn't have replaced Darren – she knew this now as an adult – but in her child's mind, it had seemed logical.

"And did she come back to normal?" Grace too seemed to think that Laura's childhood theory held some merit.

"No," Laura sighed, remembering the distraught tears that her mother would cry over any little thing. "She was worse if anything. Sometimes she wouldn't stop crying until Dad came home from work."

"And who'd mind the baby when she was upset?" Grace wanted to know.

Laura thought about this and conjured up a clear memory of playing with Orla and changing her nappy. "I suppose I helped to change her and feed her. Myself and Donal used to bring her outside and play with her on a blanket." She had a definite vision of a wool blanket with red and blue squares that they used to spread out on the grass.

"It was a big responsibility," Grace commented.

Laura grinned. "I know. You wouldn't let an eight-year-old mind a baby in this day and age but I thought I was quite grown-up at the time."

"Even taking the boys across the road to the shop was a big responsibility, really." Grace's voice held a question and again Laura felt defensive, not necessarily for herself but for her parents. They'd trusted her to bring the boys for an ice cream. It wasn't their fault that Darren had been knocked down by a car.

"The roads weren't as busy then, I suppose. People didn't see the danger the way they do now."

"But it was hard for a seven-year-old to control two small children."

This struck a chord with Laura, mainly because it was the reason she'd been holding Donal's hand and not Darren's that Sunday afternoon.

"That's true," she admitted. "Darren was quieter than Donal so I thought he'd be fine crossing the road. I thought he'd just follow me when I told him to." She smiled wryly at the folly of expecting a five-year-old to follow instructions.

Grace smiled. "Donal was less quiet, I take it?"

Laura wasn't criticising Donal for anything. "He was just a bit giddy, that's all."

"Are you inclined to think that you ought not to have let Darren go across on his own?"

Laura thought about this, not for the first time. She thought of Barry telling her that decisions can only be made using the information available at the time. This was the way they, together, made their decisions relating to the fertility treatment and she knew in her heart that, on the day of the accident, it had made sense to hold onto the half-wild Donal. But . . .

"I'll always be sorry for that. If I hadn't got an ice cream for myself, I could have been holding both of them."

Grace smiled again, a little sadly this time, as if she understood something that Laura couldn't.

"I see," was all she said.

33

By Thursday evening, nothing had changed for Donal. He was still in the bed, fully dressed, and he still wasn't even hungry. This in itself should have been a warning to him that something was radically wrong, considering that he'd never in his life gone more than four hours without food before making a declaration of starvation.

He was freezing cold too, even though he'd put the heating on when he'd arrived back to the flat on Wednesday afternoon and it was still going strong.

Orla had phoned, as promised, to see if he was feeling better. He'd assured her that he was fine but just needed a rest. Orla didn't know that all he could see in front of his eyes were the ambulances and the Garda cars and the crowds of people talking in whispers and shaking their heads.

He hated himself for wishing that Laura could have been there with him and yet he was glad that she hadn't been. He wouldn't have wanted her to see all that, but at least she would have understood how he felt, even if they hadn't actually talked about it.

He'd phoned Susan as soon as he'd arrived home, just in case she'd hear on the evening news about the accident. She'd been horrified that one of his friends had been killed and wanted to come straight over as soon as her last appointment was over. But he'd needed to be alone to get his head straight and hadn't wanted Susan to see him in this weird dazed state that he couldn't seem to get out of.

She'd phoned again this morning to see how he was and at lunchtime to tell him that she'd definitely be over after work. She'd bring dinner, she'd insisted. Now that it was almost five o'clock, her finishing time on Thursdays, he was looking forward to seeing her, in need of company and also in need of food even though he didn't seem to be as hungry as he should have been.

It was an effort even to get his legs out of the bed but Donal knew that he must look a right state with his clothes crumpled and two days' stubble to boot. A shower and shave would keep him occupied until Susan arrived.

Even the bedside light seemed harsh and abrasive when he turned it on and the fluorescent bulb in the bathroom was like being introduced to an instrument of torture. His head hurt and he was dizzy, probably, he realised suddenly, from lack of food. He diverted to the kitchen and threw two Weetabix into a bowl. It was all he could face right now even though he knew he needed to eat something proper.

He actually did feel better afterwards. The shower and shave were a bit of an effort but he felt better after that too. He even made the bed and hung his clothes up, wanting to fill the time until Susan arrived. He'd had enough time to think in the last twenty-four hours.

Susan was worried about Donal and had been kicking herself since morning for not insisting on going around to see him the previous night. All day she'd been listening to clients talking about the horrific scene on Patrick Street yesterday and the more she heard, the worse she felt that she hadn't ignored Donal's obstinacy. But he'd been definite about being on his own and Susan, for all that she felt they were getting on well as a couple, had wondered if it was a thing that he wanted to spend the evening with the drivers from Go Cars to debrief after the trauma of the day.

He'd spent the evening alone as it transpired and she'd felt guilty about this when she'd spoken to him before work this morning. Maybe he hadn't wanted to melt her head with his problems when they'd just started going out. If this was the case, then she should have persevered in her intention of going over after work yesterday.

Her own head was melted now from thinking about how shocked he must have been after the horrendous accident. She liked Donal Carmody and was surprised at just how much when she barely knew him.

Susan reached across the front seat of her car now and carefully lifted the packages of food that she'd collected from the Fine Food Emporium a few minutes ago. It would have been nicer to cook properly, she knew, but she had no idea what was in Donal's kitchen and she hadn't wanted him to have to decamp over to her house for dinner when all he must want was to be curled up on the sofa in peace and quiet.

She was shocked when Donal opened the door to her. Maybe it was her own sense of drama or her own expectation of how he might be feeling but the Donal who greeted her with his usual kiss and boyish grin didn't look at all like someone who'd suffered a major trauma in the last twenty-four hours. Far from moping in his pyjamas, Donal was clean-shaven and dressed as if they were going out for the evening. Susan, to say the least, was nonplussed and felt almost foolish that she'd been panicking all day about his welfare. The television, as usual, was on in the corner of the room.

"How are you doing?" She did feel a bit silly now that she could see he was fine.

"Grand. Starving though," he grinned and took the cartons of chicken chasseur and rice from her. The table was set, she noticed, something that made her feel slightly better about arriving with all her boxes and cartons. At least he wanted to eat in.

She set about opening the containers while he carried two plates in from the tiny kitchen and she felt better for having something to do. "So what did you do all day?"

"Not much," he admitted, looking up at her with a sigh. "Just hung around here. This smells nice."

"It's from the Emporium."

Of course it was – the logo was on the packaging. Susan felt conversation was a bit stilted this evening and was glad of the food as a diversion. It was steaming and delicious-looking on the plates now but her appetite had gone even though she'd missed her lunch in a bid to get off on time. She felt a bit superfluous and wondered if Donal would rather have been on his own after all.

"How was your day?" he asked now.

As usual, Donal was digging into his food with gusto. Susan had imagined him being shocked and dazed after witnessing such a terrible accident and had spent the whole afternoon wondering what he might like to eat. Now, she realised that a bag of chips would have been just fine. Perhaps men were different from women in this regard.

"Just the usual. It's not too bad this week because people are leaving colours and highlights until nearer Christmas. It'll be mental the next few weeks. Were you talking to anyone from work today?"

"Marge rang this morning, just to say that we'll be closed until after the funeral. And to say about . . . you know, the arrangements."

Susan wondered if he'd like her to go to the funeral with him but thought that maybe now wasn't the time to ask. Perhaps he'd prefer to be with the other drivers who'd understand better how he felt.

"Did she say how Joe was?"

Once it was out of her mouth, Susan realised just what an obvious question it was. Of course Joe Crowley was distraught at the loss of his only son – and in one of his own taxi cabs at that.

"In bits, Marge said. She went over to the house last night and she said it was desperate. She's very friendly with Ita, Joe's wife."

"Fair play to Marge for keeping the show going today. She must have known Senan very well, in that case." It always amazed Susan the way people rowed in to help others in a crisis, no matter how badly they might be feeling themselves.

Donal nodded and spooned more rice onto his plate. He'd opened two beers but his was barely touched.

"Marge is always great. She says she can't see Joe coming back for a while, though."

"Well, it's understandable, really. He probably thought Senan was going to take over the business from him eventually. Imagine what it'll be like for him now."

Donal looked surprised. "That's what Marge said. That he keeps saying it was all for nothing now."

"I can see where he's coming from. As well as losing his son, there's no future for his business either."

Donal was silent for a bit after this. "Joe's only sixty," he said eventually. "He was always on about taking early retirement but he never actually did it. Senan used to slag him about being afraid to give up all the power but I think Joe enjoyed them working together and sort of training Senan in. He'll miss all that now."

Susan knew from experience just how difficult it would be for Joe Crowley. "Remember I said to you that Mum owns a bridal shop?"

Donal stopped eating for a moment and nodded.

"Well, Julie, my sister used to work there from when she left school and she loved it. I had no interest in it so Julie would have taken over from Mum eventually. It's about ten years ago now, but Julie was killed coming home from a Christmas night out." She paused, wondering if she should be telling this to Donal at all. He looked interested though, his knife and fork immobile, so she continued. "She was only twenty at the time, two years younger than me. But what went hardest on Mum was going back into the shop. She kept saying it was like a dead end, that it was no good once Julie was gone."

"You never said anything about her before," Donal said.

"Julie? I suppose we talk about her a lot at home but I hate being morbid about her. *She'd* hate me being morbid about her."

Susan smiled at the thought of her younger sister rolling her eyes and saying "Oh, for God's sake, don't keep going on about it!" if she thought they were all dwelling too much on her departure. Julie had been impulsive and decisive and couldn't stick people dithering or mulling things over. It had been this that had got her mother back into her stride at Special Days eventually.

"What . . . I mean, how did it happen?" Donal was sitting forward in his chair now.

"The accident? God, Donal, it sounds so typical but Julie was just a bit wild, I suppose. She didn't see any harm in anything and thought everything was a bit of craic. She was coming home from a disco with a gang of friends. The fellow who was driving was plastered and got a skid coming around a corner. There was another girl killed as well."

"How many of them were in the car?"

Susan thought back now to the night before Christmas Eve ten years ago. At twenty-two, she'd felt so much older than Julie and rather than feeling grief, she'd felt angry at her sister's stupidity.

"Seven." She sighed. "I know – you couldn't believe they'd be so stupid. Not even one of them had a safety belt on. I was so cross with her for ages about that."

Grief at the loss of her sister had come much later for Susan. It was only after all the hype of the funeral had died down that she'd realised just how endearing and entertaining Julie had been. The light had gone out for the Hegartys and nothing would ever bring it back.

"And how did your mam fare with the shop? Afterwards, I mean."

"It took her a while but eventually she went back. It was what kept her going in the end. At the beginning, she couldn't see the point if there was no-one to pass it on to. But after a while, she started to see it as a job, the way anyone would."

"She was probably glad of the distraction," Donal said, standing up from the table. Susan was a little disappointed that the closeness she'd felt for the last few minutes was gone but started to clear the table nonetheless.

"Will I open a bottle of wine?" Donal was holding out a bottle that had been standing on the counter top for the past few weeks. Normally, he drank beer so Susan usually tended to drink it as well, insisting that it was a bit pointless opening a bottle just for herself.

"I'm driving so –"

"You could stay?" He was looking at her hopefully and her heart did a little dance.

"Grand so." She reached into one of the overhead presses and took out two Louise Kennedy crystal glasses. "Very fancy," she commented with a grin.

"Very Orla! She's always trying to civilise me."

"You're fine as you are."

She carried the glasses through to the coffee table and set them down before sinking into the leather sofa. The television was muted but still on. Surprisingly, Donal took the remote control and flicked it onto standby before filling their glasses. Normally, it would flicker away in the background, even if neither of them was watching it.

"Do you miss her?" he said out of the blue. "Julie, I mean."

Susan sipped her red wine and thought for a moment before answering. "Not all the time. I know that sounds awful but Julie was never part of my work, for instance. So I don't tend to think of her at all during the day. If I'm at home in Mum and Dad's house, I do. All her school photos are there, and her First Communion and Confirmation photos, so it's like she's more there than anywhere else."

"Is it hard at birthdays and things?" Donal wanted to know.

Susan was touched that he was so interested but didn't want to monopolise the evening talking about herself.

"Sometimes. Her twenty-first was the worst. And her thirtieth last June. I usually go home that day and Mum cooks dinner. We don't have a party or anything but we mark it, I suppose."

"And what about Christmas?"

"The first year was a mess, obviously. But after that, Dad decided that we couldn't just ignore Christmas. He always wanted me to go out and enjoy myself on Christmas Eve. I suppose he didn't want it to be ruined forever. I remember one year early on when I didn't want to go out and Dad told me that Miss Julie had had plenty of fun in her day and that she wasn't to put a stop to mine!"

Donal laughed quietly at this and said, "Fair play to him!"

Susan smiled too. "Even though Mum thought she was a saint, Dad knew Julie was a messer. She was always broke from going out and looking for a top-up from Dad before pay-day. One of the lads in the accident was paralysed from the neck down and Dad goes to see him every week, but he always thinks that Julie would never have been able for that kind of life."

"It must have been horrific when you think of seven of them in the car. It's a wonder more of them weren't killed." Donal had a faraway look in his eyes as he said this.

Susan agreed wholeheartedly. "It was just bad luck. Julie was always doing dodgy things like that but she'd just got away with it up until then. People often ask Mum and Dad if the driver was prosecuted but they were never interested in that, to be honest. It was a bit late for blaming people at that stage."

"They don't blame him? Even though he was drinking?"

"But Julie *knew* he was drunk, that's the thing. I'm not saying it was her own fault, I'm just saying it was a bad choice she made."

She wasn't sure if Donal got this but it was something that her parents had been adamant about from day one. Anger and blame would do none of them any good and Julie was gone, regardless. No amount of court cases and recriminations would bring her back or alter the facts.

She thought about the wisdom of this now and wondered at her parents' strength. It was lovely to talk about it with Donal, sitting here in front of the gas flames sipping their wine companionably.

"How do you think Joe Crowley will react? About the council truck and everything?" It was likely that an enormous burden of anger would overtake him at the injustice of it all once the funeral was over and life started to carry on around him.

"I'm not sure," Donal replied. "He's usually sort of upbeat about everything. Even with things like a driver crashing he just gets on with it. Once nobody's hurt he just puts it down to the insurance and that's that. This is different, though. I just can't see how he'll come back to work, even to the cab office."

"He'll need time off, that's for sure," Susan agreed, pushing her hair back from her face. "He can't just carry on as if nothing had happened. I mean, that just wouldn't be normal."

She sensed more than anything a change in Donal as he sat next to her on the sofa. She turned a little to look at him and, to her shock, saw that he was just sitting there silently with tears coursing down his face.

It was the way that Susan was able to talk so openly about her sister that first made Donal realise the strangeness of his own situation. It was almost a novelty to listen to her, a voyeuristic feeling that he'd never experienced before. It was, however, the way that she spoke about carrying on as if nothing had happened, and how abnormal that was, that had hit him like a ton of bricks.

It *was* abnormal, to the point of being ridiculous, that a five-year-old child would die and that there would be no further talk about him from the people who were supposed to love him. His eyes were closed but he could sense Susan's concern and knew immediately that she felt guilty for upsetting him, even before she started to apologise for going on about her sister. She thought it was some sort of shock after Senan Crowley's accident probably.

Donal felt a bit guilty for reacting so badly when nothing in the way he was feeling was about Senan. It was just something about the accident happening that had set him thinking about Darren and the fact that they'd all ignored him for almost thirty years. It was unbelievable that none of them had even celebrated his birthday or talked about him at Christmas. The guilt he'd felt for years was almost unbearable now and he didn't seem to be able to stop crying, something he'd never done at all since the accident.

"God, Donal, I'm sorry. I didn't mean to go on about Julie . . ."

Donal tried to tell her that it wasn't that at all – or maybe it was – but that hearing about Julie had actually made him feel good for a few minutes – but his voice just wouldn't work for him.

"Donal, it's a huge shock for this to happen," Susan said, her hands massaging his shoulders lightly.

She still thought it was all about Senan and Donal knew that he just couldn't push Darren away into the background again. He reached into his jeans pocket for a tissue and blew his nose, intent on telling Susan about his brother – his *twin* brother – who'd died aged five.

"It was a shock yesterday," he admitted.

His voice, he knew, sounded a bit shaky and he sniffed again and wiped his eyes. He was still sitting forward on the edge of the sofa with his face buried in his hands, unwilling to let Susan know how terrible they'd all been to Darren, especially himself who should have been the one to remind everyone of the times like First Communion when he too should have been there alongside them.

Susan rested her head against his and kissed him lightly on the temple. "Of course it was, Donal. It was a terrible thing to have to witness –"

"It wasn't just that." Donal didn't know *how* to talk about Darren but he had to try at least. "You know . . . how you were talking about Julie?"

"I'm sorry for going on about it –"

"No, it was good to hear about her, Susan," he insisted, although he could see how doubtful she looked. "I actually had a twin brother but he died."

"A twin? Donal, that's terrible. What was his name?"

The easy way that she asked made him feel a huge wave of guilt all over again. Even Susan could ask a normal question about Darren, yet his own family couldn't even mention his name. Unbelievably, Donal couldn't remember ever saying his name out loud since the accident, even to Laura.

"Darren," he said now, his voice breaking at the sound of it. "Darren," he said again, to confirm it and because it was so strange to hear it.

"Darren," Susan repeated. "Donal and Darren. That's nice."

It *was* nice to hear somebody saying it like that again. People had always said "the twins" or "Donal and Darren" and Donal had a sense now of relief at hearing himself described as part of a pair again. He turned it over in his mind and was surprised at how well he remembered it. *Darren and Donal. Donal and Darren.*

"What happened to him?" Susan asked gently.

It sounded so simple now to be able to tell someone, when it had all been so complicated up to now. All of a sudden, he couldn't see *why* it had been so complicated.

Donal took a deep breath. "He was hit by a car when we were five," he stated. It was out now, said out loud in words.

Susan topped up their wineglasses and sat back on the sofa, her hand stroking his lower back as if she expected him to continue. Donal felt his shoulders, tense and aching since he'd got into bed yesterday, relaxing automatically and he too sat back.

"We went into a shop for an ice cream with Laura after Mass one Sunday. When we came out she was trying to mind the two of us but she had to hold my hand because I was messing around trying to get the Flake off Darren's cone. Darren was crossing the road on his own and a car hit him."

"That's awful – it must have been horrendous for you and Laura. Was it someone speeding?"

"No. It was actually the parish priest driving the car so you can imagine the furore there was on the street with people stopping and everyone trying to help."

"The poor little fellow," Susan said, tears in her eyes at the idea of it. "Did he die straight away?"

This was something that Donal had thought long and hard about overnight. Senan Crowley had died outright with the weight of a gravel truck crushing the car. Would Darren have died instantly from the impact too?

"I don't know. I *think* so. An ambulance came and he was taken away in it but he must have been dead already. I remember seeing him lying on the road and he wasn't moving. Dad picked him up and shook him and nothing happened but I suppose he could have been unconscious."

"Didn't you ever ask your parents?"

Donal just looked at her. Then he realised that she hadn't actually met Iris and Paddy yet and would have no idea of how differently they'd dealt with the tragedy than her own parents seemed to have done. If her father had talked openly about going out at Christmas and the fact that Julie's birthday was acknowledged every year, Susan probably thought that it was the done thing to bring a dead sibling up in conversation as if it was no big deal.

Now was the time, for him at least, to start being more honest and to stop hiding Darren away as if he'd done something wrong.

"That's the thing, Susan," he sighed, "after the funeral, Mam and Dad never mentioned Darren again. We were never told what he died of or anything. I mean, if he had died instantly or later from internal injuries or whatever. It wasn't that we were actually *told* not to talk about him, it was just that Mam was in such a desperate state afterwards that Dad used to shush us if we said anything."

It sounded daft now to Donal and therefore must seem utterly ridiculous to Susan.

"It must have been desperate for her. For all of you."

To Donal's surprise, she didn't indicate that she was completely shocked. Glad that she wasn't sitting there open-mouthed, he tried to explain it a little better.

"I remember going back to school and I had no-one to sit with because we had those little school desks with the inkwells and the two of us used to sit together. I sat in it on my own the first day but the teacher made two of the other lads squash up to make room for me in their desk. During lunchtime, the headmaster came in and took our desk out altogether so I had to sit with the other lads for the rest of the year."

Susan looked as if she was about to cry. "You must have been really lost without him."

Donal thought the word "lost" was a perfect description of how he'd felt back then. "I was. I remember starting to tell Mam and Dad about it when I came home from school that day but Mam just got up and went upstairs to bed. Dad told us she was so upset that she wasn't able to be hearing things like that."

"So that stopped you from mentioning anything else?"

Donal was glad that she seemed to understand. "Something like that."

"And what about birthdays and everything?"

"It was the same day as mine so I think that was worse. Nothing was ever said. We just had a little party for me as usual but Darren was never really brought up or anything."

"You lost out on a lot really – possibly even more than Laura in a sense."

"Maybe for birthdays and things," Donal agreed, "but I think it was probably harder for her because she was minding us on the day. Imagine how she must have felt?"

"It was a big responsibility all right," Susan commented. "Even though I'm sure no-one thought she was to blame. What about the anniversary? That must be another hard day for everyone."

Donal thought about this, remembering the particular weekend in September as being of significance and recalling the tension around it.

"We just went to Mass on the Sunday of that weekend and the priest would say it was an anniversary mass for Darren Carmody. Father Hardiman was gone by then so it was probably better than if it was him announcing it. Other than that, we didn't do anything in particular. Mam wasn't able for much after it, you see."

"It must have been terrible for her, especially when it was someone local that was driving the car. And the fact that it was the parish priest must have made it worse, I imagine."

Donal hadn't really thought too much about Father Hardiman before. He had a vague memory of a big man with a red face coming into the school to ask the class catechism questions but he and Darren had only just started school a few weeks before the accident so that was only a couple of occasions. The day of the accident would be imprinted on his mind forever with some bits of it being more vivid than others. The priest had been distraught that day and Donal could still picture him getting out of his car and leaning across the bonnet with his hands covering his face. He'd been in shock, Donal imagined, with a child lying on the street so no wonder he'd been shouting and refusing to get back into his car. He told Susan this now, the details starting to flood back as he spoke.

"He was in bits and people were trying to stop him from going over to where Darren was. Maybe they knew he was dead at that stage. There was one man, PJ Madden, and he was great. It was him that Father Hardiman listened to eventually."

"And you were just standing there watching all this?"

Donal nodded. "There was so much going on . . ."

"God, Donal, I can't even begin to imagine what it must have been like."

Donal started to feel slightly guilty at all this attention. He didn't want sympathy – it was Darren who was dead, after all.

"It was but Mam was the worst of all of us." He winced now at the memory of Iris, skin and bone, with the pale face and anxious eyes that never seemed to settle.

"Losing a child has to be the most devastating thing, especially so young," said Susan. "Julie and Senan Crowley had had some sort of life."

Donal thought that this expressed his mother's desolation perfectly. "She was so different, afterwards. She just tuned out of everything, I think. She certainly wasn't able for me and Laura. And when Orla arrived, it was awful. She was always crying."

"Orla?"

"No – Mam. I think she wasn't able to cope with a baby so Laura and Dad minded her mostly."

This, at least, was Donal's memory of the aftermath of Darren's death.

"But what age was Laura?" Susan was looking at him as if he must be mistaken.

"Seven. Or eight maybe, by the time Orla came. It was just the way it was," he explained. "I mean, Mam was there but she couldn't get around to things. Something like that."

"Was she clinically depressed, do you think? I know Mum was, after Julie died. She even went on anti-depressants for a while until she picked up a bit. She says now that the depression was one of the worst things about Julie's death because she couldn't lift herself out of it. Mum says she always considered herself to be a 'coper' up till then."

Donal thought about this and figured that his mother probably had been clinically depressed only it hadn't been acknowledged at the time that this was the problem. Of course she'd been depressed, when she'd seen her five-year-old son knocked down in front of her eyes.

Donal wondered if he was stupid not to have thought of it like this before. In his head, Iris was just nervous and delicate – so much so that anything that constituted even the smallest bit of hassle had to be kept from her. Paddy had dealt with everything from school reports to minor injuries and all the bills and household decisions. He was doubtful whether his father even knew that his wife was depressed.

"Whatever it was, she never got better from it," Donal told Susan now. "I mean, she's still the same way today. You'll see what I mean when you meet her. Dad does everything for her because she gets so stressed over small things."

Susan was thoughtful. "She probably needed grief counselling at the time but never got it. People were just expected to get on with it then. Did you and Laura talk to anyone?"

Donal smiled and met her eyes. "I don't know about Laura but this is the first time I've ever even mentioned it since it happened."

"What! Ever?" Susan was clearly astounded.

"Ever," Donal confirmed. "Not even to Laura. She probably talks to Barry about it, I imagine. I hope she does anyway. It was like a big secret at home."

"But your school friends? Did they never ask about Darren?"

"We'd only just started in Junior Infants so I suppose they just forgot about him after a while. And of course the teachers and local people were probably slow to say anything in case they were seen to be criticising Father Hardiman. You know how things were in those days where priests were concerned."

"I know but it was probably no fault of his either. I'm sure he was in a desperate state over it."

"He was at the time for definite. What I said about all the shouting and everyone trying to calm him down – I think Senan's accident yesterday brought all that back. You know, the chaos and noise and people trying to help."

"It's traumatic as an adult, never mind what it must have been like at five. Especially when things weren't explained properly afterwards."

It was this vague sense of there being something that had to be hidden that was hardest on Donal over the years. He knew now that this was why he hadn't wanted Susan or even Orla to come over to the flat after the accident yesterday. It felt almost as if he was to blame in some way for this latest tragedy.

"I know," he agreed now. "I think it would have been better if Mam and Dad had been able to deal with it the way your parents did. But it was like they were pretending it didn't happen at all."

"Donal, all of that made it into a sort of mystery. Especially when you and Laura don't even know what happened fully after he was taken away in the ambulance."

Donal sighed. It *was* like a mystery. Susan, he imagined, would find it hard to believe that there were no photos of Darren on display in his parents' house.

"Maybe your parents felt guilty about it happening? I know Mum and Dad did after Julie died."

Donal didn't agree with this and was determined that Paddy

and Iris wouldn't be criticised when he himself knew exactly what had precipitated the whole thing. "I don't think so. It wasn't *their* fault that –"

"I didn't mean it was their fault – just that they might *think* it was. Parents are supposed to look after their children and if something happens, they think they haven't done their job properly."

"But it wasn't like he was on his own. Laura was minding us. If *I* hadn't been at him, trying to take his Flake, he wouldn't have taken off like that. They couldn't have been responsible for that!"

"Surely you don't think it was *your* fault?" She was looking at him as if he had ten heads and Donal had to look away.

"Donal? Tell me you don't think you were to blame for Darren getting knocked down?"

There it was, Donal thought. And all in the one sentence, at that. "Blame", "Darren" and "knocked down" – all the key words, as it were.

"Donal," she said again, this time more softly, "you were five. Of course you were messing with your brother. That's what five-year-olds do. And Laura was only seven. She couldn't have been expected to look after two of you."

"I know but –"

Susan caught him by the shoulders and turned him around to face her. "Donal, look at me," she demanded. "You couldn't have known what was going to happen. It wasn't your fault, or Laura's, or even your parents'. In those days, the roads weren't even busy. Kids were much less protected than they are now."

Donal felt so ashamed now that Susan was thinking of him as a child instead of the little terror that he'd been. She didn't know that he *would* have taken Darren's chocolate Flake if Laura hadn't called him to order. Okay, he might have given it back to him but, even now, he couldn't be sure that he would have.

"Donal, if you feel like this, imagine how your parents must have felt? Of course they feel guilty, leaving three small children off on their own. You only feel like this because nobody told you that it *wasn't* your fault."

"They never said anything about it being my fault," Donal reasoned. "I always felt that they let me away with it and I remember being glad at the beginning that no-one blamed me. Then I started to feel worse because Mam was so upset."

Susan was looking at him with serious concern now. "But, Donal, it was only normal for her to feel depressed. It wasn't something that you caused. If she'd been well enough to support you and Laura, you wouldn't be here thinking you were to blame for everything."

Donal, in fact, did think he was to blame for everything. He'd set off a chain of events by being wilful and it was something that, no matter what Susan said, he couldn't go back and change.

Almost as if she knew what he was thinking, Susan's next comment stopped him in his tracks.

"And you probably think that it's too late now to change all that happened?"

"Well, it is." Donal knew he sounded childish and obstinate but it was true.

"Donal, nothing *can* change it, no matter how many times you tell yourself that it wouldn't have happened if you were behaving yourself that day."

This made him feel even more ashamed.

"But it's not about changing it," she went on. "It's about realising that you have it all wrong. You *think* it was your fault, but your parents, and probably Laura, think it was theirs. You all can't be to blame! You're seeing it as an adult, not as a child. You were five. You were teasing your brother, which is normal. You were too young to know there would be cars coming."

"I know but . . ." he trailed off, seeing the logic in what she was saying.

He tried to visualise Lily or Rose in the same situation. Lily was definitely the more dominant of the two, just as he'd been. Would he blame Lily if something happened to Rose while they were playing? If one of them fell and got injured, for instance? He thought of Orla and knew that, for all her faults, she wouldn't for a moment forget about one of the girls if something drastic happened to the other.

He and Laura had been forgotten about in the aftermath of Darren's death. He definitely knew that. He also knew that it had been understandable, considering how bad his mother had been and how much there had been for his father to do, especially after Orla had arrived in the house.

"I suppose it was hard on everyone," he conceded. He lay back on the sofa and sipped his wine, suddenly aware of Susan and how good it was to talk about something that had been hidden for so long. "Thanks for listening."

She smiled and put her arms around him. "That's what I'm here for!"

"Seeing the accident yesterday brought it all back," he said, "but, if you hadn't spoken to me about Julie, it might all be still inside me." The moment of Darren being knocked down had been spinning around in his head for years and yet it hadn't actually come out until now.

"Most people relive things by talking about them over and over – that's what helps them to understand and accept and make sense of it. Like Mum and Dad after Julie died. They kept wondering whether they should have been a bit harder on her and not let her away with so much. She was always out and Mum felt she was to blame because she paid her so well in the shop. After a while, they realised that it could have happened no matter how strict they'd been or even if she had no money going out. But that was after talking about it endlessly, Donal."

"I suppose. Maybe if we'd talked about what happened, I'd have seen it all differently. I'd hate to think Laura would blame herself for not minding us properly. She was great, Susan. Honestly. She minded me all evening until Mam and Dad came back to collect us after they'd been to the hospital and everything."

"And she was only seven?"

"I know." Even Donal couldn't believe this now. In his eyes, Laura had been older so he'd felt safe with her. He wondered how she must have felt, being left to look after Donal in the middle of it all.

"You'll like her," he told Susan.

It was the first time it had ever mattered to him whether his family liked his girlfriend or vice versa but he knew somehow that it was important with Susan. She was sitting here next to him, her head on his shoulder as if he was still the same person. Even though she knew everything now, it looked as if maybe she still thought it was worth being here.

34

Orla breathed a sigh of relief when she pulled up outside the school on Friday morning, glad that the week was almost over. The girls were rowing in the back over a *High School Musical* glitter pen and for once she was finding their energy hard to tolerate.

"Right so. End of bickering session," she called out over the din. It was hard to believe that two such innocent-looking little girls could make so much noise.

"But Mum . . ." Lily, as ever, was unwilling to concede.

"Give me the pen," Orla instructed firmly. It was duly handed over by Lily and placed in the glove box, a place that was forbidden to the girls unless they were specifically allowed to get something out of it. "It's staying there until you can learn to behave yourselves. Now, out you hop – and don't forget the cotton wool!"

The squealing started again and Orla was almost sorry that she'd mentioned it. They were starting the preparations for making Christmas decorations in school today and each child had to bring a contribution. Lily and Rose had been sent home with a small piece of paper with "*Roll of cotton wool*" written on it.

She escorted the pair of them across the yard that she, Laura and Donal had crossed so many years ago, taking care to scan the area first in case Jessica Arnold appeared. She'd made a point of getting to the school early all week in the hope of not over-lapping with Cleo's cousin. The last thing she needed was pity for the collapsed state of her marriage when all too soon it would probably become obvious to all and sundry that Gavin's business had collapsed as well.

"Go on now, there's Miss Hunt. Run along in before you get cold."

Her heart softened when Lily turned around and asked whether she was hurrying them in case they got chilblains. Gavin had been explaining the previous evening that chilblains were something children got years ago before there was central heating and nice cosy houses. Lily, her little mind always working overtime, took everything in. Rose too took everything in and it worried Orla that they might soon start to become aware of the tension that crackled between their parents like electricity in a science lab, despite their unspoken agreement to keep their problems to themselves. Orla wondered whether it was peculiar that she and Gavin were continuing as normal in their interaction with their children, even when their own relationship was in chaos. It made her feel better, though, that both of them loved the girls enough to try to keep the status quo as best they could. Gavin, in particular, was trying his best. She had to give him that.

She smiled now and reminded her daughter that chilblains had gone out of fashion, before waving them off towards the classroom.

"Orla! Just the woman. I've been trying to catch a hold of you all week."

Orla's energy seemed to physically drain out of her as she plastered a smile to her face like a mask and turned around to face Jessica Arnold.

"Jessica! Hi."

"Go on, Claudia – the girls are gone in. Hurry and you'll catch them."

Claudia, looking for all the world like Santa in a red coat with a white fur trim, shot off after Rose and Lily. "She misses them during class time. It's a pity there are two classes this year."

Up to now, Orla would have agreed wholeheartedly with Jessica. Since last Friday, however, she'd been heartily glad that the girls were in the opposite class to Claudia as it created a distance, however small, between the two families.

"Pity," she agreed, her heart thumping.

Did Jessica know about the debacle last Friday evening in which her cousin had been discovered minus her clothes? Was she about to address the situation now? Apologise maybe, or even justify Cleo's actions?

Orla would rather that Jessica was completely oblivious of it all so that she could at least keep some level of dignity.

"Have you time for a coffee at all, Orla? I've some delicious mince pies in." Jessica looked a bit frazzled but still grinned as she made her next comment. "Mind you, I'll put my hands up at the outset and admit that they're not home-made!"

"Well, I'm not . . ." Orla started to trump up an excuse, although Jessica's reasonably upbeat manner suggested that the embarrassing state of affairs between Cleo and Gavin wasn't known to her as yet.

"I'd love if you could, Orla. I'm in a bit of a state and I'd value your advice."

This was clearly another issue altogether, Orla realised and felt able to relax, momentarily at least. Whatever was bothering Jessica, it wasn't Orla's domestic affairs.

Relieved, she smiled. "Go on then. I've no problem sampling a bought mince pie!"

It was Jessica's own assertion that she was glad she had a job that kept her busy enough to preclude baking from her household agenda, particularly as she wouldn't have been *able* to bake even if she was at home until Kingdom come.

"See you in a minute then." Jessica jumped back into her own car, a black Saab that she'd had as long as she'd been living in Barretsbridge. It was ten years old, Orla noticed – in good condition but not as shiny and new-looking as her own SUV. Maybe women like Jessica had their priorities right, minding their marriages instead of fretting over what people would think of their car or house.

Two minutes later, she was following Jessica along the short paved driveway in front of the brick-fronted two-storey that she and Peter had built a few years previously. Claudia's bike was strewn among a selection of smaller toys on the front lawn, a sharp comparison with her own immaculate house front. The Arnolds clearly weren't bothered what their neighbours thought of their home. Perhaps this was where *she'd* gone wrong.

In contrast to her own house, Orla always noticed that Jessica's was slightly chaotic with toys everywhere and the inevitable dog baskets next to the island in the kitchen. The thought of a dog basket, never mind three of them, in her own kitchen always made Orla slightly nauseous. Jessica shoved one of them out of the way with her foot and commented on Peter thinking it was a dogs' home they were running.

She had to smile watching Jessica organising the coffee. For Orla, having someone over for morning coffee was a serious event with freshly-ground beans and a treat baked that morning before the girls got up for school. Jessica, on the other hand, could have won a prize for multi-tasking. All at once she was shoving things into the dishwasher to make space on the counter, filling a sugar bowl, hitting the button on the electric kettle and checking two Denby mugs before landing them on the table.

"Always have to check for sticky fingers," she explained. "Claudia gets into everything. Now . . ." She finally brought the cafetière to the table and plonked herself down opposite Orla, who was exhausted just looking at her.

"Gorgeous." The mince pie that Orla bit into was delicious. "Where are they from?"

"Peter picked them up in town yesterday – I can't remember where." Jessica took a bite herself and murmured her agreement.

Orla sipped her coffee and thought of how nice it was to be out of the house and away from her own list of troubles, even for an hour.

"So what do you need advice on?" She was dying to know what was bothering Jessica.

"You're so lucky to be at home, Orla, I can tell you that! Nonie's been diagnosed with angina so she has to give up the after-school. I'm in a heap over it, to be honest."

"Nonie? But she's only in her fifties!" Nonie Kennedy had been minding children in Barretsbridge all her life and was the type who found it hard to say no to anyone. She'd taken Claudia from very early on so it was no wonder Jessica was in shock.

"I know. She thought it was indigestion but it persisted so she went to the GP. She's having an angiogram next week. I really hope she'll be all right." Jessica looked genuinely concerned.

"That's desperate. I presume she's had to stop working straight away?"

"Definitely, according to the GP. And you know what Nonie's like anyway – she was terrified of getting a heart attack and putting the children in danger."

Orla wasn't surprised. Nonie Kennedy was like a second mother to the children she looked after.

"So what will you do now? Have you had to take time off or what?"

Jessica sighed. "Peter took half days earlier in the week and I took annual leave yesterday and today. I saw an advert on the SuperValu notice-board for a childminder but I'd love your opinion on it, Orla." She smiled. "You didn't put me wrong the last time!"

It was Orla who'd recommended Nonie Kennedy to Jessica and Peter five years ago and she'd had no hesitation, considering the childminder's record over the years. Neither Jessica nor Peter were from Barretsbridge originally so she could appreciate how difficult it was to vet someone.

"Did it give a name?"

There were so many new arrivals to the village in the past few years that it was unlikely that Orla would know this latest candidate.

Jessica rummaged in her handbag for a moment and pulled out a little card, neatly printed in block letters.

"Sadie Kilcoyne?" She looked at Orla hopefully.

Orla's heart sank to her navel but she was glad at the same time that Jessica had had the wisdom to check the credentials before making a move.

"God, Jessica, I'm not so sure . . ." She didn't want to slander anyone but there was no way she could stand by while someone as genuine as Jessica made a mistake with something as important as a childminder. And she'd never forgive herself if anything happened to Claudia.

Jessica, she could see, was disappointed at her response. "Not all she seems on paper then?"

Orla looked at the small advert that Jessica handed her. Sadie had indeed represented herself well on paper.

"Jessica," she began, "please don't repeat this to anyone else but I really feel it might be a mistake. Sadie can be lovely, don't get me wrong, but she's inclined to drink a bit."

"Oh God, Orla . . ." Jessica looked horrified that she'd been considering her.

"You wouldn't know. Even if you met her, she'd seem fine. But she's been in and out of hospital for as long as I know her. Her son, Brian, was in my class in school and he used to live with Sadie's mother most of the time. So did his sisters. They never had lunches or anything."

257

Orla knew it sounded awful but when Sadie was off the drink she was fine. The problem was, she could never stay off it for long and could be seen banging at the door of The Bridge Inn at any hour of the day when she was drinking again.

"Thank God I asked you, Orla. That's the worst about not being local – you could land yourself in anything."

"You couldn't have known." Orla looked at the small card again. "Isn't it desperate that anyone at all can advertise? I hope someone else isn't taken in by her."

Jessica sighed and reached for another mince pie. "Back to the drawing-board then. There was nothing else on the notice-board and I can't get out of the on-call rota."

"Did you try the Post Office? They often have notices."

"Nothing there, I'm afraid, either. It's amazing how much you take things for granted when they're running smoothly."

"Well, don't be stuck if you have to go back to work next week. Claudia can come home from school with Rose and Lily and you can pick her up later. It might tide you over for a bit."

Jessica looked almost shocked. "But your whole evening would be taken up, Orla."

Orla laughed. "You must think I have a very exciting life!"

"I really wouldn't want to take advantage, Orla."

"It'd be no trouble. She could have her dinner with the girls after school. And they'd love to have someone else to fight with instead of bickering with each other all the time!"

Poor Jessica still looked bothered by it all. "Well, if it's not too much trouble, I might take you up on your offer if I haven't got anyone sorted by next week. I'm going to have a look at the notice-board in the Health Centre after lunch. And if the public health nurse is there I'll ask her in case she knows anyone suitable."

Orla's own troubles over the last week had made her a little more empathetic to Jessica's plight. In the past she might have wondered why her neighbour couldn't just give up work until the school term ended but in the past week Orla had started to see the value in having a secure, well-paying job.

"Well, see how you get on and if you don't get sorted just let me know on Sunday evening and I'll pick up Claudia with the girls on Monday. They'll think it's Christmas coming early!"

"Yeah, and you'll have to buy a set of earplugs! I'm really grateful, Orla. I mean it. And thanks for telling me the truth about this Sadie woman. I'd never have forgiven myself if I left someone like that in charge of Claudia."

"That's what good neighbours are for. And I'll have another mince pie as compensation!"

"I'll get Peter to bring another batch – you're worth a full dozen, Orla!"

35

"What time is it?" Laura was groggy but she still noticed that the light coming in through the tiny window in the treatment room was as bright as it had been before she felt the lovely, swooning sensation of the sedative taking effect. It was Monday, the day of her egg collection, and it felt like ages ago since the procedure had started.

"Half one. Are you sore?" Barry, his face a bit blurred, looked down at her with concern. He'd been sitting quietly by the narrow bed in which his wife slept for the past two hours and had been expecting her to wake up around now. It was their sixth attempt at IVF after all, so he knew the routine off by heart at this stage.

"Not too bad." Laura shifted in the bed, trying to get into a sitting position and grimaced as the slight movement caused the familiar sharp pain to shoot across her lower abdomen. "How many did they get?"

This was what it was all about, getting as many mature eggs as possible from the ovaries and, despite her discomfort, the importance of it was still prominent in Laura's mind.

"Eight. I thought there might be more but eight's brilliant.

Filip put his head in earlier to say that much but he said he'd be back whenever you woke up. Do you want a drink?" Barry was holding out a bottle of mineral water.

"Eight's great," Laura said, leaning over a little to sip greedily from the plastic bottle. "God, I'm parched. Was he happy with them?"

It was imperative that the embryologist was satisfied with the quality of the eggs collected and both of them knew that Filip, who they'd met briefly earlier in the week, would be very clear over the next few days on whether they would fertilise normally and develop enough to be placed back inside the womb.

"He didn't say. He'll have a better idea by now, I suppose."

Like his wife, Barry was anxious to know exactly how many of the eggs would be viable.

"Did you get on all right?" Laura asked now, a weak grin spreading over her face. She knew that as soon as her own egg collection process had commenced in the treatment room, Barry would have been led away to some discreet little room to produce a fresh sperm sample. This too was an important part of the process. No matter how many high-quality eggs Laura produced, they would be useless if there wasn't an equally good semen sample for the embryologist to work with.

"No bother," Barry grinned, "They gave me a great little batch of magazines and sent me back to the apartment!"

Laura smiled. "Very fancy, I'm sure." This was a new departure from the pressure of the small room at the back of the ARC clinic that they were used to.

"It's great to have the easy bit! Will I go out and get you a cup of tea to wake you up a bit?"

"Good idea." Laura pulled herself up a little more and swung her legs gingerly over the side of the bed, anxious now to hear about her eggs and get back to the apartment for a proper doze. Her shorts and top were folded neatly next to her flip-flops on the clinically tidy locker.

"Leave them and I'll help you after the tea," Barry warned, noticing his wife glancing at her clothing. He didn't want her getting dizzy and maybe having a fall while he was out of the room.

"Okay so," said Laura, lying back again.

Moments later, Barry arrived back from somewhere with her tea and a handful of biscuits, followed closely by one of the clinic's nurses who'd told them her name was Ella. Neither of them had expected the clinic staff to be mainly English but it was a bonus in terms of the absence of any language barrier.

"Great, Laura, you're wide awake. I'll take out that IV if you like so that you can enjoy the tea properly."

Laura held out her hand without hesitation, knowing how awkward it would be to manage the cup with the needle still in place.

"I'll let Filip know you're awake and he can drop in before you leave. You know you can phone over later if you have any problems, although don't be surprised if you have a small amount of bleeding. And no heavy lifting, strenuous exercise or –"

"I know," Laura interrupted with a giggle, "no vigorous sex in the next few days! As if!"

Ella smiled, aware of how many times the couple had been through this routine. "You know the score. Just take it easy, that's all. Will you have a little time off when you get back to Ireland, Laura?"

"I took three weeks' annual leave, just to give it the best chance possible. It's impossible to work, especially with the acupuncture appointments to fit in at home as well."

"It all helps though," Ella agreed, disposing of the IV gear and turning to wash her hands. "The only problem is that you end up using all your holiday time for treatment. Although I must admit that the combined holiday is one of the big benefits of coming here."

"Tell us about it!" Barry rolled his eyes at her. "We were in

Italy four years ago and haven't seen the inside of a plane until this time around."

"Well, hopefully if this works you'll be tied down for a long time to come and you won't have time for holidays! I'll leave you to enjoy your tea, Laura. And good luck." Ella smiled warmly, genuinely hopeful that after six attempts this treatment cycle *would* work out positively.

As soon as she'd left the room, Laura remarked, as she often did, on the sincerity and very real interest of the people who worked in the assisted-reproduction world.

"I know," Barry agreed. "You'd imagine it'd be like a production line for the staff at this stage but they never seem to make you feel like that. I'd –"

The conversation was interrupted by a discreet knock at the door. Barry reached across to open it and admit Filip.

"Good news so far," he said immediately, knowing that every couple was anxiously waiting for news with little time for small talk until they knew the outcome of the egg collection. "There were eight eggs collected, as I told Barry earlier, and all of them are looking good at the moment. The semen sample was perfect, with a good count and 100% motility. So we'll see what tonight brings."

This was the first positive step and the start of the waiting process.

"If you want to phone over at around 10 a.m. tomorrow, we'll know how many have fertilised and how well they're growing. Ideally, we'd like the embryos to grow on to Day Five but we'll see how they go. We can transfer them back into the uterus earlier if necessary."

"We've always had Day Five transfers before," Laura confirmed.

"I noticed that in the notes that came from the clinic in Ireland. Generally, the Day Five transfers are more successful than the earlier ones so it seems you've had quite bad luck up to now not to have had a positive outcome." Filip looked genuinely regretful. "But let's hope for a better outcome this time."

Laura smiled. "Thanks, Filip. You look after those embryos, okay? They weren't easy to come by."

"I'll do my best! We'll talk in the morning, Laura," the embryologist smiled as he turned to leave the room. "Rest up in the meantime."

"Time to get moving, I suppose," Barry said now, reaching for his wife's clothes. "The sooner we get you to bed the better."

Laura started to get dressed, feeling better now that she knew things were moving along as they should.

"Day five will be Friday – countdown starts now. You know, Bar, I have a really good feeling this time."

Her husband just smiled. "The eternal optimist, that's my wife!"

36

Donal listened to Susan banging and crashing in the kitchen and felt a sense of safety that she was there. In one sense, in seemed like an age since the accident on Patrick Street and the harrowing scenes of grief at Senan's funeral yesterday, yet in other ways it was like it had just happened moments ago, so real was the feeling of shock every time he thought about the overturned truck. It was only Monday evening, not even a week since it had happened but it was difficult to place a sense of time on the events at all.

If it wasn't for Susan making things so steady and normal, Donal thought he might just have gone back to bed again and stayed there. She'd stayed all weekend, only going out to get her clothes and some shopping and had even stood beside him at the funeral, holding his hand tightly all the time.

"Spicy or very spicy?" she called out now and Donal could only wonder about what she might produce from the staples in his little-used kitchen.

"How spicy is very spicy?" He was getting used to Susan cooking for him but still didn't know her taste in Indian and what her idea of spicy might be.

"Very," she laughed, her voice floating out to the living room over the hum of the cooker hood.

To his embarrassment, Donal had quizzed her earlier when he'd heard the unfamiliar noise starting up, never having realised that there was an extractor fan in place before.

"Just plain spicy then," he advised cautiously.

"Chicken! I'll do a Vindaloo next time."

Donal laughed contentedly and made a mental note to consult Orla about learning to cook a bit. Just in case he decided to repay Susan in kind some evening.

He picked up *The Da Vinci Code* again, surprised at how well he was able to concentrate. Susan had brought it over from her own house on Sunday evening to help him pass the time on Monday until she finished work, conscious of the fact that being alone seemed to be a little frightening for him. He was already on page 110, a miracle for Donal who claimed not to have read anything since he grew out of *The Beano* annual.

Just as he was getting back into the story, his mobile rang. If it was Orla, he decided, he'd call to her for his lunch break the following day. She'd phoned numerous times over the weekend to see how he was doing and, for once, he was grateful for her attention.

It wasn't Orla's number on the display panel but Joe Crowley's. Astonished that Joe was even well enough to be making phone calls, Donal answered. "Joe. How are you?"

"Donal, I'm glad I caught you." Joe, even over the two days of the Removal and funeral, had said very little. "You're starting back at work tomorrow?"

"Morning shift," Donal confirmed. Maybe Joe needed to focus on work, even if it was unnecessary, to distract himself.

"I was wondering if we might be able to have a bit of a chat. Before then, if you could manage it."

Donal, though surprised, had no difficulty in accommodating his boss who must surely be distraught. "No problem, Joe. Will

I come in a bit early? Or do you want me to call over this evening?" Whatever it was about, he would do whatever it was that Joe needed.

"Would you be able to drop over later? It's nothing too serious, Donal. Just a proposal, if you'd be able to help me out."

"It's no problem. I'll call over around eight, if that suits." He didn't know how much longer dinner would take and he didn't want to up and leave now when Susan had gone to so much trouble.

"That'd be great. It's just that Ita's brother has a house in Connemara and we're thinking of staying there for a bit until we get out heads together. Ita says she needs to get away somewhere quiet to think and I'm the same. I know it's a big ask, Donal, but I was wondering if you'd be able to hold the fort here for a while?"

"In the office?" Donal knew he wouldn't have a clue how to manage the cab company.

"Along with Marge," Joe amended. "She says she can manage the desk for the moment but I need someone who can deal with the drivers and sort out any problems with the cars, that kind of thing. I'd fill you in on everything and I'd only be at the end of the phone."

Joe sounded desperate and Donal really did want to help but was very aware of the possibility that he might mess things up big-time when he really didn't know the ropes. To date, all he'd done was drive and occasionally man the desk if Marge was off.

"I'd be delighted, Joe but . . ."

He could hear Joe's sigh of relief down the phone and couldn't believe that he'd just given him the impression that he was willing to take on the everyday running of the cab company.

"That's great, Donal. You get on well with the lads and you've been here so long that you nearly know everything anyway."

Donal, who'd spent the past six years trying *not* to take in

267

anything stressful or troublesome, was stunned that his boss had seen it differently.

"Call over in your own time and we'll go through a few things. And we'll have to talk money as well – I don't expect you to take it on as a 'God Bless You' job!"

For a moment, there was a tiny spark of the old upbeat Joe and Donal could see just how broken his voice had been up to now. He and Ita did need to get away and Donal couldn't refuse to help him when he needed it. Knowing Joe, it would only be a matter of weeks before he got itchy feet again. And from what Susan said about her mother, work might be what he'd need to get him back on track again.

"Don't mind about money, Joe. I'll see you around eight, okay?"

His heart now beating wildly at the idea that he'd just committed himself to something that was way beyond his capabilities, Donal dropped the phone next to him on the sofa and stared into the flames of the fire for a moment.

"All okay?" Susan was standing in the alcove that separated the kitchen from the living room.

"Joe wants me to look after the office for a bit. He's going to Connemara for a while."

"Donal, that's lovely!"

He looked at her sceptically, wondering what exactly was "lovely" about what he'd just got himself into.

"He obviously trusts you," she added, coming over to sit beside him.

"I don't know why. I haven't a clue what goes on there from day to day."

"I'm sure he'll fill you in on all that. He wouldn't have asked you if he didn't think you could do it."

Donal was doubtful. "I'll probably make a mess of it and bankrupt him or something."

"Don't say that, Donal. You'll be well able for it. The only thing is whether you want to commit to it right now. You've had a very traumatic week and obviously Joe can't know just how bad it was for you."

"Not as bad as it was for him! It's not that I don't want to help out –"

Susan came to his defence immediately. "I *know* that. Of course you'd want to help. And you're well able for the job. But will it take a lot out of you emotionally?"

Donal found it hard to admit but he was still slightly amazed at how serious Susan was about the effect that Senan being killed had had on him. Donal had spent twenty-four hours in bed berating himself for the childish way he'd reacted to the accident but his girlfriend was looking after him as if he was the one who'd had a truck land on him.

"No, I think that'll be good for me – to feel as if I'm doing something to help. I just don't want to cause Joe any more hardship, that's all."

It was better that he didn't get involved at all if he was going to be more trouble than he was worth.

Susan was looking thoughtful. "Why do you think he asked you?"

"Well, I suppose I'm around the longest, for a start."

He didn't want to admit it but he agreed with Joe that he was friendly enough with all of the drivers and, in that sense, he didn't have any worries about them taking the mick when the boss was away. And because he didn't actually socialise with any of them outside the work environment, he didn't have to worry about losing friends if anything in the line of discipline reared its head.

"He wouldn't pick you just for that reason! It's a business he's running and I can tell you for definite that if I were him, I'd be looking for someone with loyalty to the company who'd have the same outlook as myself and who I could rely on to keep things running smoothly while I was gone."

Donal had to laugh at this summing up. "Thanks. Now I have even more to worry about than I thought I had!"

"Sorry! You know what I mean. He didn't pick you for the craic of it, that's all."

In honesty, Donal thought she was probably right. Senan, of course, would have been Joe's natural replacement. Phil Conway, for instance, was way too nice and would try to please everyone with shifts coming up to Christmas if he was the one doing out the rota. Bill Buckley, driving with Go Cars almost as long as Donal, was great fun but hot-headed in the extreme if something didn't go his way. Leonard O'Dwyer, another long-term employee, had five small children and helped his wife with her auctioneering business, so wouldn't be able to commit to a heavier role in Go Cars. That left the newer lads who really didn't know what was going on.

"I suppose," he conceded. "I told him I'd go over after dinner. I'll try to get back as soon as I can."

"No bother. I'll go out and get a DVD for later, if you like."

"Sorry to have to take off when you've cooked something nice." Donal would definitely consult Orla about something simple that he could cook for Susan later in the week.

"You don't know yet if it's nice or not!" She hopped off the sofa and kissed him before heading back to the kitchen. "It'll only be a few more minutes."

Donal sat there and thought about Joe's proposal, feeling a little more confident than he had in the immediate aftermath of the phone call. He'd have to find out about the pay rates for the drivers for the Christmas Bank Holiday shifts. And he'd need to know what kind of leeway he'd have for calling in the part-time drivers for the busy nights like Christmas Eve and New Year's Eve.

Susan was right. Joe Crowley must have had a good reason for choosing him, although Donal still wasn't sure exactly what it was. In any event, he was going to do his best not to let him down.

37

By Friday, it was clear that Claudia Arnold was actually a calming influence on Lily and Rose rather than an added burden to Orla's workload. For a start, there was more for the girls to do now that they had an extra person for games and they were less inclined to fight over things for the sake of it when Claudia was there as a distraction. To Orla's relief, there was a little more time spent in the playroom and a little less of the "*Mom*, she took my . . ." to frazzle her even more than she was already.

Now that she'd straightened out as much as she could as regards household spending, things with Gavin were coming increasingly to the fore. It wasn't her usual style, but Orla for once felt like throwing herself down and admitting that she just wasn't able for it. Dealing with re-organising the practical aspects of their life had been easy in a sense, just another task to be tackled efficiently. Having to open her eyes to what had happened with Gavin and Cleo . . . well, it was just easier not to have to face it.

She knew she was tense and short with him, no matter how contrite and placating Gavin was trying to be. Unable to face talking to or even looking at him, she busied herself in the evenings once the girls were in bed, sifting manically through bits of her former life that she hoped would keep her future afloat.

Her head ached as she rifled through the huge chest freezer in the garage that she used for storing "just in case" things. She didn't even feel the cold of the frozen turkeys, labelled steaks, ham joints and reams of chops and cutlets that she'd been throwing in all year. No amount of frostbitten fingers could take away the visions of Gavin and Cleo having sex that were forcing themselves into her mind. She'd vowed that she wouldn't think like this, that it would be allowing Cleo to win. Permitting Gavin to stay had been Orla's choice. Opting to make a go of this new life in the best way she could was her choice too. She was in control and nothing that Cleo could offer would alter that.

Or so she needed to think – if only the knowledge of what Cleo *had* offered could be erased. Yes, Gavin had ended their liaison, but if Orla couldn't erase it from her mind then how could he? If Orla was thinking of Cleo day and night, then maybe her husband was too. It was this that hurt her more than anything, the fact that she couldn't get into his mind and scrub out whatever it was that had made him want Cleo enough to risk everything he had. To Orla, she'd been just another of Donal's disposable girlfriends but to Gavin . . . well, he must have seen something that he wanted so badly he could put everything else aside.

And now that Gavin and Bob had come to an agreement about the business, her husband seemed to be in front of her eyes all day. Only it wasn't just Gavin she saw when she looked at him, it was him and Cleo entwined together, over and over again.

His office upstairs, formerly used on a minor scale, was now the sole premises of Cole & Merriman and was choc-a-block with an industrial-sized photocopier and fax machine as well as every file that had ever existed, or so it seemed to Orla.

Bob, in spite of his wife's diagnosis of cancer, had agreed to finish the projects he was working on before bowing out of the business in an everyday capacity. The name Cole & Merriman would remain and after his retirement Bob would stay on as a director. For now, though, he would work from home as well. Blessedly, they'd been able to get out of their lease on the office in town so at least that was one less expense to have to worry about.

Up to now, money and the deconstruction of their life was all that Gavin and Orla seemed to talk about, discussing bills and leases and weekly outgoings over dinner as if they were business partners. It was two weeks now since the glass bubble surrounding her had been shattered and, save the night that it had happened, they'd spoken of anything but Cleo.

The painting of the bedroom and the fact that her redecorating spree was now finished seemed to be goading Orla into making the next move. She'd resurrected a deeper shade of cream in the garage than the one that had graced the walls up to now and had set to her painting job with a vengeance every morning as soon as the girls had been dropped at school. She wanted it gone, all traces of the room that she'd come home to two weeks ago, hoping that this would symbolise the cleaning out of Cleo and her getting on with her life.

Gavin, working in his office across the corridor, had said nothing about the draped furniture and coverless bed. What he didn't know was that the cream and mocha duvet cover and its expensive matching coverlet had been dry-cleaned, a worthwhile expense in Orla's estimation, and dispatched to the St Vincent de Paul shop.

Now, instead of the restful cream and mocha theme, the bedroom boasted a new deep red bed-linen set that she'd picked up a few years ago and had planned to use whenever the spare bedroom needed redecorating. Even the small piano stool at the dressing table had had its seat recovered with a half yard of ruby velvet that she'd rooted out of the stock of odds and ends she kept for entertaining the girls on rainy days. Whether it was right or wrong, she hammered in the tiny tacks that she'd found in the garage around the inside edges of the mahogany stool, recklessly aware that they wouldn't be seen once the seat was slotted neatly back into the frame. In the past, such a job would have been left to a professional upholsterer.

She'd worked manically this last week, even swapping the paintings that had witnessed Gavin's infidelity with two from the hall and sitting room that matched the new-look bedroom better.

Now though, something in Orla had ground to a halt. Her own domain was sorted but what pride she had in that was negated by the ever-present image of wild, streaky hair spread out across the pillows.

What had always been Gavin's domain was now functioning at a manageable level. And although income was at a minimum, outgoings were also at an all-time low. They had some savings, thanks to Gavin, so they would survive for now.

Orla's head had been bursting all day and despite the two Panadol she'd taken it was showing no signs of easing. Dinner would be late this evening as Gavin had someone calling at five about drawing up plans for a house. In the past, Orla would have gone mental if he agreed to a meeting so late in the evening – now she'd be waiting to hear the outcome of the possibility of future work.

Jessica would be calling for Claudia at six and Orla planned to have all three of the girls fed before then with homework done for the morning. They were playing away now after their afternoon snack and at least the civility in the playroom was heartening.

It was a strain, keeping a front up, and her shoulder and neck muscles were in a permanent state of tension. A few weeks ago, she could have gone for a massage to relax and rejuvenate or at the very least ask Gavin to give her a quick rub to relieve the strain. It was a bleak thought now to realise how narrow her options had become in every facet of her life.

However bad things were – and they were as bad as it got right now – the only thing holding her together was the fact that at least nobody knew. Her parents were oblivious, Donal, as was his way, never seemed to be aware of anything that was going on, and Laura, thankfully, was still in Barbados. The thought of her neighbours knowing of their financial position made a cold sweat come out all over her but she'd already started mentioning her intention of resuming her working life now that she'd given the girls a good start in life.

"No point in letting myself go brain-dead altogether," she'd told Hilary Lynch and Judy Burke at the school gates.

Her voice, she thought, sounded normal rather than as brittle and bitter as she felt so she'd ploughed on and signalled her aspiration of picking up something handy to start out with. "Nothing that would take up too much of the day, mind, especially when the girls are just getting established at school."

If she did have to return to work, she at least wanted it to look as if it was through choice rather than necessity.

Orla knew that she and Gavin would soon have to talk about where they were going as a couple but it choked her every time she forced herself to confront it. To be fair, he'd tried to talk about it a few times over the past fortnight but, up until now, Orla hadn't been able to go there. She'd felt calm and in control, in a weird way, doing things, achieving the sense of order that she needed to stave off the feelings of seething anger that had been building up like a rising pressure gauge.

Cleo, sexy and carefree, had the upper hand and Orla would have to acknowledge this before she could start to look at her husband for what he was – a typical, easily flattered male. Women, Orla realised in her angry moments, generally faced a crisis by overstretching and denying themselves in order to restore the status quo. Men, she now saw, used avoidance therapy in the form of affairs, alcohol or gambling. This allowed the fallback of the woman having to rescue the situation. It was a new theory, and probably a bitter and cynical one, but it fitted her own circumstances perfectly.

There would always be Cleos there, waiting in the wings. And there would always be the Gavins, needing a prop when they couldn't face the music without the human form of a hot stone massage.

It wasn't about forgiveness now. It was about what Orla wanted out of all this. She had her husband. That seemed to be a fact. But on what terms?

Was Gavin still here because of their dire financial straits and the fact that an idyllic life with a sexy, adventurous woman like Cleo was a luxury he simply couldn't afford? If there hadn't been a global and national recession involved, would her husband now be living the life he really wanted in a flat over the Beady Eye shop on Patrick Street?

For her own part, would she have demanded, in a blaze of impassioned outrage, that her husband leave Barretsbridge if the discovery of the affair hadn't been overshadowed by the frightening financial limbo that Gavin had revealed the same evening? Would a hefty monthly maintenance payment and her dignity intact have been enough for her? Did she need Gavin here only because it would be harder to manage without him?

Did she love him and want to have a loving, secure family again or was she content to live this existence of tension and anger? Did he love her, or would it be enough to pass through the house like a stranger, functioning like an automaton because there was no other way? What about Rose and Lily? What would they start to see when the excitement of having Claudia around the house every evening wore off?

It was, she knew, time to face what she'd been avoiding. Soon, they'd have to talk but the bloody anniversary dinner was ahead of her and she knew she couldn't make any decisions until that had been faced and dealt with.

She mightn't want to hear what Gavin had to say and maybe

she'd be explaining to Lily and Rose that Dad would be staying downstairs while Mum returned to the newly revamped bedroom upstairs. It wasn't what she wanted, she was almost sure of that, but she needed more time to decide what direction their future would take.

Maybe then her blasted headache would go away.

It was strange, but as soon as she'd made her decision on leaving her talk with Gavin until after the impending family gathering, Orla was able to shelve the issue and start focussing on the matter of the anniversary dinner itself. She was the one who'd insisted it had to be celebrated, so she could hardly back out of it now without raising suspicion.

It was another thing that angered her, the fact that carrying the can for her siblings seemed to be taken for granted. Even though neither Donal nor Laura ever organised anything, they were still well able to object and complain about what she came up with. Well, as soon as this particular evening was over, there would be no more pandering from Orla. It would be her turn to start sitting back a bit.

She knew full well that neither Donal nor Laura would give a hoot if the anniversary celebration for their parents never happened at all but Orla had promised Iris and Paddy that they would be getting together for dinner to mark the occasion. Making a big deal out of it was coming back to bite her now, when she and Gavin couldn't afford a meal in Chez Louis, never mind a baby-sitter and a present.

She was a little ashamed now at how disparaging she'd been about Laura's reluctance to agree to an expensive anniversary present. If either Laura or Donal were to start pressing *her* right now for money that she could little afford, what would it be like to have to explain that she just didn't have it?

In terms of baby-sitting, she knew that she could probably prevail upon Jessica for a sleepover but only if she wasn't on call on the night. But even at that, there was still the extortionate cost of the restaurant to consider, not only for herself and Gavin, but in pitching in their share for Iris and Paddy's meals as well. Orla almost laughed out loud now when she remembered her assertion to Laura that Chez Louis was good value for money, for the dining experience you were getting.

Orla wondered now about the possibility of having the anniversary celebration at home rather than at a restaurant. It would only be the family anyway and having it in the house ruled out the need for a baby-sitter. Cancelling the restaurant would be embarrassing but she'd told more than one white lie in the past two weeks. She'd do it today, which would be plenty of notice, even if she had to invent a family bereavement to gloss it over.

Now that it was decided, telling Laura and Donal that Chez Louis had double-booked them would be a doddle. Laura would be relieved at the absence of such a big expense and Donal, ever ambivalent, would simply shrug.

And the only good thing about having been so extravagant for so many years was that there was enough of a stockpile in the freezer to do a dinner party without too much extra cost.

Laura wouldn't be home until Wednesday but Donal could be phoned straight away, she thought, reaching for her mobile.

"Orla, hi, how's it going?" As ever, he answered his phone straight away.

"Grand," she lied, aware suddenly of just how good at covering up she was becoming. "How are you?" she said, sounding upbeat enough. "Feeling a bit better since last week?"

"Okay," Donal told her. "Joe's gone away to Connemara for a break with his wife so I'm manning the controls here. That's keeping me busy."

Orla was amazed that he wasn't giving out. "I thought you hated being on the desk?"

"Well, Marge is on the desk at the moment. I'm keeping order while Joe's away," he explained.

"Like, looking after the cab company?" This was the most responsibility Donal had ever taken on in his life. "How long is he going to be away for?"

"Don't sound so stunned, sister! I won't blow the place up or anything. He'll be back after Christmas, I'd say."

"It's a big responsibility. Have you to keep an eye on money and everything as well?" She had to get to the bottom of the fact that her brother had been left in charge of anything.

"Marge and I will do it together. And Joe's only on the end of the phone, even though I hope I won't have to disturb him much."

Orla was impressed that Joe was willing to give Donal free rein with the company he'd built up over years of hard work. "Well, fair play to you! Now, we'll have to have a change of plan as regards the anniversary dinner."

She waited for Donal's groan but continued quickly when she didn't hear it straight away. "The manager from Chez Louis rang to apologise a minute ago. They double-booked apparently and the other crowd were first so they had to cancel us. But I can do something in the house, if that's all right?"

"It's grand by me anyway. And I'm sure Laura and Barry will be just as happy after coming back from holidays. Did you hear from them?"

Orla was delighted that the subject of the dinner was dispensed with so quickly but should have known that Donal would have very little interest. As for Laura and Barry, she hadn't been in touch at all since they'd left, having had enough on her own plate to be texting to see what the weather was like in Barbados.

"No, I didn't get a chance to text at all. What about you?"

It was a new thing for her brother to even consider whether any of the rest of the family were dead or alive.

"Nah. I meant to give them a ring but they'll be home soon anyway."

This was unusual for Donal and Orla wondered if perhaps

he'd presumed that *she* would have been on the phone telling Laura all about the fatal accident and the fact that Donal was safe and sound. Maybe he'd expected Laura to get in contact to see if he was really all right.

In truth, if things had been on an even keel in her own life, Orla probably would have phoned Laura to tell her. With a shock, she realised that many of the interventions she made in her family were probably unnecessary, exhausting, expensive and not really her business at all.

She agreed with Donal now about Laura being home soon and reminded him that the dinner was only next week anyway. Maybe he was more traumatised over Senan Crowley's death than she thought.

"You'll be able to have a good chat with her then," she said sympathetically.

"I suppose. How are the girls?"

Donal must be a new man on account of his added responsibilities. Normally he couldn't wait to get off the phone. Now, it was her turn to cut the calls short, on account of not wanting to run up her bill.

"Grand. Quiet as mice these evenings because Claudia's coming here after school until her mother gets a new after-school minder. I'd better go here, Donal, or they'll be like demons. They always get into something if they see I'm on the phone!"

"Grand so, I'll give you a ring before next Friday. What'll I bring?"

Orla hadn't thought about this but now that Donal was offering to contribute, she knew it would be wise to accept. "Anything at all. Drinks maybe?"

"Right, I'll bring some beer and wine. I'll talk to you before then, anyway."

"Okay, bye for now." Orla hung up, pleased at the way it had gone. Maybe Laura would even offer to bring the cake.

Before she knew it, Jessica Arnold was ringing the doorbell.

Claudia and the twins had been warned about being quiet on account of Gavin's client in the office upstairs so the three of them were watching *High School Musical* in the playroom. A major protest erupted at the arrival of Claudia's mother but Orla plastered her new-found cover-up smile to her face and acted as if Martha Stewart hadn't a patch on her.

"Have a coffee if you have time, Jessica. There's only about ten minutes left in the DVD."

"I'd love one, Orla. And a bit of the serenity of this house wouldn't go astray either! I went to meet that childminder I told you about."

Orla let the comment about serenity go, wondering what Jessica would think if she knew the true situation in the Merriman household. She could see by the expression on Jessica's face that the visit had been less than satisfactory. "Not what you expected?"

"Well, if I'd been expecting a zoo, it'd have been fine! Honestly, Orla, there must have been ten kids there, of all ages. Even two babies. She seems to have two older girls of her own and as far as I could see, it was them who were looking after the children. The woman herself was cooking dinner when I called."

Orla sighed and reached for the coffee pot. It was good to hear that Jessica, despite an intact marriage and no threat of bankruptcy, had her problems too.

"Imagine what it'd have been like if she *wasn't* expecting you!"

"It's a nightmare, Orla, trying to get someone. And I'm so sorry to be imposing on you." Jessica was nearly crying when Orla turned around with the mugs.

"Jessica! Don't be panicking. Claudia can keep coming here. Honestly. Don't feel you have to rush into anything."

"But I can't take advantage forever. I just couldn't –"

"Jessica, it's only a few hours in the evening and you can drop her off here any morning you're going to work early. I know you'll find it hard to believe but the girls are far more civilised now that they have Claudia to compete over!"

"I do find that hard to believe!" said Jessica. "But Orla, we'll have to put it on a proper footing if you're going to be having her every evening. Otherwise I *would* be taking advantage."

"Jessica! There's no –"

"I mean it, Orla. I'll pay you exactly the same as I was paying Nonie until we get sorted out."

At that, Jessica named a figure that Orla could hardly believe. Nonie Kennedy must indeed be as good as everyone said she was if this was what she could command for a few hours' work in her own home.

"That's out of the question, Jessica! I'm here with the girls anyway. And she's great company for them."

"Orla, you're already feeding her and doing the homework! You're like one of those live-in nannies. It's full pay or no deal, okay?" Jessica had a persuasive smile on her face but her voice was insistent.

"Well, drop her off in the mornings then as well so Peter won't have to delay at the school. And for goodness sake, Jessica, bring her bike over in the morning! Three into two definitely doesn't go." Orla grinned, her first real, unforced smile in two weeks.

"Deal. Cheers!" Jessica raised her coffee cup and clinked it against Orla's.

"Cheers," Orla echoed and wondered what Gavin would think of this latest turn of events. What Jessica was offering would more than pay for the grocery shopping so it certainly wouldn't be a bad thing.

"You'd have had a heart attack if you'd seen the other place, Orla. It was bedlam," Jessica reiterated, relief now written all over her face.

Orla grinned happily, a little of the tension easing out of her temples. Regardless of what anyone would think about her taking on childminding, money was money at the end of the day. And at least Jessica was under the impression that she was doing a favour of sorts rather than touting for business. "It's bedlam here some days too! But Rose and Lily will be thrilled."

"Poor Claudia won't know what to do with herself. It'll be great for her to have company in the evenings."

Orla, as was her nature, would take her new duties seriously. "I'll have everything written down, Jessica. What she's eaten and whether she's had a snooze after school with the girls."

After all, she was about to become a professional childminder now.

38

Donal was delighted that the meal at Chez Louis had been cancelled. Any time he'd ever been forced to attend the stuffy, over-priced restaurant he'd felt stifled and almost choked by the formality of the venue and the inevitable tension that surrounded his own family. Later that evening, he talked about it to Susan and, amazingly, she'd understood.

"Well, it's difficult to celebrate anything when there's someone missing every time," she'd reasoned.

Donal agreed with her but didn't think that any of the rest of them would acknowledge that this was the reason if he brought it up. Iris would just put on her vague face and look at her husband for guidance on how to react. Paddy would say something jovial and placating to distract them all and move things on from a topic that would undoubtedly unsettle his wife.

Orla, who'd had no involvement in anything to do with Darren, would think that such an assertion was nonsense and would probably scoff at the idea of Donal even bringing it up. After all, to Orla, the dinners weren't even a problem anyway. Laura might be the only one who'd agree with him, although

Darren and the accident might be something that she'd filed away in her mind as Donal had done up to now. He couldn't blame her if she didn't want to revisit it, considering it was only Senan's death that had reignited it all for him.

"Are we very dysfunctional?" he asked Susan after some thought on this.

She smiled softly and shook her head. "Only the ones who refuse to acknowledge that what happened was a big thing. You're not like that, Donal. And you can't be responsible for everyone else."

"You can judge them for yourself next Friday, if you like," he told her. "Orla was on to me today and she's having a do in her house for Mam and Dad's anniversary. Will you be able to come?"

He'd been both surprised and disappointed earlier when Orla didn't get into her usual flap about numbers. He'd wanted to tell her about Susan, even though he hadn't got around to asking her to Chez Louis. He liked her a lot and had been wondering whether to expose her to the usual scenario but an evening in Orla's house would be different. She'd love to meet Rose and Lily, for a start.

"Of course I would. I'll look at the appointments tomorrow and try to get off a bit early. What time would we have to leave here?"

"Orla didn't say but I imagine it'll be at seven or something like that. I'll be talking to her over the next few days anyway."

He'd phone Orla over the weekend and let her know about Susan, just in case she was presuming he'd be coming alone.

He felt a bit sheepish considering it wasn't so long ago that he'd been introducing them to Cleo, although in this instance he sensed it'd be the last time he'd be landing in with someone new. Susan, he hoped, would be a permanent fixture.

39

Laura smiled at the idea of lying back on a beach after an embryo transfer but that was exactly what she'd done all afternoon. Now it was after eight and she and Barry were sitting in one of the outdoor restaurants finishing their dinner. Or rather Barry was, with an enormous portion of cheesecake, while Laura sipped her non-alcohol cocktail and reflected on the day's events.

The embryo transfer had gone as planned, with Filip preparing the two best quality ones for transfer into her uterus. Unlike the egg collection, which necessitated a light anaesthetic, the transfer was painless and over in minutes. Barry, ever the engineer, always marvelled at the fact that the tiny, microscopic embryos, once pushed out of the fine catheter into the darkness of the womb, were expected to find their way around and settle on a spot to attach and grow.

In the past, they hadn't done this but Laura was convinced that this time at least one of them would.

"I wonder where they are now?" Barry too must be imagining the journey that their embryos would take. He'd finished his cheesecake, she noticed.

"I think they float around for a few days so hopefully they're acclimatising to their new environment!"

Laura had a very good feeling this time, an almost high sense of hope that she thought was as a result of the altered environment in which they'd been for almost two weeks. They were both relaxed and chilled-out but it wasn't just that, as Laura kept explaining to Barry.

"I just noticed on the notes earlier while you were asleep – the test is actually on Christmas Day."

Laura thought it sounded prophetic somehow. Especially considering the number of bleak Christmases they'd spent looking back on years in which their dream hadn't been fulfilled yet again.

"Wouldn't it be magic?"

Barry knew what she meant by this. It would be special and indeed magic to see the two blue lines appearing on a pregnancy test stick instead of the lonely single one that was all they'd seen up to now.

"It would," he agreed. "It *will be,*" he restated, as determined as his wife to remain positive for the next few weeks.

Laura accepted coffee from a passing waiter and marvelled at how differently she felt this time. "It's amazing," she told her husband. "The last few times, I was exhausted by the time the embryo transfer was done. This time, I feel like it's only the beginning. And I'm glad we have time to chill out."

Barry understood as usual. "I'd say a lot of it has to do with Grace as well. Just getting everything off your chest has to be good for you."

Laura would be the first to agree that the four counselling sessions that she'd had so far had taken an enormous burden off her shoulders that she hadn't even realised she was carrying. Even Barry, for all that she'd explained over the years about Darren getting killed, hadn't been aware of the fact that she'd always felt it was her fault and that she'd let her parents down by not minding her brother properly.

Laura smiled. "It has been. Every time I thought of it before, I could see myself as an adult and I used to wonder how I didn't have the sense to mind the boys properly. Grace has made me see that I was a child at the time. I know now that I shouldn't have been expected to keep an eye on the two of them."

Every evening after one of the counselling sessions, Laura had been able to fill Barry in on the progress and just talking out loud about it had made sense of what had happened. Without blaming her parents, she was now able to see that such a responsibility shouldn't have been placed on her at all. That this was where the mistake, if any, lay.

Barry had often tried to tell his wife this before but she'd always insisted that her parents had trusted her. "I wonder if that's why your Mam is as nervous as she is? Maybe *she's* felt guilty over the years and couldn't cope with it. Isn't it mad that nobody thought of it as depression before?"

It had taken Grace to identify all the crying and panic and not coping that had befallen Iris as pure and simple grief and subsequent depression. In Laura's eye, something awful had happened to her mother and the rest of them needed to mind her. She hadn't been able to see that something awful had happened to *all* of them and that they too needed looking after.

"I suppose Mam sort of collapsed and Dad had to look after her. There just wasn't anyone left to look after Donal and me. Or Dad, for that matter. He's been ignored by all of us over the years."

Barry was adamant now about Laura blaming herself no further. "It wasn't your job to look after him."

One of Laura's sessions had been taken up by the idea that she hadn't taken better care of Donal. Barry was stunned at the level of guilt that his wife had carried all her life.

Laura smiled over at him. "I know. I just had this idea that the only one job I'd been given was to mind two children and I couldn't even do that properly. I just thought I was useless, even at such a basic thing as that."

Barry looked hesitant, but spoke anyway. "Laura, what you said just now . . . I don't mean this in a critical way or anything but –"

"What?" It wasn't like Barry to beat about the bush.

"Well, you don't think there was something . . . well . . . psychological, or something . . . that maybe –"

Laura finished the sentence for him. "Stopped me from getting pregnant?"

Poor Barry looked shocked that it was he who'd started this line of conversation.

"I don't mean that you knew it! Or that you didn't want to have kids. I *know* you do. But what if all the guilt . . . what if it was telling you that you couldn't do it or something?"

Laura sighed. Grace had suggested this too and Laura had discounted it. Quite crossly, she remembered a little guiltily now.

"Grace did mention that," she admitted.

She trusted Barry totally and knew he would never blame her for not being able to get pregnant. In fact, he'd always been the one to say that, in later years, any disease or disorder could be discovered in either of them that would explain it. He likened it to having something like diabetes, something that they could have no control over, that wasn't anyone's fault.

"*I* know you'd be a great mother, Laura. But what do you think?"

The evening was darkening around them and most of the other diners had left to go indoors where there was a combo playing traditional Caribbean music. The silence settled around Laura now as she thought about what she might be like as a mother. Strangely, for a woman who was very actively hoping for a baby, it was something that she'd never allowed herself to think about before.

Tears of anger and frustration sprang to her eyes now as she let her real feelings surface at last.

"I just couldn't let myself think any further than being

pregnant, Barry. I was afraid to *let* myself think about actually having a baby. I mean, what if I let something happen to it?"

Barry, white-faced, stared at her and reached across to hold both of her hands tightly. "How could you even think that, Laura? I'd trust you with anything! You'd never let anything happen, if we had a baby this minute. I *know* that."

Laura sobbed but no tear rolled down her cheek. She hated Barry holding her hands as if she needed to be minded. "It wouldn't be fair if I couldn't mind it properly, Barry, no baby would deserve that."

Barry kept holding her hands tightly, stopping her from pulling away. "And *you* don't deserve this. We're phoning Grace first thing in the morning, Laura, and this time, I'll be coming with you. You won't have to carry all this on your own any more. Okay?"

Laura smiled weakly, a weird sense of lightness coming over her.

"Okay."

40

Peter Arnold laid the small brown envelope on the small mahogany console table in the hall and smiled broadly at Orla as Claudia, Rose and Lily shot past him on their way to the playroom. It was Friday morning and Orla had been up at the crack of dawn getting things in order for the anniversary dinner.

"Jess said she put last week's in there as well." He nodded towards the envelope and Orla made to genuinely protest at this.

"Peter! I told her –"

Jessica's husband halted her tirade by raising his hand and interrupting her. "Jessica is ecstatic and Claudia thinks all her birthdays have come at once."

As if to prove this, his daughter's piping voice emerged in a shriek from the playroom, followed by a burst of giggles. "What more could I ask for, Orla? So no more protests."

"Honestly, Peter –"

"You're so good to be getting us out of this fix, Orla, you have no idea."

Orla felt almost guilty at all this gratitude, considering just how badly she and Gavin needed the money right now.

Admittedly, Jessica and Peter were in a fix but she would have helped out anyway, regardless of getting paid.

"Well, Rose and Lily are thrilled, I can tell you that," she conceded.

Peter rolled his eyes as the cacophony from the playroom started again. "Jess tells me you have a party on tonight so she's taking a half day. She should be here for Missy around two to let you get back to your preparations."

"Ah, Peter, there was no need for her to do that. She can't be altering her shifts to suit me. And I'm pretty organised anyway."

"All the same. We've landed on top of you at fairly short notice so it's only fair. Now, I'd better get off or there'll be a line of farmers lambasting Betty if I'm late."

Betty was the veterinary nurse who worked at Peter's practice, a glamorous blonde that Orla had met a few times at Jessica and Peter's summer barbecues. It used to surprise Orla a little that Peter would socialise with his staff but at this point she realised that she herself was now employed by the Arnolds.

Reminded now of the social climb-down that well-heeled Gaby Solis had had to make in *Desperate Housewives*, she waved Peter off and pondered on the irony that only a few weeks ago she'd been a person who employed staff. Now, *she* was the staff. Nonetheless, her new earning power had been achieved discreetly and without any loss of dignity, a fact that she would eternally be grateful for.

"Okay, girls," she called out now as she made her way to the kitchen. "Five minutes and the porridge will be on the table."

Thanking her lucky stars that she'd never started her children on sugary, processed, expensive cereals, Orla set about getting breakfast for her three charges before they were loaded into the car for the trip to school. Her list was out on the table, ready from the evening before and, as ever, she felt a sense of security and purpose when she glanced over it.

As soon as she came back from the school trip, the brown

bread for her first course would be her immediate task. A large pack of oak-smoked salmon was already defrosting on the counter, to be served later with soured cream and the fresh dill that she'd been carefully tending on the kitchen window-sill for the past week. Next on her list was the carrot and coriander soup that Gavin and the girls loved and which she had made so often that she could do it in her sleep. She knew it was probably a slightly lazy option but her parents liked it too and, as far as she could see, Donal, Laura and Barry ate anything and everything.

According to Donal, his new beau, Susan, wasn't fussy. When he'd said this to Orla over the phone, she'd been on the point of agreeing with him in a fit of black humour but had held her tongue for fear of offending him. Donal's girlfriends, she thought cynically, certainly weren't fussy if they were willing to put up with his grubby flat, filthy car and aversion to commitment. Then she thought of Cleo and the fact that *she* hadn't been willing to tolerate Donal's ways, moving on instead to Gavin with his apparently impressive job.

She stirred the pot of creamy porridge viciously now as a vision of Cleo standing barefoot on this very spot overwhelmed her for a moment. Afraid that the recurrent feeling that her world was crumbling around her would immobilise her, she pushed the vision out of her mind, along with the fleeting picture of Gavin's face last evening as he'd pleaded with her to talk to him about their marriage.

Her rage at his insistence had startled her, to the point where she couldn't even speak enough words to refuse him. She'd simply walked away, unable to deal with anything besides the practical demands of daily living, demands that had been thrust upon her so harshly that she was barely able to keep her head above water, never mind engage in meaningless to-ing and fro-ing about the state of their marriage.

Somewhere at the back of her head, she knew that Gavin meant well, that his offers to "talk" were really attempts at atonement. Most women, she knew, needed such open and frank exchanges of honesty if anything was to be salvaged but Orla was different. It was action she needed, concrete proof that her husband was willing to rebuild their life and restore it to its former status as impregnable in his wife's eyes. The fact that he couldn't see this simply served to make Orla aware of just how little he knew of her real needs.

Anger at him surged again but, like always, the immediate needs of her family took precedence.

"Breakfast is ready," she called and was gratified to hear the tap-tap of three pairs of feet racing towards the kitchen. At least one aspect of her life was running like clockwork.

"What time is the party at?" Lily was always first to get excited by an impending drama.

"It's not exactly a party," Orla reminded her, knowing that the whole school would be filled in by lunchtime. "More of a dinner party."

"But we can still wear our party dresses?"

"And put up the balloons after school?"

Rose too was in the form for a party and Orla softened. So what if anyone thought it was a simple family gathering rather than a formal dinner party?

"Definitely. And . . . ah . . . Uncle Donal will be bringing a new friend this evening," she added carefully.

She'd been putting off addressing this somewhat delicate topic with the girls but the last thing she needed was a long-winded probe on the whereabouts of Cleo in the middle of dinner this evening. Better to get it over with now so that it would all be forgotten about by seven o' clock.

"Why?"

Lily looked most put out but it was Rose who piped up with the inevitable, "Will Cleo be here as well?"

Answering both questions at once, she explained that Donal had a new girlfriend now and that they probably wouldn't be seeing Cleo again. A little fearfully, she hoped that this last bit was true.

Claudia, fascinated at the relationship between her mother's arty cousin and the uncle of her two best friends, asked if Donal and Cleo had "fallen out of love".

Orla knew it was more likely that Cleo had seen Donal's lack of potential and had dumped him in favour of Gavin, a more sure bet for an improved lifestyle, but wisely kept this to herself.

"I suppose so, Claudia love," she agreed, amused by the little girl's assessment of the situation.

Claudia went back to her porridge, thoughtful for a few moments. "We won't be related after all so," she told Lily and Rose dolefully.

"What's the name of the new person?" It took only a moment of apparent disappointment before Cleo was relegated to the back of Rose's mind.

Relieved, Orla told her Susan's name but realised that she had no other information to impart, not even her surname.

"You'll see her this evening anyway." Hopefully their curiosity about this Susan would override their interest in Cleo's immediate whereabouts. "Now eat up or we'll be late. And that wouldn't do, would it?"

"Whose idea was it to have the rest of the week off when we got back from our holidays?" Laura was stretched out diagonally across the bed, her feet resting over Barry's legs. The breakfast tray from that morning lay discarded on the floor next to her.

"Yours. And I say that definitively because I can remind you of it again in January when you need a week off and you'll have bugger all holidays left!" Barry grinned smugly at her, his hand tucked behind his head as he reclined next to her.

"Thanks for reminding me! I won't care though if I have a nice, lengthy maternity leave to look forward to."

For some reason, Laura felt it was all right to talk, even joke, about maternity leave like this. In the past, the idea of even mentioning it was anathema to her, akin almost to purposely jinxing their chances of the IVF working. Grace, her counsellor in the clinic in Barbados, had put it into her head that perhaps all this superstition about not even considering the idea of what it would be like if the treatment did work was a bit like ordering something online and refusing to believe that the item would actually arrive.

"If you put something in the postal system, you expect it to arrive at its destination within a certain time frame, isn't that right?" she'd challenged in one of the sessions. Laura had stared mutely at her before eventually agreeing.

"But you pay a lot of money to do this treatment and you don't even allow yourself to think about whether it might work. Is that positive thinking, would you say?"

Since then, Laura, instead of waiting for the inevitable letdown, had started to visualise what Number 12 Rockfield Drive would be like with a steriliser on the counter-top and a Moses basket next to the bed. For the first time ever, she felt a sense of optimism about the outcome of the treatment rather than a feeling of having to brace herself for the inevitable letdown. Even Barry was starting to be infected by her new-found enthusiasm.

"It'd be great, wouldn't it?" he said now in answer to her comment about maternity leave. "Is there anything for fathers?"

Laura snorted. "Why would there be? It's not like men have to carry around anything for nine months!"

He sighed in acknowledgement of this fact. "I can't wait to do the test."

Laura too had been thinking this. Normally, they were so by-the-book, waiting patiently until the two weeks were up before doing a pregnancy test. Sometimes, Laura's period came in the meantime, precluding the need to do a test at all.

She looked at Barry carefully now. "I wonder how soon would the test show a positive if I was pregnant?"

Barry considered this. "Well, the embryos are in a full week now."

"And they were five days old when they were put in anyway." Laura, smiled, starting to get a bit giddy and knowing that her husband wanted to do a test, even though it was probably much too early to tell.

Barry sat up a little in the bed, dislodging Laura's legs from their comfy position. "It can't do any harm, can it? Just a sneaky test . . ." His voice trailed off as he gauged his wife's reaction.

"Oh go on then," she giggled, jumping out of the bed with no further bidding. There was an unopened pregnancy test ready and waiting in the bedside locker. Grabbing it, she skidded excitedly into the bathroom, shouting out to Barry that she hoped she'd be able to piddle on demand.

"Concentrate," he ordered through the door.

As soon as she'd ripped the package open, Laura had a fleeting moment of something like guilt for not abiding by the rules. Telling herself swiftly that some people who had IVF treatment were so impatient for the results that they did a pregnancy test every day from the moment the embryos were placed in the womb and that she shouldn't berate herself at all for jumping the gun, she decided to obey Barry's orders and concentrate on actually doing the test now that she'd started.

"Is it done yet?" Barry was clearly more impatient than even she was.

Eventually, she emerged holding the little blue stick aloft. "If it's negative, we're not going to be too disheartened," she warned, laying the stick on the bed next to him. "It might just be too early to pick up a positive result."

Barry hadn't taken his eyes off the stick. "One minute gone."

"Did you ever think three minutes would be so long?"

Laura's feet had got cold from the bathroom tiles so she got under the covers again and tucked her toes into their favourite spot behind Barry's knees.

"I was the one who had to go all the way to the loo," she interjected when she saw that he was set to complain about her freezing him to bits. "So don't even think about complaining." She snuggled further under the duvet and glanced at the small clock next to the bed. One minute to go.

"Jesus, if we were on *Countdown* the time would be flying by!" The little window on the stick was facing downwards and Barry drummed his fingers on the plastic casing, his eyes now on the clock for the last few seconds.

"Okay." Laura drew in a deep breath before nodding her permission to Barry to turn it over at last.

As soon as he did, Laura knew by the look on his face that it was positive. It wasn't like in films where people jumped around ecstatically. Barry didn't even smile. There was just something in his expression telling her that, this time, things were going to be all right for them, a simple rising of his eyebrows when his eyes met hers that said everything. Silently, he held the little plastic stick out so that she could see for herself.

"Oh," was all she managed before letting out the breath she hadn't even realised she was holding.

Silently, they curled into each other.

"Do you think it's for real?" she said eventually. She could hear Barry's heart beating steadily where her face rested against his chest.

"There's another stick in the pack, isn't there?" Even he knew it was too early to get too excited. They'd both heard of so-called "biochemical positives" where a faint line could appear in the test window caused by traces of the hormones and drugs that might still be circulating in the bloodstream.

The result that Laura was looking at now was far from faint, the word "Pregnant" standing out strongly against the white background, convincing her that a newly implanted embryo and the subsequent hormone surge was activating the positive result rather than a mild trace of injected hormones. All the same, using another test might strengthen the case and allow them to feel a little more confident that this was indeed what they'd been hoping for.

Their eyes met again and Laura smiled at last. "I might manage another piddle if I had a cup of tea inside me."

"Do you feel any different?" Barry threw his legs out of the bed and shoved his feet into slippers.

"Just that I'm exhausted these last two days but that's probably down to jet-lag. I don't feel sick or anything. Though it might be a bit early for that, I suppose. Go on, make the tea and I'll stay here and mind this."

She gazed at the pregnancy test again, unable to believe that it actually said the words "Pregnant". Of all the marvellous inventions in the world, Laura thought that this must surely be one of the best. Seeing the word, right here in front of her eyes was almost unbelievable. She was gazing at it and trying to work out whether the extreme tiredness of the last two days might indeed be significant after all. In normal circumstances, a pregnancy was dated from the start of the last period. In Laura's case, it was difficult to know exactly where she was at in terms of how far into a pregnancy she might be. What she did know, however, was that once a pregnancy was confirmed she had the same chance of it continuing as anyone else.

"Still in the same spot," Barry grinned when he returned with the two cups of tea and a packet of Jaffa Cakes. He nodded at the biscuits as he handed Laura her cup. "Just in case we need to celebrate."

"Well, if you think I'm waiting for the next test to be done before I eat them . . ." Laura grabbed two Jaffa Cakes before her husband had time to object. A lightness was seeping in now, but it was too early to get excited just yet. There had been too many disappointments in the past for them to get totally carried away. On the other hand, there had never been a smidgen of a second blue line on a test before so it was hard *not* to feel the surge of hope inside her.

"Okay so. You can have them for the stress of it all then," Barry conceded. He'd already swallowed two of the biscuits himself.

They sipped their tea in silence for a few minutes, both of them slow to discuss out loud the possibility that Laura might really be pregnant.

"It's a really definite-looking word," Barry ventured, looking intently at the test stick again.

"Should I use a different type of one this time? There's a few in the drawer from the last time."

She took them out, three different brands of pregnancy test accrued from various treatment cycles that hadn't necessitated a second or third run at testing.

"That'd be good. Just in case there's a different result." Barry studied one of the brands that Laura had placed on the bed between them. "This one is effective up to a week early. Although I'm not sure whether that applies to us exactly."

"Open them all," Laura said decisively. Right now, she was determined to know one way or another if she was definitely pregnant. "We'll buy a few more later if we have to."

Barry laughed out loud and held out his own mug of tea. "In that case, you'd better finish this as well!"

By half twelve, Orla was as organised as she'd hoped for. The leg of lamb that she'd extracted from her stash in the chest freezer was fully defrosted and she was now in the process of stuffing the small slits she'd made in the skin with a mixture of fresh rosemary and crushed garlic. Roasted slowly, it would be mouth-watering with a combination of roast butternut squash, puréed carrot and Darina Allen's delicious red cabbage. Unbelievably, the whole evening's fare would be costing very little indeed – a far cry from Chez Louis and its small-mortgage-sized price tag.

And the fact that Laura was taking control of the cake was super. Orla had considered baking one but when her older sister had phoned on Thursday to say she was back from Barbados, she'd insisted on organising it. Orla would have enough to do with the dinner preparations without having to start baking and decorating a cake as well, she said. For once, Orla had agreed and was happy to accept the offer, even though she knew that Laura wouldn't bake it herself. Another time, this would have annoyed her but at this stage Orla was beginning to see the advantage of not always being quite so fastidious about her arrangements.

Laura had even offered to call over a bit early to help, another proposal that had been accepted with alacrity. The fact that Jessica would now be picking Claudia up early meant that she'd have more time to focus on the meal but Laura had said she was looking forward to catching up. A small niggle of irritation at the thought of having to listen to her sister's holiday stories had impinged on her mood for a few moments but she had dismissed the feeling quickly, telling herself staunchly that her own holiday prospects might be on hold for now but not forever if she maintained her goal of eventual financial security.

The chime of the doorbell roused her from her recurring thoughts of matters financial and she groaned out loud, not in the humour for a visitor. It couldn't be Jessica already.

Orla shoved the now-ready joint of meat into the fridge and quickly rinsed her hands under the tap, wary of spreading germs that might invade her spotless kitchen.

Fixing her hair quickly in the hall mirror, she opened the front door to find Yvonne Kelly, a mother she knew vaguely from the school gates, standing anxiously on the doorstep.

"Yvonne!" Orla's heart skipped a beat. For a moment she thought that something had happened to Rose or Lily at school and that Yvonne had been sent to fetch her.

"Hi, Orla," Yvonne began, "I hope you don't mind me calling for a few minutes but I had something I wanted to ask, if that's all right?"

Orla breathed a sigh of relief and opened the door wider. "Come in, Yvonne."

Curious, she led the way into the main reception room, conscious of the organising she still had to do and the fact that she'd have to offer tea or coffee if she brought her visitor into the kitchen.

Yvonne sat on the edge of one of the Queen Anne chairs near the fireplace. "I won't hold you up, Orla – I know how hard it is to get things done before the gang lands home from school. I hope you don't think I'm cheeky but I bumped into Jessica Arnold at work this morning and she happened to mention that you're looking after Claudia after school."

"Just for the moment while her minder is out of action," Orla began.

She remembered that Yvonne was a nurse at St Angela's where Jessica worked. Her husband, Cormac Kelly, was from the village but as far as Orla knew he was serving on an army peace-keeping mission in Chad the last she'd heard.

Yvonne took a deep breath and continued. "She mentioned that you were just obliging her but I thought I'd drop by, just in case. You see, my girls, Nollaig and Sinéad, were going to Nonie Kennedy after school too but it looks like she's not going to be able to take any of the kids for the moment with this angina scare. I've had to go on mornings for the moment so that I can be there when they come home in the evenings."

Orla thought she knew where this was going but all she could say was "Oh, I see." She hadn't thought for a moment about taking on anyone other than Claudia.

"Cormac is overseas at the moment so I'm really stuck, Orla. I was wondering if you might take the girls for a few hours after school until I get sorted?" Yvonne looked at her anxiously, her face white from anxiety. "Nollaig's in fifth class and Sinéad is in sixth so they finish at half three. And they're not too much trouble. Well, most of the time anyway! They'd cycle over straight from school so you wouldn't have to collect them or anything."

Orla's brain was working overtime trying to absorb this new chain of events. Despite the fact that she hadn't planned it, it seemed that she was destined to take two more children into her care. And it wasn't as if there was too much else on the horizon in the line of work. She hadn't heard a word from Jerry Cashman since she'd sent her updated CV into the Credit Union so perhaps looking a gift horse in the mouth mightn't be the smartest of moves right now.

"To be honest, Yvonne, you've caught me unaware," she admitted. "I mean, I'm here every evening anyway with the girls. But I hope Nonie Kennedy wouldn't think I was pulling the rug from under her . . ."

Barretsbridge was a small village and it wouldn't do to create any rivalry or animosity with someone as decent and well-liked as Nonie.

"Oh no, Orla! She'd be delighted to see the girls settled with someone reliable. I called in to see her on the cardiac ward before I left work this morning and I mentioned that I might call to see you." Yvonne smiled. "Actually, she said you had a mind like a computer when you were working in the Credit Union!"

Relieved, Orla grinned back. "I'm not as sharp now after five years away from it! Look, Yvonne, how about if we give it a go for a while? And if Nonie gets well, all the better."

To Orla's surprise, tears came to Yvonne's eyes. Sniffling, she brushed them away, clearly embarrassed. "Don't mind me. I'm all over the place at the moment from the stress of it, Orla. I'm thrilled that you'll take them. And so thankful you've no idea."

Until these last few weeks with Claudia, Orla hadn't realised what a luxury it was to be able to stay at home with Lily and Rose. Now here Yvonne Kelly was in the same situation as Jessica, vulnerable in the face of doing the right thing for her children.

"They'll be no trouble at all, Yvonne," she said firmly. "So long as they're not bored here with the smaller ones?"

"Nothing an hour or two of homework won't solve! If that's okay with you?"

"Bang on," Orla agreed. "I'll have a snack for them when they come in and they can settle down properly in the dining room with their books. If you want, Yvonne, you can give me a list of what they like to eat. I know how fussy my two are!"

Yvonne laughed, more relaxed now that she knew her daughters would be settled. "They'll be fine with whatever is going. I'm usually in by six when I'm on the day shift so they can cycle away home around then. There's a path the whole way so they'll be safe. I normally send Nonie a text to say I've arrived and she packs them off and texts me to say they're leaving."

"That's perfect." Orla was becoming more and more impressed with Nonie Kennedy's cottage industry.

"God, Orla, I almost forgot to ask you about rates and everything . . ."

At this, Orla started to laugh, knowing she'd have to become more tuned in if her childminding enterprise was to continue. "Jessica asked me the same thing! I really have no idea, Yvonne, so we can stick to Nonie's rates if you like. How would that be?"

"Absolutely fantastic," Yvonne smiled, clearly delighted with the arrangement. "Would next Monday be a good starting date for you? Or is it too soon?"

"Monday's fine. You can bring Nollaig and Sinéad over on Sunday if you like so they know what they'll be getting into. We'll be here all day."

"That'd be great, Orla. I'll have them on best behaviour! Now, I'd better not take up any more of your time before your own two get home. Or three, counting Claudia!"

Orla stood too. "We'll have time for a cuppa on Sunday if you drop by," she promised, following her latest client to the door. Already, she was intrigued to know how much money would be in Yvonne's envelope next Friday. For now though, she had her school pick-up to attend to.

"Would a sandwich do by way of celebration?"

It was half one and Laura was starving. The six pregnancy tests were spread out in front of them and despite staring at them for most of the morning, none of the results had changed. "Pregnant" announcements, blue lines, pink lines and "positive" signs – each one was different, yet they all said the same thing. It looked like Laura was indeed pregnant.

"It'll have to! There'll be no drinking champagne for you, don't forget," he reminded her with a smile.

Laura grinned back. "God, Bar, it's unbelievable. And even though I know there's no guarantees, I'm just so stunned that we've got this far."

They'd been talking about this all morning, in between doing pregnancy tests and drinking cups of tea. Both of them were clear-headed enough to know that a positive pregnancy test didn't necessarily mean that they'd have a baby in nine months' time. Right now Laura's risk of miscarriage was exactly the same as that of any other pregnant woman and they'd been told at the outset of each IVF that as many as one in four pregnancies ended in miscarriage.

"That's the thing," Barry reminded her, his mathematical engineer's brain bringing it back to numbers. "I know we could look at it that there's the possibility of a miscarriage but there's actually a 75% chance that everything will go well. Before, we had *no* chance, when the tests were always negative."

"That's the way we have to look at it," Laura said emphatically. "We can't sit here waiting for something to go wrong or we'll crack up. It's like Grace said – if you send something in the post, you expect it to arrive. So we'll just have to be positive and *expect* that everything will be all right instead of waiting for it to go wrong."

305

"In that case, I'll definitely have some champagne – Orla's bound to have some later!"

Laura shot up in the bed like a bolt of lightning. "I forgot about the cake! I was to pick it up before lunch."

"Don't worry. We'll have something to eat and collect it then. And no more sudden moves, Missus, in your condition with a baby to consider."

"I'll have a decapitation to consider if we turn up at Orla's without an anniversary cake. It's great not to have to do the whole Chez Louis thing though."

Barry nodded and threw his legs out of the bed yet again. He'd been in and out like a yo-yo all morning making tea and getting glasses of water so that Laura could do all the tests. "It'll be more relaxed, for a start, considering we've had enough excitement for one day."

Laura smiled broadly and stretched out luxuriously, not at all inclined to get up. She looked again at the line of test sticks spread out across the duvet.

"It's for real, Barry, I know it is. I just know it's all going to be fine."

And for the first time in years, she really was certain that everything was going to be just perfect.

Nervousness was a new thing for Donal so it actually took him a while to even identify the feeling. All day, he'd had a niggling feeling about the dinner at Orla's house but it was only at half one that he realised it had to do with Susan and whether Orla would be at her usual tactics of asking what she called pertinent questions, questions that demanded satisfactory answers.

It wasn't that he thought Susan wouldn't be up to the task of managing his sister's directness, it was more that he didn't want her exposed to all of that or be made to feel that she had to pass some kind of test. He hadn't actually told Susan how inquisitive

Orla could be in case it put her off going to the anniversary dinner altogether.

Now that he thought about it, the whole scenario was something that he used to be amused at. Him arriving at some function that Orla had organised and she grilling whoever he brought to within an inch of their life to see what her pedigree was. Cleo had been well able for her, whereas Amanda, his previous girlfriend, used to get completely stressed out from it. Susan, he imagined, would just be curious as to why her credentials might mean so much to Orla.

Now that he'd figured out the cause of his unease, Donal made a decision to head Orla off at the pass if she did start quizzing Susan and asking her what her plans for the future were. It would be her first time meeting everyone and the last thing he needed was Orla frightening her off just as he was getting to know her properly.

Shaking his head in bafflement at Orla's need for control over what everyone else was doing, he gathered the papers in front of him into a neat pile, placing them in order of importance so that he wouldn't be all day on the phone to Joe when he rang him to go through the events of the week. The fuel bill that had come on Thursday was on top, with the invoice for twenty-eight new tyres that had been fitted a few weeks earlier. Not used to changing the tyres on his own car all that often, Donal had been shocked at the price on the docket in front of him.

The Christmas and New Year roster was another thing that he would need to run by Joe, in view of the fact that a private bus operator had just announced a "night-line" service to cover the city area over the festive period. Donal now wondered whether they should cut their own roster back a little instead of paying drivers premium rates to cover areas of the city that would be serviced by a cheaper option. The bus service seemed to be running until 1 a.m. so perhaps a few more cabs starting *after* that time would be sufficient and more lucrative.

He glanced at the clock and decided to phone Joe a few minutes earlier than planned. He needed to get to the off-licence and collect whatever drinks he'd be bringing to Orla's later. Plus Susan had asked him to pick up some flowers that she'd ordered to take. Her own shift didn't finish until five so she'd be under pressure to get to the florist's before it closed otherwise.

Checking that he had everything to hand before he dialled, Donal scribbled "Champers" on a slip of paper before he picked up the phone. Orla, he'd just remembered, always ordered a glass of bubbly whenever they were celebrating something so perhaps he should stick to tradition. A few bottles of red and white wine would ensure that everyone was covered, so long as he remembered to get a bottle of the pink lemonade that Lily and Rose called "Pink Champagne". His nieces were definitely taking after their mother.

41

Yvonne Kelly's visit earlier in the day had loosened something in Orla. Maybe it was the sense of getting back in control that the promise of some small measure of fiscal improvement gave her, or maybe it was the idea that she wasn't just a discarded wife – that she was *worth* something – but it had nonetheless given her enough of a boost for her to consider opening her mind to the possibility of talking to Gavin.

Her mind baulked a little at the notion of an intimate appraisal of their marriage, yet she had to acknowledge that the whole state of affairs that they'd found themselves in wasn't just a financial dilemma that, once solved, would straighten everything else out as well. She thought about this on the way back from the school as the three girls bickered in the back of the car about who was going to be Gabrielle in the *High School Musical* event they were going to host in the playroom as soon as they'd had their afternoon snack.

To all intents and purposes, their financial status wasn't nearly as bad as it could be, considering that Gavin had actually started to secure some small-scale work that he could manage from home. A dormer bungalow and a small extension for the local secondary school that had been in the pipeline for months were two jobs that would be coming on-stream immediately. There was also a minor renovation in one of the city's Church of Ireland buildings that he and Bob had only tendered for out of manners as Bob's wife Deirdre was friendly with the Dean but that would now constitute a significant project as Gavin would be the sole architect dealing with it, alongside his other work.

Times had changed but at least the overheads were low now that he was working from home and that the issue of paying salaries was out of the way. It was only now when some sense of stability had returned that Orla was starting to realise just how precarious their position had been. Only two weeks ago, she'd set eyes on their credit-card bill for the first time and the extent of the credit limit had almost made her physically sick, not to mention that the majority of the purchases were hers rather than Gavin's.

Admitting that she'd been childish and irresponsible didn't come easily to Orla and apologising to Gavin certainly hadn't been on her agenda. She had, however, vowed to herself that paying off the credit-card bill would be a personal priority, even if she had to skim it off the grocery bill like a 1950's housewife.

Things were clearer now, clear enough for her to know that while they'd probably escaped from their financial crisis without the scandal of bankruptcy that seemed to be an increasingly evident feature of everyday life lately, their personal issues were at an even greater risk of collapse right now.

They'd settled into a tentative routine fairly quickly, with Gavin spending his day upstairs. He came down for lunch which Orla had ready at one o'clock and left almost as soon as it was eaten, taking a second cup of tea with him. Their conversations were almost all related to the practical matters of the day. Gavin would fill her in on what had been happening that morning and let her know in time if he had to go out to meet anyone in relation to work.

It saddened her that he now told her exactly who he was meeting and why, as well as where he was meeting them and the time he'd be back. It was as if he needed her to know that he wasn't leaving for a tryst with Cleo or any other woman and that he was being as open and transparent as possible. He was trying to make things better, she knew, but it just served to make her all the more aware of the trust that had been lost.

For her part, she tended to brief Gavin on things like how their daily finances were going, wanting him to know that she too was taking responsibility. They weren't *real* conversations, she realised, but maybe they were all that either of them could do to keep the lines of communication open.

As soon as this anniversary party was over and done with though, she and Gavin would need to look at where they were going on a personal level. They were still sleeping in the downstairs apartment but it was getting harder to justify this to the girls. The paint fumes drying out properly were Orla's latest explanation.

Tomorrow evening, if her parents could be persuaded to have Rose and Lily for a sleepover, she and Gavin would have an opportunity to sit down together and really talk. Decisions would have to be taken – long-term ones that would benefit all of them. In the meantime, the show would have to go on.

As ever, once she'd settled on something in her mind, Orla's mood lifted.

"Okay, ladies, out you hop," she instructed her charges.

As the three girls jumped out of the car, she sat for a moment and surveyed the façade of her home, for the first time seeing it as one of the secure factors in her life rather than as a show-piece to be admired from the road by a passer-by. It was theirs and it was paid for, that was what counted. She shuddered at the thought of the articles on repossession that featured on the pages of *The Examiner* almost daily now and the idea of having the whole village know the shame of their circumstances if such a thing had happened to them.

At least Gavin had had the foresight to pay off their mortgage when times were good, something that she herself hadn't even considered. Something in her had definitely softened today, now that it looked like they could keep their heads above water. In his own way, Gavin had wanted the best for them – she could see that now – it was just a pity it had culminated with the Cleo episode.

"Hurry, Mom!" Rose was yelling as she got out of the car. "We want to start our game."

"And I want to wee," Lily added.

Rolling her eyes in disapproval at this new word, Orla opened the front door. "You mean, 'I need the bathroom'," she corrected automatically. The standard of living might have to drop a little but manners would certainly have to be maintained.

Lily looked only slightly contrite. "Okay, I need the bathroom."

Orla smiled to herself and made her way to the kitchen to get together a quick snack before resuming preparations for the evening. There wasn't much left to do but setting the dining-room table would be a priority. Jessica would soon be here for Claudia and she knew well that Rose and Lily would be looking to put out the party hats and streamers as soon as their friend had departed.

Spooning three portions of tuna and pasta salad into bowls for the girls, she wondered absently why she ever thought it had to be made with fillets of fresh tuna from the fishmongers and fresh egg pasta from the deli counter at SuperValu.

Meantime, she considered which dinner service she should use. She wasn't exactly going all-out formal with the dinner so perhaps her more casual Stephen Pearse set would be best. With a jolt, she realised then just how ridiculous her ideas of necessity had been up to now. As well as her "everyday" Denby, there were three full sets of dinnerware in the cupboards, with the more formal ones saved for special occasions and entertaining Gavin's clients.

She wondered now if Jessica Arnold had more than one dinner service to her name, although she knew in her heart that the answer would be a definite "no" followed by an incredulous giggle if she even dared to ask. Jessica wouldn't have either the time or the inclination for what Orla now knew was nonsense.

It had taken a near-bankruptcy for Orla to make this seismic shift in her opinions about how one should live. Now she was thinking of taking the advice of the financial guru on *The Afternoon Show* and letting some of her "assets" go on eBay in order to clear the credit-card bill. She wondered exactly how much a full Villeroy and Boch dinner service would fetch and whether she would even miss it.

She carried the three bowls, with three glasses of milk, through to the playroom and set them down on the small drawing table. Normally, eating was reserved for the kitchen table only but today there was too much going on in the kitchen to risk the inevitable interference.

"Eat up now and no dawdling," she instructed. "Claudia's Mum is coming early today so you'll want to have your game finished."

A series of protests ensued with Claudia disappointed to be leaving her friends and the other two objecting for the sake of objecting. Orla laughed and promised that she'd delay Jessica with a cup of coffee if they presented three empty bowls and three empty milk glasses to her in the kitchen in the next ten minutes. None of the three had any real idea of time but they sensed that ten minutes was a serious challenge and dug in enthusiastically.

"Slow down! There's not that much of a hurry," Orla reassured, startled at the amount of pasta shells that poor Claudia had shoved into her mouth. Lily and Rose were almost as bad.

Orla worked ferociously on her dinner menu and was startled to see the hands of the clock show five to two when the doorbell went. She smiled to herself when she heard the dramatic groans that emanated from the playroom at the clearly unwelcome arrival of Claudia's mother. As promised, she flicked on the kettle before answering the door and hoped that Jessica would actually have time for coffee. She hadn't thought of that when she'd pledged her delay tactic earlier.

"Jessica," she greeted, "you needn't have got off this early. I'm sure you had plenty of calls on your time this morning."

To her relief, Jessica stepped into the hall and headed for the kitchen.

"How's Milady?" she enquired, although there was little need as Claudia could be heard warbling away with the others humming along.

"Flying form," Orla confirmed. "I'm supposed to delay you with coffee until their game is over." She grinned at Jessica and placed a mug in front of her at the kitchen table.

"Well, that's not a bad idea, Orla," Jessica said, her voice grave enough to make Orla turn around from where she was pouring milk from the plastic Lidl carton into her shapely Denby jug. "I had something I wanted to talk to you about – without the Little Ears listening."

Something was amiss, Orla could tell from Jessica's voice, and she sincerely hoped that her days as a childminder weren't about to end before they'd barely begun. Not that she didn't wish Nonie Kennedy all the best in her recovery but she had built her new wage into her budget and it was now an essential part of their income rather than an extra.

Gathering herself together as best she could, Orla closed the door that led out to the hall and playroom and braced herself. There was no way she could let Jessica know how much her new job had meant to her and how devastating it was to have her little bit of security taken away again.

"Is everything all right, Jessica?" Better to pretend concern than give away her need for the job by focusing on that first off. She centred her attention on pouring the coffee and hoped her hands weren't visibly shaking.

Jessica lowered her head and looked at Orla, her face serious. "Well, no, Orla." She took a deep breath and let it out with a sigh, causing Orla's heart to almost stop. "Everything's not all right. My mother phoned me at work this morning. I know about Cleo, Orla. And Gavin."

Orla didn't know if it was possible for a human heart to *actually* stop and then resume beating again but this is what it felt like to her. As if all the breath had been sucked out of her and her body was unable to function for a moment.

"Jessica!" It was a gasp but it was all she could manage. She didn't even know what she wanted to say.

"Orla, I'm so sorry. I can't believe it, really I can't . . . I'm just so . . ."

Somewhere at the back of her mind, there had always been the niggling possibility that perhaps Jessica might find out about her cousin's misdemeanour with Gavin but it was just another thing that Orla hadn't been able to consider. There had been enough to deal with, however, and as long as Jessica had showed no signs of wariness or knowingness Orla had been happy to believe that Cleo had kept her sordid little secret to herself. An affair with a married father of two wasn't something that one would be broadcasting to the world, Orla had figured hopefully.

Now, though, it was out. And Orla knew that it said something very significant about her own personality and self-esteem that the fact of Jessica knowing was almost worse than the fact that Gavin's affair had happened in the first place.

"Look, Jessica," she started decisively, determined to at least hold on to her dignity, "it happened. It's over now and –"

"God, Orla, I know it's over. Aunt Fran told Mum that for definite but I couldn't just ignore the fact that I knew." She looked unsure for a moment. "Or maybe I should have kept my mouth shut . . . God, Orla, I can't say how sorry I am. I could kill her."

Orla almost laughed out loud at the thought of Jessica wanting to kill her cousin. If anyone was going to get the chance to murder the little bitch, it would be Orla.

"I've thought of that," she said bitterly, feeling the skin of her face tighten into an unattractive grimace.

Jessica frowned and shook her head, both of her hands wrapped around her coffee cup. Her knuckles, Orla noticed, were white.

"I know it's none of my business, Orla, but I just wanted to say –"

"If you're going to say sorry again, forget it. It certainly isn't your fault." She knew how cynical she sounded but couldn't help adding, "Consenting adults and all that."

"I *am* sorry, Orla, but I wasn't going to say that again. I just wanted you to know that . . . well, if it's a thing that . . ." She paused, her face pained with the effort of explaining herself. "I mean, you and Gavin . . . just think again if you're thinking, you know, of . . . going your separate ways or anything."

Orla was utterly shocked at this. Jessica certainly hadn't struck her as the interfering, advice-offering type.

"It's just, well, I need to say this, Orla. And don't get me wrong – I'm not excusing Gavin, if that's what you think – but Cleo, well, she has a bit of a history."

Orla, for all her decision to remain calm and dignified, couldn't help but question this. She was now beginning to wish that Jessica would stop prevaricating and just get on with it. "A history?"

Jessica sighed again, a distressed look on her face. "I know she's my cousin and I know I shouldn't be giving out about her but even Mum was cross this morning after she spoke to Aunt Fran."

Orla waited for Jessica to continue, busying herself in the meantime by refilling their coffee cups. Anyone who opened the kitchen door at this moment might just think they were two friends enjoying a coffee together, so innocuous did the whole scene appear.

"There was a thing before with a surgeon while she was in college," Jessica disclosed. "Cleo was studying medicine at the time," she clarified when she saw Orla's curious look.

"Medicine?" Orla found this a bit incredible. Cleo was the typical hippy type as far as Orla was concerned.

"I know. It seems so unreal now. She's highly intelligent, you know. Mum reckons that's why she was always in trouble of some sort, because she's too highly strung or something. I'd actually finished in Med before Cleo even started so I don't know all the details but he was married anyway, which was why there was such a scandal about it."

Orla wasn't sure why Jessica thought it mattered to her that Cleo was a serial marriage-wrecker but she could see that it was being told in good faith.

"Mum rang me at work this morning because she knew how good you've been to Claudia. And how much Peter and I think of you and Gavin. She was disgusted, I suppose, that Cleo could do the same thing again."

What Orla really wanted to say was that Cleo didn't exactly kidnap Gavin but she couldn't take that step into the territory of disloyalty, not until she knew where she and Gavin stood with each other. Only an hour ago, she'd though her marriage might be something worth salvaging. Now the bitterness had returned along with a desire to physically hit Gavin for even taking away the manner in which someone like Jessica looked at her. Feeling small and somehow pitiable, she simply covered her hurt with as much blasé cynicism as she could dredge up.

"Once is an accident but twice . . ." She allowed her voice to trail off stoically.

"That's the thing, Orla. I've never told anyone this, certainly not Mum, but it wasn't just Professor Dundon."

"What?"

This was just too hard to believe. Orla wondered was Jessica suggesting that Gavin had somehow been targeted by Cleo, that this was something she did with a selection of men for . . . what . . . fun?

"I thought I'd put all this behind me, Orla, really I did. But I was just so mad this morning. I put everything together. Gavin scaling down the business and spending more time at home, doing everything he can to put things right while Miss Cleo sits on a high stool selling beads to her heart's content."

Jessica was speaking through gritted teeth now, her anger palpable and Orla was overwhelmed that she could feel like this on *her* behalf.

"I do appreciate you telling me this, Jessica," she began, heartened somewhat by the fact that the Arnolds thought Gavin had cut down on work to save his marriage, something that she felt raised her own value in a weird way. "But –"

"You don't understand, Orla," Jessica was insisting. "I know you're probably livid with him still and I know it's not as simple as just putting it all behind you. Please don't think I'm interfering. It's just that I almost went down this same road with Cleo myself. Only things didn't get quite so out of hand, let's say."

"What? You mean . . .?" Surely Peter Arnold hadn't had an affair with Cleo as well? Orla felt a dizziness overtake her, almost as if she was going to faint. Unwilling to give in to it, she lowered her head into her hands and sat stock still for a moment, heat and cold washing over her alternately. This was just too much.

"Not quite," Jessica said, anticipating the question that Orla had started to ask. "It was after the Professor Dundon affair. Things had died down a bit but Cleo really went off the rails. She was actually admitted to St Angela's for a bit. To the psychiatric wing," she explained quietly.

"My God!" Orla was now beginning to think that this Cleo was actually mad. And apart from Gavin having an affair with her, it occurred to Orla that Donal had had a narrow escape, not to mention the fact that she'd been here in this house with Lily and Rose.

Jessica was still talking, cutting short Orla's alarmed thoughts at the myriad of things that might have happened to her daughters.

"Claudia was a baby at the time so I wasn't getting out much. Cleo used to come over in the evenings sometimes, just to get out of the house. I felt sorry for her and Aunt Fran was at her wits' end to know what to do with her. It was a strange time, Orla. I was still feeding Claudia and Peter was trying to keep the practice going. We were wrecked all the time."

Orla could now see clearly where all this was going. "Jessica, I can't believe this!"

"I know," she sighed. "Claudia was up in the nursery one evening and she started crying. Cleo offered to go up and settle her. Peter was doing some work in the office upstairs that evening so he heard Claudia as well and decided to go in to her. I could hear everything on the baby monitor, Orla." Jessica looked at her, allowing the significance of it to sink in.

Now Orla was the one commiserating, remembering the exhaustion of the first few months with the twins and how wretched she'd felt. Gavin, to give him credit, had been brilliant then. That Cleo could take advantage of that with her own cousin's husband was beyond belief. "I'm so sorry, Jessica," was all she could say.

"I could hear it all, word for word, Orla. I was just stuck to the chair. Cleo telling Peter . . . how sexy he was . . . all this stuff about having a connection with him . . . it was unreal when I think back on it. Peter just sounded stunned by it all. It was the only thing that kept me going, Orla, that he actually said no."

Orla drew her breath in sharply, disappointment in Gavin hitting her like a ton of bricks. How well Peter had been able to resist!

"And don't think I'm saying that Peter resisting her makes Gavin a bad person. Peter was actually terrified. He thought she was going psychotic again because she wasn't long out of hospital. We talked about it a lot at the time, Orla, and I was really angry with him. I was so hormonal and I kept thinking that maybe he'd given her some encouragement. Looking back, I know it wasn't the case but I'd be the first to admit how easily something could happen."

"I don't know what to say, Jessica, really I don't." Orla could hear the faint banter between the twins and Claudia coming from the playroom and hoped that one of them wouldn't appear looking for something.

"I suppose I needed to tell you this, Orla, because I feel she's caused enough trouble. I know that part of this is Gavin's fault as well." She smiled suddenly, a small wry grimace. "I know if it was Peter I'd be hopping mad. But you have two children to consider, like I have Claudia, so I just wanted you to know the full story, that's all."

Orla was humbled by Jessica's honesty and knew that if the situation were reversed, she probably wouldn't have had the sort of decency that the other woman had. She wouldn't have wanted to admit that there was even the slightest crack in her marriage for a start, or that she had a certifiable, nymphomaniac cousin.

"It is good to know it although it's still hard to excuse Gavin. I thought everything was fine." It was the first time that she'd shared the burden of Gavin's affair and it was a relief somehow to talk about it, even if Jessica didn't know the full story.

"I thought everything was fine as well," said Jessica. "It never occurred to me for a moment that Cleo would do anything like that, not to me. I don't know about Gavin but Peter was certainly at a bit of a low moment. We were both exhausted and he'd slept in the spare bed the odd night if he had surgery or something big on the next day. Maybe she thought our marriage was on the rocks. I don't know."

"But to take advantage of that! We all have bad patches."

Orla wondered whether it was significant that Gavin too was going through a "bad patch" at the time of his affair with Cleo, then dismissed this thought as just another way of making excuses for him. He was an adult. He'd made a choice. He had to take responsibility for that, no matter what.

At the same time, there was a niggling voice inside her saying that maybe if she'd been a little more open, then perhaps Gavin might have been able to talk to her in the first place instead of taking his worries about the business to Cleo Morgan. And, in her own way, she knew that she too had things to take responsibility for.

Orla's head was physically spinning now. Jessica was sipping her coffee in silence, no doubt revisiting her own experience of the near-destruction of her marriage.

"Look, Orla," she said finally, "I'm not sure whether I did the right thing at all bringing this up but I won't be mentioning it again. I hope I haven't made things worse rather than better but I felt you had a right to know what kind of person you're dealing with."

Orla knew it must have taken a lot for Jessica to open up like this and she was grateful, even if it did make her more confused than ever. She reached across the table and took her hand. "I do appreciate it, Jessica. Honestly. And I think it'll help in the end."

Jessica smiled, relief written all over her face. "I hope so. Now, I've taken up enough of your time and you still have a party to organise. I wonder if the show in the playroom is finished?"

Orla stood up, glad that the conversation was at an end. Her head felt as if ten trains had crashed into each other in the centre of it. She needed time to think but meantime she pasted a smile to her face.

"Let's go and investigate."

42

Laura pulled up in Orla's drive and couldn't help but notice just how manicured the front lawn was, even in the dead of winter. There was no sign of Lily and Rose. Normally their faces would appear in the glass at either side of the front door as soon as they heard the noise of the car.

Sliding her hands across her tummy as she tried to visualise what the baby might look like inside her, she sat for a moment and savoured the wonderful feeling that she was pregnant. Knowing she had to finally allow herself to believe that she and Barry would become parents, she let a vision of herself feeding a baby flit through her mind.

It would be ages before anyone else would know, probably not until twelve weeks and definitely not until she'd had a six-week scan, but in the meantime she was going to enjoy every bit of her little secret. Already she felt a bond with this little speck, probably because she'd known him or her for so long, even as far back as an embryo growing in the lab. They'd been through a lot together already, even though it was only hours since she'd known that she was pregnant.

The cake had been collected and Barry had laid it safely on the back seat before waving her off, knowing full well that Orla would hardly appreciate him being under her feet in the kitchen as she prepared the meal with precision engineering. It would be hard enough for her to tolerate Laura "helping".

Laura had laughed at this, knowing just how right he was. Orla would have the same value on Laura as she did on Lily and Rose as far as helping in her kitchen was concerned. She hoped now that the cake would be up to her sister's standards, considering that it had been made in a bakery rather than cooked up by Laura herself. As if!

She balanced it on her hip and rang the doorbell, praying that the girls wouldn't launch themselves at her and smash the cake before it was even inspected.

"Easy, dolly-birds! Can't have the cake all over the floor," she called out as Orla opened the door and her nieces came skidding out to meet her. They giggled madly at her pet name for them and started to chant "Dolly-birds! Dolly-birds!" at each other.

"Laura, you look fantastic," Orla gushed immediately, taking the cake off her as she took in her sister's glowing skin that was enhanced by the baby-pink Parka that she wore over jeans and boots.

"Thanks. I feel mighty after the break."

Lily and Rose were looking at her expectantly and Laura started to laugh. "Will you do me a favour, girls, and check the front seat of the car? There might be two little bags there for you to open."

It didn't take much in the line of bidding to get the two of them to tear out and scramble into the front seat in search of the presents that they'd known full well they'd get from Barbados.

Orla left the front door open for the girls and ushered Laura into the kitchen.

"You spoil them," she acknowledged. "This looks gorgeous! Where did you get it? The icing is fantastic."

Laura was stunned. Normally Orla would have asked

pointedly how she managed to get the icing so perfect, knowing full well that Laura hadn't done it herself. A bought cake was now passable, it seemed.

"Mortons," Laura informed her. They were the most expensive in Cork but Laura had figured it was worth splashing out considering that they weren't going to be fleeced in Chez Louis.

"They're always good," Orla confirmed knowledgably.

"So," Laura asked as she divested herself of her jacket and stowed it in the utility, "anything exciting happen since we were away?"

"Nothing much."

Orla reached over and put the kettle on, surprising Laura who had expected a litany of things that had had to be done for Iris and Paddy in her absence. Her voice was on the slightly shrill side so there was probably a list to come over the coffee. Maybe it was the whole carry-on of hosting the anniversary in her house instead of going out but Orla seemed to be jittery in an odd sort of way.

"Only that accident in Go Cars," said Orla. "Were you talking to Donal since you got back?"

"No, I knew we'd be seeing him tonight. What happened?" Laura felt a little cold, not liking the idea of Donal being involved in an accident, even if nothing had happened to him.

Orla placed a mug and a slice of home-made tea brack in front of Laura but she barely noticed. Despite her lengthy talks with the counsellor in Barbados the word "accident" was still one that had a strange effect on her.

"Donal wasn't involved," Orla confirmed hastily, seeing her sister's stricken face. "A lorry turned over on Patrick Street just as one of the cabs was passing it. Senan Crowley, you know Joe's son, was the driver and he was killed straight away. It was desperate, all over the news for a few days. Donal was a bit shook up over it, I'd say. Even though he wouldn't admit it, of course."

Laura was shocked that all of this had happened at a time when she was coming to grips with the accident that had taken Darren's life.

"Was Donal there? Did he see anything?" Laura could only imagine how she herself would have reacted to something like this a few weeks ago, before she had started to understand the impact of her brother's death on her own life.

"He arrived on the scene all right but it was too late to do anything. The fire brigade had to take care of everything, and the ambulances of course. You know Donal. He'd only tell you the basics. Joe Crowley was on the scene as well so that must have been terrible."

"God, that's awful."

What Laura really meant was how awful it must have been for Donal to be standing there helplessly once again but of course Orla thought she was referring to Senan's father being there.

"Desperate. He hasn't been back to the cab office since so Donal's looking after it for the moment. Imagine!" Orla shook her head at the idea of someone leaving Donal in charge as she poured tea for both of them.

"Donal is? How come?" Even Laura was surprised, although she'd always had a bit more faith in Donal than Orla did.

"Not sure really. He seems to be all business about it though. He's bringing a new girlfriend, by the way." Orla rolled her eyes. "Another one."

Laura was intrigued now. Donal being "all business" about anything was a new thing, even if a new girlfriend was no great shock. "When did this start? Cleo's hardly had time to collect her toothbrush and he has someone new in tow!"

"Don't know," Orla muttered, picking crumbs of tea brack off the plate that Laura's slice had been served on. "Susan's her name, apparently."

"And I actually liked Cleo. She was different from most of the others. She had a bit of spirit to her, I thought."

Orla's mouth tightened and she reddened a bit before getting up and landing her mug into the sink with a clatter. Laura knew that she'd disliked Cleo's casual dress sense and her particular brand of confidence but for Orla to risk chipping a Denby mug over her was a bit unprecedented.

"I'd better get back to the dinner," said Orla. "Will you put the cake in the fridge in case the cream goes off?"

So much for hearing about Barbados, Laura thought wryly. She lifted the cake again and made her way to the fridge as instructed just as Lily and Rose burst into the kitchen attired in traditional Barbados beach dress. The red and yellow sarongs were tied under their arms instead of around their waists while both of them had placed their colourful headdresses skew-ways on top of their immaculate, shiny hair. They stood next to each other in the doorway, their eyes alight with excitement, waiting to be admired. And praised for getting into their new outfits so efficiently.

"Oh my word," Orla exclaimed. "You look fantastic – both of you!"

Laura too gushed with admiration. "I can't believe you put them on by yourselves, even the head-pieces!"

Rose wrinkled her nose a little and took a pretend sip out of the plastic coconut she was holding. The gaudy cocktail umbrella sticking out of it was almost up her nose, making Laura want to giggle.

"Well," said Rose, "we did have to get a little bit of help from Dad with the bows." She spun around with her arms outstretched to show off the neatly tied knot under her left arm.

"Rose!" Lily shot her sister an exasperated look and rolled her eyes dramatically when Orla raised her eyebrows.

Rose's hand shot to her mouth, as if she'd just said something she shouldn't have. "Sorry, Mom, we only interrupted him for a second!" She spouted out the word "interrupted" carefully as if it was one she'd only just learned.

Lily, ever the independent one, wasn't inclined to admit to

having had too much help. "He only supervised really. We did the hats ourselves."

"You look great. And very exotic," Laura assured them. "Gavin's off today?" she asked Orla. Normally Orla's husband kept well out of the way if she was organising a dinner party.

"Oh, he's working at home now at the moment. We have plenty of space here so he decided to give up the office in town."

"And we're not allowed to interrupt him when he's working," Rose explained.

Laura smiled, thinking there was some chance of that. "That's handy," she said to Orla, who was by now filling the two plastic coconuts with juice for her daughters.

"Did you say 'Thank you' to your auntie for your lovely presents?" she asked the girls.

"Thank you, Auntie Laura," they echoed together, their eyes on Orla and their new, flashy juice mugs.

"You're welcome," Laura grinned.

Neither of them had mentioned that there were a few packets of fancy sweets in their present bags as well. No doubt they were stashed away in the playroom to be consumed as soon as they could escape from the kitchen.

"That'll be nice, having Gavin working at home," Laura commented as soon as the girls had disappeared again. "How will it work out with the staff and everything?"

Orla was at the sink, carefully dissecting butternut squash into neat wedges with an enormous kitchen knife. Laura couldn't imagine her being happy with Gavin's employees traipsing through the house and up the stairs from early morning and, anyway, there was hardly enough space in the office upstairs except for Gavin and perhaps the secretary.

"Actually, they've decided to downsize. They were talking about it for a while but then Bob's wife was diagnosed with cancer so he needed to take early retirement. Plus, there was talk about the rent on the building increasing."

This was the first Laura had heard of it and the whole thing seemed to have happened so fast – in the last month probably, considering the short length of time she and Barry had been away. No wonder Orla was so tense-looking about it.

"Well, it's great to have him around all day," said Laura. "Although I can't imagine the girls give him much peace!"

Orla's neck veins, Laura noticed, were taut as Deirdre Barlow's in *Coronation Street* as she chopped away at the vegetables so perhaps having Gavin under her feet wasn't as desirable as some people might think. She decided not to ask anything further about this new situation, fearful of raising her sister's hackles any further.

"Now, tell me what I can do to help," she said instead. As far as she could see, everything was done but, knowing Orla, there would be important extras that Laura wouldn't have even considered.

"Well, you could peel the potatoes. I'll do champ and a few roasties as well."

Orla seemed a little calmer now that they'd moved to the safer waters of the dinner so Laura selected a knife from the knife block and set to work. "What are we having anyway?"

Orla's shoulders visibly relaxed and Laura knew they were now definitely on better territory.

"A brown bread and smoked salmon starter, carrot and coriander soup and then lamb for the main course."

She made it sound simple but Laura knew well there would be lots of *fromage frais* garnishes and sprigs of chives and dill to be prepared before the dinner was presentation-perfect.

"And the cake for dessert," Laura finished for her.

Orla hesitated. "Well, I thought I might make a quick lemon soufflé if I have time. It'd be nice and light after the lamb," she added, most likely by way of placating Laura. "And we could have the cake over coffee at the end. Donal's offered to bring the drinks, by the way."

He'd certainly turned over a new leaf in the last few weeks, whatever effect this Susan had had on him. Donal was always generous but in a completely sporadic sort of way. Laura was surprised that Orla had permitted him to take on something as specific as the drinks for the evening and she wondered if maybe she should text him quickly and remind him to include a bottle of champagne for the toast. Knowing Donal, he'd land with a trailer-load of beer. Or maybe this Susan would supervise him and his purchases.

"What way should I chop these?" Laura asked. Orla was always fussy about things like vegetables being sliced or diced in certain ways.

"Keep the nice-looking ones for the roasties," she instructed.

Laura began to separate the more evenly sized ones from the uglier ones, amused that there was a differentiation between something as mundane as spuds.

"We can cut the other ones up for mashing," Orla added.

"You've let your hair grow a bit," Laura commented now. Orla immediately looked offended so she was quick to clarify that it looked well. "The length suits you. It's lovely and soft around your face."

Normally, Orla's hair was like a piece of precision engineering, the edges sharp and defined against her porcelain skin. Today, it was pushed behind her ears, more casually than Laura had seen it in years.

"I just decided to see what it would look like with a bit of length," she said eventually.

Laura had accepted over the years that almost every conversation with her younger sister could be turned into a battleground if any hint of criticism was perceived, even if it was only as simple as a comment on her hair. No wonder Gavin kept his mouth shut so much of the time.

"All done. What's next on the agenda?" Laura could see Orla casting what she probably thought was a discreet eye over the potatoes.

"Maybe the red cabbage? You could shred it and we'll put it on now. It's always better when it's well cooked."

Laura set to work as instructed, glad of the occupation. Her mind drifted back to Gavin and the fact that he was now working from home. Was this downsizing, as Orla had described it, as a result of the economic downturn that was affecting the construction industry in Ireland so badly? Gavin had spoken a little to Barry about the general fall-off in work so perhaps it was inevitable that he would have to cut back on staff and his overall costs, in particular the prestige office space that must have been costing Cole & Merriman an arm and a leg.

It was a bit sad, Laura thought, that Orla couldn't come out and talk about this "downsizing" in a normal way to her own sister but she was far too proud of her status for that. Unfortunately, she had herself so tied up with being the perfect corporate wife that she probably hated being demoted to the ranks of Mrs Small Business. It was ridiculous in a way, as Gavin himself would more than likely talk to Barry about it later anyway.

"That's loads," Orla instructed, interrupting Laura's train of thought. "Just give it a rinse under the tap and I'll do the rest." She handed her a stainless steel colander.

Laura had just started to load the wine-red shreds into the gleaming colander when the kitchen door opened.

"Any chance of a cuppa or is there too much happening here?"

"Gavin!" Laura abandoned her red cabbage and went over to kiss him in greeting.

"Welcome back, Laura – I can see Barbados did you good."

He hugged her warmly and Laura noticed immediately that he'd lost weight. At any other time, she would have joked with him about getting in shape but felt that Orla mightn't exactly appreciate the banter. She was tense enough as it was without any further perceived jibes to snap at.

"It sure did," Laura agreed. "It's been years since we were anywhere so it took us the whole first week to relax! It was great." More than great, she thought, her mind on the little dot tucked away in her tummy.

"And the girls look smashing in their new gear. Although I had a bit of difficulty getting them tied properly." He took a mug from one of the upper cupboards and dropped a tea-bag in.

"I'll do that," Orla said immediately, turning to her husband as she spoke, and Gavin handed over his mug.

"The sarongs do look great," Laura smiled. She was always delighted to pick things out for her nieces, even if she couldn't afford the expensive toys and games that Donal was inclined to buy.

"Orla says you're working from home now, Gavin. Bet you don't miss the traffic in the mornings!"

Orla handed him a cup of tea and a plate containing two slices of the tea brack, neatly buttered and without a crumb remaining on the breadboard.

"Ta," he mumbled before turning back to Laura. "I certainly don't. I had to spend the morning in Cork and I was completely frazzled by the time I got there. And I seem to be getting more covered here without all the interruptions. I only got back an hour ago and I've heaps done since."

"Including a bit of 'dressing up' with the girls!" said Laura. She personally thought it was great that both Orla and Gavin were there during the day with Lily and Rose, although she could see that at least one of them wasn't particularly enamoured with the idea. In her own case, if all went well, she would probably have to go back to work when her baby was born considering the amount of money they'd spent on all the cycles of IVF. She couldn't see Orla appreciating that argument. Laura could just imagine her incredulous tone and the "You've waited all this time for a baby and now you won't even stay at home to mind him" type of comments from her sister. In the end of the day however, if this little baby was able to hang in there, the bills would still have to be paid, whatever Laura's own desires might be.

"Well, there can be a few interruptions here and there but I don't mind too much," said Gavin. "And of course they tend to forget all about me now that they have Claudia here after school. More entertainment value in her."

Laura had met Claudia Arnold on a few occasions and was always amused at the way she was pulled like a rag-doll between Lily and Rose insisting she should be named as best friend to one of them.

"Play-dates?" she said now, aware that Orla liked to keep well in with the children from the "better" families of Barretsbridge.

"Sort of," said Gavin. "Orla –"

"Jessica's childminder is sick at the moment so I'm helping out for a few weeks with Claudia after school," Orla interrupted. She shook a bottle of red wine vinegar over a large cast-iron pot a bit more vigorously than Laura thought was necessary and dumped the shredded red cabbage in on top. Clearly being saddled with Claudia on more than a social basis wasn't suiting Orla either.

"What time are the others arriving?" Laura figured the subject of Claudia was another one to steer clear of.

"Around seven. Or ten past, in Donal's case. I'll just put this cabbage on and then I can get the girls organised for their bath." Orla glanced at the clock. "It's getting on a bit."

"I can do the baths if you like." Laura loved the shenanigans of her nieces in the bathroom and had had enough of stepping around Orla's issues for one evening. Barry had been right about joining them a bit later.

Gavin too offered to help. "I'll finish up and I can help you with the table."

As he said this, he glanced into the dining room, only to see that the table had been long since done. He smiled apologetically at his wife. "Sorry. You're ahead of the posse I see."

Orla just smiled tightly in return. Gavin disappeared, promising to be back downstairs shortly.

Whatever was going on between them, Laura had had enough. "Will I round up the girls so?"

"That'd be great. I have everything laid out on the beds for them."

"Okay. I'll shout if I run into trouble!"

At this, Orla actually managed a grin. "Highly likely," she conceded as Laura exited.

43

Orla rested her face against the coolness of the stainless-steel fridge and wondered how her life had come to this so quickly. This morning, she'd actually started to feel something like hope of things returning to normal again, especially with Yvonne Kelly's visit bringing the promise of some badly needed income.

Jessica's revelations had put paid to this small inflation of her spirits, making her angrier than ever at Gavin for putting her in this position where she'd been demeaned as a cuckolded wife.

And now Laura was back from her holidays quizzing and questioning and no doubt wondering what had happened to reduce Gavin's business to a one-room home industry. It annoyed her that Gavin himself didn't seem to be as affected by his near-bankruptcy as she was and that he didn't seem to be taking on board the gravity of their altered circumstances.

On top of everything, Laura's comment about Orla growing her hair had really rankled. She'd studied it this morning in the bedroom mirror and had known full well that it was showing all the signs of neglect, despite her best efforts. Having to forego her weekly visit to Talking Heads had been a major blow but was one she'd been willing to accept if it meant getting some level of control back over their lives. Now though, she was sorry she hadn't thrown caution to the winds and had a quick trim this morning. It was too late now but she was irritated that Laura, whose own hair was like a bird's nest at times, had had the front to comment.

She thanked her lucky stars that she hadn't yet had the opportunity to tell Gavin about Yvonne Kelly's visit this morning or he'd have probably spilled that out to Laura as well. It was one thing to have her know about Claudia coming after school but Orla wasn't ready for just how exposed she'd feel if everyone knew about her taking on two more children and starting to guess the true nature of their financial difficulties. Her dealings with Yvonne therefore would have to be her own business for the moment, at least until she'd got through tonight.

Taking a deep breath, she stepped away from the fridge and polished away the mark that her cheek had made with a tea towel. Her head, as was the case nearly all of the time these last few weeks, was splitting. If she was to get through this evening at all, she'd at least need two Nurofen.

44

"I hope I'm not overdressed for the occasion."

Donal reached across the car and caught Susan's hand. "I'm telling you, there's no such thing as overdressed where Orla's concerned. I think you look great."

He grinned over at her, meaning every word of it. Susan looked fantastic in a slim-fitting black dress with see-through sleeves. One of the girls in the salon had done her hair before she left and it hung in a white-gold curtain straight down her back, so smooth and silky that Donal had almost been afraid to kiss her when he'd picked her up.

"Thanks. And thanks for collecting the flowers. I know you were up to your eyes today."

She glanced into the back seat to check on the tied bouquet of white lilies and white roses that she'd ordered so they wouldn't clash with any other colour scheme that Donal's sister might have going on.

"It didn't turn out to be too bad, to be honest. I got in a bit early so that made a difference. I'm beginning to agree with all the people who say that you get more done before nine o'clock than after it!"

"Well, it's true. Why do you think I go in so early? If I left it until nine every day, I'd get nothing done with the juniors getting me out to check things. At least I can get a bit of paperwork done before all that starts."

"It's great you don't have to work tomorrow. I know it probably won't be a late night but at least you can relax a bit."

Having said this, Donal doubted that there would be much in the line of relaxation for her if Orla was on her usual quest for information.

Susan smiled and reminded him that it was he who'd be relaxing, seeing as she'd already offered to be the driver for the night so that Donal could enjoy the celebration properly.

"Bad job to be dating a man in charge of a taxi fleet and still have to be the designated driver for the night!"

Donal laughed as they pulled into Orla and Gavin's driveway. He hadn't thought of getting one of the lads from the cab office to swing by and pick them up in Barretsbridge.

"It's always better to have an escape driver, just in case things get hairy," he joked.

Susan looked alarmed. "Will there be a need for it?"

"It's always a possibility," he commented wryly, only half in jest but wholly in earnest.

Opening the door to Donal and his new beau was pretty near the last straw as far as Orla was concerned.

Like a chandelier coming under too much pressure from the high tones of a soprano, her precarious nervous system started to vibrate and threaten to shatter when she saw her *hairdresser* standing next to her brother on the doorstep.

"Susan!"

Even Orla herself could hear that her voice was more of an alarmed shriek than an expression of surprised recognition.

Susan, to her credit, remained composed. "Orla! I had no idea you were Donal's sister." She smiled and held out an immaculately tied bouquet of white flowers gloriously scented and tasteful enough for Orla to know that it hadn't been Donal who'd ordered them. They were expensive too, she thought sourly, noting the perfect lilies and delicate white roses.

"Beautiful," she murmured, trying to quell the bitterness that a hairdresser could afford expensive flowers in a recession that was crushing people like herself and Gavin.

Donal, confused-looking a lot of the time anyway, looked a bit stunned that his sister and girlfriend had met already. "You know each other?"

Susan smiled. "We do indeed. I just didn't put two and two together."

Orla's hand went automatically to her hair.

"Talking Heads," she said, a little too brusquely. She *should* have bit the bullet and gone for a trim and blow-dry earlier and to hell with her budget. It galled her that Susan Hegarty might read between the lines and figure that expensive hair-do's would be the first to suffer if a financial contraction was afoot.

Donal was beaming, no doubt thinking that he could once again bow out of the tedious "getting to know the family" bit.

"That's gas! Although I'm not surprised we didn't cop on. Susan treats the salon like a confessional."

Orla hoped her brother was right about his girlfriend's discretion. "Well, come in," she instructed, trying to inject warmth into her voice through knotted vocal chords.

"Laura here already?" Donal asked.

Donal and Susan followed her through to the kitchen while Orla did her best to maintain a ramrod-straight back ahead of them.

"She came earlier with the cake. She's upstairs bathing the girls and keeping them out of harm. Mum and Dad are here too so we're just waiting on Barry."

I am mistress of my own beautiful home and Susan Hegarty can go fuck herself. Orla was shocked at the kind of foul language that had just entered her mental affirmation but she felt it was justified after this unexpected blow from left field. This morning's episode with Jessica would have flattened a lesser woman, she told herself.

"Hyper? I'll keep the Skittles for another day so!" Donal grinned happily and pulled out a chair for Susan.

Orla buried her face in the flowers and took a deep breath to calm herself. Her facial muscles felt as if they were about to rupture but now was a time for maintaining dignity. The social order had changed suddenly and Orla was having trouble adjusting. For now, the only way through it was magnanimity. And perhaps an executive decision to abandon the hostess duties to her husband for once.

"These are really lovely, Susan. I'll put them in the dining-room before dinner. Now why don't you two go out front and let Gavin get you a drink. I'll be in as soon as I arrange these."

Right now, she just wasn't able to look at her immaculately groomed hairdresser while her own hair was held together with split-end gel.

Laura had registered three rings of the doorbell by the time she had the twins dressed up in their party outfits. At least one of the chimes belonged to Barry, or so she hoped, knowing Orla would be like a demon if he was late. And knowing her husband, Laura prayed that there wasn't a soccer match on the television that might have distracted him. Orla was snappy enough with poor Gavin as it was without Barry adding to the melee.

The other two arrivals were most likely their parents, with the final ring of the doorbell probably signalling Donal and the newly fledged Susan. There was no chance that Donal would be first, she thought with a grin.

"What are you smirking at?"

Lily sounded like a carbon copy of Orla, especially the way she stood with her hands on her hips looking expectantly at her aunt. There had already been a small falling-out about Lily wanting to tie her new sarong from Barbados over her party dress.

"Just admiring my two dolly-birds looking so glamorous!"

She hadn't realised she'd been "smirking" but Lily missed very little. If she wasn't careful, the little fairy would notice her giddy good humour and draw suspicion on the cause of it. And God only knew what she'd make of Barry who'd had a grin from ear to ear when Laura had left the house.

"Are we glamorous? Should we put on some make-up?" Rose was the more girly of the two.

Laura thought about this for a moment and looked them over in their pink and white dresses with the white opaque tights and glittery pink Lelli Kelly's.

"Maybe a bit of lip-gloss. Something to match your nails, I think."

There had been high drama already over nail varnish, although at least Laura had learned by now to leave all the bright reds and pinks out of her make-up bag so that her nieces only had a choice of the shell pinks that Orla would approve of. Lily and Rose pursed their lips straight away in anticipation of the sticky lip-gloss that they loved.

"What about perfume?" Rose asked hopefully.

"Maybe a little bit, seeing as it's a special occasion."

Carefully, she sprayed Coco Mademoiselle onto her own wrist and held it out for the twins to rub their own wrists against it. This at least would stop any chance of a perfume-in-the-eyes scenario. Gleefully, they took it in turns to chafe their tiny wrists against Laura's before smelling their own dramatically.

"Fabulous," Rose announced.

Laura wondered whether she'd managed to sneak a look at Samantha in an episode of *Sex and the City*. She certainly sounded like her.

"Come on – we'd better get down and meet everyone. I think I heard Granny and Grandad arriving and we have to meet Donal's new friend."

"I hope she *does* something." Lily didn't sound too enamoured of the fact that Donal had another new girlfriend.

"Like what?" Laura was baffled.

"*You know*. Like tricks or something." Lily was looking at her as if she was stupid in the extreme.

"Cleo made jewellery out of beads," Rose said approvingly.

"Well, everyone's different," Laura told them diplomatically. "She's probably very nice. We needn't go on too much about Cleo, though. In case Susan feels . . . left out. Okay?"

"Okay, so," they chorused simultaneously.

Laura loved they way they echoed each other and wondered for a moment whether Donal and Darren had done this as well. They too had been identical and had been around the same age as Lily and Rose when they'd been separated for good. Surely Paddy and Iris must look at the girls and think of all the years of common milestones that should have been ahead of their twin sons.

She smiled as her nieces shot off down the stairs. It hadn't occurred to her that she might just be expecting twins, considering there had been two little embryos placed in her womb. She thought about this now, the way the best of the embryos were picked by the embryologist to start the epic journey to implantation. Sadly, in Laura and Barry's case, the remaining embryos had failed to make the rigorous criteria for freezing and had perished naturally, something that made Laura a little bit lonely whenever she thought about it.

As soon as she poked her head around the door of the front sitting room, she was glad that this anniversary dinner was being held here rather than at Chez Louis. Barry's eyes met hers immediately and she knew that he too was thinking the same thing. For a start, Donal was able to introduce Susan without the stiffness of the formal restaurant impeding him.

"Hi, Susan, it's lovely to meet you." Laura shook hands warmly and wondered if this elegant smiling girl would last the pace with her brother. Donal, she noticed, was beaming as he leaned over to hug her seeing as he hadn't been talking to her since the holidays. Paddy too was beaming while even Iris looked more relaxed than usual as she admired her granddaughters and smelled their wrists, cooing over the exquisite scent. Laura vowed to insist on hosting the next "occasion" in her own house as soon as Orla started planning it.

"Drink, Laura?" Gavin was hovering over the mahogany drinks cabinet waving a bottle of red wine at her.

Barry, she noticed, was already sipping a beer.

"Water's fine for me, seeing as my husband has already decided that I'm the designated driver!" This would be her excuse for not drinking for the evening.

Barry grinned helpfully at her. "First in, first served!"

"He gets away with murder," Gavin laughed as he handed her a sparkling Ballygowan in a cut-glass tumbler.

"So he should," Paddy commented, openly winking at Gavin and Barry. "The least a man can have is a drink after a hard day's work."

Laura smiled and put up a warning hand to Susan, whose eyes had widened. "Don't rise to it. Feminism still hasn't arrived in Barretsbridge."

Everyone laughed and Laura wondered why they hadn't celebrated some of their family milestones at home before instead of sitting stiffly in pretentious restaurants.

"I'll go and give Orla a hand," she said, excusing herself. It would be interesting to hear what her younger sister thought of Donal's new lady friend.

As it happened, she didn't have to ask. Orla's face was like thunder when she bounded into the kitchen. Laura had been going to quote Colin Firth in *Pride and Prejudice* and ask "What can I do for your present relief?" – a line that always made Orla laugh but she decided against it when she saw the puss on her sister.

Laura closed the kitchen door lest she be heard in the hall. "So, what do you make of her?"

Orla didn't even turn around. "She's a hairdresser. In Talking Heads where I go."

Orla sounded like a disapproving mother and, as ever, Laura was amused at the interest she took in Donal's affairs. The rest of them would be happy to see him meeting someone nice to settle down with but Orla seemed to think the whole family should have to give prior approval. Alternately, it might be the fact that Susan was her own hairdresser that irked her. Orla could be very *Upstairs Downstairs* about things.

Laura, though, was enthusiastic about her brother's new start. She hadn't had an opportunity to ask him about Senan Crowley's tragic accident but was of the mind that Susan might be a good support to him if he needed it right now.

"That explains the fabulous hair! She seems nice, though, and Donal's grinning like a Cheshire cat."

"As he does," Orla retorted grimly.

Laura had to concede that this was true at the outset of most of Donal's relationships.

"At least Lily or Rose haven't mentioned Cleo yet," she grinned. "They seemed to be very taken with her and her beads." She too had liked the free-spirited Cleo.

Orla looked over her shoulder and managed a grim smile. "The night's not over yet."

Laura decided to change the subject. "Will I take these over?"

Orla had eight plates of smoked salmon laid out along the granite worktop, beautifully decorated with capers, chives and strategically-placed blobs of sour cream. Two smaller portions, already chopped up and arranged on small slices of brown bread graced two pink plastic plates for Lily and Rose. A glow of joy overcame Laura when she saw the smaller portions. Someday, she hoped, she too would be putting tiny portions on plastic plates.

"Do, so, and I'll call everyone in."

Laura saw Orla taking a deep breath as she left the kitchen and wondered exactly why her sister was getting so stressed out. There was no doubt but that she had everything under control in the kitchen and Gavin was adept at playing host in the sitting room. As far as Laura could see, the whole thing was going swimmingly.

Donal felt strangely buoyant as he settled himself at Orla's impressive polished dining table. Susan's flowers, arranged now in a cut-glass vase, caught his eye and a small glow of pride that he hadn't experienced before came over him.

Although the setting was almost as formal as Chez Louis would have been with the rows of polished cutlery and glittering water goblets and wineglasses, the atmosphere was decidedly more relaxed. Their pre-dinner drinks in the sitting room had been the most restful family gathering of his life to date and he was beginning to wonder now whether he'd exaggerated the extent of the usual tension to Susan.

Laura and Barry were in high spirits after their holiday, probably because it was the first time they'd left the country in years. He could see that Susan was very taken with them, especially Laura who'd primped and preened Lily and Rose with perfume and nail varnish for the occasion. He'd told Susan about their long quest to become pregnant and he knew she was thinking the same thing as he was – what a waste of two great parents it all was.

Gavin was a little quieter than he usually was but that was only because Orla had him on aperitif duty. In her eyes, this would be considered a serious challenge and not just a matter of doling out wine and beer. He'd been impressed with the eclectic collection of drinks that Donal had arrived with and had immediately chilled the champagne in anticipation of a toast later. Donal knew by Gavin's approving look that Orla would be bowled over that he'd even thought to include a bottle of bubbly.

Donal had never seen his father so relaxed-looking but then Paddy's demeanour was always closely linked to that of his wife at any given time. If Iris was nervous and jittery, then Paddy was overly calm and placating. If she was upset over something, her husband would solve it immediately. As it was, she was completely taken up with Lily and Rose who were explaining loudly, in tandem, that their friend Claudia was now coming home from school to play with them every day instead of just coming for play-dates like she used to. Paddy, therefore, could sit back, sip his glass of Beamish and even make the little faux-chauvinist jokes that Laura pretended to rise to every time. At least until some minor incident discommoded Iris, in which case he'd have to intervene to smooth things out again.

It fascinated Donal that he'd thought this whole relationship between his mother and father was normal until he'd started talking about it to Susan. At some stage in the near future, he vowed, he was definitely going to try and talk to Laura about the events surrounding Darren's death. Up to now, he acknowledged, he'd hardly been able to formulate his brother's name in his mind.

"This looks delish!" he said as Orla, having ensured that Lily and Rose were settled at the table, slid in opposite him. "Can we start?"

"He's such a savage, Susan," Laura grinned, rolling her eyes at Donal.

Susan grinned, appearing completely relaxed in her surroundings. "That's why I'm mad about him. He'll eat all my culinary marvels without complaining about lumps and burnt bits!"

"Well, don't feed him too well," Gavin commented, "or you'll put the pizza place on the Quays out of business."

"Why am I being victimised?" pleaded Donal. "It's not like the rest of you aren't digging in. Compliments to the chef, is what I say."

It was the first time that evening he'd seen Orla smile properly. Paddy, half his plate cleared already, joined in the praise and reached for another slice of his daughter's wholemeal bread.

"Ten times as good as that Chez Louis place," he beamed, spreading his bread with a generous layer of butter.

"And ten times less expensive," Donal couldn't help but add. Everyone laughed in agreement, except Orla, of course, who pursed her lips in a manner that he'd become used to over the years.

"You should go into this professionally, Orla," said Barry. "Write a cookery book like Bree out of *Desperate Housewives*."

Paddy, clearly enjoying this good-natured banter between his family, joined in. "Pity that Rachel Allen is after saturating the market with her Favourite this and Favourite that."

"Pity is right," Orla agreed. "I could certainly put up with being a celebrity chef if I was making her money!"

"Never too late," Barry persisted. "Think Nigella."

Laura laughed, dug her husband in the ribs and started to collect the plates. "You *would* say that!" It was no secret that Barry, as well as Donal and Gavin, was a big fan of Nigella Lawson.

"I'm serious. Look, Orla even has candles and posh flower arrangements. That could be her angle!"

Donal was thrilled that Barry thought Susan's flowers were "posh".

"And you could be my agent," was Orla's riposte as she departed in the direction of the kitchen followed by Laura.

Donal glanced sideways at Susan to see how she was dealing with this first foray into the Carmody clan. In response, she slid her hand into his under the table, looking every bit as happy as he was.

Orla felt heat prickling under her hair. It was bad enough that all the time and effort she'd put into organising meals and nights out in lovely restaurants over the years was being made a skit of but knowing somewhere inside her that there was truth in it was worse.

She ignored Laura for a few moments, taking the plates off her in silence and scraping them efficiently before stacking them neatly in the dishwasher.

She knew herself that Chez Louis was hideously overpriced and that it had probably been a bit of a burden on the others but then, she told herself obstinately, none of them had objected or offered an alternative.

And although she herself was irritated in the extreme by the lavish praise that was being showered on the meal so far, it was equally irritating to see the rest of her family having the time of their lives while criticising the effort that she'd made for years.

"*Desperate Housewives* aside, it really is turning out to be a great evening." Laura was smiling as if it was Claridges they were eating in. "Whatever comes up next, we'll have it in my house, okay?"

Orla opened the door of the top oven and carefully lifted out the warmed soup bowls. Laura, it seemed, was getting on the bandwagon now that it was acceptable to celebrate a special occasion with nothing too special at all. And, knowing Laura, it would be a cold buffet rather than a full meal. Donal, she thought wildly, might even host a pizza and beer night for the next occasion. It galled her to see standards reaching the slippery slope, especially when she was no longer in a position to object.

"And the flowers *are* lovely," Laura continued. "That beer has gone to Barry's head but you can blame Gavin for being so heavy-handed with the drinks."

"Susan actually brought them," Orla admitted, annoyed that the bouquet was so noticeably classy. If anyone had asked her to guess, Orla would have had Susan down as more obvious "red roses" type of person.

Laura was placing the deftly filled soup bowls on a large tray that Orla had laid out on the kitchen table. "She's nice, I think."

"Well, Donal seems to like her. It's just a bit of an effort getting to know each one, though. The girls are even beginning to cop on to it."

Orla started swirling fromage frais onto the surface of the soup, carefully creating identical patterns on each one.

Laura grinned in agreement, then pointed in the direction of the damask tray cloth that sat smoothly under the bowls on the tray. "Nice tray cloth. Very Martha Stewart!"

For one mad moment, Orla thought she was actually going to cry. Here was Laura, who could hardly boil an egg, making smart comments about her home-making skills. In the past, Orla would have felt a bit superior to her less-sophisticated older sister. Now however, when she could hardly afford the grocery bill, the tray cloth seemed a bit ridiculous to her and, admittedly, a touch "Martha Stewart" as Laura put it.

"It stops the bowls from slipping," she defended, grabbing the tray from Laura in case she would spill half the contents of the bowls and negate her point that the starched damask cloth was a practicality rather than an affectation. "You bring the bread baskets," she ordered over her shoulder.

Gavin took the tray from her as soon as she arrived back in the dining room. Laura placed the bread at either end and sat back down next to Barry. An arrow of pain shot through Orla's chest when she saw the fleeting look of intimacy that passed between Barry and Laura when he slid his arm around his wife's waist. Their chairs, she noticed now, were practically pasted together.

"Uncle Donal?"

Lily, ever the drama queen, made use of the pause in general conversation that developed as Orla started to hand around the soup course. "When will Cleo be coming to do the beads with us again?"

Orla, stuck in motion with a soup bowl hovering in the air

between herself and Gavin, became effectively paralysed. Her husband, gratifyingly, lowered his eyes from hers.

"Yeah," Rose added, her voice accusing. "She promised and so did you!"

At any other time, it would have been Orla who saved the day by chiming in with something diplomatic. Startlingly, it was Donal who took control of the situation, before even looking to her for rescue as he would have done in the past.

"I don't think she'll be coming at all, ladies." Donal sounded completely reasonable while Susan had a slightly amused expression on her face.

Everyone else looked on with interest.

Almost grateful for the distraction, Orla resumed placing bowls carefully in front of anyone who didn't already have one.

Lily was expecting a better explanation than that. "Well, why not?"

Donal looked at Susan and gave an apologetic grimace. Orla watched as she suppressed a smile and winked discreetly at him. It wouldn't be half as amusing, she thought, if the people gathered around the table knew the full extent of the same Cleo.

"Well," Donal began quite comfortably, "she's not my girlfriend any more so she probably won't be coming here to visit."

The situation was beginning to dawn on Rose. "So is Susan going to be coming instead of her so?" She looked from her uncle to his girlfriend for confirmation.

"Something like that," Donal confirmed.

Susan nodded to prove it was true.

Orla hated her at that moment for being so secure and nonchalant about it all when the very mention of Cleo Morgan made *her* come out in a cold sweat.

"Fine so." Rose picked up her soupspoon, obviously satisfied with this.

Lily, characteristically, wasn't. "So what will *you* be doing for us, Susan?"

The laughter around the table erupted like a tsunami. Lily, indignant, clarified crossly that she was only *asking*. This, of course, caused another howl of mirth from the adults at which point Lily realised she'd said something funny and sat back to bask in it.

Orla was livid but held her tongue. She was sick of hearing about bloody Cleo. Gavin could direct the traffic on this one, she decided meanly. When she glanced over at him, however, his chair was empty and she realised he'd escaped to the kitchen, ostensibly to put the tray away.

"Well, I'm not too bad at braiding hair, I suppose," Susan told her helpfully. It was clear that she wasn't remotely put out by any comparison between her own skills and that of Donal's previous girlfriend.

Both girls were immediately interested and started to question her earnestly while everyone else returned to their food. Orla sincerely hoped that this new diversion would put an end to their fascination with Cleo once and for all.

"I'm sorry it keeps coming up, Orla."

Gavin was standing behind her as she carved thick slices of lamb. His voice was low so that he couldn't be heard in the dining room.

"They'll forget about her eventually," Orla responded tightly. Any other woman would have wanted to hear this contrite apology but she was at the end of her tether and just wanted an end to this constant feeling of sand shifting beneath her feet.

"I know they will." Gavin touched her shoulder lightly, making her swing around to face him as if he'd given her an electric shock. He was so close to her, looking her intently in the eyes. "But will *we*?"

She knew what he meant. *He* would be able to, if that was what was required. But what good would that be if Orla couldn't get past even the mention of her name? How could they move on at all in that case?

"This is not the time to talk about it," she hissed angrily.

Gavin had insisted on Laura remaining in her seat while he helped with the main course. Now the meat was carved but the tureens of buttered vegetables and tray of roast potatoes were still in the oven.

"We can't ignore it forever!" Gavin looked haggard and Orla glanced at the door anxiously in case Laura decided to appear and offer her assistance after all.

"I'm not ignoring it! We'll talk about it, okay? But later, when everyone's gone home."

"Fine." Gavin inhaled deeply and started to load the plates onto the same tray he'd brought out earlier. "Because we can't go on like this."

Silently, he lifted the tray and left her alone in the kitchen.

Orla stood there for a moment, sensing yet another shift in the dynamic of her life. What did he mean "we can't go on like this"? As if he was issuing some kind of ultimatum that she either accepted what had happened or else. Or else what? He'd leave? He wouldn't make any further efforts to resolve things if she didn't start engaging in dialogue?

Up to now there had been anger, seething anger, combined with hurt and betrayal and well-justified rage. Now, for the first time, fear entered the equation, stealing up her spine like a finger of cold air. Her only power had been in letting him stay with a promise of, possibly, forgiveness. But what if he didn't want to stay? What if he was done with waiting for absolution? Where was her power then?

Sick, she pulled herself together and opened the oven door. A tray of crispy squash wedges encrusted with oil and herbs confronted her. Under it was a china bowl of roasties and a tureen of creamy mash. Grabbing them carefully, one by one, she took a deep breath. For now, the show would just have to go on.

45

Whatever was going on between Gavin and Orla, they certainly weren't hiding it too well. Laura watched the interaction between them as they settled down to their main course and wondered if the strain of living and working under the one roof was getting to them. Plus, it seemed that Claudia Arnold was, according to the twins anyway, now part of the evening package.

Orla, for all that she was always demanding that Gavin spent more time at home and that she was so keen to have the girls socialising with the upper echelons, still had an overriding need to be the boss of her own home. Laura thought that perhaps actually getting what she wanted might have backfired a little for her.

Even the "Oohs" and "Aahs" around the table weren't satisfying her this evening. Usually, Orla soaked up the compliments about her cooking but she'd already dismissed Susan's rave review of the lamb and Donal's appreciation of the roasties. She and Gavin were discussing their Christmas plans with Paddy and Iris now and Laura noticed just how pale her sister was beneath her perfect make-up.

It would be lovely to be able to ask later if everything was all right but Laura knew that this was the last thing Orla would appreciate. She dismissed the idea out of hand and turned to Donal, next to her at the end of the table.

"Orla told me about Senan's accident," she said quietly. She hoped he wouldn't mind talking about it as it was only Barry and Susan next to them.

"It was desperate," he acknowledged. "I don't think Joe will ever get over it."

Barry knew only what Laura knew from Orla, that there had been an accident and that Senan had lost his life. "Hard on everyone," he said to Donal.

"It must have been awful at the scene." Laura couldn't imagine anything worse but she wanted to give Donal a chance to talk about it at least.

"It was. The fact that it was on Patrick Street didn't help. I arrived nearly straight away but I couldn't do anything." He looked at Laura, straight in the eye. "It was a bit like before, to be honest."

Laura knew exactly what he meant but couldn't believe that he'd actually said it out loud. Maybe seeing Senan Crowley dead in front of him had opened up something in him, the way the counsellor in Barbados had for her.

"I was thinking that when Orla told me about it. The ambulance and the Guards and all that." She looked at Susan, wondering if Donal had told her about the last accident he'd witnessed.

Donal was well able to read her thoughts on that one. "Susan knows about Darren. She lost a sister too."

He slid his hand over Susan's on the table and Laura could almost physically feel the connection between them. What she didn't feel was the small silence that had developed at the other end of the table at the mention of Darren's name.

"Did you?" Barry looked at her with sympathy. "As a child as well?"

Susan shook her head. "Julie was twenty. She was in a car crash around Christmas a few years ago."

"Darren was thirty years ago," Laura told her, needing to say the name out loud now that Donal had been able to say it. She knew Barry would be proud of her.

"So Donal said. At least Julie got a chance at life." Susan's hand was still in Donal's.

"It's still not easy," Barry said, knowing that the loss of a sibling in any family would be traumatic.

Susan was thoughtful for a moment. "But at least I was old enough to understand, Barry." She looked from Donal to Laura. "You were little more than toddlers."

"I know," Laura said quietly. She felt Barry's hand resting reassuringly on her thigh. Susan was right. They had been very young to experience what they had.

Donal smiled suddenly. "And at least I had someone to mind me."

Laura's breath caught in her throat as the memory of bringing Donal across the road to use the toilet at the back of the little shop struck her full force. It was the first time the events of the actual day had been mentioned between them and it was good to know that Donal had felt "minded". Barry's fingers tightened where they rested on her leg. He knew how much she worried about not having cared for her brothers properly.

Susan smiled over at her. "Donal told me how you looked after him, Laura. It was unbelievable for a seven-year-old."

Laura was struck by how relaxed Susan was with the subject and how much detail Donal had confided. She smiled, beginning to relax into the conversation herself. "It was unbelievable, full stop. We didn't really even know that Darren had died, to be honest."

"Laura!" Orla's voice cut through the air like an arrow.

All heads turned towards it and it was only then that Laura saw the expressions at the other end of the lengthy dining table.

Iris's eyes were round in her face, as was her mouth. Paddy's face was set in grim lines, the kind that Laura hadn't seen since her childhood. Gavin looked appalled, but it was hard to tell whether this was due to the tone and volume of his wife's voice or the fact that it was Lily who then broke the silence.

"Who's Darren?"

Rose, always the disciple, followed her up. "We didn't know anyone was dead!"

Laura looked around at the assembled faces, shock evident in each of them for different reasons. Iris would be shocked that the unmentionable had been mentioned, Paddy that there would be an incident to smooth over and Orla because this prohibited subject was clearly ruining her dinner party. Gavin was only in shock because he would be the one witnessing his wife's wrath long after the rest of them had departed the scene.

Laura, though, had come this far and she wasn't going to regress now. Releasing this secret from her own heart had allowed her to become pregnant, of this she was convinced. Donal too had faced the trauma of unlocking it, at the expense of seeing his friend dead in the middle of Patrick Street. There was no way that this was going back in its box now because it was somehow easier to gloss over it. She looked from Lily to Rose and answered squarely and honestly, but not before meeting her parents' eyes.

"Darren was our little brother but he went to heaven, long before you two were even born."

There had been numerous times throughout this long and tortuous day that Orla was convinced she had reached the last straw but something snapped in her when she listened to Laura and Donal talking about their brother.

"That is *enough*, Laura."

Poor Lily had opened her mouth to question what her aunt had just announced but a glance was enough to silence her. Orla felt guilty immediately but she just couldn't tolerate any more.

All day, she'd felt like she was operating in a parallel universe where everyone else was living the life of Reilly while her own world was falling apart around her. And it was she who seemed to be holding it all together and solving everyone else's problems.

Jessica Arnold had landed in this morning and whipped away what felt like her last shred of dignity but only after Yvonne Kelly's visit had made her aware of just how financially vulnerable she was right now.

Laura and Barry had returned from their holidays as high as kites to find the anniversary dinner conveniently organised.

Donal was like a spring lamb with his new girlfriend and not a care in the world. He didn't even have a mortgage to worry about, for God's sake, and yet he thought he was put upon to even have to turn up at things.

Paddy and Iris were being waited on hand and foot by her, so much so that it was almost what they expected.

Gavin, of course, defied belief with his veiled threat to walk away if she didn't toe the line.

"Orla . . ." Gavin's voice was low and placating, fuelling the rage that seemed to have a life of its own inside her.

"What?" She rounded on him, the look on her face daring him to silence her.

"Ah now, Orla . . ." This was Paddy, wanting to head off any confrontation that might upset Iris. As long as Orla had been around, Iris had never for a moment had to look after herself in any way. Who had been there to do anything for Orla when push had come to shove these last few weeks?

"I've had enough of this, Dad." It was time Paddy realised that there were more people than Iris with feelings to be dealt with. "I'm sick of this Darren thing. Sick of it."

Watching Laura and Donal a moment ago and the connection between them as they spoke about Darren made Orla's whole life flash before her eyes. She'd always felt like an outsider, excluded subtly from whatever great mystery there was about the boy who'd died. Barry wasn't excluded though. Nor, it seemed, was Susan and Orla had had enough of it all.

"What?" This was Donal, his eyes almost outside his head at what she'd just said.

"I said I'm sick of it," she retorted, no longer able to control her own voice.

Gavin looked at Lily and Rose and started to stand up.

Susan raised her hand in a silent order for him to remain seated. "Will we try doing the braids, girls? You might even have a few of those beads in that playroom you told me about."

She stood but neither Lily nor Rose moved, both of them sensing that a drama was about to unfold.

"Go on, girls," Gavin urged quietly. "Thanks, Susan."

The two started to get up obediently but were halted in their tracks almost immediately.

"*Déjà vu*," Orla spat out, her gaze moving from Gavin to Donal and back again. There was no way another of Donal's fancy women was going to worm her way in. "I can see where this is going!" she spat at her husband.

"Orla!" Gavin stared pointedly at Lily and Rose before his gaze, pleading, returned to Orla again.

She could see he was horrified that she might just be angry enough to expose his dirty little secret like this, right here in front of the girls and all her family, but she just didn't care any more. He was the one who'd done the damage, yet she was the one that everyone, even her own children, was staring at right now.

Donal, usually placid in the face of any drama, spoke up rapidly.

"For God's sake, Orla! That earring thing was nobody's fault. Susan won't let anything happen to them."

Orla realised that Donal had got the wrong end of the stick when she'd objected to Susan taking the girls into the playroom. He obviously thought that she was anticipating a re-run of the evening that he and Cleo had let Lily put an earring up her nose. If only her brother knew how much more was going on.

"Go on, girls," Gavin said eventually, more firm about it this time.

Susan nodded at them and left the table, the girls following in her wake.

Orla had never felt so wretched in all her life.

Now it was Laura's turn to pitch in. "I don't know what's wrong, Orla, but –"

"You don't know what's wrong?" Orla parodied sarcastically. "I'll tell you what's wrong! Big bloody deal that your brother died!"

"*Our* brother," Donal corrected, although all of them knew that this wasn't strictly true. Orla and Darren hadn't even been in the Carmody family at the same time.

"No, Donal, *your* brother. Yours and Laura's. Everyone's always made that perfectly clear with this whole big secret thing and not talking about him as if I was some kind of outsider that he couldn't be discussed in front of."

Paddy looked completely perplexed. "There's no secret, Orla," he explained patiently. "It's in the past, that's all."

"It's *not* in the past! Those two are down at the end of the table talking about him – so you can't say it's in the past!"

"But Orla –" This was Laura again.

"Don't 'But Orla' me as if I'm raving! If there's no great mystery then how come none of you mentioned Father Hardiman?"

Tears came to her eyes at the injustice of it all. Did they think she was stupid? She knew she was yelling now but what she was saying was all true. Not once had Darren's name ever even been mentioned in front of *her*, the man who'd apparently killed him was now dead and still she was drawing a blank. Yet Laura and Donal were allowed to discuss him freely with each other.

"What about Father Hardiman?" Iris's face, if it was possible, was even paler than usual.

Paddy's mouth was open as if he was about to say something and just couldn't get the words out. Laura and Donal were looking at her as if she had ten heads.

"This is more of it! He had to die sometime, for God's sake!" She looked at Iris now, her face accusing. "Why does everything have to be kept from me?"

It was Donal who spoke up this time. "Orla, will you listen? I don't even know what you're on about here – all this Father Hardiman stuff. You have it all wrong – this is not about you –"

"Well, that's true anyway," she retorted. She could see the shock on the faces of both her parents out of the corner of her eye but for once she didn't care about upsetting Iris or leaving a crisis for Paddy to sort out. "It's *never* about me. I'm just the one who was brought in as a replacement, to fill a gap or something. I'm just –"

It was Paddy who interrupted her tirade this time. "In the name of God, Orla, what put all this into your head? Sure there was no question of replacing him!"

"So it's all in my head? Is that what you're saying?"

At this, Gavin put his arm around her shoulder, the first proper contact they'd had in weeks, and drew her closer. "Orla. This isn't doing anyone any good," he stated gently.

Paddy, normally one to let things die down quietly, persisted in what he'd been saying. "You were always the very same as the others to us, isn't that right, Iris?"

At this, Orla was genuinely shocked and she could see Donal looking at Laura in amazement. Paddy never put pressure on Iris to deal with anything.

Iris looked from one to the other in bewilderment, her fingers grasping her throat as if she was choking. Her mouth opened but nothing came out.

"See? There's no answer, is there?" said Orla.

Orla had always known that she was second best, brought into the Carmody family after Darren had departed it, to paper over the cracks and bring the number up to three again. And for all that she did for Iris – shopping and cleaning and organising – she would never be the same as Laura who did precious little. Orla knew now that no matter how hard she worked at it, they'd never see her in the same light as Laura, Donal and their precious Darren.

"Orla!" Laura's voice was slightly raised now, probably in response to her own. "You have this all wrong. If Father Hardiman's dead, I can tell you I know nothing about it. Why do you think Donal and I know anything more than you do?"

"Well, you were *there*, for a start! At least you know what happened to Darren and why there's such a mystery." She couldn't keep the sarcasm out of her voice now.

At this, Laura's face became a mask of angry calm. "Orla, you're such a silly girl, do you know that? Of course I was there. I was the one who was bringing him across the road, for God's sake. I was seven, though, so forgive me if I can't figure it all out."

Orla was gob-smacked at this. Laura never got cross and she'd certainly never have dared to call *her* silly before. And this was the first she'd heard of Laura actually being involved in the accident. They stared at each other down the length of the table until Donal spoke up.

"I was there too. Acting the maggot so that Laura had to take hold of me. That's how Darren was crossing on his own."

Orla felt a weird sense of deflation at Laura effectively telling her to grow up. She wondered whether she and Donal were telling the truth about not knowing that the priest who'd mowed down their brother was dead. And now here Donal was talking about the accident with no trace of his usual jokey immaturity.

"Is that it? He just got knocked down crossing the road?" She'd imagined over the years that there must surely be something more to it. Even Denis Brett had made it clear that there was some level of blame or guilt around Father Hardiman. It *couldn't* be all in her head, as her father had suggested.

"What do you mean 'Is that it?'?" said Laura. "He was five,

Orla! The same age as Lily and Rose. Don't tell me you'd think it was that minor if something happened to one of the girls!"

"I just thought –"

Donal cut her explanation short. "It was horrendous for everyone. Laura had to look after me when everyone went off in the ambulance. We were on our own for hours, Orla. So it might sound fairly simple to you that he just got knocked down but it wasn't that simple at all."

Most of the surging emotion had gone out of Orla now, leaving her feeling weak and almost exhausted. And not a little foolish. Maybe all the little comments and references she'd heard from outsiders over the years *had* been built up in her imagination. There was still dessert, coffee and the anniversary cake to serve, she remembered with a slight feeling of panic.

"But why did it all have to be such a mystery?" she insisted, looking from Donal to Laura, both of whom were staring at her as if they'd never seen her before. "Why are there no photos of him up or anything? And none of you ever mention him when I'm there. I know it was bad, of course I do. But why should I have to be left out of everything as if it was my fault that I didn't make things better?"

She stared accusingly at Paddy and Iris suddenly and directed her final comment in their direction.

"I don't know why you bothered adopting me at all!"

Laura turned and looked at Barry, knowing that he too would be stunned that Orla had carried such issues around with her for years, just as she herself had. She hadn't even been there, yet Darren's death appeared to have weighed as heavily on her sense of herself as it had on Laura's. And perhaps on Donal's too, for that matter.

Donal caught the look that passed between Laura and Barry and wished that Susan was here beside him instead of braiding hair in the playroom with Lily and Rose.

"We adopted you because we wanted to. And Darren had nothing to do with it."

To say there was a stunned silence around the table was an understatement. None of them, except perhaps Paddy, had ever heard Iris speak so decisively before. Nor had any of them heard her say Darren's name out loud.

All heads turned towards her and Orla could see that Barry and Gavin were looking at her as if she might detonate at any moment. They, of course, only ever saw a certain side of their mother-in-law, the side that Paddy's attention and protection created.

Orla didn't know what to say to this. Now that Iris had spoken, perhaps it was best to let her continue. Paddy would know what to do if she became upset or distressed.

"That's right, Orla." Paddy spoke now, his eyes on Orla rather than on his wife as would normally be the case.

"Oh."

Orla couldn't see how her own adoption was unrelated to the loss of her brother but she wasn't used to asking the kind of difficult questions that might upset her mother.

Iris was looking at her curiously, her thin, pale hands resting on the table at either side of her half-full dinner plate.

"It was all sorted out before anything ever happened to Darren. You were supposed to come the next day but they wouldn't let us have you straight away, with the funeral and everything."

"What do you mean?" Orla looked at her open-mouthed. What Iris was saying didn't make sense.

Paddy sighed deeply as his wife looked at Donal and Laura before explaining.

"We went out for a spin in the car after Mass. We were going to have the ice creams and tell the others about the new baby that was coming the next day."

"You were adopting me anyway? Even before the accident?"

The bottom fell out of Orla's world as she digested this. Everything in her life to date had been built on the fact that she had been adopted to fill the gap in her family after another child had died. She looked at her brother and sister now to see if they had been aware of this all along but she could see from their faces that it was news to them too.

A small tear rolled down Iris's cheek and, strangely, Paddy didn't even seem to notice. "It was all my fault," she said in a voice that was smaller than any of them had ever heard.

"Now, Iris, there's no need to go into all that." It was always Iris that Paddy was worried about upsetting but on this occasion he was looking anxiously at Laura, Donal and Orla.

"I should have gone into it long ago, if this is what Orla thinks about it all. That there's some sort of mystery about it all."

Suddenly, the wind went out of Orla's sails and she felt a huge sense of shame sweep over her. She'd made a mess of everything. Her marriage was a shambles, her indiscriminate spending had brought them almost to bankruptcy and now she'd alienated her entire family. Neither Laura nor Donal had spoken a word since Iris had opened her mouth.

"It's all right, Mum, you don't have to . . ."

Her voice broke as she tried to put an end to what she'd started and the rest of the words just wouldn't come. Unbelievably, she felt Gavin's fingers wrap firmly around her own clenched ones. She looked at him helplessly and felt his grip tighten, his eyes telling her that everything would be fine.

"I *do* have to. I wasn't satisfied with everything I had and that was why Darren got killed."

"That's not true now, Iris, we –"

"It *is* true, Paddy." She looked around the table. "After the twins were born I was very sick and I had to have my womb removed."

She looked apologetically at Barry and Gavin at this point, no doubt thinking it was somehow indelicate to bring up such a thing.

"I thought we were going to have a big family so I was very

upset over it, even though I had the three of you. It went on so long and I couldn't get over it so I got it into my head that we'd adopt a child. So we put our names down for a baby."

So many different thoughts went through Orla's head on hearing this that she thought she might actually faint.

I wasn't an afterthought. It wasn't that nobody really wanted me.

I tried so hard to make them all want me in case they'd send me back.

"If I'd been satisfied with the lovely little family I had already the accident mightn't have happened at all," Iris stated firmly.

Orla wondered what Iris was trying to say. That she should have been happy with Laura, Donal and Darren and not gone down the road of looking for another baby at all. That she would have been better off not being *given* a baby at all?

"Anyone else would have been happy with three healthy children but I thought it was the end of the world. And then I was so delighted when we heard we were getting you. When the accident happened, I didn't sleep a wink in case they decided not to let us have you. It would have been like losing two children."

To think that Iris had bonded with her even before she arrived shocked Orla. But that she would have considered losing her on a par with losing Darren was unbelievable.

"I thought . . . I thought . . ."

Orla could hardly string her words into a sentence now but she knew she needed to apologise for her outburst as well as the thoughts she'd harboured for years.

"I *know* what you thought, Orla love, and I'm sorry you were thinking that. And I know I wasn't much of a mother to you after all that happened."

"That's not true!"

Now that she thought about it rationally, Orla wondered how she would cope if she lost either Lily or Rose. It was no wonder that Iris had been so fragile all these years.

"I should never have let you all off to the shop on your own."

Orla looked up and saw that her mother was talking to Laura and Donal now.

Once again, Paddy intervened before either of his older children could speak.

"It's all in the past now, Iris. There's no point in going over it again."

"We should have gone over it long ago," Iris repeated. "There's not a day goes by that I don't ask myself what I was thinking letting them cross the road on a busy Sunday with all the cars coming up after twelve o'clock Mass."

Paddy lowered his face into his hands, defeated. "But don't forget, Iris," he said, a bitter edge creeping into his voice, "that they went across that road many a Sunday, the same as every other child in Barretsbridge. Times were different. And if it wasn't for that lunatic and he full of brandy –"

Iris looked at him as if he had ten heads. His three children and their spouses were staring at him too. None of them had ever heard Paddy raise his voice.

"Paddy, we promised we wouldn't talk about him any more." Iris, after decades of suppression, seemed to have found her voice.

"Well, we might have been wrong, if this is what it's come to! What's this, Orla, about Hardiman? How did you come to hear that he was gone?"

Orla was starting to feel cold now, as if she was going into shock. Her father, it seemed, knew nothing about Father Hardiman's death, which meant that Iris probably didn't know either. Nor, according to themselves, did Donal or Laura.

"Orla?" Laura prompted.

Orla felt the warmth of Gavin's fingers wrapped around her own, a little of his heat seeping into her. "It was in *The Examiner*," she said, her voice sounding meek after the outburst she'd just had.

"When?" Paddy asked. His eyes were steely and she could see just how strong he'd had to be for all of them over the years.

"A while ago." She looked at Laura. "Before you went on holidays – the day you took Mum to Cork."

"I see." Paddy's voice was grim. "Well, that's the end of an era. Orla was right about there being a mystery, that's for sure," he said to the table in general.

"Dad?" Donal was starting to feel as if he'd been a bit simple all these years, thinking that Darren's death had been forgotten by everyone but himself. He'd thought Orla was mad to be thinking that there was something going on that she was excluded from but now, the way his parents were acting, he wasn't so sure.

Paddy sighed. "The man was a complete alcoholic – the whole village knew it. There wasn't the same clamp-down on drinking and driving in those days as there is now, especially where a priest was concerned. He was blind drunk that day, out shouting and yelling around the road until a few people got him back into his car. PJ Madden drove him home before the Guards arrived."

Orla drew her breath in sharply. This is what Denis Brett had meant when he'd spoken about some people having a lot to answer for.

"Was he prosecuted?" she asked now.

Iris shook her head, a cynical expression on her face. "I suppose you could call it a cover-up. Nicky Kelly was the Guard dealing with it – apparently he couldn't do anything because Father Hardiman wasn't breathalysed at the scene. I suppose people thought it was a good idea at the time. To get him out of there."

Laura was curious now. All of this was new to her and she found it amazing that she'd attributed so much blame to herself for all those years. She thought of the little baby growing inside her and vowed to protect him or her from the harsh realities that she and her siblings had encountered. "So he got away with it?"

"That's about the size of it," Paddy admitted. "He was sent off on a trip to Rome fairly smartly. PJ Madden was always sorry about his part in it. I suppose I should have followed it up properly but we had a new baby coming into the house and that was more important." Paddy smiled at Orla then, making it clear that, while he was aware of his own role in all that had happened, she'd been as much of a priority as any of the others.

"Things were different then," Orla reminded him. "You would have been fighting the Church." It was liberating, somehow, to be a part of this and to know that Laura and Donal were equally new to it all.

"We can't turn back the clock now," Iris agreed. "But it's time we came out of this limbo. Colman Broderick was right. We can't keep ignoring it forever."

Orla saw Paddy's mouth open in what looked like disbelief and she could see that Laura and Donal were also baffled as to what the local solicitor had to do with anything. Ironically, after all the years of tip-toeing around her for fear that she'd break down in some way, Iris was the only one of them who seemed to be gathering strength as this unprecedented family catharsis took place.

"Mam, what has Colman Broderick to do with it?" Laura sounded exhausted and her colour was almost greenish, reminding Orla a bit of the way the girls looked if they were sick with a tummy bug.

Iris looked at her husband, a look of inevitability passing between them before she began to speak again.

"After the accident, there was a whole thing with the Guards, an investigation of some sort into what happened. Father Hardiman was going at an awful speed and the dogs on the street knew he was drunk but it was impossible to prove anything – or so we were told. That didn't matter to us one way or another. Darren was gone and there was no bringing him back."

Orla wondered whether she and Gavin would have the same sense of finality if they were ever in that position.

Iris, on a roll now, was still addressing her children while Gavin and Barry sat like silent partners in a boardroom. Orla looked down at her left hand where Gavin's fingers still clasped hers. Her engagement and wedding rings looked the same as they always did, solid and glittering and reminding her that they meant something to her and Gavin when he'd placed them there.

"The Bishop sent a letter to say he was 'looking into the matter' but we gave it to Colman Broderick and he sorted everything out. We didn't want anything to do with it, especially a court case and going over it all again."

Iris shuddered at the memory of it and looked at her husband.

"What your mother is trying to say is that there was a settlement eventually from Bishop Holloway, all done through Colman's office. I can't even remember how much it was, it was so long ago, but we didn't want it anyway. Nothing was going to bring Darren back and we were lucky enough to have Orla after everything that happened."

Orla had a strange sensation of humility that her parents thought they were *lucky* to have her.

Iris sighed and looked around the table. "Now I know it was foolish to have ignored it for so long but it seemed all wrong to be given money when it was my fault that I let him get killed. So we left it all to Colman over the years, even though he kept telling us that we'd have to deal with it if he ever retired." She looked shamefaced then, as if this was something she'd needed to get off her chest for a long time. "We knew he invested it but I used to throw the statements in the fire every year without even opening the envelope. I couldn't bear to look at them," she finished apologetically.

"We should have faced up to it before now but it all came to a head when the government started talking about this bank guarantee scheme," said Paddy.

Orla wasn't quite sure what this guarantee scheme meant and kicked herself once again for the way she'd been effectively ignoring the recession. She knew vaguely that the major banks had been about to collapse under the strain of enormous loans which property developers could no longer repay. She also knew that the precarious situation had put in jeopardy the savings of many ordinary people who'd thought their money was in safe hands and that the government had been forced to guarantee the safety of those savings up to a certain value. What that value was, she had no idea, probably because it hadn't infringed on her own safe little world at the time.

Her father, though, seemed to be more than *au fait* with it all.

"Colman insisted we come in to the office when it was all happening because he was obliged to advise people on where they stood with investments. We didn't know anything about the investments or what they were worth because I always just signed whatever papers he gave me whenever he asked. As far as we were concerned, whatever money was there would go to you three after our time."

"That way, we didn't have to have anything to do with it but it might come in handy for you at some stage," said Iris. "It didn't amount to much but it was going to be there for you anyway."

Orla felt sorry that her parents had had to carry the burden of their son's death all these years, so much so that they were unable even to deal with the practicalities that would be bound to arise. She thought of Donal and the way that Joe Crowley had had to walk away from his taxi business. He too was unable to face the tasks of everyday life, especially when he too would be confronted with insurance details as if Senan had been any other employee. It didn't bear thinking about.

Iris's mouth was set in a grim line as she continued the tale.

"We know we were wrong now. We should have used the money to do some good, maybe brought you all on a little holiday or something to help you get back to normal. I see that now but I couldn't at the time. I could see nothing but that road and your father lifting Darren up to try and save him."

Iris's voice broke a little and Orla reached over and laid her free hand over that of her mother. "It was a very hard time, Mum."

"It was harder for you three," she countered. "And I didn't think of the effect it might have on you. When I see them all on the telly now talking about grief counselling, I wonder how you managed at all."

"That was the way it was in those days," Laura reminded her. "People thought it was best not to keep going over things."

"I know that," Iris agreed. "But it's not too late to do something good. Colman Broderick was very loyal to us over the years, even though we were very hard to deal with. There was a lot more in the account than we ever imagined so Colman is going to arrange to give a donation to the Road Safety Authority in Darren's name."

"Your mam and I are going to go on a little trip to Rome for ourselves but we want you three to take what's left and do something nice to remember Darren by."

"But Dad –" Orla protested. It was enough for her to finally know she was as much a part of the family as Laura and Donal and Darren. She didn't need anything else.

Both Laura and Donal started to speak at the same time but Paddy raised his hand before anyone else could protest.

"If we knew that Sunday how little time we had left with Darren we'd have made the most of it. Well, that's what we want you to start doing now and hopefully the extra few bob will help. Let this be the start of better times," he finished decisively.

Iris looked around, her whole demeanour altered now that the secrets of the past had been brought out into the open.

"That's right," she echoed. "The start of better times. And there's plenty of time to talk about this again."

Paddy smiled proudly at his wife as she said this. "True. Now what about dessert and that cake the girls were telling me about? We could all do with a good cup of tea."

"Don't mind about tea," Donal grinned. "There's champagne as well, don't forget."

"So there is," Orla grinned as she rose from the table to call her children and Susan in from the playroom. She turned as she reached the door and looked with pleasure at her family gathered around the table. Gavin gave her the smallest smile.

She smiled back. It was time to face the future now.

"Isn't this so much better than Chez Louis?" she said.

The Following September

LAURA: Three Wishes

"I don't know what you're moaning about! Look at the poor woman in California who had eight of them!"

Barry smiled up at his wife as he struggled, red-faced, to manoeuvre Finn's legs into his third outfit of the day.

"Well, good luck to her," Laura retorted. She broke the seal that had developed around her left nipple and eased the breast pump away from her breast.

"Not bad," she reported, holding up the pump to determine exactly how much milk was in the bottle. "If we bring whatever is in the fridge we should have enough to tide us over until the speeches are done with."

"Daisy's a bit of a savage though," Barry commented with a grin. Anyone who'd minded their youngest daughter for more than an hour remarked that she'd inherited her always-hungry genes from her father.

Laura capped her almost-full bottle and started to disconnect the plastic tubes of the breast pump for washing. If she didn't buck up, they'd be making the noisiest entrance possible at St Manchan's.

"Catriona says she's in the middle of a growth spurt but even *she's* beginning to think that excuse is wearing a bit thin."

Laura glanced into the cradle nearest to her where Daisy, despite only having gone to sleep two hours previously, was already mooching again.

"No wonder she gained 500 grams!"

The Public Health Nurse had smiled when the little minx had increased so much at her weekly weight check, considering she'd already explained that 200 grams was the recommended weekly weight gain for a premature baby.

"Poppy hasn't a notion of waking," Laura commented.

It was almost one o' clock and she needed to have all three of them fed before she even considered getting into her outfit. The last thing she needed was a big dribble of milk trailing down the back of her dress.

"I'll pull back her blankets a bit and see if it'll stir her."

Finn was now rigged out in a pair of pale blue trousers and matching shirt and jacket that Orla had bought him as a Christening present so Barry laid him carefully back in his cradle before tackling his younger sister.

Poppy didn't even budge when he peeled back her cotton blanket and opened the fasteners of her Baby-Gro. A typical middle child, she always seemed to wait until her siblings were fed and sorted before she made any attempt to look for food. Even when Laura was pregnant, she'd been able to identify the constant movement of the others while Triplet 2, as the obstetrician called her, didn't exactly over-exert herself.

"Will we have a quick sandwich? She might wake enough for even a short feed if we give her a few minutes," Laura called from the kitchen.

She had the breast pump washed and placed in the steriliser and was already peering into the fridge to see what they could have for a quick lunch before they left for the wedding. The meal wasn't being served until six and she knew well that Barry would be ravenous before the Mass was even finished.

"Definitely. You know what Father Maddox is like!"

The priest who'd married Orla and Gavin was performing the ceremony today and neither of them were hopeful of it being anything shorter than an hour and a half.

"We can always phone for room service when we get to the hotel."

Laura had everything planned to precision, a necessity now that she was suddenly the mother of three children. She'd already called to Broomfield Hall to check out the room that they'd be occupying for the night and had made sure that there would be three cots ready and waiting, as well as an empty mini-bar to store a supply of bottles for Kevin and Noelle to call on.

The logistics of travelling, even to somewhere as near as Broomfield Hall, was immense and involved the breast pump and steriliser being brought as well. Thankfully, they had two of everything so Barry had been able to pack the car in advance.

"That's a good idea," Barry agreed. He popped a slice of ham into his mouth and started to butter bread, knowing that if he didn't hurry, Daisy would probably wake up and demand to be fed before he'd eaten. "Kevin said for us to text them as soon as we check in and they'll come straight up to the room. We could order something and have it in the room while we're getting sorted out."

Their friends had proved to be a marvellous support to Barry and Laura from the moment the triplets had arrived and would be invaluable today of all days. Having them come to the hotel to sit with the babies would allow Laura and Barry to enjoy the wedding properly without having to bring the babies down to the reception room. They'd been advised by the paediatrician of the risk of any or all of them getting bronchiolitis over the winter months and a stuffy, over-heated wedding reception was just the place to pick up the necessary bugs. Premature babies were particularly prone to the RSV virus and Laura and Barry were determined to keep their precious children out of hospital if it was at all possible.

"Noelle says Kevin is really revved up for the evening," Laura grinned.

It would be good practice for both of them to look after three children for the evening, even though it would be a different ball-game than what they would expect for themselves in the next few weeks.

Barry laughed. "I hope it doesn't put him off the whole idea!"

Kevin and Noelle would be travelling to Vietnam on the first of October to meet the baby that they'd been awaiting for so long. And even though she would be three months old by the time she arrived in Ireland, they expected Tam Li to be a little smaller and more delicate than the average three-month-old. Hence their eagerness to get in as much practice as possible with the Gordon triplets before their own baptism of fire.

"Well, if we can manage three, I'm sure they'll manage one. I think I'll change Poppy and get her started before Daisy gets going."

Laura gulped down the last of her sandwich, stowed her plate in the dishwasher and brought her cup through to the living-room. Feeding themselves had become as big a part of their day as feeding the babies was, as they'd found out the hard way. In the early days, they'd been concentrating so much on getting a routine established with their new family that Laura and Barry had neglected to look after themselves. It was only when Laura's supply of breast milk had started to dwindle a little that Catriona, their Public Health Nurse, had tutored them on the importance of looking after themselves as well.

"Come on, Pops, up you get!"

Laura smiled at her little girl and marvelled at just how different she was from her sister, even though they were actually identical. It still amazed her that she hadn't really considered the possibility of a triplet pregnancy when they'd set out for Barbados.

It was something they'd been warned about every time they

did an IVF treatment, yet the reality of it hadn't hit home until their first ultrasound scan when their midwife in the Assisted Reproduction Clinic in Cork had announced the fact with a smile. Both Laura and Barry had actually started to laugh, having tutored themselves for the fact that there might be twins inhabiting the uterus. Now, however, Finn, Poppy and Daisy were part of the household and Laura couldn't remember what life had been like before they arrived.

"I'll hit the shower so," Barry called out, already halfway up the stairs.

Co-ordination was everything and Laura knew that her husband would bottle-feed Daisy and dress both of the girls in their fancy dresses and frilly knickers while she herself finally got glammed up. Her days of going to the hairdresser for a blow-dry before a wedding were long gone. Simply getting into Cork to buy something to wear had been luxurious in the extreme.

"Grand so," she called back. Poppy was looking at her with wide, dreamy eyes that made her a little sorry that she'd had to disturb her cosy sleep at all.

"We have a wedding to go to, Poppy," Laura reminded her with a kiss. "You can't sleep your life away."

Poppy gave her a wide smile as if to say, "Oh yes, I can."

"Now, get a good little feed or you'll be starving by the time Father Maddox gets through the Mass," Laura advised her as Poppy latched on to her right breast.

For a baby that was as laid-back and easy-going as Poppy was, she was well able to feed strongly. Laura felt the familiar tug and sat back in her armchair to enjoy the feeling of feeding her daughter.

It still amazed her that her wish to breast-feed had actually materialised. Granted, she had to supplement her own milk with formula to a certain degree but she was happy knowing that each of her babies got a certain amount of expressed milk and at least one full feed from her breast every day. It required a certain amount of juggling and literally anyone who so much as passed the door was invited to feed a baby but Laura was happier than she'd ever been in her life.

Poppy sucked away quietly as her mother marvelled at the laws of nature that had given her such a wonderfully complete little family. Finn, fed and settled by his dad, snoozed peacefully in his cradle while Daisy, always half-awake in case there was food going, chattered and gurgled in the run-up to a full-scale cry for sustenance.

Laura thought about Darren now and tried to visualise what he might be like if he was here to enjoy today with them. He'd look like Donal, of course, and might even have the same almost-horizontal personality type – the same one that Poppy appeared to have inherited. Would Darren be married by now, maybe even with children himself? Or would he have stayed a bachelor as long as Donal, especially when they would have had each other as companions all these years?

Maybe it was the fact that her hormones had definitely been awry but Laura had spent a good part of her pregnancy, especially in the aftermath of Orla's cathartic dinner party, speculating as to what all of their lives would have been like if Darren hadn't chosen that one particular moment to dart across the road in 1979.

She'd talked about it a lot with Donal, with both of them now able to recognise the effect of that one devastating second on everything they'd thought and believed about themselves. The level of blame that her brother had carried over the years had shocked Laura beyond belief, especially when he'd explained the guilt that he felt every time he achieved anything. However small, it was something that Darren would never have the chance to achieve, so he never allowed himself to enjoy anything or move forward in any way.

She thought now of all the times that she and Orla had disparaged their brother for his lack of initiative. Neither of them had understood that, for Donal, to celebrate an excellent exam result was to gloat over what Darren didn't have an opportunity to do. To be successful at work, buy a house or get married would have been passing Darren by when there was no possibility of him catching up, thanks to Donal's shenanigans on the day he'd been killed.

"It sounds so stupid," he'd said repeatedly to Laura, "but that's how I saw it. Every time something good happened, even getting a present, I felt awful because Darren couldn't have the same."

It was all in the past now and the transformation in Donal had been astounding once he'd got it into his head that he hadn't been to blame for his brother's death. Yes, he'd been acting the maggot and had to have his hand held crossing the road. But if Laura had been holding Darren's hand, then Donal might have been the one to scurry across unaided. It was a matter of chance, unfortunately, like Julie being the one to die when others in the ill-fated car weren't wearing seat belts either, as Susan had pointed out. That moment *had* altered all of their lives, yet nothing could alter the fact that it had happened as it had.

Lately, Laura had begun to look at the positive things that Darren's death had brought to all of them, over thirty years after the event. It was too late to say that each of them had wasted years in their own grief-stricken exile. That was a fact of life that each of them had to accept and move on from. Laura had a new life ahead of her with Barry and the children, while the future for both Orla and Donal was only just beginning too.

Iris and Paddy too had become the kind of people that they'd never allowed themselves to be. Doting, involved grandparents with a life of their own to live as well. Whether it was their eventual acceptance that acknowledging the compensation payment wasn't a betrayal of their son or whether it had been the liberating openness that occurred at Orla's dinner table, either way a mantle had been lifted from them both.

Susan, in the aftermath of the dinner-party when Lily and Rose had gone off to bed, had given all of them a new perspective on their reactions to the events of September 1979.

Paddy, in particular, gained a level of absolution when he'd talked about the guilt that had plagued him over not ensuring that Father Hardiman be properly taken to task. It was an easier road, he'd explained, to just let it go rather than attempt to take on the closed ranks of the Church. Especially when it was impossible to prove that the priest had actually been drunk, thanks to the good citizens of Barretsbridge who'd removed him from the scene before the law arrived. Even in those days, however, "leaving the scene of an accident" had been a crime, yet he hadn't had the will to insist that Colman Broderick follow it up on their behalf after Garda Farrell had misplaced the official photographs of the accident scene.

Susan, having been through this with her parents in the wake of her sister's accident, was quick to point out the wisdom of not getting embroiled in what would most likely have been a fruitless and prolonged battle with the Church. There was precious little chance of a parish priest being prosecuted for *anything*, much less drunk driving and the unlawful death of a child. The conflict, she reasoned, would have detracted from the real priority of looking after their remaining children as well as creating a legacy of anger and bitterness that would have festered for years. Like her own parents, Paddy had made the right decision for his family instead of engaging in a gratuitous and unwinnable war. Laura had seen the relief on her father's face as Susan had reinforced this firmly, her voice calm and reasonable, and was grateful to this serene and confident girl for her empathy.

For Laura and Barry, Darren had been able to play a part in the lives of Finn, Poppy and Daisy in the most important way ever. Any sacrifice, of course, would have been possible where the triplets were concerned, yet Laura had moments where she wondered how they would have managed had it not been for the large sum of money that Colman Broderick had transferred over to her in the course of her pregnancy. Maternity leave payments had ended all too soon and the idea of returning to work would have horrified her. For now, at least, she had the glorious luxury of staying at home and caring for her children without the financial worries that so many parents of multiple births experienced.

She looked up at the small framed photograph on the mantelpiece and thanked Darren silently for making it possible.

Orla: Tír na nÓg

"I'll have my phone on silent in the church," Orla instructed, "so just text me at any time and I can nip home, although there should be no problem. Nonie will sort out anything that crops up, I imagine."

Orla was standing in the small kitchenette while Sheila and Lori had their early lunch. It was the first time that she'd be gone for such a long period and she needed everything to run smoothly on this of all days.

"No problem, Orla."

Sheila had been with her right from the beginning and was well capable of working out any issues that might arise, even if Nonie Kennedy wasn't arriving to oversee Tír na nÓg for the afternoon.

"Jasmine's mum will be here a bit early so just make sure she's ready to go. They have a doctor's appointment to make for three. And don't forget that it'll be Claudia's uncle that'll be picking her up – he's on the file as a named person and I've already checked with Jessica. Dan's his name," she added, wanting to reiterate the importance of protocol with her employees.

Orla was very strict about collection arrangements for the

children in her care, especially at a time when things like the abduction of children were never out of the news. Even acrimonious separations and divorces could impinge on who was authorised to take a child out of a child-care facility like hers so it was important that any diversion from routine was cleared properly first.

"That's fine, Orla," Lori confirmed. "Are the girls still very excited?"

Lily and Rose had the day off school and had spent much of the morning "helping" in Lori's room with the toddlers.

"They're upstairs getting dressed now but I don't know how I'm going to keep them clean until we get to the church. Gavin has them bribed as far as I know but that'll only last so long!"

Orla had brought the twins down to the hairdresser in the village only an hour ago to have their little white roses and pearls pinned in while her own hair was being blow-dried. The importance of not disturbing the arrangement had been stressed again and again but now that they were gone from her own stern watch, Orla wondered whether they'd be like scarecrows when she went up to check on them.

She was just about to take her leave when the buzzer went and Nonie Kennedy's face appeared at the reinforced glass panel of the door.

"Oh great, Nonie's here. I'll take off and you can fill her in on the small things." Sheila nodded, her notebook already out in anticipation while Lori opened the door to Nonie.

"All ready to go, Orla?"

The older woman greeted her with the beaming smile that Orla had become well accustomed to. On days like this, she was glad to have Nonie temporarily on her team, even though she'd officially retired from childminding.

"Almost. I just have to slap on a bit of make-up and step into the dress. And the girls are just getting organised as we speak."

Orla smiled to herself at the idea of Gavin dressing the girls in preparation for a wedding, something that would have been unheard of a year ago. Now though, she'd learned the hard way that doing everything herself didn't necessarily mean that it would be done *better*.

"Fair play to him," Nonie commended. "Why don't you take off now and get your glad-rags on? I'll go out and let Kerrie in for her break."

It pleased Orla that Nonie was as much on the ball as if the children in Tír na nÓg were her own particular charges. Kerrie, the newest member of staff, was supervising the fifteen-minute "TV Time" that Orla scheduled in on Fridays as a treat. The three babies in her care were being watched by Sheila through the sliding glass panel that separated the kitchen and the Nursery. All three were sleeping soundly in their cots while the little breathing sensors under their mattresses clicked away rhythmically.

"Grand so," Orla agreed, happy that everything was in order and that she was confident that Nonie and the girls could cope with whatever cropped up. Nonie would lock up at half six as soon as the "after-schoolers" had departed and the premises had been tidied and prepared for the following working day. "See you all on Monday."

A chorus of instructions about enjoying herself echoed after her as Orla opened the heavy fire door that separated Tír na nÓg from the main house.

Nonie, she reflected now, had been a godsend in more ways than one this past year. There was something motherly about the older woman that made her feel at ease. Her trademark kindness had made it easy for Orla to talk about her family's past and the lamentable manner in which her brother's story had been buried for so long.

"But it was understandable," Nonie had articulated. "The loss of any child is a tragedy but the way it all happened made it worse. Nobody in the parish even talked about it because they knew how it happened."

"I just can't understand how so many people, even our own

neighbours, knew he was drunk and said nothing. You'd think they'd be outraged, especially all the ones who had children of their own!" Orla couldn't understand the veil of silence that had protected the priest from facing the law.

Nonie had just shaken her head and reminded Orla of just how tight a grip the Church had exercised over Irish society.

"Look at the way the Church has fallen from grace these last few years with all the child abuse scandals. Nowadays people are more open with criticism but back then it didn't do to speak out against the parish priest. He was on the Board of the primary school, remember, so people had to deal with him over their own children. Unemployment was high around that time as well and a character reference from the parish priest would always help with a job application. So you can see how there was almost fear involved when it came to sticking your head above the parapet."

"I suppose," Orla had conceded, recalling the way they had to stand to attention in their classrooms at school if the parish priest, Father Hardiman's replacement, deigned to pay a visit. "But PJ Madden? How could he live with himself after what he did? If it was now, he'd probably be prosecuted for taking someone away from the scene of an accident!"

Nonie, characteristically, was able to shed light on this for Orla in her own compassionate way.

"He was the sacristan at the time. It was his *job* to look after the priest as well as the church itself. He thought he was doing the right thing."

"I can't see how!" Orla thought this was a bit outrageous.

"Depends on how you look at it," Nonie remarked. "We talked about it once, years ago. Around the time of the Bishop Casey scandal. Everyone knew Father Hardiman had a problem with drink but PJ saw it as an illness and was always trying to support him. Imagine he used to call to him every morning to make sure he was out of bed in time for Mass. If he was worse for wear he'd even make his breakfast for him."

PJ was a good man, this Orla did know. Which was why she found it so hard to reconcile the motivated Community Council chairman with the actions of the man who'd driven a killer away from the scene while a child lay dead on the road.

Nonie seemed to know what she was thinking. "The day Darren was killed, PJ was trying to stop Father Hardiman from making a show of himself. He was plastered, out on the street shouting and roaring. He thought he was preserving his dignity in front of his parishioners. He was the sacristan, doing his job. It didn't occur to him that he was doing anything wrong."

"He told you that?" Orla knew she would never be able to have this conversation with PJ himself but Nonie was so reliable that her version of events was good enough for anyone.

"He did. It was the reason he gave up the job in the end, even though it took him years to realise what a cover-up it all was. Did you know that Bishop Holloway was going to make some sort of presentation to him when he retired but he refused it?"

Orla, of course, hadn't known this. It was difficult but she was starting to understand how complex the power of the Church had been in Ireland until very recently. PJ, in refusing to be commended by the bishop for protecting Father Hardiman, had atoned in his own way for his imprudent, if well-meaning, actions.

The ability to forgive and let things go was another thing that Orla had learnt this past year. Some things were worth fighting for, like her marriage and her family. Other things, like anger and resentment and bitterness had no place in her life now.

Life was all about progress, moving on from the past and the future being better than what had gone before. Her new and thriving business was the living proof of the kind of progress that had indeed been made.

She couldn't help but marvel at the fortuitous nature of having the space to start Tír na nÓg the way she had, and when it had been most needed. In hindsight, it had probably been an expensive folly to build on a separate apartment in anticipation of Paddy and Iris ever coming to live with them. As a ready-made childcare facility, however, it was inspired.

The kitchen was there already, as was the large bathroom. The former bedroom and living room were now in daily use, as was the generous conservatory she'd added for extra space at the outset. On sunny days, there was enough space fenced off from their own garden to facilitate outdoor activities, with everything in compliance with the regulations laid down by the Health Service Executive. The few renovations she'd had to make were minor, considering that her new premises actually had a separate entrance of its own to begin with.

The first thing she heard now as she mounted the stairs was a stern "Absolutely not!" from Gavin. It was bound to be Lily he was talking to, Orla surmised with a grin.

Passing the bedroom door on the way to get into her own gear, she observed the stand-off between Gavin and Lily, who was attired in her white frilly dress but holding aloft a pair of stripy red and orange woolly tights.

"They're my *absolute* favourite," she was insisting, dramatic as ever while Rose looked on, already dressed in her own white, lacy tights.

Orla rolled her eyes, glad it wasn't she who had to rein Lily in. Gavin, his voice grave, started instructing Rose on how to manage flower girl duties on her own – if it was a thing that Lily decided not to dress in the proper flower girl outfit. Moments later, Orla heard a resigned snort.

"All right so," Lily told her dad brazenly. "Just this once. But I'll be wearing them *every* other day."

"Fantastic," Gavin praised. "Hurry up now or we'll be late. Everyone will be dying to get a look at the flower girls."

This was enough to send both of them into squeals of excitement at the thought of what was to come – *millions* of people all coming to see them walking up the aisle strewing their rose petals.

Orla started on her make-up, fascinated at the reverse psychology that Gavin used with such effect, especially on the more wilful Lily. Orla herself would have been using reason and persuasion, tactics that Lily had become wise to at this stage.

"They're on a five-minute warning," Gavin grinned, catching Orla's eye in the dressing table mirror a few minutes later. "Is everything okay downstairs?"

"All sorted," Orla confirmed.

She slicked a layer of gloss over her lipstick and rose from the tiny piano-stool. Her dress was hanging in the walk-in closet, newly dry-cleaned for the occasion. Tights, shoes and jewellery had been laid out earlier in the day, in the event of some unforeseen crisis occurring in Tír na nÓg. "Nonie's there for back-up, just in case."

"Will we have a quick snack before we go? You know what Father Maddox is like!"

"It's a three-course meal we'd want to sustain us through one of his Masses!"

Gavin laughed, his hand resting lightly on the small of his wife's back as she passed him on the way to the dressing room.

"I'll see if there's anything 'clean' I can give the girls to eat. There might be some pasta salad or something in the fridge."

Orla thought back to Father Maddox and their own wedding day as Gavin departed with the girls trailing down the stairs after him. They'd been through a lot since then, the whole "for better, for worse, for richer, for poorer" thing that had gone over her head at the time proving eerily prophetic in the last year.

In the end of the day, it had been honesty on both their parts that had made them stronger and more together than they'd ever been.

Each of them had changed, that was inevitable, but it was all change for the better. The night of Paddy and Iris's wedding anniversary, at a time when Orla felt her whole world was caving in around her, had been a turning point for both of them. She hadn't known it at the time but things had been at rock bottom with the only way out being up. Their marriage had reached its lowest point as had her own confidence and sense of place in her family. Financially too, they were at their lowest ebb. And although she hadn't even been aware of it, Orla's health was also at breaking point.

Scenes from the anniversary evening rushed through her head now as she stepped out of the casual linen trousers she was wearing and reached for the lacy underwear she'd be wearing under her sheer purple dress.

Calm had descended after the confusion of Paddy and Iris introducing the existence of the compensation they'd received following Darren's death. Strangely, the evening had finished in a civilised manner with coffee and dessert being served as if Orla hadn't just blown her head off over being excluded from the family circle. There hadn't been a circle, according to Laura and Donal, or certainly not an intact one. Nor, it seemed, had her parents had any concept of Orla being different from their other children.

Admitting that it had all been in her head had come surprisingly easily once she'd realised that her siblings had also been prohibited from discussing Darren. Being left out in the cold wasn't so bad at all once she realised that there were other people out there too.

She looked at herself in the full-length mirror now and thought back to the kind of person she'd been the last time she'd worn this dress. The Architectural Society Annual Ball in Broomfield Hall had actually meant something in the kind of life she'd been living back then. Even the fact that she was wearing the dress and the matching Louboutin heels today was testament to the changes that had been wrought in the past year. She'd starved herself to look good in this dress a year ago in order to impress people that she barely knew. She'd thought it mattered that they were sitting beside the right people.

What she hadn't known then was just how badly her health had been suffering from the stress and strain she'd been putting herself through. And that had been ever before she'd known about Gavin's affair or their dire financial straits. Her blood pressure had been dangerously high for a woman of her age, as she'd found out when she'd finally attended her GP for something more effective than the over-the-counter headache pills that she was taking more and more of.

She was lucky, she knew, that she didn't have to go on medication. A rethink of her priorities had been enough. That and the renewed bond that she and Gavin had achieved in the aftermath of the seminal anniversary dinner.

She now remembered that last occasion in Broomfield Hall just how bad her headache had been and how Gavin had taken her home early with the minimum of fuss and the maximum of care. It had barely registered then but that was the part of her marriage she should have valued, not the part that was played out as Mrs Orla Carmody-Merriman, wife of Gavin Merriman of Cole & Merriman, Architects.

Through everything that had happened over that fateful dinner party, it was the way Gavin had held her hand in his as she expressed her anger and isolation to her family that had imprinted itself on her brain and had formed the basis for all that had happened since.

Orla stood still in front of the mirror, unable to define what it was that was different about her now. She *looked* the same, as far as she could tell, with her jet-black, shiny hair and her creamy, flawless skin. Her outfit, as soon as she donned the full-length organza coat that she'd wear in the church, would make her appear identical to the Orla that had swept up the granite steps of Broomfield Hall what seemed like a lifetime ago.

What hadn't been there before, however, was the sense of peace and contentment that was now an integral part of her life in every way. The night of the anniversary dinner had been the start of her life as she now knew it.

That was the night that she knew her marriage to Gavin would survive – and that she *wanted* it to survive. They'd talked long into the night after everyone else had gone and had made love in their own bed in the early hours of the morning.

Everything had come out and, surprisingly, Gavin had understood why she'd needed that feeling of having to make something of herself, to prove that she was as important and needed as Laura and Donal. She'd tried to make herself indispensable to everyone around her, even to Gavin, with her perfect wife and perfect mother routine. Her spending habits had been part and parcel of that, a refusal to see that there was anything beyond the perfection gained by decorating herself, the children and the house.

Gavin, for his part, had been able to admit to the escapism that had led to his affair with Cleo Morgan.

"I thought I was letting you down," he'd told her, shamefaced. "All the things that were important to you would be gone. And all the things that Lily and Rose would need. I know you find it hard to believe after what I did but you and the girls are the best thing that ever happened to me and here I was almost bankrupt with no way of turning things around. I was just so ashamed to have to tell you, Orla."

Orla knew that he wasn't making excuses. She wasn't sitting there taking all the blame but she did know how it felt to have a sense of inadequacy and failure, emotions that had driven her life until now.

"With Cleo . . . it wasn't that I didn't want *you*, Orla . . . it was just . . . it's hard to explain . . . it was like the way some people take to drink to block things out. It's the best way I can explain it and I know it doesn't make much sense but that's how it was."

Orla had understood this in a strange sort of way. She knew that many women would think she was giving in or letting him off the hook but she also knew that every situation was different.

Gavin, she felt instinctively, hadn't gone out purposely to dupe or destroy her. He too had been living a lie, based on the notion that his value in his family was based on what he could provide for them. And if he couldn't provide to that same level, then what was his value at all? Having spent her whole life insecure about her own value, Orla could understand the concept only too well.

That night, they'd vowed to look at the things that were really important to them – Lily, Rose and each other – and to make a different sort of life for themselves. Whatever they did would be together, decisions, plans and a way forward that would be right for all of them.

Orla smiled now as she listened to her family clattering around in the kitchen below and knew that she and Gavin could take credit for *most* of the changes but not all of them.

Darren, the Lost Boy for so many decades, had reappeared in their lives in a way that connected him in the most tangible way possible. It was Darren who'd made Tír na nÓg possible and for him that she'd chosen its name – the Land of Eternal Youth. Darren would forever be five years old but he would no longer be relegated to the past, especially if Lily and Rose had anything to do with it.

Fascinated by the fact that there had been another set of identical twins in the family, they pumped Iris for information so innocently and so straightforwardly that it seemed natural for her to oblige with the answers.

"Did you ever mix them up the way Mum mixes us up sometimes?", "Who was the oldest?" and "Was there anything different about them, the way we have different belly-buttons?" were some of the less-complicated queries she'd had to contend with.

The fact that they thought Darren was their blood relation

made Orla feel more connected than she'd ever been, especially since the arrival of Laura's babies, two of whom were also identical.

Orla descended the stairs to find Lily and Rose sitting quietly at the kitchen table scribbling away with their pencils.

"No markers," Lily confirmed, just to show how serious they were about keeping their dresses clean.

"And we only had water in case we spilled juice on ourselves," Rose added piously.

"You're two super girls," Orla praised as she took the mug of tea that Gavin held out to her. "As soon as the photos are over you can have as many treats as you like. I'm dying to try the wedding cake."

"We're going to be allowed to take off some of the little horseshoes as soon as it's cut," Rose told her excitedly.

"And we're going to put them in our handbags and keep them for our own wedding. Claudia says we'll have to have a Double Wedding 'cause we're twins."

Claudia had become an authority on just about everything as far as Lily and Rose were concerned. She still came every morning and evening, only now it was to the playroom in Tír na nÓg. Orla had come a long way since Jessica Arnold and Yvonne Kelly had tentatively asked her to look after their children. She had a proper business now and a lucrative one at that.

Gavin was making sandwiches to tide them over until the wedding meal was served, although the girls had already decimated a feed of pasta, if the two empty bowls on the worktop were anything to go by.

"No coleslaw in mine," Orla warned him. The last thing she needed was a blob of mayonnaise down the front of her dress.

"You look lovely," he complimented, handing her a plate of ham and cheese, cut up in small triangles as if she was a child. "Easier to manage," he explained with a grin.

"Thanks!"

"Mum, come and look at our list," Lily was insisting. Orla

had wondered what they were poring over and she could see Gavin suppressing a smile.

"We've made a list of names," Rose explained. "It's for Susan, just in case she's thinking of having a baby."

"Well, I'm not sure . . ." Orla was at a loss as to how to deal with this statement.

"It's only a few. Listen to this. Heather, Hyacinth, Violet . . ."

Lily was on a roll and Orla almost had to turn away to stop herself from giggling. Donal would really appreciate this.

"We have Laurel on it as well, even though it's more of a plant than a flower." Rose was leaning over so that she could read the list herself.

"It's a *shrub*," Lily intervened. "But I think it's okay to put on the list, seeing as we have Holly on it as well."

They'd become obsessed with the concept of names when Claudia had pointed out that both of them were named after flowers, as was their Granny Iris. The whole thing had taken on a life of its own as soon as Laura had produced two girls.

Finn had been lucky to get named after Barry in a shortened version of Finnbarr, his father's full name. Poppy and Daisy had been the creation of Lily and Rose's new fixation with flower names and it was just as well that both Laura and Barry had actually liked the ones they'd chosen. Otherwise, there might have been full-scale anarchy.

Gavin, leaning over the sink in order to hide his mirth at the idea of Donal being in charge of a child called Hyacinth Carmody, mumbled something about Mrs Bouquet of *Keeping up Appearances* fame.

"What about Pansy? Have you got that on it?" Orla was now getting into the spirit of it.

"Or Petunia," Gavin suggested with a dead-pan expression. "Uncle Donal would love that."

Rose was writing furiously now, the list extending well beyond anything they'd ever imagined. "Will you photocopy it for us, Dad? We'll give one to Donal and Susan and keep one for ourselves – just in case they lose it or anything."

Gavin, smiling at the idea of Donal and Susan being presented with the list on today of all days, told them it was a great idea.

"Quick though, or we'll be late."

Orla watched the three of them tearing out of the kitchen, Gavin almost as giddy as his daughters, and wondered how she ever thought she didn't have a proper family.

DONAL: Let no one put asunder …

Donal almost wished that he'd brought some kind of a seat as it seemed a little strange to be standing at a time like this. He would have felt more relaxed, for one thing, as well as less conspicuous. It was quiet here, which was a good thing, considering that the rest of the day would probably be chaotic.

He read the inscription again and allowed it to infiltrate his consciousness, half afraid that something would happen.

"Darren Patrick Carmody"

"3/6/74 – 16/9/79"

The small, marble gravestone was white and remarkably well tended to with snowy marble chips spread evenly between the white marble that bordered the plot. Not a weed had appeared here since his last visit, an indication that someone came here regularly. His mother? Paddy? Or both of them, perhaps? Donal made a mental note to find out, now that it was no longer an unreasonable thing to ask.

In films, people talked out loud at the graves of loved ones when they had something important to say but Donal knew that he wouldn't be able to speak like that here today. Anyway, it wasn't as if he had anything in particular to articulate, it was more that he wanted to just be here for a few minutes before he moved on to the next stage of his life.

It was good to be able to do this and mentally let Darren know that he would have been involved already, if he'd been here. Before, Donal's solution had been to simply not do things at all. That way, he hadn't had to face the imagined hurt and betrayal of his brother.

As he'd done the last few times he'd visited Darren here in the cemetery in Rathmollin, Donal replayed in his mind all the things that were happening in his life so that his brother could hear them. Logically, he knew he didn't have to come to a graveyard to have his thoughts heard but it seemed more like a conversation here, as if it was a proper visit for a chat he was making.

Work was something he'd been thinking about a lot these days, especially when he was going to be away for two weeks. Joe Crowley had been oddly pleased when Donal had suggested gently that it would be of great benefit if *he* kept an eye on things for the fortnight, just in case there were problems that needed to be ironed out straight away.

Darren was privy to Donal's thoughts on Joe already and would know that Joe was a new man now that Donal had taken the burden of Go Cars off his shoulders permanently. As Paddy had pointed out when Donal discussed it with him at the outset, the whole transaction would be done with Darren's blessing anyway.

It still shocked him a little that he was the owner of an actual business but then again, there had been lots of things to shock him in the past year.

The very idea of his father discussing Darren as part of a normal conversation was one thing, the concept of Paddy insisting that the money accumulated over a period of thirty years be used to allow Donal to enrich his life was quite another. It was a bit unreal, the way everything had happened in tandem but Susan was a great believer in the elements of the universe coming together at just the right time.

Things had started to change, even before the bust-up at Orla's house that had blown all of their pre-conceived ideas out of the water. He'd already opened up to Susan about Darren, although that had been precipitated by Senan's accident. Which had resulted in him being in charge of Go Cars and getting a feel for what it would be like to run it full-time. In truth, the chain of events that led him up to today had been well underway anyway, even before Orla had thrown her wobbly the night of Paddy and Iris's anniversary dinner.

Donal had been a big fan of the *Back to the Future* films in his teenage years and he wondered now what today would be like if he could just zap back for Darren and land him into the middle of 2010. It would be handy to have him here as a best man, for a start.

It was Susan's idea that they should leave space in their wedding ceremony for both Darren and Julie, who would no doubt have been Susan's bridesmaid. Donal, to whom fuss was anathema at the best of times, thought it was a great idea. He would wait alone at the top of the church for Susan, with the rings tucked away in his inside pocket. Susan's dad would accompany her up the aisle, with Lily and Rose ahead of her spreading their petals where Julie would have walked.

It would be their only tribute to their siblings and Susan's mother had laughed when they'd told her their plans.

"Just as well," she'd smiled. "Can you imagine what Jools would say if you gave her a 'Minute's Silence' at the reception the way some people do?"

Paddy and Iris too had accepted the idea with equanimity.

"But I hope you're not doing it to please me?" Iris had queried. She accepted now that she hadn't coped very well in the aftermath of the accident and acknowledged the burden this had bestowed on her husband and children.

Donal had assured her that it was what both he and Susan wanted. There was no question of them being afraid to mention Darren – it was more that his presence would be felt at the altar by the people who mattered.

Donal looked heavenward now as if Darren could see him and let him know whether he approved of all this. Susan had been certain that Julie would and didn't need some sort of sign to be confident of this.

He looked at his watch now and realised that it was definitely time to make tracks. Knowing how efficient Susan was, she'd probably be *early* rather than fashionably late. The tiny townland of Rathmollin was quiet as he closed the wrought-iron gate behind him and headed for the car. Even on a Friday afternoon it was like a ghost town, definitely one that the Celtic Tiger had bypassed. Apart from Donal's, there was only one other car parked outside the little shop that doubled as a Post Office.

"Hey Mister, you look like a penguin!"

Donal looked down to see a small boy coming out of the shop, an ice-cream cone clutched tightly in his hand.

"Eric! That's bad manners," his mother admonished, looking mortified.

Donal just laughed, having forgotten that he was actually walking around in full Black Tie regalia.

"You're right – I *do* look like a penguin. But you'll have to wear this gear when *you* get married some day."

He smiled at the mother and hopped into the car, a newer Volvo these days but a Volvo nonetheless. Other people had best men to ensure that they got to the church on time. Just before he closed the door, he noticed that little Eric was still standing there looking at him, the ice-cream cone dribbling down his wrist.

"What age are you?" Donal asked.

Eric stuck out his chest proudly. "Five."

Donal just smiled. "The very best age in the world."

Eric's mother ruffled her son's hair and beamed at Donal. "Have a wonderful day."

Donal started the car and set off for St Manchan's, knowing that it would indeed be wonderful.

He didn't need to wonder any further about what Darren would make of his Big Day.

CLEO: The Last Straw

Cleo suddenly became aware of the chill on her bare arms. The duvet cover had slipped a bit because of all the twisting and turning she'd been doing since she first laid eyes on the photo and she was only wearing a light, sleeveless nightie.

She held it up in front of her face again now to study it properly and felt only shame at the sight of so many smiling faces. Did any of the people in the photo feel like this? Certainly not Laura and her extraordinary and hard-earned little family. Or Donal, innocent still, she imagined, of the hurt and disharmony she *must* have caused. Gavin perhaps had as much to regret as she herself did but it was Orla's radiant face she was focusing on now, having dissected all of the others one by one.

She knew from past experience that this early morning waking wasn't a good sign but as soon as the overwhelming tiredness that captured her into sleep in the early hours of the evening had been sated by a muggy sleep, her eyes seemed to open at will at 6 a.m., her mind ordering her to face up to the things she'd done and maybe even take a little responsibility, painful as that was.

"Stupid, stupid girl," she groaned to herself, crumpling the scrap of newsprint into a ball yet again. It had been balled up and smoothed out so many times now that it was in danger of disintegrating altogether, something that actually brought a small smile to her face. Stupid was what she'd been, on more than a few occasions and she wondered now if it was too late to make amends. She couldn't turn back the clock, that was for sure. And she couldn't visualise any conversation with Orla that would end in a teary-eyed forgiveness. She couldn't blame Gavin's wife if she hated her – what she'd done was inexcusable and torturing herself this past twenty-four hours was driving her bonkers.

"I'm sorry," she said out loud, directly at Orla, practising for a time when it might be possible to say it to her face rather than to a photo in a newspaper. The broad smile that looked back at her humbled Cleo beyond belief, something that had been a constant since she'd come across this picture of the group of Shiny Happy People in the social pages of *The Examiner* yesterday.

Orla's outfit in particular surprised her. It was the same one she'd worn the first night that she'd been in Gavin and Orla's house, on the evening of some ball in Broomfield House. She and Gavin had been left to their own devices in the good sitting room while Orla instructed Donal on childminding in the kitchen. They'd clicked, an immediate banter springing up between them that she'd found both thrilling and comforting. Gavin was a nice guy, or so she'd thought until he'd left her standing naked in his kitchen like a prostitute while he made amends with his wife upstairs.

Everything about this Carmody family photograph was so far removed from what she'd chosen to believe that she was shocked at her own naïvety. She wondered what trait she possessed that made her fall for every sob story in the book and come out the far side of it the worse for wear.

Orla, for instance, was beaming in the snapshot as if she didn't have a care in the world. Yet according to Gavin, they'd been on the point of bankruptcy less than a year ago, a lot of it on account of her love of spending. All the while she'd been going out with him, Donal had been spouting on about Orla being high-maintenance and using any occasion to splurge on expensive clothes and extravagant accessories. Gavin too had talked about this being a problem, yet here she was in the same purple dress, organza coat and stunning purple shoes – her own brother's wedding and she hadn't bought a new outfit.

Maybe Gavin, on whom her eyes settled now, had made it all up. *My wife doesn't understand me.* It was the oldest line in the book and she had clearly fallen for it yet again. The full-page article underneath the colour photo clearly stated that Orla was the proprietor of a busy child-care facility. How was it then that Gavin had given the impression that as well as Orla being a big spender, she was the type who wouldn't be able for the sudden shock of having to go back to work once she found out the full extent of his financial difficulties?

It seemed to Cleo that Gavin had been more deceptive with his sob story than she would have believed possible. Not only had his wife been able to return to the workforce, she'd actually gone and started her own bloody business! And good for her.

As Cleo knew only too well, setting up a business required *capital* as well as determination and perseverance, which made her wonder just how real Gavin's financial woes had been at all. She wondered now whether the sob story was some kind of stock item that married men used routinely to get susceptible women into bed.

"Silly simpleton," she berated herself, her eyes moving to her ex-boyfriend who was now, according to the article, a respectable married man. She wondered when the transformation had occurred – this change from his devil-may-care nonchalance and staunch refusal to conform. Now here he was being lauded as a "Popular businessman", getting married in conventional tie and tails regalia as if he was the most staid and sensible of citizens. Had Donal always been like this? Was it just she who'd wanted to believe he was a free spirit like herself? Cleo now found it hard to believe that Donal, who purported to spend everything he earned as a taxi driver on pizza and beer had overnight become a scion of society. He'd clearly been a rock of sense all along, with his Little Boy Lost persona being simply a figment of her own imagination. What was it about seemingly needy yet charming men that attracted her attention time and again?

Reading now about him and his new wife, also the owner of a successful business, embarking on an exotic honeymoon before returning to their home in Glasheen really made her question her own judgement. She presumed his untidy bachelor flat was a thing of the past now. Donal, it appeared, had moved on with his life. How long had she, Cleo, remained stagnant?

Seeing them all there like that had changed something in her. It underlined the fact that she really was a fool of the highest degree. She'd wasted her life while everyone else was moving on with theirs. How her mother had found out about her affair with Gavin Merriman was still a mystery but her head was reeling even now with the lecture both her parents had delivered.

To call it a lecture was putting it mildly, considering it was the first time she'd ever heard her father raise his voice. Ashamed of her is what they were, ashamed and disgusted. Had she no thought for anyone? It was bad enough that time with Professor Dundon, her father had pointed out, but at least he'd had his family reared. Gavin Merriman, they knew, had two small children.

Cleo's mother had spoken a lot about her daughter having to pull herself together at some stage of her life. She'd been blessed with brains but no sense. What way had they brought her up if this was going to be the carry-on of her? What did she think was going to happen with these men? Did Cleo think it was some kind of game to see if she could get them?

They'd landed on her doorstep to call her to order after they'd found out about Gavin and Cleo could still feel the shame. It was bad enough that she'd done all these things – she felt dirty and scared every time she even thought about the havoc she must have wreaked – but to think that her parents knew was just too much.

The fact that they didn't seem to know about Peter was a testament to her cousin Jessica and the fact that she was obviously a better person than Cleo ever would be. Jessica's discretion was just another thing that highlighted the kind of person that Cleo should now aspire to being.

She had spent the better part of the night trying to make sense of how she'd ended up as an inpatient in the mental health wing of St Angela's in the first place and wondered time and again what sort of madness had led her to make a pass at her own cousin's husband. A cousin who, mortifyingly, had been better to her than any sister or friend could have been.

She'd pushed the whole thing to the back of her mind, preferring to pretend that none of it had ever happened. All she knew was that it had been Christmas and she had been alone. Jonathan Dundon was preparing for Christmas with his loving wife and family while she roamed around the house in her dressing gown thinking of the two-day trip to the hospital in Hampstead that had cost her the little life inside her.

St Angela's hadn't helped at all. Nobody there had been able to see the emptiness inside her. Or maybe they had and that was why they'd filled her up with drugs. Jessica had been her only support and she wondered now whether her life would have been different if she'd been brave enough to confide in her cousin instead of keeping to herself the horrible deed she'd perpetrated on an innocent, tiny speck of a baby.

Cleo's stomach rumbled loudly, reminding her that she needed to eat something. She had eaten Weetabix earlier but now the hunger pangs were kicking in. All this time lying in bed gazing at a crumpled photo was all very fine but she needed to motivate herself now and pull herself together as her parents had so forcefully recommended.

Laura Gordon, for instance, was getting on with her life in a way that was a clear affront to the chaos in Cleo's. She and Barry had had their problems yet here they were with not just a baby but *triplets*. A full three lines of the article were dedicated to Finn, Poppy and Daisy Gordon, born by caesarean section at thirty-four weeks.

How was it that someone like Laura could move ahead and deal with whatever problem she had in an organised manner? Laura wasn't going around having affairs with married men. Laura wasn't being carted off to St Angela's at the drop of a hat and having to be bailed out by other people time and again.

A sense of inadequacy assailed Cleo now as she looked at the image of Laura holding the little boy in blue while Barry grinned proudly as he cradled the two little mites in pink frilly dresses. They looked so in control, as if they were deliberately emphasising the mess that *she* had made of her life.

Even the fragile Iris, who Donal believed was some sort of nervous wreck, stood proudly next to her only son in a heather-coloured silk suit and a matching feather Fascinator. It was far from frail she looked, in her elegant outfit with her husband at her other side and her family around her. Who did Cleo have beside her?

Her parents were right. She was wasting her time, trying to siphon away other people's lives. Jessica, always her staunchest ally and the one who'd forgiven her an enormous sin on account of her traumatised state at the time, had turned against her as soon as she'd heard about the affair with Gavin Merriman. Her parents, although still talking to her, had stressed the need to "paddle your own canoe" on almost every occasion she spoke to them. There had been firm talks from her brothers, Nick and Paul, across the airwaves from Barcelona and Ontario and Cleo knew that they weren't even aware of the half of it.

Something was igniting in her mind now, something that had been there this last twenty-four hours and maybe even since the evening her parents had confronted her about Gavin. She knew now it wasn't anyone else's fault that she was lying here in bed alone, embarrassed and upset by the way she'd lived her life up to now.

Yes, she knew that the termination of her pregnancy was something done in fear and confusion and that regret and trauma had precipitated her admission to St Angela's. Who was it but herself that had led her into a sordid affair with a married man in the first place? Was it really Jonathan Dundon's fault that she'd had to go to Hampstead alone in a web of lies and excuses? He hadn't known she was even pregnant, after all. And she had told him it was "sorted" that time he'd asked her if she was on the Pill.

There was no excuse for what she'd tried to do with Peter Arnold – none at all. She had been genuinely depressed, she wasn't denying that, but how had she got there and what had she done to help herself? Having an abortion had been the worst decision of her life and was something she would regret until the day she died. But it had been *her* decision and she would have to live with that.

Gavin Merriman was also her decision and yet another thing she would have to live with. She took one last look at him now with his arm around Orla's waist and their two shiny girls in front of them.

It was time to let go of the past, she knew. Maybe what she saw here in this photograph wasn't all there was to the extended Carmody family, just like there was more to *her* than the carefree face she showed. What if there was more behind the shiny façade *everyone* presented to the world?

Cleo sat up and swung her legs out of the bed, the now-decrepit piece of newspaper flying unnoticed to the floor.

Chaos and confusion wasn't all there was to her. There was more to her, this she knew.

What if she was able to start again, fresh, today?

THE END

If you enjoyed *A Moment in Time* by Mairead O'Driscoll
why not try
Where the Heart is also published by Poolbeg?
Here's a sneak preview of Chapter One

MAIREAD O'DRISCOLL

Where the Heart is

POOLBEG

Chapter 1

Emily Gordon closed the back door quietly so that her mother wouldn't hear her leaving the house. The last thing she needed was an audience, however supportive. She set off down the road, glad that the village was reasonably quiet for her reconnaissance mission.

Rathmollin was a passing-through village, often described as "starting at one end and finishing at the other". Apart from the few cars racing along the main street on their way to somewhere other than Rathmollin, the place was quiet. Just as well, considering that her innocuous stroll would probably be the talk of the place if she was spotted by Aggie Lenihan, the local gossip. As it stood, Emily reckoned that she'd provided Aggie with quite enough mileage for one year and wasn't prepared to offer any more of her life up as a sacrifice to her hobby. She'd already answered more than her fair share of "innocent" questions about The Wedding that Never Was.

Apart from a large extension to the rear and a line of three neat prefabs along one side of the yard, St Ciaran's primary school looked much as it had the day Emily first walked through its front door at the age of five. It had only been a matter of months before she'd broken a little hole in the hedge that divided her parents' house from the school and after that the yard had become like an extension of her own home. Her parents had tolerated the gap as it allowed Emily and her brother to go to school without having to incur the risks of the main road. It was still there.

The school door was painted red now and the front windows were overflowing with a profusion of petunias and lobelias in heavy terracotta containers. Even at this hour, six o'clock on a Sunday evening, there was someone there. She could hear the rhythmic grate of gravel being shovelled and wondered what new project the Parents' Council had on the burner.

Harmony Cottage was at the far end of the village. Having spent the better part of the day just lying on her bed, the short walk would actually do her good. Something about the badly focused photo of the little house in *The Examiner* had made her feel as if she might actually have a future, not a bad thing considering that up to now she hadn't been able to see anything past a black hole when tomorrow or next week or next year was mentioned.

She walked on, past Curly Locks hair salon, Connolly's Master Butcher and Mac Gleeson's Grocery, her hair blowing away from her face in the blustery March wind. Richard used to love the feeling of her unruly auburn ringlets tickling his face when they were out walking, or at least that's what he'd said at the time. Emily wasn't sure now what had been true and what had been a lie but at least she was beginning to wonder about it less and less.

She was nearing the cottage now and was almost starting to feel scared that it would be a disappointment in real life. She knew how the property pages could pump up a house so that it was the Taj Mahal you were expecting by the time you viewed it.

She could just imagine what Richard would say if he knew she was considering a house that was probably a hundred years old but it was a bit late now to be worrying about what *his* advice and opinions might be. Maybe a shift away from a state-of-the-art, all-mod-cons show-house was what she needed right now. And, thanks to Richard, that was just about all she could afford.

Emily lifted her chin in the manner that she'd learned to adopt since that fateful moment on New Year's Eve and strode purposefully towards what she hoped might be her fresh start.

Sandra Coyne was glad of the excuse of picking up Dylan's bike from the pathway outside her parents' house and for the feeling of the fresh air on her face. Her father had been on at her about Paul again and she was finding it more and more difficult to defend him, especially when it was gone six o'clock and she'd had no account of him since lunch-time.

New Year's Eve had been wonderful, an emotional if somewhat drunken reunion with the father of her child, her first great love. Her only great love, come to think of it, considering that she'd barely been out of the house in the last eight years. Now, over three months on, Sandra wasn't so sure.

She and Paul had made a pact to put the past behind them and start again and she'd truly wanted to let bygones be bygones and start from scratch for Dylan's sake. As Paul had pointed out on New Year's Eve, Dylan had a right to know his father and Sandra knew it wasn't fair of her to deny him that.

And despite everything, as soon as she saw him again in The Stone's Throw, the old familiar attraction had come back to her as if the intervening years had never happened. She'd always loved the height of him – the way he towered over her made her feel somehow cherished, like a china doll next to his muscled bulk. The wide grin and bright blue eyes that were now so familiar in her son reminded her that they used to be a family and could be again if she let it happen. But it was the comforting weight of his arm where it rested across her shoulder that night that had made her believe it was possible to start again, that and the way he made her laugh with tales of his life in London. A life that he was prepared to leave for another chance with Sandra and Dylan.

He'd been happy to move into the small council house opposite the school with them and had been raring to go when Sandra mentioned to Jack Rooney the following Saturday night that Paul would be looking for work. They'd had a drink together in The Stone's that night and Jack had been happy for Paul to start the following Monday.

It had been great those first few weeks, a honeymoon period that had given her a new lease of life. Somehow, though, the shine had worn off a bit. The ritual of daily life was getting harder and she was beginning to wonder if she'd made a mistake in rushing into things with Paul once again.

It wasn't the first time that he'd let her down, her father had warned her a few minutes ago. He knew that Paul spent more time in The Stone's than was strictly sociable, but what he didn't know was how easy it was to irritate him when he came home late and how his drinking was eating into Sandra's already tight budget. It was all very fine saying "I told you so", but in actual fact nobody *had* told her so. It was up to her now to make the best of it, for Dylan's sake if not her own.

She leaned against the front wall, reluctant to go back inside and face more of her parents' weary disapproval. Then a huddled figure walking towards her caught her attention – a chance perhaps to delay the inevitable return inside.

"Emily!"

It had been ages since she'd spoken to Emily Gordon. Sandra knew from her mother that an engagement had been dissolved in the last few months but it would be the last thing she'd mention – unless of course Emily herself brought it up.

"God, Sandra, I was dreaming there – I hardly noticed you. How are you?"

Emily looked pale, but then she'd always had an ethereal sort of look. The creamy skin (its light sprinkling of freckles well concealed) and dark auburn curls had always reminded Sandra of the kind of paintings that had naked ladies and cherubs in them.

"Great. Just tidying up after Dylan – he's a terror for leaving things all over the place."

"He must be big now. Eight?"

Emily had a way of screwing her face up that made Sandra feel old in comparison.

"Next week. I can't believe it. Are you home for a bit?" As far as she knew, Emily was still working in Dublin.

"For the moment. I'm working in Cork now so I'm starting to look for my own place."

"Any luck? The new ones over the road look nice."

"Expensive though – they're all well over three hundred thousand."

They both glanced across the road to where the stone entrance of Sycamore Drive was blocked off for the night by a strategically placed excavator.

"I actually came up along to have a look at Ina Harrington's cottage. I saw it in *The Examiner* yesterday."

To Sandra, the rundown cottage was little better than the small council house that she herself was renting at the other end of the village and she was surprised that Emily was even thinking about it, considering that she had a college education and a good job as a social worker.

"I noticed it was for sale," she said. "Would it need much work, do you think?"

"I've no idea. It's worth looking at though."

Sandra wasn't sure that it was but couldn't exactly say so to Emily who was gazing towards Ina and her sister Minnie's old cottage with a wistful look in her eyes. Besides, to Sandra, the idea of owning her own home was as far from reality as flying to the moon and she envied Emily her ability to have such a thing within her reach, even if it was Harmony Cottage she was considering.

She was just about to ask Emily about her job when Dylan appeared around the corner.

"Mam? Can I go over to Tim's for a while?"

"It's a bit late, Dylan. You'll see him at school tomorrow anyway."

Sandra wasn't sure where her son's burgeoning friendship with Tim Kelleher was going, in light of the vast differences in their financial status. Jennie and Vincent Kelleher lived in Rathmollin Woods, the village's most desirable residential location, unfortunately too close to Dylan's grandparents' house for Sandra's liking. It wasn't that she had anything against Tim – he was great – but the fact that he had everything she couldn't afford for Dylan bothered her enough to wish he hadn't picked him for a best friend.

"I'll only go for a few minutes." He was pleading now, mad to get over to his friend's PlayStation for an hour before bedtime.

"He'll be getting ready for bed by now. We'll be going home soon anyway. Go on in and get your things together while I'm talking to Emily." Sandra glanced at Emily and winked as Dylan skulked off in the direction of the house, disappointed that his great idea was out of the question.

"He's a lovely little fellow," Emily commented and Sandra had to admit with a smile that she was right.

"He's great, to be honest. Even when he was a baby he was easy to manage." Again, she had the feeling that she was so much older than Emily, who looked much the same as she had as a teenager. She was as slim as ever while Sandra was still threatening to lose her "baby weight" eight years on.

"I'd better keep going and let you get back inside," said Emily. "You never know – your mam and dad might have a neighbour yet!"

"They'd be delighted if it was you, you know. There was talk

412

of a housing development going up in the field behind them and the cottage being knocked to make an entrance. The last thing they need is a load of houses overlooking the back garden."

"That'd be desperate all right. Hopefully this whole property boom thing will slow down a bit soon or I'll never be able to afford anything."

After Emily left, something like dismay set in for Sandra at the thought of the property boom. It all seemed so far removed from her own life – a million miles if the truth be told. It occurred to her that even with a degree in Social Work under her belt and a good job, Emily was talking about house prices being prohibitive. In that case, she wondered, where did that leave *her* in the grand scheme of things?

It was just as well that Sandra had decided against letting Dylan call over to Rathmollin Woods to play with Tim Kelleher. By the time Emily had satisfied herself that Harmony Cottage was a true reproduction of the picturesque image on the property page and Sandra had gathered up as many of Dylan's toys as possible from her parents' sitting-room, Jennie Kelleher was on her way to the A&E Department with Tim and his younger sister bundled into the back of the car.

It was typical, Jennie fretted as she waited impatiently for the painfully slow parting of the electronic gates, that Vincent would be out of the country for this latest episode in their children's lives. And it was unfortunate that Lucy should come out in an inexplicable rash on a Sunday evening when both her father *and* the baby-sitter were out of bounds. Tim, therefore, had to be brought along for the expedition to the A&E.

There had been no sign of the rash that morning when Jennie was helping Lucy get dressed. It was only when she'd hopped the pair of them into the bath after supper that she'd noticed the rash covering her daughter's tummy and chest.

"Are you itchy, love?" Her voice was casual but she could

hardly believe that Lucy hadn't been unwell at all during the day with such a profusion of spots covering her torso. She had complained about being too hot when she and Tim were trying to see who could bounce the highest on the trampoline but Jennie had merely whipped off the five-year old's light cotton cardigan and thought no more about it.

"No. They're funny," Lucy giggled, examining the rash now that her mother had drawn attention to it.

Tim too studied the small clusters of spots. "Pocahontas died of measles!" He was ecstatic at the thought of his sister having the same disease as the exotic heroine. "Maybe they're measles!"

Lucy's face fell at the idea of a possible untimely death and her lip started to wobble. "Mum! Is it true?" she asked tearfully.

Her older brother looked on with some satisfaction, the prospect of their bedtime being delayed by an interesting diversion uppermost in his mind. At eight, he was allowed to stay up a full half hour later than his sister but any small extension would be a bonus.

Jennie had to diffuse the drama. "No, no, no," she said. "Anyway, it can't be measles – you both got an injection against measles when you were small."

Lucy looked relieved, Tim disappointed. Jennie lifted her daughter out of the bath and began to dry her efficiently, checking surreptitiously under her arms and in the creases of her legs for any more spots, as the meningitis leaflets often advised. Or maybe it wasn't the meningitis leaflets that said it.

Light was the thing – children couldn't tolerate bright light if they had meningitis. How bright was bright, she wondered as the children continued to chatter away about Lucy's fascinating spots. If only Vincent was here to talk it out with.

Without letting the fear that was in her chest come out in her voice, Jennie lifted Lucy onto her hip and carried her to the walk-in closet in the spare room, leaving Tim to dry himself. It was the only place in the house that didn't have a window. Before her daughter could start complaining about not being allowed to herself, Jennie flicked on the fluorescent light in the poky little room, flooding it with brightness and praying that Lucy wouldn't react.

"I'm not sleeping in here," Lucy whined, wriggling to get out of Jennie's arms. "All my things are in my own room!" She ran off naked towards the small pink room at the front of the house lest there be any question of her missing out on her books before bedtime.

At least she doesn't have photophobia. The ominous-sounding word came back to her now that some slight relief had set in.

Jennie remained in the pale blue and beige guest room for a few minutes, her mind frantic as she tried to plot her next move. The pair of them, for once, were in their pyjamas before she had to threaten a withdrawal of all toys and DVDs. For Lucy's sake she needed to act normally but she still wasn't satisfied about the rash.

"Okay – downstairs now and you can watch *Toy Story* for a while."

"Two! Two! I want *Toy Story 2!*" Lucy was yelling her head off in her anxiety to get her demand in ahead of Tim's.

They had a rule that whoever said something first got the choice. Tim, defeated on account of not being quick enough with the shouting, resigned himself to foregoing the original film and followed his sister. *Toy Story* was a bit babyish for him but Tim was a diplomat and knew he'd be able to get a bit of *Spiderman* in as soon as Lucy was packed off to bed.

Their mother, meantime, collected the sodden towels from the bathroom floor in a bid to allow herself thinking space.

There was a test with a glass that she'd read about in the GP's surgery a few times but she couldn't remember what exactly was supposed to happen when you pressed the glass against the skin. Was it more dangerous if the spots disappeared or if they *didn't*

...n't remember and vowed now to watch the
... on television from here on in if Lucy was
...le disease.

...less phoning Vincent in Dubai for advice. For one,
... wouldn't know any more than she did about
me... ...s. And whether he did or he didn't, it would be horrendous
to alert him to the fact that one of the children was sick when he
was so far away and unable to actually do anything.

Jennie's mother or her older sister Molly were the only other
people she could ask, but she couldn't bear the thought of them
criticising her afterwards if it was a false alarm. Vincent's mother
Elsie, efficient as ever, would probably have a definitive answer,
but Jennie hadn't actually rung her even once in all the years she'd
been married to her son and she wasn't about to start now. Even
Maxine, her best friend, was away tonight at some sort of
gardening thing with her husband. Jennie was on her own and
she'd just have to deal with it herself.

The children had settled themselves in front of the television
by the time she'd selected a plain water glass with a flat base
from the kitchen cabinet.

"Show me the rash again and I'll do a trick!" Maybe the
correct procedure would come back to her if she placed the glass
on the skin.

Lucy, delighted with all the attention, pulled up her pyjama
top and stretched straight out on the couch, as self-important as
if she were being examined at a high-profile medical conference.

"Can I do the trick as well?" Poor Tim was feeling left out.

"Course you can, love. We'll see if it's different on boys than
on girls."

Lucy let out a yelp as soon as the bottom of the glass was
planted on her bare tummy and Jennie's heart froze. She almost got
weak with relief when the children started to giggle with Lucy
shrieking her head off, "That's freezing!"

Her tummy was wobbling now with all the laughing and

Jennie was finding it difficult to tell if the spots disappearing or not.

"Stay still, Lucy, or I won't be able to see it."

Lucy immediately stiffened out like a board, causing Jennie to look up in alarm.

"Can you see now?" Lucy asked obligingly, holding her tummy as rigid as she could. Jennie had thought she was about to get some sort of seizure and tried to calm herself enough to look at the glass. The skin of Lucy's abdomen was pale where the glass pressed into it but the small spots were still faintly visible. Defeated, Jennie removed it, still as wise as ever regarding the seriousness of the rash.

"Next we'll have to take your temperature," she announced officiously, the way she did when they played "Doctors" and the children were the unfortunate patients.

"You never checked *my* tummy!"

Tim's plaintive whine made Jennie smile to herself – despite being three years older than Lucy, he seemed younger in many ways than the sassy Lucy.

Less meticulous this time, she did the glass test on Tim and sped off to the kitchen for the ear thermometer while Lucy made room for Tim on the sofa and they got themselves ready for their examination.

She did Tim's first this time, hoping to get some sort of baseline to compare Lucy's to.

"Very normal, 37 degrees. Next, please."

Lucy tilted her head this time, anxious to see if her temperature was as normal as her brother's, notwithstanding her spotty tummy. To her mother's relief, the thermometer again rested at 37 degrees.

For the millionth time, she wished that Vincent was at home. He might not know what to do next either but at least they could decide together. The Nurseline that the health insurance company provided was the only other option open to her. Leaving the children to

Story, she made her way to the kitchen so
hear her making the phone call. All the literature
said to look at the child and see if they were off
neither of which Lucy was. Yet she couldn't ignore
even if the temperature was normal. And she still didn't
know the significance of the glass thing.

The voice at the other end of the phone was calm and reassuring but as soon as she mentioned that the rash hadn't disappeared when pressed under a glass, her worst fears were confirmed.

"You really need to take Lucy to your GP or to the nearest A&E."

"But could it be meningitis?" Jennie had phoned so that she could hear out loud that she was worrying unnecessarily – instead she was being told that her child needed to see a doctor immediately.

"It's a possibility, along with normal childhood illnesses or even a simple viral infection. She needs to be examined by a doctor to rule it out."

"Thank you, I'll get her seen straight away." Shocked, she sat for a moment on one of the kitchen chairs, trying to decide what was best to do. If Lucy really did have meningitis, then the time lost waiting for the GP could be crucial, particularly if he was out on a call miles away.

The A&E would be better, especially if there was any sudden deterioration in her condition. She'd seen parents on television telling their story and recounting how their child was a lively infant one minute but hooked up to tubes and wires in the ICU the next. She couldn't let that happen to Lucy.

A new sense of urgency came over her suddenly and she headed straight for the playroom, car keys in hand, her mind already plotting the route to St Angela's. She'd already lost precious minutes with all her checking for signs and symptoms.

"Come on, you two. We're going on an adventure to get rid of Lucy's spots."

The question came as one voice, incredulous. "In our pyjamas?"
"Yes, in your pyjamas."

Jack hammered away at the bottom of an old fish-pond that had been closed off even as far back as his own schooldays, oblivious to the fact that it was practically dark. He'd switched on the light at the gable of the school so that he could finish the job that he'd started three hours ago but the beam was poor and he was working almost on instinct at this stage.

The base of the old pond had been filled with concrete, a far cry from the PVC pond liners available today and he repeatedly cursed the original craftsman's primitive efforts.

Despite the fact that any normal person had more to be doing on a Sunday evening than hacking out a ton of concrete, he ignored the painful ache that was starting in his shoulder muscles and kept going. If he didn't, then the load of topsoil that he needed to have removed from the Sycamore Drive site further up the street would have to go elsewhere, meaning that the reality of the school having its own herb garden would be yet another unfulfilled dream for the Parents' Council.

The only available site for the educational garden was the spot he was now working on, a spot that was mercifully almost clear now of the solid layer of concrete that had covered it a few hours ago. He straightened to admire his handiwork – although it was now almost too dark to appreciate it. The evening air was still fresh and crisp and he felt the coolness of it kick in as he stood there.

Moving the discarded shards of uprooted concrete was going to be another job but that could be tackled later in the week when the long-suffering parents had levelled out the topsoil to their liking. Jack had decided that he'd just barrow it to one side to make room for the excavator that would land the topsoil in the designated area

Minutes later, having collected his tools and switched off the outside light, he was done. The village was quiet as he walked the short distance to the solid two-storey house that he'd inherited from his parents. He was fantasising about a hot shower even before he opened the door. His personal rule about working on the weekends was rarely broken but, on this occasion, he'd actually got satisfaction out of the strenuous physical labour.

It was a long time since he'd felt the need to burn off excess energy like that but all that day the events of the previous evening had glowed in his brain with an annoyance that he could never have imagined Heather igniting in him.

It wasn't the loss of her that bothered him, as much as the manner of it. Even almost twenty-four hours later, it still surprised him just how little he'd actually known her. As far as he'd been concerned, after six months their relationship had passed the early stage of merely getting to know someone, although it was still nowhere near the stage of talking about the future or how they really felt about each other.

It was Heather who'd suggested they stay in on Saturday night instead of going out for a meal in town the way they usually did. It had suited Jack at the time, considering it was the first Saturday he'd worked past lunch-time in years. He'd decided to cook dinner for them, knowing that Heather would be staying over as she had on most of their recent Saturday nights, her smart navy Saab parked discreetly near the back door to avoid the gossip that the inhabitants of most small villages seemed to thrive on.

"I have a reputation to protect," she was fond of saying and Jack had appreciated that this was indeed true. The classic green and gold frontage of the Sutherland & Lucas office was very much an institution of Rathmollin's main street and the personal life of one of its senior solicitors would be considered juicy gossip, especially in terms of where she'd spent the night and with whom. On the other hand, it was probably well known that he and

Heather were in a relationship but as far as Heather was concerned, discretion had to be observed at all costs.

And as she was always so keen to point out, with Aggie Lenihan prowling around the village first thing every Sunday morning, there was nothing that didn't get logged on the gossip register. Now, after what had happened the previous evening, Jack was beginning to wonder about the real reason that she'd insisted on theirs being such a discreet liaison.

While he liked to cook, Jack was a man with a limited repertoire and had expected to see Heather roll her eyes in amusement at the two steaks sitting beside the grill pan awaiting her arrival. Gratin potatoes were already bubbling in the oven and his usual accompaniment of steamed vegetables, onions and mushrooms were just reaching culmination in various pots and pans around the hob.

In place of amusement, he immediately saw the reserve in her eyes and sensed that their evening wasn't about to go as he'd planned it. Food, he reasoned, wasn't a priority, but it was certainly a distraction so he went on with preparing the meal, somehow doubtful as to whether it would be eaten at all.

He was right, as it transpired. Heather had started to talk almost straight away, as if she needed to get it out as quickly as possible.

Gerard, she told him, was someone that she'd been very close to in college and for a few years afterwards. He'd moved to London, ostensibly to gain experience in family law in the context of the new divorce legislation in Ireland, but more so to spread his wings and put some space in what he'd described at the time as a "prematurely mature" relationship with Heather.

The relationship had fizzled out but now it seemed that Gerard was back and conveniently installed in Sutherland & Lucas in an office adjoining her own. The last few weeks had been cathartic for them, she told Jack, and there was a chance that they could restore their former bond. It occurred to Jack that things with Gerard hadn't been so life-shattering that she hadn't been able to share Jack's bed and make love to him in the inter-vening weeks, but he imagined it would have been less than gentlemanly to say this out loud to her over the kitchen table. Instead, he just sat and listened while she tried to make him understand that it was all for the best anyway.

"And it's not as if *we* were going anywhere anyway, is it?"

"Sorry?" Jack wasn't sure what she meant but wasn't about to make the deception of the past few weeks easier for her, if that was what she wanted.

Reddening just a little, she spread her hands expansively in an attempt to explain. "Well, you know what I mean, Jack. It was never going to work out really. I mean, we're so different – our lifestyles and everything . . ."

Here she trailed off, leaving Jack in no doubt as to what she meant. She'd obviously considered him to be some kind of "bit of rough".

"I see," he'd said evenly. Why prove her right and act like the boor that she seemed to have him down for? "Heathcliff Syndrome." He hated sounding so cynical but the reality was that, despite his wealth, Heather wanted someone more educated with a fine-tuned accent to settle down with.

She'd blushed at that – to know she'd treated him appallingly was one thing but to know that he was wise to it was another. *And* the fact that he'd made her aware that he might not be as well educated as Gerard but that he wasn't exactly as thick as a plank either.

"I'm not saying . . ."

She was blustering all of a sudden and Jack had actually felt sorry for her. It was a solicitor or someone she considered to be of equal status that Heather wanted, he realised. Not necessarily Gerard, who had already treated her dreadfully by her own account, but definitely not Jack. Notwithstanding his wealth being significant by anyone's standards, the fact that he was a mere builder was obviously not on. He wondered, with a slight tinge of bitter amusement, if perhaps he should start describing himself as a property developer.

He'd felt a little sorry for her then. "I know what you're saying. Really I do, Heather. I wish you and Gerard the best of luck." There was no point in expending his energy on a relationship that had no chance of survival.

She'd left shortly afterwards and Jack had spent the night tossing and turning, alternating between indignation at his now-ex-girlfriend's elitist attitude and curiosity as to why she had wasted her time in a relationship that she had no value on and a man she clearly had no respect for.

Now, almost twenty-four hours and a session of hard labour later, he was feeling more resigned to the situation. He was only twenty-eight, he consoled himself. There was plenty of time to meet someone who would actually accept him for who he was.

·-•-·

If you enjoyed this chapter from

Where the Heart is by Mairead O Driscoll

why not order the full book online
@ www.poolbeg.com

See next page for details

·-•-·